DREAM VACATION, SURPRISE BABY

ALLY BLAKE

THE MAVERICK'S BABY ARRANGEMENT

KATHY DOUGLASS

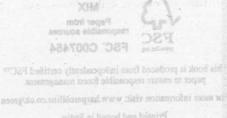

MIX
Paper from
responsible sources

FSC
www.fsc.org

FSC C007454

This book is produced from independently certified FSC™
paper to ensure responsible forest management.

For more information visit: www.harpercollins.co.uk/green

Printed and bound in Spain
by CPI, Barcelona

MILLS & BOON

First Published in Great Britain 2020
by Mills & Boon, an imprint of HarperCollinsPublishers,
1 London Bridge Street, London, SE1 9GF

Dream Vacation, Surprise Baby © 2020 Ally Blake
The Maverick's Baby Arrangement © 2020 Harlequin Books S.A.

Special thanks and acknowledgement are given to Kathy Douglass for her contribution to the *Montana Mavericks: What Happened to Beatrix?* series.

ISBN: 978-0-263-27894-1 AW

0020

DREAM VACATION, SURPRISE BABY

ALLY BLAKE

Dedicated to Em. For the bit about the horse.

Oh, and the trips to Byron, the alternative creative outlet, the seat next to me at the movies, the hugs, the friendship, the true love, the village—all that stuff too.

But mostly for the horse.

PROLOGUE

My desk buzzed.

Or, to be precise, the fancy intercom my gung-ho interior designers had embedded *into* my new desk.

So embroiled had I been in the utterly delightful photographs my private detective had sent me, I might have flinched. Which, as I am nearly seventy-six years of age, could be a health hazard.

My assistant's voice followed, carrying the slightest hint of defeat, as if it wasn't the first time she'd tried to rouse me. "Vivian? Ms Ascot? Your ten o'clock is here."

I swiped crooked fingers over the hidden touchscreen, in search of the appropriate button with which to answer.

"All these new-fangled technologies," I muttered, rolling my eyes at my little dog, Max, who peered up at me from his personal, antique chaise longue beside my office chair. "In the olden days a simple knock at the door sufficed. Yet another sign the world is overtaking me." Then, to my assistant, "And whom might my ten o'clock be?"

A whisper through the speaker, tinged with a hint of hauteur, replied, "The ghost writer."

"Oh! Excellent. Let him up."

I had been approached more than once over the years to write my autobiography. *"Your life!"* those in charge of such things had expressed. *"Your charitable work! Your support of the arts! A woman—"* gasp! *"—in charge of such a stupendously successful company!"*

But this was the first time I'd entertained the idea. The first time I'd felt as if I had something of worth to share. I was quite looking forward to their shock when they realised it had little to do with my net worth.

Knowing it would take a minute or two for the writer to

make it up the lift to my office high atop the Ascot Building in central London, I went back to enjoying the photographs of my lovely young friend, and most recent recipient of the Vivian Ascot Scholarship to Life—a delightful Australian girl named Aubrey Trusedale—arriving safely and stepping off the plane in Rome. First stop on the international adventure my scholarship was funding.

"You remember Aubrey, right, Max?" I said. "And Jessica and Daisy? They are the ones who rescued you when you leapt from my arms at the annual Ascot Music Festival when it was held in Copenhagen. Stopped you from being trampled to death."

Max's delightful little ears pricked. Perhaps at the thought of being trampled to death, but I chose to believe he was remembering the good part. The way those three girls had fawned over him. The way they didn't make me feel silly for being so upset when I thought he'd disappeared for good.

I paused the slide show on one photograph. Sat forward. Squinted. Not sure how much worse my eyes could get before my glass lenses became so heavy they'd make me hunch.

Back when we first met, Aubrey had been a little on the wild side. With a mass of head-turning auburn waves and the trust the world would catch her if she fell. The result—I felt—of having three burly older brothers who adored her to pieces.

As I look at her now, beneath a hat too big for her head, the auburn hair poking out beneath was more a shaggy bob. She seemed a little lankier, too. Chin up, grin plastered across her elfin face as she traipsed through the airport, hands gripped tight to the straps of her battered backpack. All joy, gumption and grit. But changed.

No wonder, after all she'd been through.

I could only hope the infusion of funds from the Vivian Ascot Opportunity Legacy—better? Or too much of a mouthful?—would give her the chance to find her feet again.

"Max," I said, a strange kind of melancholy coming over me, "is it wrong of me to envy her? Not for her youth, or her loveliness, or her excellent eyesight. But for the fact she is about to experience Italy for the first time. The impossibly green hills of Tuscany, the ancient architecture of Rome."

And the men, I said, only this time to myself. For Max was a sensitive soul. Nowhere else in the world makes men quite like those of Roman blood.

Max's greying muzzle twitched as he looked up at me, limpid brown dachshund eyes a little rheumy, pitying even. I could all but hear him saying, *Vivian, dear, it's not like you to be so schmaltzy.*

Well, he'd feel schmaltzy too, if he was finding himself looking back more than he was looking forward. Such as now, as I found myself drowning in the bittersweet memories of a single summer spent under the Chianti sun.

It was why the Vivian Ascot Endowment Fund for Most Excellent Young Women had been born. Yes, I quite like that one!

The reason I'd endowed those young women with the means to achieve their dream? Instinct.

I couldn't see the future, or sense the lotto numbers, or lead police to dead bodies like that lady on the television. But I could *sense* what people needed, if they needed it enough. Not need as in a little extra deodorant wouldn't go astray. But deeper. Transformative. That one thing that would make a person feel whole.

Whole, I thought, my hand going to my chest. To the strange bittersweet sensation that had taken up residence therein the moment I had seen the first picture of Aubrey in Rome.

I'd been twenty or twenty-one when, in a trattoria in Florence, I'd found myself face to face with the most beautiful man I'd ever met. Tall, dark, Italian. He'd smiled at me, as if he'd known exactly how he'd affected me—

I shook it off.

It was a long time ago. I had no regrets.

I might never have married, or had children of my own, but I'd travelled and laughed and imbibed and inhaled and delighted and felt great wonder. My life was, and had been, wonderful. People wouldn't be throwing so much money my way to hear about it otherwise.

Not that I needed the funds. I had amassed a fortune the likes of which no one person could ever hope to spend. None of which I could leave to Max as I fully planned on outliving my darling boy.

And so the endowments to the lovely Jessica, Daisy and now Aubrey. I had been biding my time, waiting for the right moment to pounce. I mean *help*. Nudge—gently, generously, benignly—towards that which might allow them to shake off the fears holding them back, so that they might truly thrive.

"Ms Ascot," my assistant called through the speaker in my desk. "Your ten o'clock is here."

"Let him in."

The door opened with a soft click and an electronic whir. All this technology really was a bit ridiculous. Just another sign that perhaps my time in the corporate world was coming to its natural end.

"Hi?" the writer called, his head poking around the door. Hand-picked from one of the few glossy magazines still in print, he was young enough the whiskers on his muzzle were golden and sparse. "I mean hello there, Ms Ascot. I mean… Sorry."

I pushed back my chair, moved around the desk, and held out a hand. "Call me Viv."

"Viv," he said. "All right. Though I'm not sure I've ever been quite this star struck."

"Star struck?" I repeated, quite liking that. I gave Max a look, to find he was pretending to be asleep.

"You are *the* Vivian Ascot," the writer intoned, arms spread wide. "Head of Ascot Industries. Benefactor of the Ascot Music Festival. Ascot Music Awards. More galleries and performing arts scholarships and publishing endowments than we likely even know. You, ma'am, are a true patron of the arts."

"You have done your research, young man."

The young man smiled, and I saw a flicker of determination behind the soft face. "Why?" he asked.

"Why do I spend such a large portion of my hard-earned money on pursuits in the arts? Because without art, without beauty and invention and elegance and verve, what is there to live for?"

"No, I mean why do you want to write a book?"

Because I had a story to tell. A story of kindness, and hope, and love.

"Well," I said, "the idea came to me the weekend I met three lovely young women at my music festival in Copenhagen…"

CHAPTER ONE

AUBREY TRUSEDALE HAD imagined this very moment—meeting him for the first time—more times than she could count.

She'd known her fingers would tingle as they did now, imagining how he'd feel to touch. Her blood rushing heedlessly around her body. Heart skittering in her chest. Spotting him across the crowded room; his size, his infamy, his sheer masculine beauty taking her breath fair away.

At over five metres tall, all marble, muscle and might, the David did *not* disappoint.

After around her seventeenth sigh, Aubrey glanced behind her to find the tour group who'd been milling about when she'd arrived had moved on.

Leaving her alone.

With *him*.

Growing up, her three older brothers had had pictures of cars tacked to their bedroom walls. While she'd had notes, sketches, and printouts depicting paintings by Monet and Waterhouse.

But the poster of the David had had pride of place right over her bed.

Yep. A naked man on her wall. Among her mates, it had been quite the coup.

Now, he was so close. This infamous study of the male form: shadows, indents, veins, muscles, strength, shape... He was honestly the most beautiful thing she had ever seen. If she fell down dead, right here, she'd die happy.

Not that she planned to fall down dead. A lot of clever people had spent the past two years of her life making sure that would not happen any time soon. So, she was pretty determined to stick it out.

Aubrey took a step closer. And another. Till she was all

but leaning over the surprisingly small barrier. It wouldn't take much to reach out and touch—

She curled her fingers into her palms.

The number one rule in these places was no touching. Longevity, future generations and all that. But the guy *had* survived outdoors for nearly four hundred years before he was moved into this space.

Would he feel cold? Rough? Dry? Surely a fingertip couldn't hurt. Maybe a gentle sweep of her palm over his—

She glanced over her shoulder to see Mario the security guard strolling by. Heat creeping into her cheeks, she gave him a wave.

Mario grinned back. And hid a yawn behind his hand. He'd worked at the Galleria dell'Accademia for nearly seven years. He had four teenaged daughters. All of whom made it difficult for him to get to sleep at night.

She knew because they'd chatted for a bit when she'd first stepped inside the gallery doors. People opened up to her. Always had. Made them happy to do things for her. Go the extra mile.

Like the time at the Ascot Music Festival in Copenhagen when she'd first met her very best friends in the entire world, Daisy and Jessica. After rescuing a cheeky little sausage dog from being trampled by thousands of unknowing feet they'd also taken care of Viv—the dog's owner— when it turned out she'd twisted her ankle, badly, in trying to chase little Max down.

While everyone else fretted over Viv, off Aubrey went, found a guy with a golf cart who was meant to be ferrying around VIPS, and convinced him to schlep Viv away to the medical tent instead.

Crazy to think they'd only just this summer discovered that their friend Viv was none other than Vivian Ascot, billionaire head of the Ascot Industries and sponsor of the music festival!

Ask questions, and actually listen to the answers and

you never know what might happen. Such as two years later waking up to a legal letter telling you that you had been gifted a bottomless, all-expenses-paid, first-class world trip by that very same billionaire, who would not take oh-my-gosh-you-are-so-lovely-but-I-can't-possibly-accept for an answer.

Something her brothers could learn—the asking, the listening. It was a wonder any woman had married them. Much less had their children. Their gorgeous, roly-poly cherubs. Thinking about how much her beautiful nieces and nephews would grow while she was away had been the one thing that could have stopped her from going.

And yet, some time away from those beautiful babies, all that they represented, all she'd never have, was the very reason she'd had to go.

Realising she was on her tippy toes, Aubrey let herself sway back onto her heels. Consoling herself with the knowledge that the air she breathed had wafted over the David. It was enough. Unless she planned to be arrested for fondling a priceless piece of art before being extradited home on day one of her magical fantasy trip, it had to be.

A couple came into the room, took one look at the David, and kept walking. *Philistines.*

Knowing her one-on-one time with the love of her life was too good to last, Aubrey plonked herself down on the floor, stretched open her backpack, pulled out a sketch pad and the stub of a fine charcoal pencil, looked back up at the David, and breathed.

Which bit to sketch first? That dashing profile? The whorl of his ear? His foot—the one that had lost a toe when some crazy had chopped it off with a hammer?

The hand.

It was his fault she'd always had a thing for hands. Strong hands. With veins and scars and strength and a story.

Aubrey stared at the David's hand for another few seconds before putting pencil to paper. With a sweep of charcoal across the page, there was no going back.

Drawing had always been her bliss. Sketching with a stick in the dirt in their hot, dry inner Sydney backyard, using her toe to create sand animals on their biannual trips to the beach. It had been a way to escape into her head when she'd needed time out from her boisterous family of six.

First money she'd made had been as a precocious eight-year-old, setting herself up on the sidewalk outside her family's Sydney auto shop, Prestige Panel and Paint, selling pictures she'd drawn of the vintage cars inside. She'd put the money in a tin she'd marked *Plane Ride*.

Resolute, even then, to see the world.

Her dream had seemed ill-starred, when, two years earlier, while finally on the trip she'd saved for her entire life, just after the Copenhagen festival, she'd been cut down by a mysterious infection that doctors had told her family would most certainly be the end of her.

Realising her pencil had stopped moving, Aubrey blinked to clear her eyes, then tipped her dad's old fedora further back on her head and smudged a little graphite shadow into a groove of David's wrist with her thumb.

It *hadn't* been the end of her. She'd pulled through. After two long years of obstinate recuperation, she was back. Only now she carried with her one slightly damaged heart.

She looked up at the David—*the David*, right there in front of her—and thanked whatever gods out there might have helped pull her through. Asking them if they could stick around, keep an eye on her, make sure nothing happened to force her home too soon this time.

Not that she believed it would. This time things seemed fortuitous, sprinkled as they were with Vivian Ascot's particular brand of magical fairy dust. The timing could not have been more perfect, coming as it had right on top of the most recent bombshell from Aubrey's doctors.

When Viv had stated—tongue in cheek, Aubrey was almost sure—that the only provisos were that she was not to deny herself a thing, that she luxuriate and spoil herself rotten, and that she start her trip in Florence, staying in a hotel Viv herself owned, what choice had she had but to accept?

Dante. Machiavelli. Da Vinci. Michelangelo. Galileo. Of the greats, only a small number were born in Florence or spent time there. If this trip was to be Aubrey's renaissance, her chance to envision her life beyond her condition, and all it had taken from her, this was the city to do it.

"I don't know about you," a deep, male voice said from behind her, "but he's always bigger than I think he'll be."

Aubrey flinched and the charcoal slipped, leaving a bold black streak right across the page.

"Well, poo," she said.

"Whoa, sorry," the voice said. Australian, she realised. How funny was that?

Aubrey shrugged. Mishaps were a part of the story. They did not define it. "No worries. It's hardly a Rembrandt."

Shadow fell over her as the owner of the voice moved in, blocking the light pouring into the room from the huge glass dome above as he looked over her shoulder. "No," he said. "But it's damn good."

Aubrey held onto her hat and turned. Looked up. And… hot damn.

Talk about bigger than you expected! It was difficult not to gawp. For the man was tall. Built. Dark chocolate hair raked into devastatingly sexy spikes. Sunglasses hooked into the collar of his pale grey T-shirt that did little to hide the shape beneath. The man behind the voice was handsome enough to have her blush, just a little, as big, handsome guys always had.

"Thanks," she said with a quick smile, shoving her stuff back in her vintage backpack, yanking the frayed leather strap around the opening to tighten it up. She slung it over her shoulder and got back to her feet as gracefully as possible, which in short overalls and floppy sandals wasn't graceful at all.

"You sketch the big guy a lot?" asked Mr Tall Dark and Aussie, his gaze roaming around the big room.

He'd moved away again. Not crowding her. *Handsome and thoughtful,* she thought. *Nice.* Nice and big and beautiful, with a nose Michelangelo would have wept over, a hard jawline, and lips she'd kill to sketch.

"First time," she said, blinking ten to the dozen when his gaze moved back her way. "But it won't be the last, I hope. He's magnificent. Bucket-list stuff, right there."

"Hmm," the stranger hummed. The deep sound seeming to reverberate through Aubrey's chest.

"You don't agree?"

"Me? No. He's…fine."

Aubrey tried not to sputter. "*Fine?* He's perfection."

That earned her a raised eyebrow. If anything, it made the stranger even more ridiculously gorgeous. Her toes curled into her sandals.

"Marble's not my medium," he said, his gaze on the statue looming anciently over them.

"What is?"

"Wood."

At that, Aubrey tried not to look at David's bits. She really did. But with the stranger's declaration bouncing about inside her head, and David's bits staring back at her three times normal size… She was only human.

"Intimidated?" she asked, her cheeks tugging into a smile.

There was a moment, a beat that felt like a thud deep inside her chest, before his eyes narrowed. Then he lifted his chin and said, "Nah."

"Ha!"

At her bark of laughter, he swung his eyes her way. And the last of her breath left her lungs in a whoosh. His eyes were ridiculous. Deep blue, and dark and mysterious, like a river at night. Eyes a girl could drown in.

She'd use a well-sharpened pencil if she sketched him. Or a fine black pen. She'd need to get the sweep of each individual eyelash just right. The defined angle of his jaw. The chiselled curve of that seriously enticing mouth.

And those eyes, the flash of blue that might well turn a piercing aquamarine out in the sunshine, the thought of studying them enough to do them justice, made her feel light in the head.

In accepting Viv's generous gift, Aubrey had made herself a promise. To use this amazing opportunity to find a new normal, now that the future she'd always believed would be hers could not be.

No time like the present to begin.

She held out a hand to the most beautiful—flesh and blood—man she had ever seen and said, "Aubrey Trusedale. Of Sydney."

A beat later, he took it. Said, "Malone. Sean Malone." No qualification as to where he'd hailed from. *Melbourne,* she thought, taking in the cut of his clothes. The effortless style. *Definitely Melbourne.*

Taking a pause seemed to be a thing for him. A moment in which to make a decision. Find the most famous statue of a naked man in the world intimidating, or not. Talk to the strange girl, or not.

When the heat from Sean Malone's hand spread into hers, the unexpected calluses on the pads of his palms rubbing against the matching ones on hers, she smiled. And meant it.

"I'm very glad to have met you, Malone."

A half-hour later, Sean found himself unsure as to how he'd ended up in the Piazza Della Signoria having a coffee with a stranger he'd picked up along the way.

Or had she picked him up?

One of them had mentioned being starving, which, on reflection, didn't sound like him.

So here he was, sweltering beneath a bright yellow sun umbrella, at a rickety wrought-iron table, palming a cooling espresso, and packed in like a sardine with a zillion other sun-baskers doing the same.

While she—the stranger, Aubrey Trusedale of Sydney— was leaning over the back of her chair, chatting with the South African couple at the next table about their travels— and jobs, and families, and favourite books—leaving Sean to wait, and muse, and remember.

None of which he was keen to do.

But first... "Aubrey."

She held up a staying finger. "Just a sec."

Sean held out a hand in supplication, but nobody was paying him any heed.

So, he leaned around the table and grabbed the woman's backpack. It was wide open. Without even trying to see inside he spotted paper, pens, wallet, sunglasses, what looked like spare clothes in a Ziploc bag, and a lacy G-string sitting right on top.

He pulled the strap that scrunched the bag closed— mostly, the thing was built for pilfering—before squeezing the bag between the table leg and his own.

And waited. And mused. And remembered.

Having lived in Florence near on five years now he'd visited the David more than once, but playing tourist had *not* been how he'd planned to start his day.

The email. The email had knocked him off course.

Once his team had arrived at the workshop he'd built beneath his place in the hills overlooking the city, the sounds of saws and music spilling through the open windows, he'd walked out of the front door. Leaving his dog at the villa, for the day was far too hot to lug Elwood down the hill.

The height of summer had descended over Florence, bringing with it the usual humidity and plague of tourists, so by the time he'd hit the city his head was no clearer. The answer to the email still unformed.

So he'd kept walking. Meandering the back streets; lean, shadowed caverns between the old stone buildings it was easy to get lost in. It was what he'd loved most about the city. He'd lost himself there years ago.

And he'd found himself outside the Galleria dell'Accademia—its unassuming wooden door tucked into the side of an unending row of beige buildings—as the sun had truly begun to burn.

Taking a break from the heat, he'd gone in. Made his way to the most famous artefact in the place, and found her sitting there—Aubrey Trusedale of Sydney—cross-legged, in the middle of the gallery floor.

Short overalls over a white T-shirt covered in faces of black cats, one strap half falling off her shoulder. Sandals only just clinging to her feet. Her back to the room. Her backpack on the floor beside her, wide open.

He could have moved on. Kept walking. Made his way back to the air-conditioned bliss of his city showroom. Answered the email and moved on with his life.

But something about the way her shoe had been half falling off, and her hat was too big for her head, had made him stop.

Florence was a great city, but like any city—any place—bad things could happen. And something about her screamed trouble magnet.

Not that he had a knight-in-shining-armour complex. He intentionally kept out of other people's business and appreciated them doing the same for him. But the bag—he had to say something. Only when he'd moved in did he notice she was sketching.

Her fingers had gripped so tight to a charcoal pencil her knuckles had gone white, and yet the sweep of movement over the paper—it had been arresting. Her style loose and easy. The lines bold yet graceful.

She was very good.

He'd have recognised the subject anywhere. The David's right hand. Famously larger than it ought to have been. Supposedly a nod to the man's inner strength. Though it messed with Sean's architectural brain.

A bespoke furniture designer by trade, he sketched all the time. Mostly on grid paper—straight lines and precise curves. Shapes he could build. Shapes that were comfortable to the eye. And the backside. Shapes that had people on wait lists for his designs.

Yet he had none of her light hand. None of her sense of freedom. Her effortless speed. And he'd found himself entranced.

He'd watched her pencil fly over the page for a full minute before he'd heard a voice. Surprised to find it was his own.

Then she'd looked up at him. All big brown Bambi eyes. Eyes full of spark. Eyes that had taken one look at him and warmed all over. Clear that she'd liked what she'd seen, and that she'd had no ability—or, perhaps, intention—of hiding it.

Only then had come the accent. Australian.

Of all the days...

For the email that had sent him walking had been from back home. Hidden, innocently, between the usual—invitations to gallery openings, to guest lecture at tech schools and museums, to present a TED talk, even a nudge to see if he might be keen to co-host a renovation show on British TV.

The email was a commission enquiry for a custom memorabilia shelving unit for a pre-eminent Australian Rules Football club.

It wasn't his usual thing. His custom pieces tended to be more specialised. Twelve-foot doors. Monolithic tables. In the past year he'd been called on to build a throne. His sister used to call this sideline of his vocation Shock and Awe.

Sean blinked at the vision of his sister's face, blaming

the damn email anew. Then downed the last of his coffee, holding onto the bitter aftertaste.

The email had been sent by a friend of his father.

His father whom he hadn't seen in half a decade. Hadn't spoken to in, what, a year? More? Was it a coincidence? Or could it be his old man's way of reaching out?

Laughter brought him back to the now.

A waiter had joined in the conversation on the other side of the table. Telling a story, in broken English, that had Aubrey and her new friends in stitches. The young man held a menu in what looked to be a most uncomfortable position, high above his head so that it stopped a shard of sunlight between the umbrella edges from hitting Aubrey in the face.

Mid smile, she reached for her bag. Found it missing. She spun on her chair, Bambi eyes wide.

Sean lifted the bag and passed it over the table.

And her eyes met his. Direct. Warm. Zesty. Filled with laughter and suggestion and temptation. Heat swept over him—inevitable and true. Heat that had nothing to do with the bite of the summer's day.

She fixed the strap of her overalls that had slipped off one shoulder. Mouthed, *Thank you*. Then ferreted around inside the bag till she grabbed what looked like a mint and tossed it back with the last of her coffee.

She paused mid swallow as she caught his eye again; this time her expression was far more guarded. She ran a finger over her lips and said, "Special vitamins."

He nodded. Waited for her to turn back to her new friends. And breathed out.

That was how he'd ended up here.

Back in the gallery, her eyes on his, head cocked, her hat slipping off her head to reveal short, shaggy auburn waves. Freckles on a fine nose. Dark smudges beneath those warm, inviting eyes. Lips that might seem too wide for such a delicate face, unless a person had seen them smile.

The squeeze of her hand reminding him he hadn't let her go.

"Is it just me," she'd said, "or do you also feel the urge to jump over that little fence and touch the big guy?"

After a moment Sean had shaken his head.

"It's like a current running under my skin. You really don't feel it too?"

He'd felt something. Concern, he'd told himself, at the fact her backpack now slowly eased open as she jumped from foot to foot, energised by that current under her skin.

"Maybe I'm just hungry. Do you know a place?"

And here they were.

Across the table Aubrey said goodbye to her new friends and turned to him, her expression chagrined. "Sorry, they were about to leave for Rome this afternoon and hadn't seen the David. I felt like it was my mission to convince them they must."

"Success?" he asked.

"Success," she said, those wide lips stretching into a huge smile. Then she dropped her hands to the table, leaned forward and said, "So, now what?"

Her focus was sharp. Her smile encouraging. And for a second Sean felt as if the current she'd spoken about flickered deep inside him.

He lifted his hands deliberately from the table and pushed back his chair. "Now I have work to do. What are your plans?"

The edge of her smile dropped, but she rallied quickly. "You know what, I'm exhausted. I think I'll head back to my hotel, get a good night's sleep and start anew tomorrow."

"Lead the way."

"It wasn't an invitation for you to join me there," she said over her shoulder as they threaded their way through the tightly packed tables, the glint in her eyes making it clear she was joking.

"I'm aware."

"Are you sure? I wouldn't want to hurt your feelings."

"My feelings are just fine."

"I mean, we've only just met. And you aren't a fan of the David. And this is my first day in town so I really should keep my options open."

Hands in pockets, Sean followed. "Sounds like a good plan."

Sean would escort her back to whatever backpacker place she was booked into and on the way he'd give her some sage advice on the areas to avoid. Recommend she ditch the backpack and simplify what she needed to take out with her into the streets.

And feel safe in the knowledge he'd done all he could to make sure a stranger he'd once met lived through the day.

Aubrey fell back on the lush king-sized bed in her opulent suite.

Viv had made it very clear that she was not allowed to take a single cent back to Australia with her. That it all had to be spent. On luxury accommodation and gastronomical feasts, on gondola rides and hot-air balloons and helicopter flights and every sensory experience a person could possibly imagine.

Aubrey closed her eyes, breathing in the singular scent—like snow and freesias and spun gold—and replayed every second of her first day in Florence.

Firenze. The city of flowers. Of Machiavelli and the Medicis. Of Michelangelo and Rembrandt. The freaking David!

And Sean Malone.

She wriggled on the bed, the current she'd felt under her skin in the gallery back with a vengeance. She'd assumed it was due to the man on the stand. Maybe it had more than a little to do with the real live one instead.

She bit her lip to stop from grinning.

Who'd have thought? First day and she'd already met

some tall, dark handsome stranger, had a coffee with the guy, while a statue of a Medici on horseback looked over them, and a fountain depicting Neptune and a bunch of sea-horses bubbled ostentatiously in the background.

It had been an overload of sensation. The warmth on her skin. The effusive banter in Italian, flowing and tripping all around her. The smooth dark flavour of the coffee.

She might have pinched herself. Twice.

Despite the jet lag and her usual fatigue tugging at the corners of her subconscious, she sat up, bounced her way to the end of the huge bed, and grabbed her phone. Hoping somewhere in the world one of her friends would be awake.

The first to answer the video chat was Jessica. Diligent to the last.

"Aubrey!" she said, rubbing her eyes and yawning.

"Oh, no. Did I wake you?"

"Hmm? No, it's fine. I must have fallen asleep on the couch. We were watching *When Harry Met Sally*. Jamie and I are on week two of a New York rom-com binge."

Aubrey's eyebrows lifted. "He agreed to that? Jeez. He really must be love struck."

Jessica attempted to glare but she was way too sweet, and way too in *lurve* to pull it off. "Tell me, what's happening in Aubrey land?"

Aubrey lifted the phone, twirled it slowly about the insanely glamorous suite Viv had put her up in, then carried the phone to the window, pulling back the floaty curtains to show off her view. The Arno river. The Ponte Vecchio. The buttery sunshine pouring over the ancient architecture.

"Oh, my gosh!" Jess's voice came through the speaker. Then a little muffled, as she turned away, to talk over her shoulder. "It's Aubrey. She's in Florence."

"Hey, Aubs." That was Jamie. Jessica's wonderful new suit-and-tie guy.

Aubrey had spoken to him a handful of times since he and Jessica had fallen for one another and she loved him already. For Jessica. He wasn't *her* type. Too straight up and down. Too smitten.

Aubrey wouldn't turn down the chance for a little romance while on her trip, a fast and fiery meeting of the souls—but until she figured out what the next phase of her life would look like she wasn't dragging some poor lovestruck guy into the picture.

"Hey, Jamie!" she said, moving to sit on the floor, leaning against the velvet banquette at the end of her bed. "How's it hanging? Or should I ask Jessica when you're out of the room?"

The wide-eyed look he gave her matched Jessica's to a T. Made for one another, those two.

"Have fun, Aubs," he said before heading out of shot.

"Planning on it!" Aubrey called, her voice echoing in her massive suite.

Jessica's face returned; she was biting her bottom lip to stop from laughing. "So tell me. What have you been up to so far? Eaten your weight in pasta? Accidentally touched any great works of art? Fallen in lust with the man of your dreams?"

Sean Malone's handsome face slid into her subconscious, and Aubrey's heart shifted. Or squeezed. It moved in a way she was not used to, and wasn't looking for. She had a love-hate relationship with the reliability of that particular organ. She gave her chest a bump with her fist, told it to settle down.

The shock must have shown in her face, as Jessica's brow knitted a moment before she rolled her eyes. "I meant the *David*! Did you get to see the David?"

"Oh! Right." Aubrey laughed, letting her hand fall away from her chest. "And yes. Yes!"

She crawled over to her backpack—a gorgeous, deep, soft, vintage-green suede thing she'd bought online that looked as well travelled as she one day wished she would be. Sure, it didn't close all that well, which Mr Malone had mentioned more than once as he'd walked her home, but it had the perfect inner pockets for wallet, phone, wipes, spare clothes, passport and, most importantly, her meds.

She scrounged around till she found her sketchbook, turned to the page where she'd sketched the David's hand, with its raw, angled knuckles and beautiful roping veins. She held the picture up to the phone.

"Wow, Aubrey," Jessica breathed. "Just…wow. Jamie! Come see what our girl drew!"

As she flipped through the pages for her captive audience, she found herself imagining the hand turned to flesh. Tanned, male, brute strength evident in the curl of the fingers as they rested loosely around an espresso glass. Short square nails, dark stains in the creases of his knuckles. Not dirt. Oil? Varnish? And scars. Several scars.

She remembered the feel of that hand wrapped around hers. The heat humming beneath the surface. The rough calluses creating an echo, a scraping sensation, in her belly.

"Aubrey?" Jessica's voice drifted into her subconscious. "Aubs?"

Daisy's voice joined in. "Is she okay? She looks flushed. Why are you flushed? Are you okay?"

Aubrey dropped the sketchbook and her hands flew to her cheeks to find them warm. Dammit. The last thing she needed was the girls worrying about her. On day one!

"Daisy!" she said, leaning forward and flapping her hands at the small camera. Distraction was one of her better skills. "Oh, my gosh, is that rock star Daisy Mulligan?"

Daisy rolled her eyes. "Are you okay?"

"I'm fine. Fabulous. It's just a zillion degrees here. I've been out, absorbing fresh air and sunshine."

"How was the flight?" Daisy asked, eyes narrowed.

"The flight. Was that today?" Jessica asked. "Must be an awfully long flight from Australia. Make sure you rest."

"Any time you can," Daisy added.

"Mum. Dad," Aubrey said. "You can stop fussing now."

Both of her friends cringed.

"Sorry," said Daisy, resting her chin on her hand till her lovely face was squashed. "Tell us about the hot city-boy Italians. I missed that being out in the country. Do they *ooze* sex appeal? Can you walk straight what with your trembling loins?"

Aubrey glanced to Jessica's face on the other half of the screen and pointed her thumb at Daisy. "You'd never believe she writes hit lyrics for a living."

Jessica laughed. "Don't change the subject."

"Okay, fine! The guard watching over the David's name is Mario. He has four daughters and occasional gout."

"She's trying to distract us," Daisy muttered to Jessica.

"I concur," Jessica said. "Meaning she's holding something back."

Aubrey loved her friends dearly. Even though they lived in different parts of the world, they were so close. They could open up about things, fears, failings, in ways they couldn't to those closest by. Or maybe that was why. But sometimes she kind of wished they didn't know her so well.

"Okay, fine. But I'll need vocal lubrication for this." Aubrey took her phone to the tiny pod-coffee machine by the window and made herself an espresso. Over the whir she told them about Sean Malone.

When she finished she waited for the good-natured ribbing. But while Jessica looked doe-eyed, Daisy appeared furious.

"We said she should have done a tour," said Daisy. "Stayed with a group. Had a buddy. Been on a list that had to be checked off hourly. She's too trusting."

"Far too trusting," Jessica conceded, blinking away the romance in her eyes.

"Is that what you were wearing?" Daisy asked.

Aubrey glanced down at the white T-shirt covered in black cats she wore under her shortie denim overalls. "Jessica gave it to me last Christmas."

"Exactly!" sad Daisy, as if that proved the fact that Aubrey should not be let out of the house alone. "What if he's some kind of weirdo? A stalker? A…predator?"

"You think?" said Jessica. "He did take her out for coffee."

"Hello!" Aubrey called, drawing focus. "I'm right here. Sean Malone did not take me out for coffee. I drank coffee. He drank coffee. We sat on opposite sides of the same table. And he pretty much spent every spare moment telling me how to stay safe."

That was right. The conversation hadn't been at all romantic, come to think of it. He'd given her the rundown on tourism safety while she'd nattered on about all the things she planned to do on this trip.

But not the why. People always turned weird when they found out she'd been so sick. Her body so scourged she'd had to relearn how to walk. Her joints sore. Her muscles weakened. Much of her long curly auburn hair had fallen out. Her mother had cried when, a year ago, she'd shaved it off.

Another reason she loved her girls so much. They thought she was just as fierce and fabulous now as in the Before. Which was why they wanted her to pace herself. They knew it wasn't her nature.

"He told me how to hide my money and papers under my clothes."

"He did what?" Daisy shot back.

"*Told* me. Not showed me. Jeez." Though the thought of those hands sliding up under her shirt, or tugging at the beltline of her shorts, was not a terrible one.

"Well, that sounds nice," said Jessica aka Miss Always Look on the Bright Side. "Not stalkerish at all."

"Yep. Just a nice Australian guy, helping another Australian." So why did that make Aubrey suddenly feel as if she'd run over a nail with fresh new tyres?

"What was his name again?" Daisy asked.

"Malone," Aubrey said distractedly. "Sean Malone."

"And he's Australian. Why is that name familiar?" Daisy brought up her phone, thumbs flying over the screen. "I've been reading a lot of true crime of late."

When Daisy's eyes went wide, Aubrey had a pretty good idea she'd found him. Daisy held up her phone. "This him?"

One look at the swish of dark hair, the chiselled jaw, the lovingly carved lips, the deeply romantic blue eyes burning into the camera and Aubrey felt her cheeks go hot once more. "Mm hmm."

"Whoa," said Daisy. "He's—"

"I know, right?" Aubrey breathed.

"I mean he's really really…"

"Gorgeous," they said in tandem.

Then they laughed, and any tension that had been there as a result of her favourite girls looking out for her just a little too much dissipated.

"Says here he's a well-respected furniture maker. Born in Melbourne. Based in Florence."

"So he *lives* here."

"Has for several years, it seems. He's kind of famous, actually. His stuff has ended up in houses of movie stars, presidential meeting rooms, a palace or three. His medium is wood—tables, chairs, fancy architectural stuff—oh, my God! That's where I know him from! My Jay has a couple of his chairs, big manly beastly things, all square arms and leather seats, he wanted to bring to the cottage till we realised they wouldn't fit through the doors. Well, there you go!"

Jessica and Aubrey let Daisy's super-sweet "my Jay" comment go. For all that she was super well-known now, she was deeply private and had a tendency to go underground if she felt cornered.

"Wood," said Aubrey suddenly, as Sean's comment from earlier suddenly made sense. She laughed out loud. Laughed until she felt breathless.

"Okay," said Jessica, "I don't care if I sound like your mother, I think it's time we let you get some rest."

Daisy glared into the camera. "Check in whenever you can so we know you're making good choices."

"Not a chance! Love you guys!"

"Love you too, you terror," said Daisy before signing off.

"Enjoy yourself," said Jessica. "Soak up every second. Just… Take it from me, and I'm sure Daisy would say the same, while Viv's gifts have been life-altering, they can come with a sting in the tail. And after all you've been through, the last thing we want is for you to find yourself stung. Again. So, take care, okay?"

Aubrey nodded. "Promise."

When they both signed off Aubrey let go of a long slow breath.

And the exhaustion she'd been holding at bay came over her in a wave so strong she had to sit. The travel, the heat, the sensory overload, the David, and the guy. It was a lot for one day. A lot for a girl from the suburbs whose highlights from the past two years had been getting the doctor's permission to have butter on her movie popcorn and being given the green light to drive again.

While meeting the likes of Sean Malone had been unexpected, to all intents and purposes, he was as real to her as a marble statue.

And that was okay.

Aubrey crept back onto the bed, the hotel room such a perfect temperature she didn't need to crawl beneath the blankets. She simply curled up in a ball, her head sinking onto the downy pillow.

While her eyes began to flutter, she scrolled through old folders on her phone till she found the last photo taken of her before she'd fallen ill.

She was holding her phone at the end of her outstretched arm, auburn curls tumbling over her shoulders, cheeks fuller than they were now, a huge grin on her face. Behind her, on the hospital bed, sat one Vivian Ascot. Beside Viv, Jessica and Daisy. Max the dog's little face peeked out from inside Aubrey's jacket.

On a whim she texted the photo to the girls. And then also to Vivian Ascot.

Then she sent a few quick Proof of Life pics to her family. A selfie with the David. The view from her room. The table at the café, with its glossy cappuccinos and red checked tablecloth, one Sean Malone cropped out of shot. A photo of one of her sketches.

She let her phone drop to the bed and closed her eyes. Seconds later she was out like a light.

CHAPTER TWO

AUBREY DRAGGED ONE eye open, then the other, to find herself face up in a big soft bed; a fresco of a dozen naked cherub babies with wings hovering high above.

The sight of their chubby little legs gave her a massive twinge, right in the ovaries. Meaning it took her a few extra seconds to remember where the heck she was.

She rubbed her eyes, rolled over and sat on the edge of the bed. Through the gap in the gauzy curtains leading out to her balcony, her gaze settled on the sight of Ponte Vecchio, one of the most famous bridges in the world, right outside her window.

And it all came back to her.

Viv's exorbitant gift. Convincing her parents, her doctors, herself that she *had* to take it. The lo-o-o-ong, exhausting flight. Landing in Italy on a sweltering summer's day. The three-hour drive from Rome to Florence with a driver who did not seem to know how to use his brakes—

And, the David. Her life-long crush. In all his marble glory.

Feeling much better about the world and all things in it, Aubrey tipped down onto the floor, padded to the coffee machine and booted it up. Yawning as the coffee poured, hot and dark, into her glass.

And, as she had done every day for the past year and a half, she checked in with herself. Hand over her heart, eyes closed, as her psychologist had taught her. She waited till she felt her heart beat. Even and sure.

Next her fingers. No numbness. Her legs were a little worn out. A slight ache behind her eyes. Not surprising considering her last couple of days and the amount of things she'd jammed into them. It was a lot, even for a normal person.

Perhaps heading out into the heat to explore the moment she'd reached the hotel hadn't been the smartest choice.

She pictured her mother, hands wringing out a kitchen rag, eyes on the mobile phone propped in the stand her oldest grandchild had made at kindy. Her brothers pacing by their phones, waiting for Proof of Life. Her father, working at the auto shop, pretending he wasn't laying a hand on the phone attached to his tool belt with a clip she'd painted, so he wouldn't miss the buzz.

Should she stay in for a day? Recoup her energy? Rethink her beautiful vintage backpack as Sean had suggested, while she was at it?

"Oh," she said, the word catching in her throat, as Sean Malone came back to her in a whumph.

Grumpy, bossy, quite famous furniture builder and all around hot guy. Imagine if she'd stayed in the day before and missed that?

Question answered, she squared her shoulders. Grabbed her phone. Took a quick photo of her view and added it to the family chat with the message My view is better than yours! then tossed her phone onto her bed and padded to the bathroom, which was bigger than her apartment back home.

Showered and dressed, with her vintage backpack over her shoulder, she headed out into the beautiful summer's day.

If she couldn't run with the bulls, or drink herself under the table, or boldly touch a piece of art that connected her to centuries of masters who subsumed themselves to the wonder of beauty, then what was the point in dreaming big at all?

She just had to find a way to do all that, while not wearing herself to collapse, before her world tour had barely begun.

And she knew just where to start.

* * *

Sean sipped on an espresso, his elbows leaning on the counter-top in his showroom in the Via Alighieri, his mind a million miles away.

Or, to be precise, a couple of hundred metres away, where, on the opposite bank of the Arno River, stood the Florentine Hotel where he'd left one Aubrey Trusedale the afternoon before.

The Florentine was no backpacker joint. It was six-star, with views of the Ponte Vecchio and across to the Pitti Palace. What a girl in cut-off overalls and flappy sandals was doing staying in a place like that, on her own so far as he could tell, was a mystery.

A mystery he had no intention of spending another moment concerning himself with after he'd done all he could the day before to send her safely on her way. And yet, here he was, spending moments. Plural. Thinking about those warm, unfiltered, golden brown eyes.

But it was either that, or stew over the email from back home. The one he'd yet to answer.

Through the cracks in the stone walls Sean could hear the faint echo of applause from the ten o'clock tour group, no doubt packed to the rafters watching the leather-stamping display in Bella Pelle next door.

Distraction. That was what he needed. Noise, not quiet. Not time inside his own head.

He moved around the counter, boots scuffing the ancient mosaic floor, and Elwood lifted his smooth silvery head, solemn blue Weimaraner eyes looking at Sean.

"Walk?"

The dog's chin slid back to the floor.

"Maybe later."

Sean propped open the glass door, using a wooden wedge—an offcut from a table he'd made years ago. The summer air hit like a furnace blast, tendrils leaking around him into the air-conditioned comfort beyond.

Summer in Florence was a testament to the city's draw; the heat enough to make a person squint, but not enough to turn them away.

Leaning in the doorway, letting the Italian sun thaw him out, he hoped the heat, the noise, the colour, the life outside his door would burn away the thoughts that refused to clear.

Turned out half the proprietors in the laneway were doing the same; leaning in their shopfront doorways, eyes on the street as it thrummed under the weight of the summer tourist infestation.

Enzo, the restaurateur, called out the daily specials to those who wandered by. Offered free wine, free garlic bread, free hugs. A couple of people took the hugs, more still fell for his charm and found themselves swept inside.

Gia, the leathersmith, shooed the tour group out of the door, while wiping a hand across her brow.

Roberto, the jeweller, was no Enzo on the charm front, but his wares were inducement enough. The man was a true artisan. He even had another shop on the Ponte Vecchio itself.

Sean knew their stories. They were vocal about their successes. And their heartaches. For they were a bold bunch; effusive, emotional, happy to be all up in one another's space.

But they did not know him. Or his story. Polite hellos. Discussions about the weather. That was his limit. He didn't do sharing. It was not his way. Not here. not any more.

"Gian!" called Enzo, snapping his checked tea towel over one shoulder. "You look hungry! What can I bring you?"

Sean shook his head, and lifted his espresso glass to show he was good.

Enzo scoffed. "I'll bring you *tiramisù*. Or *cassata* Siciliana...*panna cotta*...*babà*...*tartufo di Pizzo*..."

It was a play they had acted out so many times he could recite it by heart. Enzo trying gamely to feed him, the Italian way of bringing someone into the fold. And Sean resisting.

"I'm fine," Sean called, stepping back as a group of young female tourists scurried close, giggling behind their hands.

"Ah, you hurt me. You really do," Enzo cried, all drama, before turning his decidedly unscathed attentions to the paying customers.

No one came to Sean's door. His spot was a display case rather than a shopfront. A stage on which to show examples of his team's more esoteric pieces. The current range his most daring and difficult yet—chairs and coffee tables made of wood warped and shaped in flowing, twisting lines that had them appear as if made of ribbon. Some simplified form of which would soon trickle down into his wholesale lines.

But more than that, it was a place to get away to when the energy of the workshop became too much. Just as the workshop was a place to get away to when the energy of the street circled too close, his life a constant balancing act of punishing work, and solitude.

When Roberto the jeweller looked as if he was building up enough steam to hurtle himself through the crowd and across the laneway, Sean pressed himself away from the doorframe. "Elwood," he said with a whistle. "Time for a walk."

Elwood huffed, then unfolded himself from his spot beneath the air-conditioning vent and lolloped to the door. Sean grabbed and pocketed a lead. Dogs, by law, were free to roam in the city but the Australian in him was too strong to go so far as to take Elwood into a café, or a museum.

He locked up—the cool lighting in the showroom permanently on—then spun out into the lane only to run smack bang into someone coming the other way.

Arms flailed.

Elwood barked.

The stranger swore rather magnificently in English, then dropped to a crouch, collecting sunglasses, hat, bag and any number of things that had gone flying.

Sean froze. Something about the top of the head—the short, shaggy auburn waves—looked familiar.

"Aubrey?"

She looked up, while shoving things inside her ill-advised backpack before attempting to drag its fallible opening closed.

"Malone? Is that—? Oh, my. Hi!" Big, liquid brown eyes beamed up at him. The colour of unstained cherry wood. The colour of home.

Elwood sat on his foot, tail wagging as he panted gently up at their interloper, and when Aubrey caught the dog's eye she lit up, leaning down to ruffle Elwood's ears. "Oh, hello! Aren't you beautiful? Such a good boy. And a *big* boy! Whoa!"

She laughed, all easy grace as she got a nose to the crotch.

"Jeez, Malone," she laughed. "Your dog's a little fresh. I wonder where he learned that move."

Before he could hope to respond, out of the corner of his eye, Sean noted that they had an audience. His fellow vendors were no longer trying to out shout one another. They all hovered in their shopfronts, watching. Patently intrigued by the fact he had a visitor. Or a customer. Or that he was engaging in conversation at all.

Aubrey stood, her eyes finding his once more. "How funny is this? You and me, finding one another again while I was out and about following my feet and… Hang on a sec. My phone!" Aubrey spun on the spot, smacking at her right butt cheek, eyes frantic.

Sean found it beneath Elwood's wagging tail, face down, the case detailed with a photo of what looked like a heart made out of stained glass. Looking closer, he saw it had been painted onto the hood of a muscle car.

He turned it to make sure the screen wasn't damaged, to find the phone on, open to the map. A little red pin pointing right at his showroom.

Following her feet, was she? A muscle flickered in his cheek as he handed the phone over. He watched her eyes widen as she realised she'd been sprung.

"Okay, fine," she said, "I wasn't following my feet. I was kind of stalking you."

"Stalking me."

Out of the corner of his eye, Sean saw Gina hustle over to Enzo, and stage whisper "stalker" while pointing his way. Enzo nodded effusively, as if that made far more sense than him having an actual acquaintance.

"Well, my friend looked you up online, you see," Aubrey was saying. "My other friend is too nice to do that kind of thing. She's Canadian. We kind of drag her along for the ride."

Sean opened his mouth to ask what on earth she was talking about, then thought better of it. The way her eyes moved over his face, the sigh in her voice, transparent, unbridled, he had a pretty good feeling what her conversations with her friends might have entailed.

Aubrey spun to watch an older woman on a Vespa curl in and out of the crowd meandering down the centre of the alley. Her face was bright, alive, as she said, "This place is wild. Crumbling yet posh. You know?"

Figuring it better not to indulge her, he said, "Were you stalking me for a reason?"

She caught his eye, and blinked. "Surely one doesn't stalk a person on a whim."

He lifted an eyebrow and waited.

Eventually she puffed out a surrendering breath. "Okay, then. Here's the truth. Since you're the only person I know in this city, I was hoping you might be able to point me in the direction of a chaperone."

"A chaperone?"

"What? No. Not a *chaperone*. Pfft. I'm a grown woman living in the twenty-first century."

She cocked a hip.

"Look, I hate even asking, because I *am* a grown woman living in the twenty-first century. But I'm here on my own. And while that *was* my plan, to do this trip alone, to own it, you know, to follow my curiosity and soak in every ounce of adventure that fell my way without having to ask permission, it was actually kind of nice, yesterday, having someone to hang with. Someone to remind me to stop and have a cuppa rather than go go go till I collapse."

She waited for him to respond. But he had nothing. Whatever she was asking he was the exact wrong person to ask.

"I don't have a natural off switch, you see," she went on, rocking from foot to foot now, her energy levels ramping up. "Which is totally part of my charm. But Florence is my very first stop. I'm in this travel thing for the long haul, and I don't think packing my days quite so full is a recipe for longevity."

When she looked at him, beseeching him to say something so she could stop, Sean ran a hand up the back of his neck, and glanced down the laneway. "Do you need me to hook you up with a tour company? Gia, next door, the leathersmith, has a lot of groups go through her door."

Aubrey stopped her swaying, and gave him a look that was both direct and shrewd. "You know what? Forget it. I don't know what I want, clearly, and you shouldn't be the one to figure it out for me. Just because we're both Australian, and you clearly find me delightful, doesn't mean we're friends. You hardly know me! I mean, what's my last name?"

"Trusedale."

"Oh. *Oh*," she said again, the second time softer than the first. "You *were* paying attention." Her face came over all sweet, with a good dose of canny, and Sean wished he'd kept his trap shut.

Just then, a bunch of well-dressed young Florentine men burst from the entrance to Enzo's bistro. Laughing, jostling. One of them bumped Aubrey as they passed.

A couple of the men turned to apologise. When they saw who they were apologising to—a long-legged beauty in short shorts, with glowing skin, huge smiling eyes, who was lapping up every ounce of attention—they moved in. All apologies, promises, playing up their accents for the pretty tourist.

Her backpack slid from her shoulder, the lip opening wide. And before he even felt himself move, Sean stepped close, and reached out for the handle; his finger tracing her shoulder, skin warmed by the sun, as he slid it down her arm and into his hand.

He moved in front of Aubrey as he yanked the cord tight, and turned to the men. *"Vai avanti,"* he said. *"Vamoose."*

The young men bowed, held up hands in supplication, one stopped to pat Elwood, who panted blissfully, his tail wagging once in the heat, and off they went.

When Sean turned back Aubrey's eyebrows were half-way up her forehead. Her lips clamped between her teeth as she waited for an explanation.

The fact was, he didn't have one. Not one he cared to verbalise.

So he went with, "Maybe a chaperone is exactly what you need."

"Ha! Sexist much."

"My observations," he said, "have nothing to do with your being a woman and everything to do with the fact you can't keep your damn bag closed."

She held out a finger and he draped the loop of her backpack over the digit. When his finger grazed hers, the lightest imaginable touch, he felt a crackle of electricity.

She gave the cord an extra tug, as if he'd been about to rifle through the thing. But her smile... She liked him. She liked the tension strung between them. That much was crystal clear.

He'd be lying if he said he didn't feel the pull, a leaning towards her effervescence, but, while she was so full of light it was hard not to squint, he'd been burned hollow a long time ago.

"*Gian! Caro amico!* Did those young men bother your friend?"

Sean looked up to find Enzo descending, eyes locked onto Aubrey—his conduit to a conversation outside food, or whether or not it looked like rain.

"Not at all," said Aubrey. "They were hilarious."

"Ah. *Bene. Bene.* That is good."

Knowing the older man would burst if he was not at least given an introduction, Sean said, "Enzo, this is Aubrey, my—"

"Your friend! *Sì.* It is so nice to see you with a friend. And a lovely friend at that!"

Not a friend. Barely an acquaintance. Absolutely a thorn in his side.

In the end, Sean corrected with, "She's a fellow Australian. Aubrey Trusedale, this is Enzo Frenetti. The owner of the fine bistro you see across the way."

"Oh, how brilliant," Aubrey said, reaching out to shake Enzo's hand. "Cannot wait to eat there!"

"So, you and Gian are *not* friends?" Enzo queried, expression near comical in its confusion as he took in the gap between Sean and Aubrey. Or lack of gap more like, as Aubrey had leaned into him until the barest sliver of daylight peeked through.

Sean inched away. One hand curling Elwood's leash tighter, the other shoved into the pocket of his jeans.

"That's right," Aubrey said, grinning. "We are most definitely *not* friends."

"Then… Are you here to check out Gian's wares?" asked Enzo.

"His wares, you say?" Her big Bambi eyes turning his way before glancing down to his shoes then back to his face. Not even trying to hide the fact she'd just checked him out. "Sure. Why not?"

Sean cocked his head. *Really?*

She shrugged. The tiniest movement of her shoulders. *So sue me.*

"*Sì,*" said Enzo, chest puffed out, missing the subtleties entirely. "This young man is one of the most talented artisans I have had the pleasure to meet in my entire life." Was that a tear brimming in Enzo's eye? "He is a marvel. A visionary. Florence is lucky to have him as our adopted son."

"Visionary, you say?" Aubrey was no longer trying to hold back her grin. It was pure sunshine. Utter delight. "Do tell."

"Another time," said Sean, before the two of them steam-rollered him with their combined enthusiasms. And he'd already engaged in more conversation than he usually did in an entire day.

Enzo took the hint. "Another time. Till then, I shall leave you young people to your adventures."

With a bow of his head he backed away, banging into Roberto, who was hovering behind him. Enzo flapped his hands at Roberto, chastising him in *presto* Italian as they scuttled off to their respective shopfronts and began beckoning passers-by as if nothing had gone on.

The sounds of the crowd bustling around them crept back in as Aubrey turned his way. She took in the dog now leaning against his leg, and the lead gripped in his palm. "So, we are walking, yes?"

Sean baulked. He could just as easily claim work, and head back inside the air-conditioned comfort. Pull out his laptop. Get some admin done. Answer a certain email—

Chances were, she'd follow her feet right inside his showroom and settle in for the day.

"We are walking," he said, regretting the words the minute he said them.

Till her lovely face lit with delight.

"Any place in particular you'd like to go?"

"Every place." She bounced on her toes and clapped her hands and pointed in every direction till he picked one.

"Would you like me to show you my favourite things to do around Florence?"

"Really? That would be grand. I can't imagine why it never occurred to me to ask!"

Sean almost laughed. Or more that he remembered how it felt to do so. "Okay, then. Let's go."

CHAPTER THREE

AUBREY EXPECTED THE delicious Mr Malone to take her some place obvious, like the Pitti Palace or the Uffizi Gallery.

Or some hidden gem of a spot known only to the locals. Some place special to Dante, perhaps. For Sean Malone had a definite sense of a tragic poet about him. All dark hair raked by frustrated fingers, the constantly furrowed brow, the deep voice with that seriously sexy Italian accent as he said things such as *"mi scusi"* and *"grazie"* as they edged their way through summer crowds.

But the man seemed to be wandering, meandering nowhere in particular. Slowly. She tried clicking her fingers at his big beautiful dog in the hopes he'd speed things up. But alas, the velvety grey pup was clearly made for his ambling owner.

Was he trying to shake her off? It was a possibility.

Then again, she *had* tracked him down in the hopes of a little company to slow her down.

Yeah, right, her subconscious perked up, *that's why you tracked the hot man down.*

And yet… More than that, Aubrey was anxious to do the things. To see the places. To experience every experience. To have at the world before…

Before she accidentally pinched herself and awoke from this fairy-tale dream.

Or before something bad happened. And the dream was taken away from her, yet again.

Not that she feared contracting another heart-harming virus. But she could get hit by a Vespa. Bitten by one of the zillion dogs that roamed the city. A piano might fall from the sky and land on her head!

If it happened, it happened. But she would not die knowing she hadn't lived her life with every ounce of joy and fun and heart and purpose and communion she could. She was going to fill her life with wonder if it was the last thing she did.

"You okay?" Sean's voice rumbled into her subconscious.

She came to from her macabre imaginings to find he'd slowed even more, and was looking at her a little askew. "Hmm?"

"You're jumping from foot to foot. Need me to point you in the direction of a rest room?"

"What? Pfft. No! Where I work, I'm the only female in a place with unisex bathrooms. I have the bladder of an ox."

A beat, then, "Do oxen have particularly good bladders?"

"I've no idea. Yes. Probably." She nibbled at her lip, then thought to hell with it. "I know you have this austere aesthetic going on, but if this is your favourite thing to do in Florence you really are easily pleased."

His hand played absently with his dog's velvety grey ears; the eerily pale canine eyes looked at Aubrey in quiet expectation. The human eyes, on the other hand, those depths of the most stunning blue, watched her in a way that made her feel jittery. As if she were balanced on the edge of something. And could fall either way.

"I wasn't aware I had an aesthetic," he said, his voice like oil over gravel.

"Oh, you totally do. Don't get me wrong, it's fabulous. All *hands off the merchandise*. Dark and broody and spare."

Something flashed behind those eyes. Though she had no idea if it was exasperation or a visual version of that same crackle and snap she'd felt when he'd slipped her backpack from her shoulder earlier. Like static electricity ramped up to eleven.

But then he ran a hand over his jaw and looked off into the middle distance. Elwood tugged on the lead and they started ambling once more.

A few steps later, a drip of sweat wriggled down Aubrey's temple. She drew her tank top away from her belly and gave it a flap.

She'd always been on the smaller side. Her brothers joked they'd taken up all the hearty DNA and she'd got the left-overs. Until she'd fallen sick and those kinds of jokes had dried up overnight.

Back then, being small had led to her being famously cold at all times. When she was nine, she'd made them all sign a form promising that—when she died falling off the top of the Eiffel Tower or helicoptering over the Grand Canyon—they'd bury her with her socks on.

Now the sweat dripping down her back was just one thing to get used to in her new "normal". As if she had to relearn herself even at a cellular level.

While Sean looked so cool, so crisp, as if he had his own personal air-conditioning unit under his clothes.

Not that there was spare room for such a thing. His polo shirt fitted just right. Snug around impressive biceps, kiss-ing his wide pecs and flat belly every time Elwood yanked on the lead. *Good dog.* His jeans moulded to him as if they never wanted to let go.

"Aren't you hot?" she asked, when she had to wipe sweat out of her eyes.

He looked at her as if he'd forgotten she was even there. *Super. Brilliant plan, Aubs. This is going just beautifully.*

"It's summer. In Florence," was his response.

"Is that a yes? You are hot?"

Say it.

"Yes, I'm hot."

Aubrey held up her hand for a high five. "Gotta love a man with confidence."

The look she received was a killer. Part warning, part glint of humour; as if he *might* finally crack a smile. Would there be dimples? Just one would be more than enough. Two and her ovaries would likely self-destruct.

Not that they were of any use to her otherwise these days.

At that, her heart clenched. Enough for her to wince.

She closed her eyes a moment and shook her head. Trying to shake off the memory of her doctor's face as she'd delivered the news.

No. Not now. Distract! Look at all the pretty Florence. Look at the pretty man!

And so she looked. Distraction the key.

No dimples, but definitely eye creases. Meaning he must know *how* to smile. Unless he was a serial squinter.

Sweat trickled down the side of her face. Her palms burned. Her tongue felt parched. When she took a step the ground didn't quite reach up to meet her.

Dammit.

She hated being forced to say, "I know we've been on a snail's pace, but can we...can we pull up for a bit?"

"You okay?"

Chaperoning her because she'd tricked him into it was one thing. Having him look at her as if she were a delicate flower was quite another.

"You need to promise me something."

A single eyebrow twitched. "What's that?"

"No more asking if I'm okay."

"Right."

"It's a pet peeve." *It really was.* "I'm well aware I look part pixie, but rest assured I'm tougher than I look."

"I have no doubt." His mouth twisted one way, and then the other. "So, coming to me with the request to find someone to carry your bags—"

Hold the phone. Was that sarcasm? She felt the smile start in her belly, a warm hum before it hit her mouth. "Oh, shut up."

He held up both hands in submission.

And she laughed. Actually laughed. For the beautiful broody man had snark.

"Come on," he said, his voice deepening. "We'll stop at the next café."

He held out a hand.

Not for her to hold, she realised, when she went to take it, but to herd her ever forward.

She snapped her hand back into her side. "Sorry. I thought… But, no. I hardly know you! So *that* would be totally weird."

He gave her one more look, measured, reckoning, as if he was not blinded by her sense of humour. As if he was, in fact, figuring her out far too quickly for comfort. Then he walked on.

And Aubrey followed. Her next breath out was a little shaky, and it had little to do with the heat. It was those eyes. Stunners, both. Beautiful even. A deep, mesmerising cerulean blue.

No, Le Mans Blue.

Pearlescent Le Mans Blue, no less.

Le Mans was an absolute classic colour when it came to vintage car paint. Favoured by sixties Chevy owners. Camaros and Corvettes. Elegant and timeless and sexy, it was a favourite for custom paint jobs at her family's auto shop.

And pearlescent paint? Containing mica, a kind of powered crystal that reflected and refracted light, it created sparkle and shimmer, splitting into myriad rich colours depending on where you stood. It was her absolute favourite paint to work with, but super high-maintenance.

She risked a long glance. Took in his preppy hair, his short neat fingernails, the stubborn set to his chin. Yep. High maintenance for sure.

Used to being the boss man. To getting his way. Add deliberate. Not fanciful at all. And she was certain he'd be a right handful.

Why he'd agreed to let her follow him around she had no idea.

She could daydream it was because he'd developed an instant mad crush on her. Something along the lines of the floofy feeling she got every time he looked her way.

Wouldn't *that* be fabulous? A Florentine Fling. Sounded like a cocktail. Or an Agatha Christine novel.

Following through would mean more time in doors, for one thing. Less hours spent walking the streets. Less time out in the heat of the day. Her mother would be delighted.

Laughter curdled in her belly at the thought of video-chatting with her folks. *Hey, Mum! Dad! Meet Sean. He's kept me strapped to my hotel bed for the last week!*

Yeah—no. The occasional Proof of Life pic sent to their group chat of her smiling in front of some fabulous monument was more than enough. They needed the break from worrying about her as much as she needed her independence. Whether any of them were truly ready for it or not.

Pressure suddenly building behind her ribs, Aubrey stopped. Checked in with herself as she'd been taught. Hand over her heart, eyes closed.

Her heart was holding up fine. It was her head that needed sorting out.

She sat on what looked like a plinth meant to hold a pot plant. It could have been a thousand years old. She unhooked her backpack from her shoulder and let it slump to the cobbled ground beside her feet. "Where are we going, exactly?"

Sean's gaze remained glued to her bag—as if it might be about to sprout a head—as he said, "Some place simple. If you're looking for tourist traps, I can take you back to where we started. You'll find some of the best leather and textiles in the city."

"Nah. I'm not a 'stuff' kind of girl. Experiences. Textures. Tastes. Beauty. Art. Inspiration. Feelings—"

The more Sean's face didn't change, the deeper she went.

"I'm here to drench myself in intangibles till they are absorbed into my very skin. Add in the occasional nap, coffee, and time to sketch and I'm golden."

By the end of her rant she was sure she spotted a flicker in those dashing blue depths. Some small measure of recognition at her mission statement. Or maybe he had a dog hair in his eye.

He did the whole looking-off-into-the-distance thing one more time—his hard jaw clenching, his nostrils flaring—then he seemed to come to some sort of conclusion. "Okay, then. Without in any way implying that you're not one hundred per cent okay, if you can carry on another minute I can promise you all of the above. Then coffee."

Aubrey hauled herself to her feet, ignored the way her brain seemed to take an extra beat to catch up, and said, "Done."

He held out an elbow.

"Is that for me to take?" she asked. "After the hand-holding debacle I just want to make sure this time."

This time she got a twitch of his lips for her efforts. At this rate, she'd crack a smile from him in no time.

"Are you always so forthright?" he asked, the oil over gravel back in his voice.

"I'm a Leo," she said. "Your elbow?"

Sean reached out, took her hand and slipped it into the nook.

It fitted there like a glove. As if it had been made to live in that exact groove. Or maybe that was wishful thinking, because he was *so* nice to hold. Built like an championship diver who smelled like cinnamon and wood shavings. Big too. Big enough she felt as if, under his shelter, she could poke her tongue out at any passers-by and they'd not do a thing.

Not that she would poke out her tongue. She was a grown woman living in the twenty-first century.

Because of that she could take on the world, all on her own, just fine.

So why aren't you? her subconscious chimed in.

Because while she'd spent the past two years vibrating with the need to reassert her independence, she also didn't want to do *anything* that might cut her trip short and send her home too soon. Before she had had some idea of what that life back home might look like now that all her original dreams were no longer hers to dream.

If a handsome Aussie wood-wrangler was the fulcrum between both those needs, then so be it.

"So, I'm trying to think how I might repay you for your kindness. I'd offer to show you around Sydney whenever I get back there, but that's a tad moot, considering your accent. Where in Australia are you from?"

A muscle jerked in his cheek. His jaw clamped so tight he could be mistaken for sudden onset rigor mortis. "Melbourne."

"I'm sorry."

He lifted his voice. "I said, Melbourne."

"No, I heard you. I'm just sorry."

That made an impact. His face registered actual surprise. Maybe even a little amusement! Aubrey actually loved Melbourne. What she didn't like was feeling as if she were banging her head against a wall.

"So, that's how it's going to be?" he asked, his voice dropping. The deep tang of it creating goosebumps all over her arms.

She nodded. "Sydney is the pre-eminent Australian city. Better weather. More landmarks. And the Harbour. I mean, that's where I drop my mike."

"Pick it up. There's not a city in the world that beats Melbourne for the mix of culture, sport, food, architecture, design—"

"Then why are you here?"

A shadow descended, as if a dragon had flown low overhead. Before he had the chance to lean into it, she changed the subject. Closing her eyes tight, she begged, "Please tell me the one thing you want to show me before we find coffee is a copious amount of pizza—"

Sean pulled to a stop. "Open your eyes, da Vinci."

So she did.

To find they had stopped at the end of a cobbled lane. The small thoroughfare opened up to the edge of a huge market. Foods, textiles, trinkets. Hustle and bustle. Noise and energy and commerce.

But she saw all that out of the corner of her eye as Sean had propped her in front of a column at the corner of the square in which a three-foot-high sculpture of a man—biblical, in a loin cloth—resided. Carved into a squared-out alcove in the stone.

Come at it from any other direction and you'd miss it.

And it was glorious. It was everything she had asked for. The movement, the execution, the torment in the twist of his body, the agony of his face.

She took a step closer, her hand sliding out of the protection of Sean's arm. Blackened in the creases, nose and toes worn away, it must have been there for centuries.

"Touch it," said Sean. "I know you want to."

Aubrey laughed. Then laughed some more. "Saucy."

Sean smiled. For a split second. No teeth, but eye creases galore, and, oh, my God, a dimple. Just the one. And it was perfect.

As if he hadn't seen it coming, as if he would have stopped it if he had, Sean pulled himself together. But not before a seriously adorable flush grazed his cheeks.

"Don't get distracted," he grumbled. "You wanted to absorb, so absorb."

Aubrey was absorbing, only the statue was not her subject. She could happily have been distracted by Sean Malone's face all day long. To say he was sketchable was an understatement. Those cheekbones. The depths of his eyes.

When he tilted his head, his eyes widening, his expression increasingly exasperated, she flapped a hand at him. "Fine…fine." And turned back to the statue.

No velvet ropes here. No signs telling her what she wasn't allowed to do. She moved in, reached up and placed a hand over the statue's foot.

Closing her eyes, she committed to memory the cool of the stone. The mix of rough and smooth. The bumps where the chisel had slipped. The chips that time, and weather, and human interaction had worn away.

It could have been seconds or minutes later when she lifted her hand and opened her eyes.

Around them people milled. Talked. Haggled. Ate. Bought bags, belts, single red roses, soaps in the shape of the pope.

She felt Sean move up beside her.

"That," she said, her voice more than a little rough, "was pure magic. Thank you."

"You're welcome." A beat went by before he added, "I make wood furniture. Chairs, tables."

"I know," Aubrey said. "I cyber stalked you, remember?"

"So you did," he drawled, his voice a rough burr. "I endeavour to make pieces that are both beautiful and comfortable. Solid, artfully crafted, using old, trusted techniques. Pieces that will last. But they have nothing on the carvings you'll find scattered in such inauspicious places all over this city. Picture frames leaning outside shops. Frescos tucked into sconces in the walls. The durability is astounding. The accessibility astonishes. Exquisiteness is so interwoven into this place it's easy to miss it. So I made it my mission to see it."

It was more words than she'd have thought he had in him. And she knew she'd never forget a one.

"Pizza?" he said, and all she could do was nod.

Aubrey held the door open for the little old man with the walking stick she'd befriended while looking over the menu outside the pizzeria.

"*Grazie,*" he said.

"*Prego,*" she returned, holding the door a little longer when her waiter appeared holding her pizza. Well, hers and Sean's, but she'd have no compunction fighting for the last piece.

She followed the pizza with her nose, taking in the thick airy crust. The sauce a gorgeous oily red, big juicy basil leaves scattered atop. It was so fresh out of the pizza oven, the mozzarella still bubbled.

When she sat Sean held up the pizza cutter, his eyes asking if she was all right with him making the cut. She nodded, too busy holding back the drool till he passed her a slice.

Holding it in two hands, she bit down. "Oh, my God," she managed through a mouthful of crispy slippery goodness, "this is so good."

They didn't speak again, not till the pizza was nothing but crumbs and they were both sitting back, hands on bellies, enjoying espressos.

Elwood—curled up in a ball at Aubrey's feet—made a loud harumph.

"One thing I've noticed in my day and a half here," said Aubrey, "is the number of dogs."

"Late twenties, the Florentine government made it legal for dogs to accompany their owner pretty much everywhere. Only place they're not allowed is the Teatro del Maggio Musicale—the Florence Opera House."

"Hope Elwood's not a big fan of Puccini."

"All good. He's more a metal fan."

Aubrey grinned. Sean frowned, as if disappointed in himself for having made a joke. And her heart kerplunked dramatically inside her chest cavity.

She mentally told her heart to pull its head in.

The man sitting across from her—supremely gorgeous and broody and self-aware as he was—was not to be her test case.

He was Australian. He was here. He actively tried to help her keep her bag closed, meaning he was not about to rob her. He was nice to look at. They were the reasons she'd roped him in to help her out.

She had no intention of letting her crush get away from her.

Her heart was…untried in its current state. It had been through the wringer the past couple of years. The virus had brought about a barrage of damage. It had stopped more than once. It had been on a pacemaker. And she still took meds to keep her arteries nice and open.

Even if she told her family she was good as gold, even while her doctors had signed off on her trip, no one could tell her how much longer it would take to heal, if at all.

Meaning she had to check in, to listen to her body, to trust her instincts. Her instincts said, when it came to Sean Malone, she had to be hands off.

Which shouldn't be a problem as he clearly had no clue what to do with her.

Sure, there was *something* there. For both of them. A lovely kind of sizzle, purring away deep below the surface. So long as they both refused to act on it, the friction would keep things kinetic. Unstable. No chance they'd be on the same beat, the same breath, and their nascent friendship— yes, *friendship*—could simply kick on.

"You done?" asked Sean.

See. To the point. No room for misunderstandings. She liked that.

"Yes, Malone. I am most certainly done."

Sean wiped the napkin across his mouth. Aubrey didn't stare at his lips as they curved up at the edges. Or the moons that creased his cheeks, more evidence he did, in fact, know how to smile.

Nope. She stood and grabbed her backpack and definitely didn't stare.

As he pressed back his chair, and uncurled his big frame to standing, Sean's forehead creased into perfect horizontal lines as he gave her a look. "What?"

"What, what?"

"I can feel you thinking. Why do I feel like I need to brace myself?"

"What? No! I was just thinking how we are, in fact, most definitely, friends."

Something flashed, dark and mysterious, behind his deep blue eyes. "Friends."

"Yep. We're beyond acquaintances, certainly. Elwood took care of that when he sniffed me in the you know what."

Elwood gave her a look, his tongue lolling lazily out of the side of his mouth. She rubbed him behind the ears. Good boy. An ally after all.

With a wave towards the guys behind the pizza counter as he ushered her around the tables and out into the street, Sean said, "I've seen the way you make friends, picking them up like found pennies everywhere you go."

"I do not. I'm very discerning."

She was! She *got along* with most anyone. She loved hearing people's stories. It had been her way of living vicarious adventures when she'd not been able to afford her own.

But friends? With three big brothers, and working in the automotive industry, most of her acquaintances were male. In fact, nowadays, especially since she'd spent so much time in recovery, Daisy and Jessica were pretty much it when it came to friends she'd class as truly close. Did it help that one split her time between Canada and New York, while the other was British and constantly on tour? What did it say about her if it did?

"Right," said Sean. "The security guard at the museum yesterday."

"Well, I mean, he looked awfully bored. It was only right to try to add a little sparkle to his day."

"The South African couple yesterday. And the waiter. The little old man you helped through the door just before we ate. What do you know about him?"

Aubrey pressed her lips together. "Fine. He's ninety-six, single and has never left Florence. Not once! I'm interested in people. In their stories. In what we, as global citizens, have in common. Aren't you?"

If she could also use her time here to survey as many people as possible in order to find out what made them happy, as she set about figuring out her new normal for when she went back to real life, then so be it!

She felt a small tug, as Sean's hand gripped her backpack, stopping her from stepping out as a family of cyclists zoomed past the pizzeria. She stumbled till her back met his front. A wall of warmth. Of strength. Of Sean.

"Not really. No," he said, his voice close. Close enough a wash of warm air brushed the back of her neck. "I can happily go days without seeing a single person. Just me and Elwood, good coffee and a roof over our heads. That's my bliss."

Aubrey shot him a look over her shoulder to find he was even closer than she'd imagined. Close enough to see the streaks of chestnut in his dark hair. The unreal clarity of his eyes. The way his Adam's apple bobbed when he swallowed.

"I admit the don't-feed-the-bear vibe is a huge part of your appeal," she said, her voice gravelly and not even close to friendly. "And yet… Why do I not believe you?"

Sean's gaze travelled slowly over her face. The touch of his eyes set off spot fires in the strangest places: behind her ears, the backs of her knees, under the balls of her feet. When his eyes once again met hers, the pupils were inky black.

His voice was a burr, scraping against her insides, as he said, "You don't know me, Aubrey. What you choose to believe, or not believe, doesn't affect that. If that fits within the bounds of what you consider a friend, then sure, we're friends."

Knocked a little off her game by the veracity in his eyes, Aubrey rolled her shoulder and Sean let her backpack go.

She moved out into the sunshine. Into the waft and sway of tourists and locals mixing and mingling in the square.

She tried to soak up that energy; that melting pot of joy, of vitality, of life was her bliss. But instead she found herself in a tunnel. Every part of her focussed on the quixotic man, the beautiful puzzle, behind her.

She turned to face him, right as he reached out, his finger sliding beneath the strap of her backpack, lifting it to untwist it and lay it flat. His fingernail scraping over her shoulder as he pulled away.

It was an intimate move, over the hill and far away from merely friendly. In fact, if he was a fraction less the determined isolationist, the deliberate pushing of her buttons when it came to her choice of bag would have felt a hell of a lot like a dare.

"Happy now?" she asked, keeping her chin high.

"Marginally. Though I'd be happier if you weren't wearing it at all."

"Saucy," she said, and this time the look he shot her was less surprised. More cautionary. A warning that she was playing with fire.

Thing was, Leos loved fire.

Maybe Sean was right about one thing. Maybe they weren't friends. Maybe friendship *was* a little too simplistic for their unique and nimble dynamic.

Maybe they were flint and stone. A spark in the night.

Maybe a Florentine Fling wasn't such a silly idea.

A one-night stand. Maybe three. Plenty to see in Florence, and she wasn't in any real rush to move on imminently. She had bottomless funds, enough to keep travelling till the end of time if that was her desire.

And it had been a while since she'd…you know. Before she fell sick, as a matter of fact. No wonder she was feeling so frisky. Out in the world, having handsome Sean fall into her lap.

Surely it would be like riding a bike. So to speak. A big

bold way to shed the old her and step into the new. Physically. Mentally. No need for her healing heart to come into it at all.

Sean's phone rang with the famously moody opening strains of "Nessun Dorma". Elwood might like metal, but Sean was an opera man. *Seriously. Could he be any cuter?*

He excused himself before checking the caller ID and answering with a brisk, "What's up?" Then his face came over all frowny; the horizontal lines in his forehead deepening. "Right. No. Of course. I'm on my way." After which he hung up.

For all his lone-wolf, Elwood-and-me-against-the-world vibe, turned out he had people after all.

Though when he stared at his phone, the background was black, bar a clock. No social apps. No goofy picture. Hers had a photo of her and all her nieces and nephews. What looked like a dozen of them in various stages of panic, tears or tantrum as her family tried to get them all in one shot.

She felt a pang at their distance, the little ones in her life. Scrumptious little bundles that they were. And now that the chances of her having her own family were dust, her role as Auntie Aubrey was an even bigger deal. But she wasn't much use to them until she felt useful to herself.

Travel. Experience. Knowledge. Information. The space to build herself some new foundations. To push outside her comfort zone, as it was no longer a place she belonged.

"Malone?" she said, thinking *friends, not flings*. She'd never had a friend she also had a little crush on. But this adventure was all about new experiences, right?

"Sorry," he said, running a hand through his hair. "I have to cut our tour short."

"Problem?"

"Work. I have to go to work. I have my car today, parked in a garage near the shop. I'll drop you back at your hotel on the way."

"Cool. Except you work for yourself though, right? I mean, you're the big boss."

He shot her a look.

"So no one would have a problem if you brought a *friend* along."

He opened his mouth. Shut it. He was a man of few words, but still she quite liked that she'd rendered him speechless.

"Excellent," she said, rocking up onto her toes. "I get to see what the great and wondrous Sean Malone does when he's not playing tour guide. Besides, I'm excellent in a crisis. I might even be of use."

CHAPTER FOUR

Sean's car was gorgeous. Her brothers would hate it.

Too pretty. Too European. If they found out she was hanging out with a guy with a Maserati—aka not a Ford—they'd never let her live it down.

Aubrey, who considered herself more open-minded, took a three-hundred-and-sixty-degree tour of the late-model sedan. Metallic black paint. No custom flash. Big shock.

She leant over to peer through the tinted windows to the red leather interior, racing car seats, the big soft rug on the back seat covered in grey dog hair, before standing upright to find Sean watching her over the top of the roof, his keys swinging on the end of a finger.

"Something wrong?" he asked.

"Nope. It's clean-cut. Sophisticated. With just a hint of grunt. It's you."

His eyes narrowed. She wondered which part he had a problem with.

Before she figured out that part was her, she pulled open the door and slid inside. Sean opened the back door for El-wood, who bounded in and licked Aubrey right up the front of her face the moment he saw his chance.

By the time Sean slid into the driver's seat she was sputtering and coughing.

"You—?" He stopped himself right in time.

"Am I what?"

"Can't say. You told me not to."

Aubrey grabbed the edge of her shirt and lifted it to wipe the spit from her tongue. "Seriously? Don't you think that was an occasion that warranted it?"

"You tell me."

Aubrey peeked over the top of her shirt hem to find Sean looking…strangled.

"Can you put your shirt down, please?" he gritted out.

"Why?"

"Because… I can see you."

Aubrey had a gander. Her shorts were high-waisted so there was a smidge of skin showing above her belly button and below her bra. Far less flesh than the world would see if she was wearing a bikini.

She glanced up at Sean and scoffed. Only to find him now gripping the steering wheel and looking out of the front window as if his life depended on it.

Meaning he was trying even harder to keep the sizzle between them locked down than she was.

She cared less about the why than she did about the *oh, my*.

Sean Malone was keen on her. Super-keen. Friend? Fling? Maybe it was best to not put a label on it and just enjoy.

She slowly let her shirt fall back over her belly, and turned a little on the seat. Her voice dropping a smidge. They were in a small confined space, after all. "I know you're this super-straight, upstanding guy who goes around rescuing women he believes might be damsels in distress, even though they are fierce and strong and perfectly fine thank you very much, but I didn't pin you for a prude."

A muscle twitched in his jaw. His lovely hard jaw. It matched the pulse now beating rather strongly in his throat. When he turned to her, the heat in his eyes was anything but prudish. In fact he looked as if he wanted to ravish her then and there. As if the barest scruple was all that was holding him back.

As if a switch had been flipped and the curtain she'd been standing behind dropped away, all the feels she'd been denying shot to the surface. She wanted it. Wanted him to lean over, slide a hand behind her neck and kiss her. Just the thought of it made her head swim, her palms go clammy and her heart shudder.

It was her heart that stopped things, as it always did. A flicker of panic deep within its damaged depths. Like a big old wall keeping her safe from harm.

Aubrey gave her shirt an extra tug south. "Just in case."

Sean laughed. Except it was really more of a groan. He ran a hand over his mouth before letting it drop to his lap. "If I'd known you would be this much trouble I'd never have piped up at the *galleria*."

"Yeah," she said, leaning back against the cool leather head rest and batting her lashes at him. "You totally would have."

Muttering, mumbling, in Italian no less, the accent doing things to Aubrey's insides that she couldn't hope to contain, Sean faced front, switched on the car, gunned the engine, not once, but twice, before taking off fast enough to press her back into the seat.

Air conditioning flooded the car in glorious cool air in moments but she barely felt it, too surprised by the realisation Sean Malone was using his car to prove a point. He wasn't quite as upstanding, cool-headed, or nearly as strait-laced as she'd led herself to believe.

They were out of the city surprisingly soon, Sean's gorgeous car sweeping them up into the hills. The houses got bigger the further they went, the land plots larger and the landscaping more lush.

Sean eventually turned into a long, curving driveway, passing terraces covered in shrubs and scattered in statues, one boasting a crystal-clear infinity pool, ancient stone walls holding them all in place.

At the top stood a large stuccoed villa. It was at least three stories, with wings and pitched rooves, wrought-iron window frames and Venetian glass lamps. It was like something out of a Cary Grant movie.

The car rumbled to a halt right out front.

"We're here?" Aubrey asked, rather redundantly when first Sean then Elwood leapt from the car. "*This* is where you work?"

"This is where I live."

Aubrey moved slowly, taking in the details anew, with wide open eyes. "Melbourne Schmelbourne," she muttered. "This is bloody fabulous."

Showing a little speed now he was on a mission, Sean hustled her inside.

Forgoing the ostentatious front steps, they made their way through what had probably at one point been a servant's entrance. It led to a rabbit warren of rooms and halls and stairs, with bits added on over the years, till they burst into a huge open-plan room with shiny wood floors, a big modern kitchen and mis matched wooden chairs around a huge round table.

Aubrey gasped. And not just at the sight of the unbelievable coffee machine. Five times the size of the one at her family's garage. Her brothers would salivate if they saw it.

But the view...

Through the floor-to-ceiling windows tossed open to the elements was a vista of lush rolling green hills covered in classic Italian conifers spearing towards a hazy blue sky. And in the distance, a brown smudge with a couple of recognisable buildings peeking out of the top, Florence proper.

"Aubrey," Sean's voice cut into her reverie, "will you be all right if I leave you here a moment?"

"Yes," she breathed. *You can leave me here for the rest of time.* "Absolutely. Give me the chance to get acquainted with your delightful coffee machine."

"I wouldn't touch her; she's temperamental," said a voice with a strong Italian accent that was *not* Sean's.

Aubrey spun to find a foursome of impressively strong, healthy-looking humans heading up the stairs; two young men and two fabulous young women who looked like Wonder Woman's cousins, all of them in work boots and covered in wood dust with face masks dangling around their necks.

"Hey there," said Aubrey, going for friendly only for her voice to come out as a squeak.

The woman in front, the one who'd spoken—hair pulled back in a severe ponytail, dark eyes wary—gave her a knowing smile. *Pitying.*

"Aubrey, this is my staff," said Sean. "Taking a break, I see."

"We saw you driving up," Wonder Woman's cousin said, a curious gaze flickering between her boss and his unexpected guest.

Sean said nothing. Didn't even budge. How interesting. Aubrey had felt a distance between him and the lovely Enzo back in town. She'd figured it came down to the fact not everyone had her incessant determination to connect. But now, even here, with staff who clearly knew one another well by the way they lounged about his living-space room, she could feel the divide.

Aubrey stepped forward. "I'm Aubrey. Nice to meet you all."

"Flora," the leader said grudgingly, taking Aubrey's hand and squeezing for all she was worth. "The big redhead is Hans, the skinny one is Ben. The one who looks like me is Angelina."

"We're twins," said the other twin, a winning smile creasing her striking face.

"Yes," said Flora, rolling her eyes. "I believe that was implied. What we really want to know is where you came from."

"Flora," Sean chastised.

"*Che cosa?* What?" Flora said, her face all innocence.

Aubrey turned to find Sean leaning against the bench, arms crossed, gaze flat, lit with warning. Telling Flora to back down.

But Aubrey didn't need defending. She might be a half-head smaller than each of them, and they all looked as if they could bench-press her, but she could take care of herself.

She lifted a hand to the mask dangling around Flora's neck, added, "Your face mask. Looks like it's good for gas, paint, vapours dust, mould. Is it an FreshAir 2000?"

Flora's mouth opened before she looked over Aubrey's shoulder to Sean. "I... I have no idea. Boss?"

Aubrey felt Sean shift. Felt him amble towards her. Felt him stop less than a metre to her left. Felt him as if he were millimetres away, not feet. All tension and bridled heat.

"It's an FreshAir 3500," he said. And, for the first time since she'd made his acquaintance, Aubrey saw a spark of unchecked curiosity light his eyes. "How on earth do you even know that?"

"We use really similar ones in my family shop. The full face, though. Not the half."

"What kind of shop?" That was Ben. Skinny. British accent. Pale skin blotched with pink.

Focussing on him was easier than on Sean, who remained a warm, dark presence at her side. "My family owns an auto body shop called Prestige Panel and Paint back in Sydney. We pimp vintage cars."

"Serious? That's wicked."

"Totally wicked. My dad's a panel beater. Highly respected, countrywide. Race cars were his thing in his youth. My brothers are the spray painters. I'm the details girl. I do the finicky work. We all have to wear these super-sexy suits, like Hazmat suits. Full air masks. Paint, metal dust. Safety first!"

Sean's four workers nodded along. Even Flora seemed less full-on, now that Aubrey was one of the Face Mask Gang.

While Sean... Sean was looking at her differently. And she soaked it up like a sponge. Even while he was still steadfastly resisting her charm, she was a moth to his flame.

Metal shavings to his magnet. Her woman-who-hadn't-been-in-a-relationship-for-over-two-years to his hot man.

"Details," he repeated, after doing the blinking thing, taking his customary "Sean moment" to absorb. Though with that new glint in his eye she felt as if he'd absorbed enough of her to become saturated. "You mean…flames down the sides? Leopards on the hood?"

She rolled her eyes. "And you a supposed '*visionary'*," she said, trying Enzo's accent on for size, waving Italian-esque hands for good measure.

Flora snorted. Then hid it, by clearing her throat.

Aubrey brought out her phone, opened the auto shop's webpage displaying her work, and held it out to Sean.

He took it, his thumb sliding over hers in the handover. A little more slowly than seemed entirely necessary. Was it accidental? Was it deliberate? Not that she was complaining.

He took his time, scrolling. Looking at her work the same way she'd looked at the statue in the square—with time, and respect.

"This is you?" he eventually asked, brow furrowed, all delicious concentration. "You did all this?"

"Mm hmm."

He turned the phone over. To the stained glass heart on her phone case. "You did this too."

"Sure did. My friend, Daisy, is a musician. She used that pic on a single cover, then had the phone case custom made for me for Christmas a year ago, just before I finally went back to work."

"Back?"

Oops.

"Long story." Not one she had any intention of sharing. She was having far too good a time being Aubrey the Un-avoidable, rather than Aubrey the Sick.

She moved in closer. Her shoulder happened to rest against his arm as she slid a finger over the screen till it stopped on her favourites. A photo of her putting the final touches on the petrol tank of a Harley Davison made to look as if it were covered in lace. A Camaro decked out to look as if it were covered in snake skin.

"Let me see," said Flora, finding a way to shuffle between them, forcing Aubrey to take the phone and Sean to let go as he moved away.

After a few long moments Flora turned to Aubrey, her eyes accusing as she said, "You are very talented."

It was so unexpected Aubrey laughed. "Damn right I am. But thank you."

Flora gave her a nod, mouth downturned. *Respect.* Before reverting to Italian, turning her back and moving in on Sean to say, *"Il capo. Il telefono."*

And Sean's face came over all broody and dark. Like an island in a storm.

Making Aubrey realise how much he'd lightened up over the past few hours. She allowed herself the little glow that came with being pretty sure she had something to do with it.

While Sean and Flora talked in fast, furious yet muted tones, the rest of the crew hovered. Shuffling from foot to foot. Waiting for instruction. Deferential.

Which was when Aubrey realised Flora's vibe wasn't possessive. It was *protective.* Making her wonder why big, strong Sean Malone would need protection. Especially from the likes of her.

"Hey, guys," Aubrey stage-whispered, "I'm going to make myself a coffee. And I'm happy to make more if anyone's keen? Don't mind a little temperamental." She edged towards the fancy coffee machine, wriggling her fingers to encourage the shufflers away from the talkers.

Angelina, Ben and Hans all nodded, following the promise of caffeine. While Sean shot her a grateful smile. Not huge. More a tilting of the lips. A warmth around the eyes.

Still she might have stumbled just a little at the sight of it. Actually stumbled. As if she'd tripped over non-existent shoelaces.

He knew it too. The smile deepened. A sudden flash of teeth, a crinkle around the eyes before he turned back to Flora, who was looking at him as if he'd grown an extra head.

Aubrey bit her lip to stop from grinning like a loon. Then set to searching through what turned out to be some well-stocked cupboards to make the team a bunch of very fine cups of coffee.

All the while realising that Sean Malone was perfectly aware of how he affected her. And he let her stick around anyway.

"Aubrey," said Sean as he ambled up to her spot leaning against the kitchen bench where she had plonked herself a good hour earlier, taking the time to send pictures to family and friends when the others had all moseyed downstairs.

Fine, so she might have explored first, away from all the loud banging and whirring coming from the workshop, nosing around the place to find a lot of locked doors. And even more traces of elegantly shabby unfurnished space. As if Sean lived out of only two or three rooms like some kind of mythical prince, trapped in his castle.

Though from what she could discern it was self-inflicted. His refusal to settle in, to open up, a choice.

Did people really just accept that? Or was she that much more bullish when it came to making herself seen—the product of being the youngest with three loud big brothers? If so, she was glad of it. He was worth the effort.

"Hey," she said.

He moved to lean against the bench beside her. Not too close. But not too far either. "Sorry that took so long."

"Hey, you came here to deal with whatever that was. I'm just a stowaway."

Sean gave her a look. Considering, measuring; little sign of the wall he usually held in place. Because he was home?

Or because of the series of infinitesimal shifts in their dynamic that had happened since?

"Tomorrow," Sean said, leaning in a little; his voice deep, soft, intimate.

"Tomorrow?" she parroted back, her voice more than a little rough.

"I'll make up for it."

"Oh. Okay." Not one to look a gift horse in the mouth... "How? I need details."

"I'll take you places. Touristy places. Places Machiavelli once stood. Michelangelo. Galileo. Places you can stop, and sit, and sketch. Or try to touch works of art when the guards aren't looking. Places so rich with history and touristy splendour you'll forget the David's name."

Aubrey gasped. "Never! He's it for me. My one and only. Once I figure out how to help him down off his perch, the two of us are outta here."

"Nevertheless."

Aubrey nudged her chin towards the stairs. "Are you sure? Your crew looked plenty filthy. And I heard noises. Clearly there's some actual hard work going on...somewhere within the walls of this crumbling palace of yours."

The edge of Sean's mouth tilted. "It's no palace, believe me."

"A little big for one guy, perhaps?" she said, not exactly pressing for personal info about his relationship situation, yet totally pressing.

"Mmm. It was the huge wine cellar that sold it," he said, rubbing a hand over the dark grit that now shadowed his chin. "Since the place is built into the side of the hill, the basement has exterior access—two big old wooden doors lead right onto the driveway, which is perfect for pickups and deliveries so I had the cellar converted into a workshop."

"Sacrilege," she whispered.

"I think you mean ingenious."

And once again, she saw a flash of teeth as he smiled. She'd wished it, but now she wasn't sure she could handle it.

She looked away so that she could control the air in and out of her lungs. "You don't have to. Tomorrow. This afternoon has actually been exactly what I needed. A rest day. Just focus on whatever it was that brought you zooming back here in your fancy car, okay?"

He ran a hand through his hair. Giving it a hard tug at the end. It was telling. A sign things were not totally cool in Sean World. "It was nothing."

"Nothing. Okay. If you say so."

He gave her that look. The one that warned her not to push.

But the thing was, she was a Leo, the youngest of four, and the only girl; pushing was the only way she knew to get things done. "If you're determined to keep spending time with me, you will tell me eventually. You know that, right? I'll niggle till you spill. It's a big part of my charm."

Sean's hand dropped to the bench, his little finger curling over the edge a hair's breadth from her own. The look he gave her was hooded. Sexy lines furrowing his brow. Lips tilted at the edges.

Nobody should look the way he looked when he was trying not to look like anything. It really wasn't fair to the rest of the human race.

Then a shadow passed over Sean's eyes before he dragged his gaze away to look out of the big picture windows, to the sky beyond. She thought that might be it. Conversation closed.

Till he said, "We—in this space—work on commissions. Creating, from concept to completion, everything from a single nursery chair for a royal baby, to a boardroom table that had to be sent by ship, then hauled to the thirtieth floor of a skyscraper in Qatar by way of a crane. The Malone Mark on a piece carries weight."

Not an ounce of apology for his success. She loved it.

She leant her chin on steepled fingers and begged, "Tell me more."

A cough of laughter. His shoulders relaxing a smidge lower. The furrows in his brow easing. It was quite lovely to watch him unwind. To know he felt comfortable enough to be that way with her.

Then he said, "If you keep your trap shut longer than half a second I will."

Aubrey mimed buttoning her lips, even while her heart thudded at the sudden flash of authority coming her way.

Sean's gaze dropped to her mouth. Where it stayed. Lingered. His chest rising and falling. His jaw tightening.

And any *comfort* she might have felt disappeared as fast as a drop of rain on a hot car roof.

She might have made a sound. A squeak. A moan. Enough that Sean breathed out hard and lifted his eyes to hers. If he didn't see spades of lust therein he wasn't looking hard enough. And from where she stood he was looking. Hard.

"The Malone Mark?" she said, her voice scratchy against the tight confines of her throat.

"Right," he said. She wondered if he knew he'd had to physically shake himself back into the conversation. "I received an email yesterday morning. A commission request. I'd yet to respond as I'd yet to decide if it was something I could do. The…person making the enquiry followed up. Phoning here. From a private number. Flora took the call as the only person who ever calls the landline is her dad."

"If it's a private number how did this…commissioner get it?" she asked, but only after unbuttoning her lips. And once more it caught Sean's gaze.

This time when he looked away he ran a hand over his face. "He's an old friend of the family. Only person who'd have given him the number is my father."

"Right," said Aubrey, even though she didn't understand at all.

Sean's voice was solemn. Sombre. The word *father* dropped like a lead balloon.

She got that family could be a code word for chaos. How fraught those connections could be. How fragile and how fierce. Her own family was mad. But she loved them so much. Enough that they were absolutely her Achilles heel.

They were all in, each and every one. From her mum and dad, to her brothers, their wives, their gorgeous growing broods of kids.

The fact that she loved her family so ferociously was half the reason she'd taken Viv's gift.

While Viv's only proviso was that she begin in Florence, Aubrey's only proviso was that before she spent a cent on her trip, she'd pay her parents back every cent they'd lost in taking care of her when she was ill.

It had been a big ask. But Viv had been adamant that her gift was giving her more joy than she could explain—and that she had billions to spare and no one to pass them on to bar Max, her dog.

It had served as a wonderful distraction. Showing her parents their flush bank account, then scooting out of the door and into the cab waiting to take her to the airport.

All that in mind, Aubrey treaded carefully, keeping her voice light as she asked, "Is his being friends with your family a good thing? Or no?"

"It's…complicated."

"Of course it is."

"Are you mocking me?" he asked, shooting her a hot dark look that made her knees give out. Just a bit.

"Constantly!" she shot back.

Sean laughed that time. Really laughed. A rough rolling release of energy that barrelled through him till he had to bend over, hands on knees, to breathe.

"You okay down there?" Aubrey asked, her voice just for him.

He stood and she stood with him, eyes locked. Leaving

Aubrey feeling a little light in the head. She could have put it down to those baby-blue stunners, but her low blood pressure was another thing she had to manage nowadays. And it had been a while since she'd eaten.

She leant back against the bench to regain a semblance of balance. Covering the slow return of blood to her head with fast talk. "By the intense back and forth earlier, I'm thinking Flora wants you to take the gig."

"It's not her call."

"Of course, Mr Boss Man Malone decides where the Malone Mark goes. But it's clear she cares about the business." And the crew. And him. Even though even now Sean stubbornly refused to give. "What's her take?"

"It's good exposure."

"And you don't want to take it because…"

"Family. Complicated. I thought I'd made that clear."

Definite hot button. "Flora is close with her family?"

"Flora and Angelina are Enzo's daughters."

"Enzo? From the *bistro*?" Enzo who Sean acted as if he barely knew? Jeez, talk about complicated.

"His wife died not long after I arrived. I heard him tell the others in the street that the girls were at a loss. Flora especially. She refused to step up, to take her mother's place in the bistro, which broke his heart anew. While Angelina broke more plates than she served and he didn't know what to do with her. I'd met them both once or twice. Knew they were capable. So I offered them work."

It might well have been the first time in Aubrey's life that she'd been rendered truly speechless.

She stood there, facing him now, and took him in. This man. This walking dichotomy. This fascinating complicated creature she could not resist doing everything in her power to unravel. Because she could sense, at his core, he was something truly special.

"It seems you have quite the collection of damsels in distress."

"Try telling Flora that."

"Yeah, no."

He laughed again, but this time it was contained. Measured. He had himself back under control. Pity.

While Aubrey felt as if the foundations beneath her feet weren't quite as steady as they had been a few moments before.

She'd thought she had him figured out. Big, serious, knight-in-shining-armour complex. But in looking after the likes of Flora—in seeing in her a need and filling it—he hadn't done so because he'd thought she was weak. Or broken. Or because he was tight with her father. He'd taken her in because he was there. Because he could. Because it was the right thing to do.

Sean Malone might be deeply sexy, but he was also a very good man.

And Aubrey found herself forced to admit there was more that drew her to him than his ridiculous hotness. Or the urge to mess with his adorable uprightness.

It was the shadows that called to her too. The darkness in those beautiful eyes. It hooked her right through the gut. Whatever was going on with his family had a grip on him. It haunted him. This was a man who'd known loss. And guilt. Two emotions she knew intimately.

"Seems it's been a tense couple of days," she managed.

"I had no idea how tense, till laughing gave me an actual stitch." He lifted a hand to his side. His T-shirt lifted to reveal a quick flash of skin. Muscle. One side of a ridiculously defined V dipping into his jeans.

Aubrey's mouth went dry. "Can you put your shirt down, please?"

"Hmmm?" He realised after a beat she was throwing his own words back at him. Only this time there was no room for misunderstanding. Or mocking.

He slowly let his shirt drop and when his eyes met hers the heat was real. Matched by her own.

"So," she said, pausing to lick her lips. "I do believe you've been using me these past couple of days, Sean Malone. As a distraction from your real life."

Lines flickered over his nose a moment before his eyes filled with apology. He was far too easy.

"Relax," said Aubrey with a flap of her hand. "I've totally been using you, too. I thought that much was clear."

Then she gave him a punch on the arm. Because…three big brothers. And because—for all her bravado, her ability to talk to strangers, and ask questions, and stand up for herself—her heart… Her damn heart was pounding. And she wasn't ready for it to be tested like this.

She simply didn't trust the busted muscle beating in her chest would hold up under real pressure. And there was too much she wanted to do, wanted to see, wanted to be at peace with in her life, before she put it to that test.

"Coffee?" she asked, moving away from the man, back to the safety of the big machine with its noise and busyness. "I worked in cafés for a while. Coffee art was my thing. Watch this. I have skills."

Sean stepped in closer. Only she knew he wasn't watching the cool, double-layered glass in her hand as she slowly poured the hot frothy milk into a shape. He watched her face. In a way that made her think it was simply a thing he liked to do.

"Before or after the custom-paint-job gig?" he asked. His voice different. More intimate.

"As well as. I'd been saving up the big bucks for a world trip. Got as far as a music festival at the Faelledparken in Copenhagen a couple of years back."

"The Ascot Music Festival."

Coffee art forgotten, Aubrey dropped both glass and jug to the bench. "Yes. How do you even know that?"

"It's how I met Ben. I was heading to the Opera House to see something by Verdi—*La Traviata*—when I stumbled on Ben and the girl he'd been travelling with, right after they'd been robbed. Bags sliced open on the train. They were frantically emptying their bags in search of their tickets to the music festival. It was sold out. No other way in. I offered to shout them tickets to see the Verdi instead. Took them about half a second to accept. Good sports."

"Opera over pop?"

"For me, well, yeah. My mother played nothing but when I grew up. It's…familiar." The shadows were back. His voice a little faraway as he said, "Only one band I can remember wishing I'd seen there. Not the headline act, another one—"

"Dept 135?"

"Ah, yes, actually. One of the band members owns a couple of my chairs, which is pretty cool. That was the night they first played with Daisy Mulligan, you know?"

It was Aubrey's turn to laugh. "Daisy is one of my absolute best friends."

Sean's disbelief was clear.

"Seriously! She's the one who searched the internet for you. Who turned me into your stalker. Who used that heart picture on my phone on one of her single covers."

"You know Daisy *Mulligan*."

Aubrey pulled out her phone, scanned till she found the picture taken during that same festival, the day the girls had visited Viv in the hospital.

Sean leaned to look over her shoulder. "That's Daisy Mulligan."

"No. Where?"

Sean was too discombobulated to join in the joke. "And that… Is that *Vivian Ascot*?"

Aubrey turned, just a fraction. But enough to find Sean's face devastatingly close to her own. Close enough to count his thousand perfect lashes. To see stubble sprouting all over his perfect jaw.

Aubrey tipped her phone away, and moved, just enough so that her breath no longer mingled with his. "Sure is. And that's it as far as my famous friends go. We all met at the festival and stayed in touch since. It's no 'I make furniture for royalty', but I'll take it."

Sean leant back against the bench, ankles crossed, his arms doing the same. "What do you mean you only got as far as Copenhagen? What happened in Copenhagen?"

Dammit. How had she let herself lead the conversation there again? There she was telling herself it was her mission to loosen him when he kept doing the same to her.

Making her forget. For a while.

When she was with him, it was all about the now. Soaking in his calm. Deciphering his micro-expressions. Seeing how far she could push him before he pushed back.

With him, she felt like herself for the first time in a really long time.

"I had to go home," she said when the silence stretched out too long.

"Because?"

"Reasons. Now stop distracting me with your questions. And your shirt flapping. And your handsome face." She went back to her coffee. Heated up the froth again and started over. "There."

She presented him with the glass.

He looked at the "art" as instructed, only to find no palm leaf or heart as they were no doubt wont to do down at his local, but something far more R-rated.

His gaze lifted to hers. Humour, connection, heat.

"Seriously?" he asked, his voice a rumble.

"Told you I have skills."

CHAPTER FIVE

LATER THAT EVENING, after the crew had all insisted on popping their heads upstairs to say goodnight to Aubrey, who had plied them with coffee—and coffee art—all day long, Sean found Aubrey sitting at the small table on the balcony by the lounge, arms wrapped around her knees, feet tucked up on the chair, as she looked out over the city.

The sun was slowly sinking lower in the sky and the gauzy heat of the day was gentled by a cool breeze.

He could have offered her a lift home, at any point. But he hadn't.

He could have insisted, using work as an excuse. But he didn't.

He'd kept her near. Aware that his crew had fed off her quirky energy in a way he'd never seen in the workshop before. They were jovial. Chatty. Including him in their ribbing, which they never did, ever.

He thought of the South African couple at the café in Piazza Della Signoria the day before. The security guard at the Galleria dell'Accademia.

Aubrey had a way of drawing people out. In following Aubrey's lead, his crew had found permission to be themselves.

Which was on him. He knew that. He'd fostered that sense of distance. Of work and no play. He'd not moved to the other side of the world on a whim. It had been a huge risk. A massive undertaking. Yet he'd had no choice but to create a new foundation for his life after his last one had been ripped out from under him.

Sean's eyes drifted closed as his sister, Carly, once again snuck into his subconscious. Memories bobbing up like treasures weighed down below the surface. The kind incessant tides eventually set free.

Only one thing had changed in his landscape to make those weights no longer function as they had. One person causing him to lose that grip.

If he was smart he'd have said, "Big day tomorrow. I'll take you home."

Instead he said, "Hungry?"

She turned, her face relaxed. And so very lovely in the dwindling evening light.

If *she* was smart she'd yawn and say what a lovely day it had been but she needed her beauty sleep. Instead she gave him a long, direct, discerning look, before saying, "Famished. What does the palace cook have in store for us?"

He leant his forearms along the back of the chair beside hers. "Coffee first? Then pasta. I'll make both."

Hands locked behind her head, she watched him from beneath her lashes. "Got anything stronger?"

"I remember seeing a bottle of wine somewhere. Left behind by the last people who owned the place. Might be vintage. Might be vinegar."

"Stronger," she said, her eyes not leaving his.

"What's the thing these days? Aperol Spritz?"

She scrunched up her nose. "Too dry."

"A Bellini? Negroni?"

"Now you're talking. You have the goods?"

"The crew think I haven't noticed the gear they've snuck into my pantry over the years. Serves them right if we clean them out."

Aubrey let her feet drop to the ground, before unwinding herself from the chair. She lifted her arms in a stretch, swaying as if moved by the last breath of the light evening air.

He'd picked up such a strong sense of vulnerability, seeing her sitting on the floor of the gallery, sketching away. Now he saw grace and gall, straightforwardness, doggedness, kindness. There was more vitality, more life, in her little finger than he'd lived in a year.

When she sashayed past him and headed inside she left him feeling restless. As if he were ruled by currents. Stormy winds. Eddying and swirling. Begging for release. Release in her.

But he held back. Years of self-denial had left his will-power strong. Burnished to a sheen.

Moving to the kitchen, looking to the world a normal man, he found what he needed. Poured the gin by eye. Campari. Vermouth. Mixed, then poured into two glasses over ice.

"You've done that before," she said.

"You worked in cafés, in between times. I worked in bars."

"Of course you were a bartender. I've always had a thing for bartenders."

He grabbed a fresh orange one of his guys had no doubt picked from one of the trees in his orchard out back, adding a spritz of zest at the end. He licked a drop from the palm of his thumb, made eye contact, and said, "Because they're good for a chat-up line?"

"Because they're good at making cocktails."

A smile. He felt it start in his throat before it hit his mouth. A tightness and a release. "True. I made my fair share through uni."

"Chat up lines?"

"Cocktails?"

"Ah. You were studying…?"

"Architecture."

"Of course. All the hot, upright guys study architecture."

He'd known this woman a day and a half. years to feel comfortable enough with one In his world—private schools, old money, parents on the board of the Opera Foundation, dinner at the dinner table every night at seven—it took people another to be that honest. If ever.

Ask him and he would have said he preferred those people. Found ease in the aloofness. Yet his truth was that he found every single thing about Aubrey as refreshing as all get out.

"What gave you the idea that I'm upright?" he asked, holding eye contact, his voice a little rough.

"I... Well..." She swallowed. Rendered speechless for a brief moment.

He slid her drink across the counter. Waited till her fingers wrapped around the glass before letting go. "Sit. Drink. I'll have dinner ready in fifteen."

He pulled out the sauce he'd made the night before, and popped it back on the stove. Filled another pan with water, salt and penne.

Then smiled, feeling unusually good about the world, as he watched the water come to the boil.

A half-hour later they sat next to one another at the round table, digesting.

Candlelight flickered over Aubrey's face, creating hollows in her cheeks, picking out flashes of red in her hair. It was romantic as hell. Till Elwood groaned as he rolled over on his bed in the corner.

"So architecture wasn't for you in the end?" Aubrey asked out of the blue.

Sean picked up his drink; a fine local red she'd somehow had delivered to the villa during dinner using an app. "My mother's father was a cabinet maker. He taught me how to hold a chisel before I could hold a pen. After the first couple of years of uni, I...decided the hands-on part of design— shaping, honing, pushing the envelope—was where I fit best. It made sense to shift."

Aubrey gasped and sat forward, eyes wide and delighted. "You mean you didn't *graduate*. That so doesn't fit with the Sean Malone aesthetic. Why?"

Sean looked into the swirling shadows of his drink.

"Well, that was a longer than normal pause, even for you. Meaning you have no intention of telling me."

He looked up to find her watching him. No accusation in her warm gaze. Just interest. A seeking of truth.

The truth was that that was the time his sister, Carly, was getting into real trouble. His parents, people whose lives were built around how things appeared, let her get to the brink before admitting they'd lost control.

The instant he'd found out, Sean had deferred uni and moved home to help. To reconnect. To talk some sense into his little sister. It seemed to help, too. Carly moved back home. Stopped seeing her boyfriend. Seeing progress, Sean, who'd not been raised to sit on his hands, had leapt at the chance of a side hustle to fill his time. He spent all his time brushing up on his woodwork skills and took up where his grandfather had left off.

First product show he'd entered he'd hit the market with a splash. The success a counterpoint to the desperate quiet of home he'd sought to escape. And he'd lost sight of why he'd come back at all…

The sense of weight back in his belly, Sean shook his head slowly.

Aubrey's smile twisted. "You're deeper than you look, you know."

"You have no idea," he said, hoping she might take heed. Realise how very different they were.

Instead she shivered, as if the thought of hidden depths was delicious.

He'd known she was trouble the second he saw her. A sixth sense warning him of danger. It had never occurred to him *she* was the danger. That he was the one in trouble.

"Fine," she said with a roll of her eyes. "I won't go rummaging around in your shadows, so long as you know that means you also get zero access to mine."

"Your shadows."

"Baby, I have shadows like you wouldn't believe."

Her voice was pure sass. But a flicker behind her eyes told him she wasn't all quips and lip. That there might be something hidden there after all.

He lifted his drink and took a sip. Was he okay with that? With not knowing? When he'd worked so hard to keep his life simple. Disconnected. No deep connections meant no drama. Meant no heartache. No loss.

Aubrey nibbled on her bottom lip and his concerns became muddled. "If I can't ask why you didn't graduate, or why hearing from your father's friend has you in such a tizz, or why you clearly love red wine but had none in the house, then what can we talk about?"

He leaned back. "The weather."

"Great. It's bloody hot, right? Okay, now we've exhausted the weather. How about…? The Malone Mark. I'm going to be indelicate here."

"Big shock."

"I know, right? The pieces you are working on downstairs are seriously lovely, but unless you sell each for tens of thousands, how can you afford this place? Not to mention the car. And that pretty window right in the centre of town."

"The Malone Mark—"

"Carries weight. Yes, you did mention that, in a rare yet refreshing brag."

"I was going to say, is only a small part of my business. The custom pieces are the wow factor. Perfect for Instagram. Creates name recognition. Desire. That trickles down into my wholesale business."

"Right. I get it. Like the way car manufacturers release drool-worthy, futuristic concept cars that make we poor slobs go out and buy their regular street version in the hopes of having a little of that lustre rub off on us. Smart thinking, Malone."

"Exactly."

His family had never understood. Telling friends about his big commissions but not the fact they probably all plonked their backsides daily onto his wholesale stools in their kitchens. The same way they'd talked up his big accomplishments, over Carly's smaller ones. Not that he'd ever called them up on it. Not in time, anyway.

Sean shook the thought away. Said, "It was all fairly organic really. Once I became focussed. One chair in particular found traction. Became a bit of a thing when it was featured heavily in a popular TV show—"

"Oh, my God. You designed the Iron Throne!"

"What? No. It was used by the hosts of a morning show in the States. My designs are based on form and function. Not fear and pain."

"Right. Sorry. Go on."

Laughing now, relaxing, and rather amazed at both, Sean kept talking. Talking more than he remembered talking in years.

It was all due to her. Her gift was born of genuine interest. But after the "you'll never know my shadows" comment he wondered if it was also a way of not having to reveal much of herself.

"Several manufactures tracked me down after that chair. Offered to buy the design. Never much wanted to work for someone else, so I took a risk. Went into manufacturing it myself. I now have three plants building reproductions back in Australia."

"Hell of a commute."

"No commuting. This is my base now. The operations back home are run by highly competent people. I oversee remotely."

"You *never* go back?"

"I never go back."

She gave him that gaze, the one where all the shimmer stilled. Where she focussed. Every part of her direct. Where he felt like a fly caught in her amber.

"Did you run away from home, Sean?"

"I thought we agreed not to touch on that."

"So that's a yes. And I agreed. You didn't. Tell me about your family."

"Tell me about yours."

"Are we going to do this now?"

Were they? Before he could form a thought, Aubrey leant forward, challenging. Said, "My dad, Phil, is a panel beater."

"Old news."

"You want more? Okay. In his spare time, Dad paints. Abstracts. Wild gorgeous colourful things. He's the one who gave me my love of art. He'd give anything to come here, to see the greats. But he busted his knee a few years back and wouldn't be able to handle the travel. He's so thrilled I'm finally here, that I'm doing this—"

At the last, her voice cracked. Just a little. A hint, perhaps, into the shadows she made him promise not to nudge. Only now he knew they were there, they reshaped his understanding of her. Made her feel less like a flash of light blinking in and out of his existence. And far more real.

"Mum, Judy," she said, pulling herself back together, "is a homemaker. I have three brothers, all older. Have I mentioned that? I tend to, pretty quickly. They do loom large. I'm twenty-six and I'm sure our mum stays up till she hears we're all safe and sound."

Her next breath was deep and shaky, the challenge with which she'd started the conversation having dulled from her eyes. Sean felt a strong need to put a stop to this, whatever it was.

"Aubrey," he said, his voice unexpectedly raw.

But she stilled him with a look. As if she wanted to get this out. *Wanted* him to know. To see her. To understand her. To know that this—whatever it was that was happening between them—wasn't normal for her either.

"So," she went on. "My brothers have produced a zillion children between them, each of whom I could eat up in one gulp, they are that delicious. I miss them all desperately.

And have no doubt they miss me as I am the most amazing auntie there ever was."

Something dark flickered in her eyes then. Something so big she swayed with it. Heartache? Sorrow? No, it looked a lot like *defeat*. But, it couldn't be that. He couldn't imagine Aubrey allowing it. She'd look it in the eye and say, not happening.

And while pressing back, asking questions, opening up, letting her in, was miles outside anything he'd done in a while, in years, watching this woman flounder was enough for him to say, "Their names?"

"Hmmm?"

"Your brothers. What are their names?"

A light flickered in the darkness. "Adam. Craig. Matt."

"They good to you? When they loom?"

"Phenomenal. And annoying." The pain in her eyes eased. The light returning. "They could take down the likes of you with their little fingers."

He leant forward. Putting his glass next to hers. So close it clinked. "Left or right?"

A muscle twitched under her eye, and the edge of her sweet mouth curled into a devastating smile. The kind that took a man's legs out from under him. "Take your pick."

"Mmm."

"Now it's your turn."

Sean's next breath burned. Helping her play was one thing, but it wasn't a game to him.

Yet something in her face, the slight tremble still wavering beneath the bravado, fractured something inside him. Shearing away a great chunk of the wall he'd built up inside, like the edge of an iceberg falling into the sea.

"Margot," he said, speaking his mother's name out loud for the first time in nigh on five years. He held eye contact as if Aubrey were a life preserver and he a man who'd suddenly found himself lost at sea. "My mother's name is Margot. She's a lady who lunches. And sits on charity boards.

She was an interior designer. A very good one. Inherited my grandfather's eye for shape."

"And your father?" she asked, her voice unusually soft, her gaze rich with empathy. "The one with the friend."

"Brian." Sean felt his head squeeze as he tried to push away the vision of the last time he'd seen his father. Broken, in utter shock, a shell of the man he'd once been; sitting in their big cold house, Carly's wake going on around him while he held tight to a photo of his only daughter when she was just a little girl.

"He was—" Sean stopped, cleared out the frog in his throat "—is a financial advisor. Straight-laced. Clear morals. When I decided to throw every cent I had at the chair that made my name, I was sure he'd try to talk me out of it. But he supported it all the way."

"Of course he did," said Aubrey. "If he's anything like you he's both savvy and intrepid. If he saw the light in your eyes when you talk about your work, I'm sure supporting your idea was a cinch. How about siblings? Any brother or sisters who drove you crazy?"

Sean shook his head. He wasn't going further. He wasn't going *there*. In fact he'd gone a mile past his limit. Carly wasn't something he talked about. To anyone. No single person he'd met since moving to this country had heard him speak her name.

Yet this slip of an Australian had him on the verge of divulging the whole sordid story. And his part in it. His deep, cavernous sense of shame…

No. Just no.

Sean pressed himself to standing. Fast enough his chair rocked.

While Aubrey sat, knees together, hands clasped on her thighs. So still. So slight. Her face a blend of delicate curves and tiny freckles and warm, pretty eyes that belied the strength beneath. The furious energy. Determination. Grit.

She sat there as if she hadn't just come achingly close

to tearing him open with nothing but soft words. Her refusal to back down.

He glanced out of the window, where Florence glowed in the valley below. The River Arno was lit up along her banks, the Duomo a glowing golden beacon.

"I should take you home," he said, several hours—and two drinks—too late.

"Generous offer, but Sydney is miles from here."

"I meant your hotel."

"Ah," she mocked. "I'm following you wherever you go today, remember? So are *you* going to my hotel?"

He opened and closed his mouth, like a fish out of water. Then he ran both hands over his face and growled.

She was impossible. And sublime. She terrified him. How she made him feel. How she made him smile even when he didn't deserve to smile.

And he didn't want to see her go.

"Look," she said, tipping forward, before stretching to her feet. "I don't know what happened to you, Malone, to send you so far from home. And it's okay if you don't tell me. But I'm a really good listener if you ever need to talk. Right now, though, I'm just going to hug you, okay?"

She reached out with both hands. Moved in. Sliding around his waist, slowly, as if she was giving him every chance to refuse her touch.

Then one hand slid up his back, the other moved between them, clutched at his shirt. She kept moving until she was pressed up against him. Her cheek turned against his chest. Her head fitting just under his chin.

What was he to do, but slide his arms around her too, cradling her close? She smelled of warm days and cool nights. Of citrus zest and sheets just off the line. Her hold impossibly soft, yet at the same time it was as if she was holding him upright. As if she were his very spine.

He tilted his head to rest his lips upon her hair. "Aubrey—"

"Shh. It's okay."

Sean laughed, even while his chest felt tight and his head was swimming. Caught as he was between the urge to put space between himself and this rare creature who deserved far more than the shell of a man he'd become, and the instinctive, survivalist need to soak up whatever life force she could spare.

"You can stay. There is a spare room in use. Staff have crashed here once or twice when a commission neared its end date and they weren't yet done."

"I'm not staff."

"No, you're not. In fact you're the first person I've let in the front door whom I don't pay."

"Hey, whatever gets you through the night."

It took him a moment. "Jeez, Aubrey, I didn't mean—"

"Mocking!" She lifted her head, her big whisky-brown eyes soft with desire. "God, you're easy."

No, he *wasn't*. He was hard, and stubborn, and fractious. He'd created a life in which he gave away little and asked for less. "Aubrey—"

She snuck a finger to his lips. Pressing so he had no choice but to hold his breath.

"Just shut up, okay?" she said, her eyes bright. "Stop trying to get rid of me. You might think you're all that, that you can out-stubborn me, but you have no idea who you are dealing with."

"Neither do you."

Her head tipped to one side, her breath leaving slowly between soft lips, she said, "You knew what you were doing when you 'let' me follow you around today. You knew what you were doing when you 'let' me jump in the car with you. You know what you're doing now. Now prove it."

Her words were big, calling him out in order to elicit a reaction. But he could feel the quiver beneath them. The fear that he might deny her. That she might yet be made to look a fool.

She was feeling this too. The speed of it all. The sense that it was out of their control.

But Sean was *all* about control. It was his anchor. It had saved him when he'd not been certain he deserved to be saved. And he was done letting anything take him places he wasn't ready to go.

So he reeled it in. And held on tight.

He lifted a hand to Aubrey's chin, cradled it, looked from one of her bright beautiful eyes to the other. "Come to bed."

She stilled. "Which bed?"

His thumb ran down the side of her cheek, the feel of her skin—warm and soft and giving—creating whorls of heat inside him. "This is not the time for mocking. Come. To. Bed."

"Are you kidding?" she said. "It's the *perfect* time for mocking. Otherwise you will totally fall in love with me and we can't have that because I'm on holiday so will be gone before you know it. And you'll be stuck here, pining, and—"

Sean quieted her with a kiss.

It was the only way.

It was a soft kiss. No more than a meeting of the lips. Breaths held, eyes open.

Then, with the sweetest moan ever known to man, Aubrey softened. All over. Her hand flattening against his chest, her body melting into his.

The kiss, so sweet, so soft, soon turned into something more. A flood of relief. Of release. Of reckoning.

No more tiptoeing around the escalating attraction that had been brimming between them from the moment they met. It was a tidal wave, no holding back. He bore the full force of her want. Her need.

Her words echoed in his head.

"You knew what you were doing when you 'let' me jump in the car with you. You know what you're doing now. Now prove it."

He lifted her into his arms, shocked to find how little

there was of her. Her delicacy hidden by the sheer force of her personality.

Kissing her still, he carried her into his bedroom. His curtains were open, an eerie mix of moonlight and the final breaths of daylight falling over the room.

He kissed her once, then, holding her tight, helped her onto the bed. And followed.

Her hair splayed out near his pillow. Her eyes, dark in the low light, looked up at him.

What he saw there floored him. The sheer honesty of her feelings. Her desire.

Her hand reached up to his face. Her fingers traced his bottom lip. The line of his nose. The curl of his eyebrow. Her thumb returned to his mouth, tracing his top lip this time. Her gaze following.

"I will be compelled to draw you one day," she said, her voice husky, and low. "I'll capture a moment, when you're not expecting it. So you don't pull a face."

"Stalker."

"That I am."

"Just so long as you don't compare me to him."

"Him?"

"The David."

A beat, then, "Who?"

"Atta girl."

When her fingernails scraped up the sandpaper edge of his jaw, he sucked in a breath. Only to see her smile.

"You look so sweet," he rumbled, "but it's all an act."

"I know, right?"

Sean laughed. *Laughed.* Joy flowed through him, freely, unfettered. It had been so long since he'd experienced the emotion, he no longer had the skill to temper it.

He gently brushed her hair away from her face as they drank one another in. Savouring the bittersweet ache of waiting on the brink, when their bodies, their eyes, said *now*.

Then he kissed her cheek. Her nose. Her chin. When

his teeth grazed the side of her neck she lifted off the bed. Gripped his back. And groaned.

Needing more, needing skin, needing to assuage the heat, the joy, the guilt—yes, guilt, for it was there still, a constant companion, a bitter tang to every breath he took— merging inside him, he slid down her body. Nipping at her shoulder, her collarbone, the edge of her bra through her clothes.

She writhed under him, gripping his hair. Guiding him. Fearless. Wanting.

When he reached her belly, he nudged her shirt with his nose, and pressed a kiss to the right of her navel. Then the left. The sounds coming from her making his vision hazy, his body, coiled tight for so long, burn.

When he slid his hand beneath her shirt, meaning to ease it away, she pulled the hem back down.

When he tried again, she wriggled out from under him and flipped him over. Straddled him. Her hot wild gaze drinking him in. Eating him up.

Something in her eyes made him pause. Some flicker of doubt. But considering all the big emotions he was grappling with, he couldn't blame her.

"Aubrey, we don't have to—"

Then she tucked her hands into her hair, twirling it into a knot. Her hips moving against his till his eyes near rolled back in his head. Purely deliberate. Nothing sweet about it. No indecision at all.

He reached for her, his thumbs pressing into her hip bones, guiding. Slowing. Watching her. Watching her eyes, drugged and lush with desire. Rolling with her till her breath hitched, her eyes dragging closed.

Her hands fell to his chest. Nails digging in. Biting her bottom lip so tight he feared she'd draw blood.

When she called his name, a keening desperate plea, he reared up, slid a hand behind her head and captured her mouth. Kissing her slow. Deep.

Losing himself. Spiralling.

Oh, hell; the tang of salt. Of iron. He slid his tongue along the seam of her lips, finding the spot she'd bitten swelling already.

"Sean," she gasped, her head tipping back, knees spreading, sliding herself along the erection locked in the confines of his jeans.

Then with a roar that seemed to come from the back of her throat, she pulled back, pressed him to the bed. Pointed at him and said, "Stay." Then she rid herself of her shorts, twirled them around a finger and flung them across the room.

Before he had the chance to even think about laughing, revelling in her abandon, her hands were at his fly, unbuttoning, unzipping, and setting him free.

Fearing it would end before it had begun, he rolled her over, and said, "Stay." He grabbed protection from his side drawer, sliding it on with a speed heretofore unknown.

"Yes," she said, watching, relishing, as if she knew he needed to hear it. "A thousand times yes."

And while it took every ounce of strength he could muster, Sean began to slow. His kisses, his touch, the roll of his hips. To pay attention. To be in this. Before it subsumed them both. His hands learning every inch of her body. Until she breathed when he breathed. Her eyes unable to focus. His name a prayer on her lips.

When he finally slid inside her, she cried out—in pleasure, in relief. The power he'd been holding in check detonated as he was sheathed in her, to the hilt.

Then her eyes found his. Locked on tight as they moved.

Lost, together, to the slide of heat. The flood of sensation. The taste, sweet and spicy. And the yield.

The way she gave of herself and the way she gave in. Accepting and following, open and accepting and demanding, till she dragged him under with her.

Under. And over. And undone.

* * *

Aubrey lay sleepily tangled in the sheets of Sean's bed, her head up one end, his up the other. Hand over her heart, eyes closed, she checked in.

Her heart, well, it was taking its time to settle, but no wonder. It had been put through its paces. At least it felt even, and steady, and strong. In fact, it felt indomitable.

"You awake?" Sean's deep voice crooned from the other end of the bed.

"Almost."

"I was just thinking."

"About?"

"When I saw you sitting on the floor of the museum. Backpack open, back to the room, I figured you were a disaster waiting to happen."

"And now?"

"I'm sure of it." He let out a short sharp breath, lifted up onto his elbow, the sheet pooling around his waist, arms and chest on display. And what a display. "You have a tattoo."

"More than one," Aubrey said.

"Words," he said, pointing to his side. "I didn't stop to read them. Was too busy."

"The fact of which I am most appreciative."

Sean nodded. "You're welcome."

Aubrey pulled down the sheet, and lifted her T-shirt just enough to show the words scrawled across the bottom of her ribs. The shirt she'd managed to keep on the entire time they'd made love, without him making a peep of complaint. Meaning he wasn't a boob man, or he was a man who took consent seriously. Considering the way he'd moved around her body, she figured it was the latter.

Sean leaned over her to read, *"Be in love with your life. Every minute of it.'"*

"Jack Kerouac."

He took a "Sean moment" before lifting his eyes to hers. "Apt."

Aubrey's smile started behind her ribs. "One of the kitchen staff in the—"

She stopped herself just in time. Feeling all loose and lovely, her brain still a little fuzzy around the edges, she'd been about to say, *In the hospital in Copenhagen*, which would only bring questions. Leading to answers that would change everything. He'd made love to her as if she was strong. As if she was whole. She wasn't giving that up for anything.

She went with "—this place I stayed in Copenhagen, was really into quotes. She'd write them on little notes and bring them to me with breakfast. She could hardly speak English, I can't speak Danish, so I think she found them on Pinterest and copied them out. Some were hilarious."

"Such as?"

"Ah. *'You are the gin to my tonic.' 'Coffee doesn't ask me stupid questions in the morning. Be like coffee.' 'If we're not meant to have midnight snacks why is there a light in the fridge?'*" I quite liked that one too. Just thought it might be a little long for the space."

Sean's smile was indulgent. Delicious. What had she done to deserve ending up in this place with that face? Must have rescued ten, twenty children from a burning building in a previous life.

That's the good. What did you do to deserve the bad?

Aubrey closed her eyes, squeezed the voice out of her head.

"You said there was more than one," said Sean. "Tattoo."

There was. Including one he'd never need to know about. Too much explaining to do there.

That was okay though, right? To keep things from him. It wasn't as if they were promised. They were…having fun. And tattoos that covered scars did not—on the whole—fit into the fun category.

Opening her eyes, concentrating on that face of his, she lifted a foot to show her ankle, and the dragonfly thereupon. Super fun! "I was sixteen, pretended I was eighteen. My mother nearly had a fit, which was, of course, the point. Last of four kids, you gotta do what you gotta do to get the attention."

Sean took her foot in hand, pretended to pay the tattoo close attention. All the while his thumb pressed into the soft arch of her foot, making her groan.

Then he pressed his lips to the tattoo, before making his way down her leg. Or was it up her leg?

Whatever.

She closed her eyes, lay back on the bed and let him go up, go down, wherever he damn well pleased.

CHAPTER SIX

AUBREY'S PHONE RANG. Video call from Jessica.

She nibbled on her bottom lip, cocked an ear, heard the shower still running.

She wrapped herself in a sheet, rolled onto her tummy, set up her phone on the pillow and answered. Waited for Jessica's sweet face to centre on the screen. The sound of laughter and music blurred in the background.

"Hey!" said Aubrey. "What time is it there?"

"I'm not sure. Midnight perhaps? I'm at a party in Manhattan."

"Wow, you animal."

"Hardly. Jamie had a table at an industry book awards charity thing earlier tonight."

Daisy joined the conversation, pushing Jess into a smaller space on the screen. She rubbed her eyes. "Jeez, girl, it's ridiculous o'clock."

"Sorry but this is important. It's about Vivian."

Daisy went from half asleep to focussed in half a second flat. "Our Viv? Is she okay?"

"Yes. I think so. It's just…" Jessica leaned so close to the screen she was a nostril and half an eyeball. "There have been *rumours*. She signed up to write a book for Jamie's company. An autobiography of sorts. Single woman runs the world type thing. But news just came through that she pulled out, citing ill health."

"Oh, no!"

"Right? Except I'm not sure I believe that's the entire story," said Jessica. "She sent me a strange message earlier tonight."

"Give me a sec." Aubrey minimised their conversation. Checked her phone. There it was. A private message from

Viv asking for updates. Saying how much she was enjoying Aubrey's photographs. That it was bringing back memories of a special time she'd spent in Florence when near the same age. How lucky she was to have all three of them fall into her life.

"She doesn't sound unwell. But she does sound…"

"Odd," said Jessica.

At the same time Daisy said, "Like she's been on the herbs."

"I'll call her later," said Aubrey. "I've been in contact with her quite a bit once we figured out she was the one who'd given us our crazy gifts."

"Super," said Jessica. "Let us know what you find out."

All too late Aubrey realised the shower had stopped. The door to the bathroom opened, and in came Sean, a towel draped around his waist.

He gave Aubrey a slow smile, his gaze travelling down her back. After the night spent together, she'd yet to find her shorts.

It registered somewhere far back in her brain that she was in the middle of something, but the rest was completely taken up with ogling the miles of sculpted chest and broad brown shoulders and the smattering of dark hair leading down towards his—

He crawled up onto the bed. His gaze determined. The man's focus was unparalleled. She knew. He leaned down to press a kiss to her mouth, stopping mere millimetres from touchdown.

"Ah, hello," said Sean, his breath sending trails of warmth over her cheek.

"Hi," Jessica's voice whispered from the phone.

Aubrey's face spun to her phone to find Jessica waving, and Daisy with her mouth hanging open.

"I'm Sean," said Sean.

"Jessica."

"Daisy."

Sean clicked his fingers, his face breaking into a rare smile. "Holy hell, that's *Daisy Mulligan!*"

Daisy looked over her shoulder.

Sean laughed. His face creasing into a smile. An honest to goodness grin. The shape of which made Aubrey's heart stop. Not literally of course. Been there for real. Knew the difference. More like from one beat to the next her heart was no longer quite the same as it had been before.

"Well, what do you know?" he said. "I've leave you to it, shall I?"

"Don't leave on our account," Daisy said, while Sean shot Aubrey a look, making sure she knew there would be hell to pay once she got off the phone.

She watched him walk away, his towel slipping a smidge so she could just see the rise of his glorious butt cheeks over the top.

"Who on earth was *that*?" Daisy asked, twisting her face as if trying to see around the edge of the phone.

"Him? Just some guy I picked up in a museum."

As she said the words she regretted them. Jokes aside, it just felt...wrong. He wasn't some guy. He was Sean. Malone. A man she'd wanted to hold, and kiss, and unravel more than she'd wanted to do those things with another living person in the history of her life.

"No, he's not," said sweet Jess, looking highly affronted. "He's the wood guy. The one you looked up online!"

"Oh," said Aubrey. "The wood guy. I *thought* he looked familiar."

Daisy snorted. "Well, he looks fine in a towel, which isn't to be sneezed at."

"To think," said Jess, "when I travel I lose my luggage and get my phone stolen."

While Daisy said, "Look at you."

"Who, me?" Aubrey queried.

"You're all flushed and floopy and...dare I say smitten?"

Aubrey frowned. "Pfft. Not *smitten*. Just appreciative. Of the man's…bits. And ways. And talents. And all that stuff."

"Well, you look happy, which is lovely. It's all either of us want for you. Just…" Jess leaned into the phone to whisper. "I hope you are being…safe."

Aubrey got the implication, but she hid it well. Holding her chin, looking confused as she said, "*Safe?* Whatever do you mean?"

"I mean I hope you were…protected."

"Protected from…"

"Pregnancy! STDs! Did you use condoms?" Jess stated, then sat back and glared at the phone. "There. I said it. Happy now?"

"God, Mum," Aubrey moaned, "you can be so embarrassing sometimes."

Daisy laughed so hard she fell out of the screen.

Aubrey hoped her grin held up. The moment Jessica had yelled pregnancy her insides had twisted in a way they hadn't for days. Not that she could explain it to them. She'd yet to fill them in on the news from her doctor, feeling that once her girls knew it would make it really real.

"On that note, gotta go," said Daisy. "Get back to the party, Jess. See what you can find out about Viv, Aubrey."

"Will do."

Aubrey blew them both kisses then hung up. Laid back. Shook off the malaise the word "pregnancy" might well always and for evermore cause to descend over her, and stretched her beautifully achy body from head to toe.

This was lovely. This was good. This was something she could still take into her new normal. For while it had been some time since she'd salsa'd—horizontal or otherwise— the man's athleticism knew no bounds.

But they *had* been safe. The first time. And the second. Though it was a bit of a blur as it had morphed, blissfully, wildly, and more than a little naughtily into the third. But yep, yep, yep—safety first.

She was naturally small, with frenetic levels of energy, her periods had always been irregular, and the meds she'd been on kept her weight right down, which had made her cycle near non-existent. Add all the other drugs that had been pumped into her, the coma, the damage—her system was in recovery, and might be for a long time.

She'd taken it all as best a person could. Stubbornly refusing to let it break her.

Hearing, from her beloved psychologist, that despite her recovery, she was to prepare herself for a life in which motherhood, conception, and carrying a child were not on the cards had been brutal. That had broken her. Snapped her in two. She'd researched. Tried negotiating with her doctors. Sought second opinions. And sobbed. For weeks.

Then one day she'd woken up and made plans. To be in love with her life. Every minute of it.

She ran a finger over the ridges of the tattoo, one that Sean knew about, then lifted her fingers to trace the tattoo he did not. Both inked in the sweet spot of time between removal of her pacemaker and just before starting her "vitamins", the blood-thinning meds she was still on today.

Aubrey glanced up to make sure Sean was still out of the room, then she leaned over the edge of the bed, grabbed her backpack, riffling through one of the many pockets till she found her angiotensin-converting enzyme inhibitors.

Her doc had said she could stop before she left. But then he'd wanted her to wait around to see how she went. They'd compromised, her dose as low as it could be. A weaning of sorts, from old life, to fully new.

Yep, she was being super-safe.

By the time they roused themselves to actually leave the house, the team had already arrived. Sean whistled and Elwood uncurled himself from his bed in the cool corner of the kitchen and followed him down to the workshop.

Hans quickly turned the music down and four pairs of

eyes landed on Sean. Edgy. Hopeful. Trying to decipher if he was the old Sean, or the one who'd shown up the day before. Without Aubrey there to facilitate, Sean didn't have the language to answer.

"Can you guys watch Elwood today? I'm heading into the showroom. Not sure when I'll be back."

Flora nodded and answered for the group. "Of course, boss."

Sean turned to leave, only for his feet to screech to a halt as Angelina called out, in Italian, "Tell Aubrey the *gelateria* near the Ponte alla Carraia is the best. A bit of a walk but worth it."

He glanced over his shoulder to see Flora glaring at her sister, who shrugged back.

"She's still here, right?" Angelina stage-whispered, as ingenuous as Flora was calculating. "We all saw her earlier."

Old Sean would have frowned and walked away. Not played into the drama. Instead, he gave Angelina a smile and said, "Ponte alla Carraia?"

"Sì."

"I'll let her know. *Grazie.*"

And as soon as he left the room, all four of his crew burst into laughter, the music turned up nice and loud and they got to work.

Once back upstairs he found Aubrey tying up a sandal, her foot on a chair. An early model he'd made in the first year he'd lived in the city. Delicate, diagonal arm rests. Not good enough to sell, but beautiful enough to lead him to the next design that did. In the thousands.

Her hair was tied back in a short ponytail with a big scarf. She'd changed into clothes she must have had in her backpack. Dark denim shorts that showed off every inch of leg. A white T-shirt with *I'm With the Band* scrawled across the front, tied in a knot at her waist. Sandals that twisted up her calf like a Roman soldier's.

Her skin—lightly gilded by the Florentine sun—was shiny with sunscreen. Such an Australian thing to see.

She grinned at him before biting down on a peach she'd nabbed from the bowl on the bench.

"God, you're cute," she said, giving him a lazy once-over.

Sean looked down at his loafers, knee-length khaki shorts, and linen button-down rolled up to the elbows. "Okay."

She sauntered away from the chair, snuck up onto her tiptoes, and grabbed him by the chin, bringing him down for a kiss.

She tasted of toothpaste and peaches and sunshine and sex.

And Sean's mind spun from it.

"You promised me primo tourist stuff. So let's go, boyo." She slung her backpack over her shoulder, the lip closed tightly, for now, and made her way down the stairs towards the informal entrance.

Sean blinked, once again wondering how on earth he'd ended up there. With an impudent, effervescent woman with the most voluptuous ability to seek out joy. She knew Daisy Mulligan, for Pete's sake! Daisy Mulligan, who'd met him while he was wearing nothing but a towel.

Carly would have loved that. He pictured her eyes growing comically wide, as if he'd just told her of his meeting with an actual rock star. If she'd only stuck around long enough to hear it.

"Time waits for no man!" Aubrey called, her voice wafting up from below.

Sean ran a hand over his face, collected himself, called, "Jeez, woman! Give me a minute."

A beat went by before her head popped around the corner of the landing. "You might think I would be offended by that tone, but you should know it actually has me considering forgoing the Uffizi right now, just so I can drag you back to bed." A moment, then, "You are taking me to the Uffizi, are you not?"

"Of course I'm taking you to the Uffizi."

She punched the air, then jogged back down the stairs, her voice carrying behind her. "If you don't hurry I might start doodling pictures on your car!"

He laughed, and ran a hand over the back of his neck.

It would behove him to keep the words he'd heard her say to her friend on the phone—*just some guy I picked up in a museum*—on a loop in his head.

He knew she'd been joking. But there was a truth to it all the same. A truth to hold onto.

"Shall we get a table?"

"It's cheaper if you drink your coffee at the counter," said Sean, nodding at the barista as he got his change for their espressos.

"Seriously? Ha. That's awesome."

Aubrey glanced at the barista, who shot her a flirtatious smile and said, *"Sì. Sei Australiano?"*

"Sì," she said, in affected Italian, smiling back.

While the barista set to making their coffees, Sean fought the urge to drag her out of the café and find coffee elsewhere.

Just some guy I picked up in a museum, he reminded himself.

She was here in Florence on borrowed time. A world trip lay ahead of her. Late the night before she'd told him her plans to ride a camel in Egypt, walk the Great Wall of China, visit Jim Morrison's grave. About how she'd met Vivian Ascot and the unexpected gift that had led her there.

She would meet people along the way. Many, many people. Collecting them like ticket stubs.

The barista said, *"Signorina?"*

She turned to grab their coffees, curtsied her thanks, leaving Sean to muse that Carly would have been smitten by her.

Dammit. He hadn't thought about his sister this much since when it all first happened.

When Aubrey passed him his drink he downed it in one, the fresh brew scorching the back of his throat enough that he coughed.

"Are you okay?" she asked, patting him on the back.

"I thought we didn't ask that."

Aubrey blinked. "You don't. I can ask whatever I want."

He shot her a look, to find her face was sincere. Sincerely adorable. From her upturned lips to her wide whisky eyes, it was a face he enjoyed looking at very much. A face he'd miss when it was gone.

That face broke into a smile, as if she knew exactly what he was thinking.

"Drink up," he growled. "I'm taking you to the Ponte Vecchio."

"Yes! Quick, quick, quick." She sipped and sipped until she'd downed the coffee, then thanked the barista, who gave her another smouldering look.

"Sorry," she said, pointing at Sean with her thumb. "I'm with him."

Then shooting Sean a wink, she led him out of the café.

Two *carabinieri*—Italian police—lounged against the railing at the entrance to what had to be one of the most famous bridges in the world, chatting to tourists.

"Are they for real?" Aubrey said, gaping.

"What?" Sean asked.

"The knee-high black boots, fitted black pants, the hats sitting jauntily on the backs of their heads; they look like Italian Chippendale dancers. I have to get a picture."

She ran up to the pair, waited till they'd finished giving

instructions to the tourists before her, and then motioned the international signal for selfie.

Grinning, they held out their arms and welcomed her. She snuggled in between them, imagining how Daisy and Jessica and Viv would love the picture.

"Here," said Sean sidling up to them. "Let me."

Handing over her phone, she splayed her now spare hands at her sides, imagining it looked as if she were gripping the young police officers' thighs. By the twitch in Sean's cheek as he took the photo she figured she was right.

"*Grazie,*" she said, when they were done.

Both men doffed their caps and said, "*Prego.*"

She ambled over to Sean, who was holding out her phone. "What?"

He herded her onto the bridge proper. "I didn't say a thing."

"And yet I can feel it. The waves of jealousy pouring off your skin. You have nothing to worry about. I am all yours. Here." She reached out and wrapped her hand around his.

He looked down at it, as if it was something entirely foreign.

And she felt a sudden wash of vulnerability. Heat flashing along her cheeks at the very real fear he give her a look that said, *Honey, that's not what we are.*

Instead he shifted his grip so that he held her more fully, then looked ahead, along the bridge, and began to walk.

Relief flooded through her, brisk and cool. And disturbing. So they'd slept together. In between splendiferous bouts of not sleeping together. But nothing had changed. Not really. They were still ships passing in the night.

"See those tunnels above?" Sean said.

Aubrey pretended she'd been listening, not having a quiet panic. "Mm hmm."

"That's called the Vasari Corridor. Built by the Medici family, so that they could cross the river on horseback high above the rest of the riff-raff. The bridge itself used to be the place to find a good butcher, but the Medicis didn't like the smell, so they moved in jewellers instead, and that's how it remains today."

"Did you know all that, Malone? Or did you do some research some time over the past twelve hours, knowing you were bringing me here?"

Sean's pause told her all she needed to know.

She took her hand and slid it into his elbow, snuggling herself tighter. And he let her. She felt a little bittersweet as they ambled along the bridge, pausing to window-shop. And to talk to anyone who caught Aubrey's eye. She loved finding out where people were from, why they'd chosen Florence of all the places in the world to visit, and what one thing she had to see before she left.

In one jewellery shop a single chair sat in one corner, with what looked like a real fur pelt draped dashingly over the corner. Aubrey ducked inside, went straight up to the chair and checked the back to find the mark she was looking for.

"I knew it! It's a Malone! Did you know this was a Malone chair?" she asked the young woman behind the counter, who gave her a surprised smile.

"Mi scusi?"

Sean moved in, his hands going to Aubrey's shoulders as he attempted to herd her away. "It's a reproduction. A wholesale piece. Likely picked up from a furniture store in town."

"Well, it's still lovely."

"Thank you. I try."

"He's Malone," said Aubrey. "He designed that chair."

The young woman's gaze moved to Sean and stopped. *"Sei Malone?"*

Sean answered in fast, furious, dashing Italian while the more he said, the more the sales assistant swept her hair behind her ear and nibbled her lip and generally gave every indication she might be about to melt into a puddle of lust on the floor.

Huh. If Sean was trying to get her back for the barista, and the *carabinieri*, then he succeeded. An achy discomfort had swept over her. Which was nonsensical. This was a holiday thing. Which would cease any moment. In fact, she might choose to move on to Rome the very next day, meaning, in all likelihood, she'd never see him again.

Rather than that make her feel better, the achy discomfort only heightened.

"I think it's a sign," Aubrey interjected, "that I need to buy something from this shop. A souvenir to remind me of my days here. So I don't ever forget the time I went to Florence."

Sean laughed. A soft sound of complete understanding. His stunning, darkly handsome face shifting into something infinitely lovely as he indulged her utter lie. She'd never forget. This place or him. And he was self-aware enough to know it.

"She likes you," Aubrey said. "You can get her number if you'd like, for when I'm gone."

The smile disappeared. His eyes hardened. "Thanks, but I'm fine."

Aubrey held up her hands in submission, before pretending to check out the wares. Her mind was buzzing. Her skin felt too tight. And it wasn't the heat. Or her heart. At least not the ball of gristly muscle keeping her alive.

She quickly found something—a small gold ring in the shape of a flower—and paid the sales assistant—a delightful girl named Sasha, who was an only child from a tiny little town in northern Chianti, who worked in the shop while studying commerce at university—before finding Sean outside the shop, hands loose in the pockets of his shorts, leaning against a lamp post, watching the world go by. Nose tipped to the sky, he was soaking up the sunshine on his face as if it had been a long time since he'd noticed there was a sun at all.

He turned, his face relaxed, content. "You good?"

And the superficial ache that had come over her earlier shifted and settled, deep inside. Was she good? Not so much. In fact she believed she might be in quite a bit of trouble.

But she nodded. No need to worry the man.

He held out his elbow. She slid her hand back into the crook.

Things remained quiet as they continued along the bridge. Till another *carabiniere* strolled past. Aubrey *might* have sighed.

And Sean chuckled. "Wait till you get to Vatican City. Their uniforms were designed by Michelangelo himself."

Vatican City. Could you imagine? Only she'd have to leave this place to get there. Which was what she wanted. Most of all. To see everything. To open herself up to new experiences so that she might be able to put her old dream behind her and create a new one.

"Now you're just trying to make me self-combust with lust," she joked.

"You do know that's my new mission in life," he said, his voice a low rumble.

She tripped over nothing. Pretended there was a loose paver on the roadway.

Sean's laughter was real. Deep. All hers. And she knew she wasn't going anywhere. Not yet. The Vatican could wait.

Their night together didn't have to be a one-off. Or a three-off, to be fair. She could handle a little more of this, of him, before heading off into the sunset, alone. Couldn't she?

"You can stop the foreplay you know," she said, removing her hand and moving to walk backwards in front of him. Flirtatious. Fun. Keeping things light.

"Is that what this is?" he asked.

And shivers skittered down her neck and into the backs of her knees. "Just take me to the big show, Malone. I need the Uffizi, now, please."

"Done."

"Woohoo!" And as they headed towards the famous museum, Aubrey kept her little shopping bag in the hand nearest him. Figuring it best to keep her hands to herself. For now.

Aubrey was like a cat on a hot tin roof on the walk to the Uffizi Gallery, chatting ten to the dozen and keeping just out of reach.

When all Sean wanted to do was touch her. Fix her scarf before it fell out of her hair. Hold her backpack. Duck into any one of the dark alcoves they passed and kiss her till her hands gripped his shirt in order to stay upright.

"I have to find *The Birth of Venus*. It was commissioned by one of the Medici family for their cousin, did you know? Mine's lucky to get a text on his birthday. And Caravaggio's *Medusa*. My first ever commission was painting my version of the Medusa on the bonnet of my boyfriend's beat-up Corolla."

"You've done your research too, it seems."

"I had a bit of spare time up my sleeve of late. Reading about all the places I could visit kept me sane."

"Then why did you let me go on and on about the bridge?"

"I like your face when you talk about this city. You're so serious most of the time, but when you forget to brood, when you actually start to enjoy yourself, you become quite animated."

"I do not."

"Okay." A few beats slunk by. Then, hovering closer, she murmured, "You're like a little kid, pointing out all the things he wants for his birthday."

With a growl Sean took his chance, finding her hand and twirling Aubrey back into his arms. She laughed as she grabbed onto him. Such easy release. And now he had her, her hand slid over his shoulder and into the back of his hair, the other curled around a button on his shirt.

He wondered if she even knew how she curled into him.

Locking herself into place. As if once she had him she didn't want to let go.

"One of these days," said Sean, his voice a low growl, filled with heat and want and all the possessive feelings she brought out in him, "you will mock me one time too many, then look out."

Something flickered behind her eyes. Something wrong. Sean moved to assure her he was kidding, that he'd never hurt her, when he realised that wasn't her concern.

One of these days, he'd said. As if she were sticking around. When she'd been at great pains to make it very clear she had miles to go before she slept.

Which was the only reason he'd let her in. Let her deep. So fast.

Because when she left it would not be a shock. It was a given. Built in.

He reached up and ran a thumb over the creases above her nose. "You can relax, Trusedale. I am well aware that one day I will wake up and you'll be gone. And that my life will have to go on as it did before, only with a you-sized hole in it."

Blink. Blink-blink.

She took longer than usual to compose herself, but her chin did finally lift. "Good. Because that's *exactly* how it's going to happen. Though I'll probably get my foot caught in a sheet, and make a right ruckus when I hit the floor, busting my knee. So you'll have to pretend you're asleep, okay? So as to allow me to limp out the door with a modicum of grace."

"I can do that."

"Wait, I'm not done."

Of course not.

"You must then fall into a deep depression, for a week, maybe two, when you realise how much you do in fact miss me. But you'll come out the other end a new man. Forged in the fires of my condescension. You name a chair after me. Perhaps a whole collection. Then—"

Sean kissed her to stop her talking.

It was the only way.

His hands to her cheeks, holding her close. He kissed her and she kissed him back. The sun warmed the back of his neck. The sounds of the crowd milling past them—all wolf whistles, and laughter—was a hazy soundtrack to the feel of the woman in his arms.

He pulled back to find her eyes fluttering open. Oaken eyes. So full of truth and heat and questions. Always with the questions.

Dangerous questions. Questions that he could not... *Would not* answer.

How could he whisper in her ear that she made him feel both light and full, human again, that he felt something akin to *happy* for the first time in years, without her misunderstanding? He didn't have the capacity to keep this level of contentment going.

Her eyes flickered between his, searching, before she slowly let him go and took a step away. Her face unreadable, for once. Her eyes distant.

"Oh, look," she said, breaking away.

In the nearest nook was a short tunnel, the ceiling trailing in ivy, and at the end a gate. She gave it a shake.

"Aubrey," Sean warned, "you can't go in there. It's private."

Aubrey gave the lock another jiggle and it sprung open. Her eyes, when they met his, were daring, and a little sharp, as she said, "Live a little, Malone."

Live a little. When he'd been doing his very best to live as little as humanly possible. Stopped by how freaking unfair it was his sister no longer got the chance to live at all.

She stepped through the gate.

And it was his turn to follow her.

Into a tiny courtyard surrounded on three sides by the

backs of stone buildings, typical of the area. Tins of paint were stacked under a small awning of one building. Washing hung over the railing on one. Not much in the way of beauty, pure utilitarian.

And yet Aubrey moved to a small stone wall and grabbed her sketchbook out of her backpack. Then, crouched like that, she set to copying some intricate designs etched into the stones.

"You do realise *The Birth of Venus* is three minutes from here," Sean said.

"I know. But how is this not as valid? Just because some old white guy didn't commission another white guy to carve it, what makes that picture of—?" She leaned closer, her hair falling half over her face as she got a better look.

When she sat up, her lips were caught between her teeth.

"You were saying?"

"Fine. Yes. In amongst the curlicues is the carving of a penis. But it's still art. There's another one. They're everywhere." She looked around at the buildings, the light in her eyes dancing. "Oh, my gosh, how brilliant. Do you think the people who live here know? Do you think they've ever noticed?"

Sean ran a hand over his face. Then coughed out a husky laugh. "You are a true original, Aubrey Trusedale."

"I try," she said, before going back to sketching her own version of the "art". Focussed on that the joy of it.

And Sean figured focussing on joy just a little more, for another day or two, surely couldn't hurt.

In bed that night Aubrey drew circles on Sean's chest, her gaze following the glint of the delicate ring she'd bought on the Ponte Vecchio. Loving it when the ring caught on a hair and Sean flinched.

Proving he wasn't completely unreal.

She was becoming unduly fascinated by him. There were the oodles of lust to contend with, yes. But it was his layers, his edges, his choices that really had her caught. That was what kept her spinning about his axis. Locked in his orbit.

The wondering.

One of those wonderings was how hard it might be to spin away. When the time came.

The thing she was realising was, with the luxury of time and money, there really was no rush. She hadn't made further bookings, or set plans. Viv owned the hotel she was staying in, and when Aubrey had messaged to let her know she might stay longer than originally intended, Viv had insisted she stay as long as her heart desired.

She was travelling to follow her curiosity. To forge a new life path for herself. And right now she was curious about Sean Malone. And all the ways he could make her sigh. All the ways he made her feel so very alive.

Her senses were open as they'd never been opened before. She could see colours, pick out aromas, feel textures, enjoy sitting and breathing in a way she'd never been able to do. First because she'd been in an all fire rush to grow up, always looking forward, and then because she'd been spending every spare second trying not to die.

Or maybe it was all Sean Malone.

For all the amazing things she'd see and do on this trip, she knew she'd never forget the sound of his voice. The deep, rough burr; never raised, but often exasperated. Calling her name from another room. Murmuring on the phone. Making grand promises in her ear and then, oh, the follow through.

She might have tugged a little hard, for Sean's body jolted beneath her touch.

Oh. She'd put him to sleep. That wasn't going to do her any good.

Another tug and he woke with a snuffle, his head tipping to face her, brow furrowed. The moonlight pouring through his huge windows creating slashes of shadow and light across his beautiful face.

"Did you just pinch me?"

Aubrey nodded. Slowly. Then leaned over him to kiss the spot.

"You're gonna wear me out, Aubrey Trusedale."

"Maybe," she said, rolling onto her back as he slowly moved over her, "but it'll be totally worth it."

CHAPTER SEVEN

A WEEK WENT BY, then another. Working hard and stealing time to scout out new places in the city to explore with Aubrey, Sean found a balance he'd never thought achievable. Not for him.

"Hey," Sean called, his phone open on the webpage he'd been scrolling through. "I'm thinking of trying this new restaurant someone has opened not far from here."

It was a little kitsch. Set up to feel like a dinner party, with everyone eating around the one big table. When Sean had read about it a couple of weeks back, just before he'd met Aubrey in fact, he couldn't think of anything worse than having to make polite conversation with strangers. But Aubrey? It would be her bliss.

So long as he was beside her, his knee nudged against hers, his hand along the back of her chair, good food on the plate, knowing they were five minutes from home, from his waiting bed, he could handle anything.

"Aubrey," he called, not finding her in his bedroom, though the en suite bathroom door was ajar, the light on.

"What do you think of this?" he said, pushing the door open a smidge to find her, hands gripping the edges of the sink, head slumped. Her bohemian yellow top had slipped off one shoulder, the blade poking out sharply. The veins in her arms struck blue in her pale skin.

"Aubrey," he said, hearing the thread of dread in his own voice and not liking it one bit.

She looked up, catching his eye in the mirror. And what he saw there made his stomach muscles clutch. Fear, pain, and concealment battled in her gaze. Swimming over the top, like living mercury; her silent pleas that he not ask if she was okay.

For a moment—a heartbeat—he considered backing out and closing the door. Giving her the privacy she clearly wanted.

It was the easier move. The one with the best chance at salvaging some form of self-containment.

But he'd been there. Opted to trust. To respect boundaries.

And lived to regret it.

He pushed the door open with more force than he'd intended. And found himself asking words he'd never wanted to utter. "Aubrey, what's going on? Are you…sick?"

She flinched. Then, with a stubborn lift to her jaw, said, "I'm fine."

Sean looked closer, taking in the dark smudges under her eyes. Wisps of her hair curled against her forehead, as if she'd been sweating. And a whole bunch of small signs he'd blithely let slide coagulated into a telling tale.

"The vitamins you claimed to be taking… They're not vitamins, are they?"

"Have you been through my stuff?"

"Of course not. Have you been lying to me?"

She flinched again. As if she was barely holding herself together.

Her phone rang right at that moment. A picture of a smiling couple, the ID reading *Mum and Dad*. Without a pause she sent it to voicemail and turned her phone over. Other times, when he'd found her talking quietly on the phone, she'd signed off as soon as she'd spotted him.

He'd thought she didn't want whoever was on the other end to know about him. Now, he realised, she didn't want *him* to know about *her*.

"Aubrey, you're so pale I can see through your skin. Talk to me. Tell me what's going on."

A muscle flickered in her cheek. Her lean shoulders squared. As if she was preparing to take him on. Or run.

But she stayed, catching her own eye in the mirror, shaking her hair off her face, attempting to rally. "There's plenty we don't know about one another and that's okay. We've made no promises, Malone. This has all been so lovely. Fun. Light. And I know you'd rather keep it that way."

It was his turn to flinch, at her assessment of his character. But she was right. Or he would have said so only a few weeks before.

But now, the not knowing, the keeping everything locked up tight, it didn't sit right. It felt shallow. And it felt untrue.

"My name is Sean."

She blinked. Her brow furrowing.

He moved deeper into the bathroom to stand beside her, leaning a hip against the bench so she had to look at him directly. Not through the haze of the mirror.

"I was named after my grandfather, the one who taught me woodwork. My middle name is Eric. I had a lisp until I was ten and my front teeth grew in. I didn't learn to drive till I was twenty-one because I lived in uni housing so had no need. I haven't spoken to my parents in over a year. Before that I ignored their calls, emails, and carrier pigeons for as long as I could before checking in. Even then the contact was brief, loaded with agony as we've known tragedy in our family and the only way I knew how to deal with it was to put it behind me. Literally. And I know why you call me Malone."

She looked like an animal, trapped, all wide eyes and fidgets.

He knew, as deep down inside as he'd ever let himself see, that she needed this. She dreamt of jumping out of a plane over the desert, swimming with sharks, and already she talked to any stranger who caught her eye. But, he was coming to realise, intimacy, revealing the parts of herself she believed people might not find so charming, scared the hell out of her.

Seeing her tremble and sweat overrode every instinct to

turn his back. To not become involved. He held out a hand. "Come with me."

While her innate stubbornness rolled in, like a storm over the ocean, she eventually turned and put her hand in his.

He took her into the bedroom, motioned for her to sit on the end of his unmade bed, the sheets still tangled from a night in her arms.

She sat, tucking her hands beneath her, her pinkie fingers poking out from beneath the hem of her short denim skirt.

From a drawer in his clothes chest—beneath his spare change, scraps of notepaper and passport, as if it were so much detritus—Sean found a small photo album.

His mother had had it made. A copy for her, a copy for his father, and a copy for him. He knew she'd done it in some effort to help. To show them all that the good years had far outweighed the one year of truly bad.

But it had only pressed home how deeply, how unutterably, he'd failed.

Curling his fingers around it for the first time in years, he moved to the bed, sat beside Aubrey. The spine of the album made a cracking noise as he opened it up.

The first picture was of him—kindergarten age—wearing a cowboy outfit for his fifth birthday party, his mum and dad's faces pressed up to his cheeks. His hair was lighter, his eyes brighter. He looked happy but ready to bolt from the frame to join his friends on their bikes.

Aubrey's finger hovered over his face. Then those of his parents. "Your mum… She looks like she could eat you up. And your dad's hot."

A laugh rose inside, but was quickly snuffed. He knew what she was trying to do. Her humour was her secret weapon for keeping intimacy at bay.

Sean flipped the page. Next came a picture of him at around age eight. A little girl with pigtails hugged him like there was no tomorrow.

"Who's that?"

"That," said Sean, running a thumb over a smudge on the page, "is my sister, Carly."

"Carly. Have you mentioned a sister?"

Her words didn't have their usual bite. Either she was too exhausted by whatever it was that had her slumped at his side, or she knew him well enough to understand he wasn't sharing this lightly. That now was not the time to mock.

"I haven't. I don't talk about her. Or my family. If I can help it. It's…difficult. Carly died; a little over five years ago now. Drug overdose."

"Oh. I… I have no idea what to say."

And so she said nothing. Simply encouraged him to turn the pages. There he was, throwing Carly in the pool. The two of them at a restaurant somewhere—Carly's eyes crossed, his cheeks puffed out like a blowfish. The photo of him in the shed felt like yesterday; looking earnestly at their grandfather while they worked on some basic lathing, while Carly lay outside, sunning herself, reading a book.

The last photo had been taken about six months before Carly died. It was a candid shot of the family at a trade show in which one of his chairs—a fluid, sweeping, laid-back cantilever that seemed to defy gravity—had won a big prize. It was during the time Sean had believed she was better. But in the photo it was clear she was not. The light in her eyes was dimmed, her cheeks sallow, her fingers curled into claws as she fussed with her bitten-down fingernails.

Aubrey's head slowly moved to lean against his upper arm. A warm body at his side. And it was enough to loosen the perpetual tightness in his throat.

"I was the firstborn. A good kid. Always doing the right thing. Making good choices. Good grades. My friends were all honour students, athletes, achievers. Carly was always wild. And brave. A daredevil. A risk taker. It enticed a darker crowd. Kids who craved attention from the shadows. But even as she began to change, to move away from us, to me she was always Carly. My brilliant, bratty little sister.

"When I went away to uni things got bad, fast. Drugs. Petty theft. A guy who didn't treat her well. Chatting with Carly, she seemed fine. Brushed it off as a little light rebellion. My parents—who are not the kinds of people to show when things are hard—didn't even let me know how bad things were till the night they came home to find their front window broken, their TV missing. They didn't need to beg me to come home. I came. Instantly.

"Carly seemed to rally, having me around. I was her ballast. No judgement, with me she could take her time to find her way back. She could breathe. She dumped the guy. She held down a job. We all had dinner at our parents' place three times a week.

"I got more and more antsy at being home. I'd given up my degree. All my doer friends were off doing and I was playing babysitter. As for the family dinners—the best thing I can say about them is they were polite, three courses, and on time. And Carly seemed better. My business was taking off. I revelled in being busy. I became less available each day.

"I figured my parents would let me know if things began to shift off course. But they, being the kind of people they are, again tried to shoulder it on their own.

"My little sister was twenty-three when she died. OD'd at a party held in an abandoned warehouse on pills she'd robbed from a pharmacy with her junkie ex-boyfriend."

As he said the words, Sean felt a fog shift over him. His voice, to his ears, coming from a mile away. Then he felt Aubrey shift beside him. Heard her sniff, before her hand moved to quickly swipe at her eye.

He slowly closed the album. And looked at her. Waited till she looked at him.

"I won't do that again, Aubrey. I won't deliberately put myself in a position where I can be sideswiped. Tell me about the pills."

Her eyes, red-rimmed and wholly devastated, looked

deeply into his own. This woman who adored hearing people's stories, who absorbed them like warmth from the sun, was hurting. For him.

The urge to reach up and cup her cheek, to kiss away her tears, to own her pain, was overpowering.

But he had worked too hard to create a life in which his responsibilities were simple and clear-cut. In which he did not take on more than he could bear to lose.

The wound of losing his sister still burned—open and feral and for ever. And the guilt... The guilt had stripped him bare.

Realising, then, how much he'd let slip these past few weeks, how easily she'd found a way in, he hardened his heart before saying, "Tell me now, Aubrey, or I'll call a car to take you back to the hotel. And that'll be it. I won't see you again."

"Wow," she said, the warmth in her eyes cooling, as if she was adding a few new walls herself. "You're sexy when you're bossy."

"Aubrey—"

"Okay! Okay. Okay."

She pushed herself off the bed, went into the bathroom, rummaged around in her backpack and came back with the little container in which she kept her "vitamins".

She rolled the bottle in her hand a few times, before handing it over.

A lot of chemical gobbledygook and brand names with *angiotensin converting enzyme, ACE, inhibitors* written in bold.

From what little he knew of such things an inhibitor reduced or suppressed...something. Was it a thyroid thing? Something as simple as that?

"I'm not a chemist, Aubrey. You're going to have to translate."

"Angiotensin converting enzyme inhibitors relax the

blood vessels so that the heart doesn't have to work quite so hard."

Her *heart*? The hardness around his own took a hit. "And why would your heart not need to work so hard?"

She looked down at her hands, her fingertips and thumbs running over one another in a nervous dance. Then she breathed out hard and said, "A couple of years back, right after the music festival in Copenhagen, in fact, I collapsed. I ended up in a Danish hospital for several weeks while they tried to figure out why. They were stuck on believing I'd taken something at the show, you see. That it was an allergic or toxic reaction to some dodgy ingredient cut into some dodgy drug."

Aubrey shot him a look then, piecing together his story with hers. Her eyes filled with mortification and sorrow. "It wasn't like that! I promise. I'm not into that kind of thing. A cocktail, yes. But before the collapse I'd avoid even taking paracetamol."

Sean said, "I believe you. Go on."

"My parents did what good people do and listened to the doctors. When questioned, as I lay on a ventilator by that stage, they admitted I was headstrong. A little wild. Not so good at following rules. They…believed it was my fault."

Sean's fingers curled into fists in the effort to sit still and listen. To not react. Or comfort. Or cut his losses and walk away.

"Anyhoo, since they were on the wrong track, I went downhill fast. Ended up in the ICU. Even an induced coma for a period before they diagnosed me as having myocarditis. My heart, by that point, had taken a beating. I went into heart failure."

Sean's eyes felt so gritty, he forced himself to blink.

"My folks… They've never forgiven themselves for not trusting me. Not pushing harder, faster, for a correct diagnosis. Then they started blaming themselves. Figured it was something to do with the paint we used at the shop.

That they hadn't provided good enough safety equipment. Or the right size.

"Truth was I'd not told anyone about the shortness of breath, or the occasional missed heartbeats I'd felt leading up to that day, figuring it was down to excitement that I was finally heading off on the trip I'd been saving for since I sold my brothers' Lego to other kids at school when I was eight years old. I didn't want anyone to tell me if I was sick I couldn't go. But turns out I had a virus. The virus caused the myocarditis.

"They pumped me full of all kinds of gear—anti-viral corticosteroids, inhibitors, beta blockers, now the meds to reduce the risk of blood clots forming in my heart. I'm only on a tiny dose now, working towards coming off them, which is great. But—"

After a few long seconds, Aubrey pulled down the top left shoulder of her shirt and he finally understood why she'd never removed her shirt any time they'd made love.

There was a scar, about an inch long, just above her heart. And above it? A tiny tattoo, etched along the top. The zigzag of a heartbeat, looping into a broken heart, then a zigzag again.

"I had a mechanical pump inserted inside me for a while, until they decided I wasn't in need of a transplant. Then I went home. Not well enough to drive, work, go out and be in the world for months. Can you imagine? Me cooped up? On bed rest?"

Sean attempted an expression that showed he understood, but he was still attempting to absorb the image of the scar; puckered, pink, and clearly recent.

"So I hunkered down. I ate my veggies. I did my rehab exercises. Saw a psychologist who helped me more than anyone. Dry wit. Honest. Gave me great practical tools. I loved her. Till she told me I can't have kids."

Aubrey said the words in the same tone as if she were telling him a funny story about one of her nephews, but her body… She all but crumpled before him. Her face falling into her hands.

Sean's next breath squeezed from his lungs. He wished he'd never found her in the en suite bathroom. That right now he was booking dinner someplace light. And fun.

And yet…

Knowing this, knowing her truth, having shared his, everything had changed. He felt in it now. Grounded. The urge to keep moving, doing, exploring, to stay out of his own head simply dissolved away.

"Aubrey," he said. "Sweetheart. It's okay. You don't have to say any more."

"No!" she said, sitting up, her eyes a liquid gold as they held onto his. "I want to. I have to. It's like an animal trying to claw its way out of my chest."

"Okay then. Let it out. I can take it." It was his turn to absorb her story. As best he could with his limited experience. His limited means.

She nodded. Licked her lips. "She told me that having children… They never say never. Fear of getting sued, I guess. She said the chances are infinitesimally small. She gave me pamphlets about freezing eggs, and egg donation, and the legalities of surrogacy. I'm for all that. Whatever it takes for a family to have a kid or a kid to have a family. It's just… The dream I had of *my* future was so simple. It didn't seem like too much to ask. And to be told no. Just no. It…it's been challenging to see the way forward."

"Tell me about it," said Sean. "Tell me your dream."

Aubrey looked at him anew. Her brow furrowing. As if she was trying to figure out if he was merely indulging her. Then she looked up at the chandelier hanging over his bed, and breathed out a shaky sigh. "You, with your grand life, you'd think it was silly."

"Not a chance. I promise."

And so she told him. Travel, a nice guy, house, yard, kids. Weekend barbecues with her brothers and all the nieces and nephews. Grandparents involved every step of the way. That was it.

It sounded…loud, messy and chaotic for a guy who grew up in a house in which there was no running, no dirty shoes. Where the backyard was a showpiece kept by the gardener, with a sister who was glared at any time she burped at the dinner table. The older he'd become, the more it had felt as if it weren't real, more some halcyon existence people used to sell SUVs and home loans.

"How about you?" she asked, catching him off guard. "Do you want kids?"

His, "No," was quick. And honest.

Even before the shadow of Carly's death, trying to carve out a life of his own, one that felt real, and true, had been challenging without a model on which to base it. The thought of bringing kids into that felt unfair.

For Aubrey, he gentled. "I didn't grow up with the same kind of family you did. Our life was more…structured. Composed. Less barbecue, more dress for dinner. I like kids. I was one once, if you can believe that. But after Carly… I just don't see how parents do it—live with the fear, every second, that no matter what they did it could still end in tragedy."

Aubrey blinked. "Hate to tell you, but that's Parenting for Beginners. My oldest brother still holds a mirror to his son's sleeping mouth to check he's breathing before he himself goes to bed."

"Was that meant to change my mind?"

"No," Aubrey said, letting go a laugh that was more of a sob.

Then she reached over, and took his hand. Hers was small. Cool. He curled his fingers around it. She waited till he looked her in the eye.

Her eyes were clear. So clear he felt he could see a mile past the surface, right into her deepest depths. To find someone complicated. Searching. Determined. Kind. Empathetic. And drawn to him, still.

"Don't want kids if you don't want kids. Just don't be a fatalist," she said, her voice no longer wavering. "It doesn't suit you."

"Then what does suit me?"

"Linen," she shot back without pause. "Those jeans, the dark ones, that hug your backside just so. The colour blue. The look you get when you think I don't know you're watching me. All hot and simmering, full of ideas of what you'd like to do to me when you next get me alone. I like that on you best of all."

She nudged him with her shoulder, trying to perk *him* up.

Sean snuck a finger under her chin, tilted her face till she looked him in the eyes. "What do you need me to do?"

Her mouth opened, and closed. "Not a single thing. This has been perfect. Lovely. Magical. You, Sean Malone, have been an antidote."

Sean's fingers slid around the edge of her chin. His thumb tracing her jaw. "That's right, you're using me."

"I'm totally using you. And don't you forget it."

Something shifted in the air in that moment. Like an invisible string curling around them.

"The thing is though, Aubrey, I know you like to take on the world as if daring it to even try and stop you. But you're not invincible. None of us are. It's okay to make mistakes. To take a day. It's okay to slow down."

A smile flickered across her full lips. "I know. I do. Just—"

"Just?"

"If you treat me differently after this, Sean, as if I'm some fragile flower, I'm not sure I'll handle it."

"Never."

"You sure? First time I saw you I thought, *Hot damn*. First time you saw me you thought, *She's gonna be mugged*."

That was true. But hot damn had followed right on after for him too.

"I will never treat you as if you are a fragile flower," he said. "I promise."

She swallowed, her eyes locked onto his. Fierce and damaged. Wary but warm. The most beautiful contradiction he'd ever known. And those eyes—those brimming oaken whisky eyes—drank him up. He'd never in his life had anyone look at him the way she did.

And Sean felt the last vestiges of the protective shell around his iron heart shudder and shift, dissolving in places, floating away in others, not sure if he'd ever be able to reforge them again.

Then she straightened her spine, leaned into him, and lifted to gently press her lips against his. She kissed him softly, again and again, until he had no choice but to kiss her back.

It was an elixir. She was an elixir. A giver of life. But he had been empty for so very long, his well dry, he did not want to deplete her.

So he broke the kiss. Pulled away.

She rested her forehead against his chin. "That was intense."

"Little bit."

"Let's say we don't do that again for a while."

"What's a while?"

A single shoulder shrug, her shirt falling a little further down her arm. "Not sure. A bit longer. Maybe. If it's still okay with you."

"Sure. Why not?"

"That's the spirit." She moved up onto her knees, straddling him. Both hands on his shoulders, she gave him a shove, pushing him back onto the bed. Then she leaned over him, lips hovering just over his. "You and me, we are both allowed to make mistakes. We are both allowed to take a day. And we could both do with a little fairy dust."

Another kiss, deep this time. Her warm body melting into his.

Sean's arms went around her, his hands sliding beneath her loose top and up her bare back to find her hot, lush and a little sweaty.

She pulled away, panting slightly, her eyes dark and determined.

"Let's agree, here and now, to be one another's fairy dust. To keep this thing easy and light. A holiday fling. No promises, no debts. No knight-in-shining-armour concern for my busted heart. Trust me when I say I've got this. I'm all over it. I'm *fine*. Is *that* okay with you, Sean?"

"It's okay with me." Heaven help him, as he said the words he'd half believed them.

Till she had to go and call him by his name.

Not Malone. Sean.

He slowly rolled her over, till they were side by side, legs intertwined. "Show me your tattoo again."

"What? No."

"No promises. No debts. But no more secrets either. Show me."

Nostrils flaring, eyes brimming with vulnerability, she slowly pulled down the neckline of her shirt to reveal the tattoo. And the scar.

His heart, now unprotected, beat hard against his ribs. "Does it hurt?"

She shook her head, not meeting his eyes. "It can pull a little. Can be tender when it's cold out."

And while the thought of why it was there tore at him, his anger was stronger still. That someone so lovely and kind and bright could be so struck. Could feel untethered for so long.

Breathing deep, he leaned down and kissed her, just above her scar, on the tattoo she'd been too afraid to let him see lest he treat her as if she was breakable. Right on her broken heart.

She shuddered.

When he pulled back tears were streaming down her face. Emotion so raw and real it was more than he could hope to name. And while it felt light years beyond easy, beyond light, beyond a holiday fling, he drew her to him, anyway, losing himself in her.

They never made it out to dinner.

The next morning, Aubrey woke to find herself alone in bed.

Mind you, it was nearing ten in the morning, after an emotionally exhausting night, followed by the most wonderful, tender, glorious make-up sex.

The sound of whirring machinery told her there was work afoot deep below the villa.

She stretched herself out to the four corners of the bed, groaning as bits and pieces of The Conversation came back to her. For all the lovely that had come after, it had been so hard admitting the truth of her condition to Sean.

Finding out could have easily been a tipping point for him. The man was a grown-up. With strong opinions. And limits as to what he would accept. And she'd pushed those limits pretty hard. Regards his staff. And the people in the laneway. And his family.

She groaned, flinging her arm over her eyes.

What a fool she'd been.

Not only to assume his greatest benefits were his pretty face. And clever hands. But to suggest they agree, out loud, to keep things easy and light, no promises, no plans.

When her feelings for Sean Malone had grown to be anything but easy. Anything but light.

Because last night she'd finally seen into the man's heart. And what a massive beast of a thing it was. Deep, soulful, caring, steadying, protective, understanding. And forgiving. During The Conversation, that strength had more than made up for the restraints of her own faulty ticker.

Despite his own pain, his own self-confessed limitations—

and what sounded like some deeply held survivor's guilt—he'd listened, he'd respected, he'd held her close.

Because he cared. For her. Not because she was the kind of girl who'd always had the ability to convince people to do things for her, but because he wanted to. Wanted *her*. More than he wanted the peace and quiet of the lifestyle he'd carved out before she'd stumbled raucously into his life? Maybe. Just maybe.

Holding tight to that thought, she rolled out of bed feeling…airy. As if a huge burden had been lifted off her shoulders.

After showering and changing and repacking her backpack—having picked up a couple of changes of clothes from her hotel the day before—she opened the bedroom door to find Ben slowly pacing the floorboards as if he'd been doing so for some time.

"Ah, hello?"

He flinched. "Aubrey. Hi. Morning."

"You're not Sean."

"I did mention you might notice that."

Mention. Meaning Sean knew he was there.

Aubrey moved to sneak around Ben, only to have him lean to block her. She held out both hands. "Whoa there, partner. What's going on?"

"Um, Sean has to work today. Commission deadline. Admin. All piled up. I thought… I offered to show you some stuff today. Around town."

"Did you now?"

"Yep." Ben looked up and away, classic sign of lying.

She'd have felt sorry for him if all the lovely, warm, exciting, new feelings she'd been revelling in not that long ago weren't now caught up in a massive messy jumble.

Aubrey slid her phone from the outer pocket of her backpack and called Sean. What would she say when he answered? *Are you avoiding me? Because I'm sick? Did the cold light of day bring all we said into sharp, all too real relief?*

She swore she could hear the faint shrill of the ringtone from downstairs, yet the phone rang out.

So she typed in a text. Showing it to Ben. "Too much?"

Ben shook his head, then nodded, all while looking as if his eyes were about to bug out of his head.

She hit send.

What's the haps, Malone? You seem to have shrunk. And your hair changed colour. And when I kissed you, you tasted different.

Sean texted right back as if he'd been waiting for it.

Funny girl. I have to work. You have to play. That is how it is written. So I've given Ben the day off to show you his Florence.

Aubrey felt the air leave her nostrils in a frustrated steam. She showed Ben his boss's response. He looked so pale she might have worried he'd faint if she weren't feeling so furious.

"Next time, do a better job of keeping your stories straight, okay?"

"Okay," said Ben.

Aubrey scrunched up her face in chagrin. "Sorry. This isn't on you. Not your fault your boss is a stubborn so-and-so. And I'd actually love to see your Florence. I'm imagining less walking, less opera."

Ben laughed, then ran a hand up the back of his neck. "I was thinking food and a vinyl-record store I haven't had a chance to check out."

It was enough for her to refrain from showing Ben her next message.

You do remember what happens when men show me their Florence, right?

A few long, heavy beats slunk by as Sean took that one in. His eventual response?

I remember.

As she imagined the word in his deep intimate voice, Aubrey's belly filled with butterflies. Goose bumps skittered all over her skin.

They had something. It was deeper than either of them would admit. And clearly, considering he was giving himself some space, Sean was struggling with it as much as she was. Could she blame him? Should she call him on it? Or give him a day? Give him whatever time he needed?

Sean filled the gap, texting.

Dinner. The best fettucine of your life. I'll tip the waiter to serenade you. You can even pick the song.

Aubrey coughed out a laugh.

And she closed her eyes as she told her heart to stop fussing and settle down.

Sean was a grown-up. With strong opinions. And limits as to what he would accept.

But so was she.

She ducked around Ben and darted down the stairs to the workshop where she found Flora and Sean arguing. Arms flailing. Boisterous Italian bouncing off the ancient stuccoed walls.

When Flora saw Aubrey she stopped, her face reddening. Muttering, only slightly less loudly than she'd been shouting, Flora threw up her hands and turned away.

Sean spun, his dark eyes catching on hers.

Her heart fluttered, coughed, caught on the look in his eyes. The caution. The concern. Before he blinked and it was gone. His face clear. His expression blank.

"Problem?" Aubrey asked.

"We were just arguing over...the shape of a table leg," Sean assured her.

Flora snorted. And the concerns Aubrey had pushed out of her mind came back with a vengeance.

"Okay, so I just wanted to check in before Ben and I head off. We're going to have the best time! Right Ben?"

Ben, hovering on the bottom step, muttered, "Um, sure. We'll have a nice time. Average nice. The regular kind."

"Sure you don't want to play hooky and join us, Malone?"

Sean's cheek twitched at her use of his last name. His eyes dark, unreadable. No smile. No mocking come back. No sign of the man who'd held her so close the night before.

"Okay then, bye," Aubrey said, backing away before the tickle in the backs of her eyes turned into something.

As she ducked out of the workshop doors into the light of day, she wished she'd never caught the look in Flora's eyes. Full of sorrow and regret. As if she'd seen this version of Sean before.

Sean followed Aubrey to the double doors leading out to the drive. But even while a thousand words crammed into his throat—from *Wait, I'll take you* to *I am a damn fool*— he said not a word.

He watched as Ben helped her into his Fiat. Watched as she smiled up at the lanky kid. Said something that made Ben laugh. And blush. And run a hand up the back of his neck.

Aubrey did not wave as the car drove away. Or even look back. He could picture her jaw, tight and strong. Her shoulders back and fierce. Her clever brain ticking over all the reasons he might have sent her off without him.

"Dammit," he muttered, the word tight in his throat.

Part of him wanted to message her, to ask if she had the answer. Because he sure didn't. Not with any real clarity.

All he knew for sure was that from the moment he'd seen her gripping the edge of the sink the night before, her face pale, sweat dappling her brow, something huge had shifted inside him, and was still shifting. Knocking, crushing, rearranging him at the cellular level.

After hours of it, he felt a bruising ache. All over. Every breath hurt. Every feeling stung. The thought of holding her, agony. The thought of letting her go even worse.

She was right. He *had* sensed it—her fragility—that first day. For all her strength, her confidence, her determination, it was something she'd carry with her always. The same way he'd carry Carly's death.

A shadow. A ghost.

Being with her, letting her light warm him when he'd been in the cold for so long, he'd been sure he was inured against her like. That his experience had tempered him to a point of invulnerability.

Aubrey was something he'd never counted on.

"Sean?" Flora's voice called, flatly. "Malone." Then, "Boss?"

Sean turned.

"If you're done mooning, can you please give me the instructions you simply had to give me this morning, the ones that were so important you sent Ben in your stead? Or can I go back to doing what I already do perfectly?"

"I… Sure. Maybe."

Flora moved to him, smacked him in the arm. "Focus. If she messes with your head, boss, we all suffer. We need the work, just as you do. So pull yourself together."

"Flora!" Angelina exclaimed, while Hans furiously cleaned the crevices of a turned table leg with a toothbrush.

"He needs to be told!" said Flora. "For his own good! As he looked after us when we needed it most, now it is our turn to look after him."

Sean looked at her, then at his crew, all bar Ben, who was hopefully driving safely down the hill with his precious cargo in tow.

To think, only a few weeks before they'd all been so polite. Yes, boss. No, boss. Three bags full, boss.

Flora would never have punched him, much less roused at him, or sassed him. Now they were all at it. Ribbing him about Aubrey. And castigating him if they thought he could do better. Coming to him with ideas, telling jokes, and sharing their own stories.

Giving him space if he needed it. And a knock to the head if he needed that too.

As if they were family.

Aubrey, he thought, her name a clutch in his belly. Aubrey had done that. The seeds had been there. In the good people he'd chosen to be around. The wish, on their behalf. She'd yanked them all together in a way he'd not had it in him to allow before.

Aubrey, with her scars. Far more literal than his own.

Aubrey, with her already badly broken heart.

He was the one who had to find the strength to let it in. To let her in. Fully. None of this light, easy, no-promises guff.

He had to give this thing a chance, or his actions would be truly unforgivable.

CHAPTER EIGHT

THE NEXT COUPLE of weeks rushed by in a flourish with Aubrey filling two new sketchbooks with studies of tiles, fabrics, faces and graffiti.

Now that she wasn't in such a rush to do all the things, she found herself noticing the world in a different way: flowers and notes tucked into the carvings in walls, children playing in the streets, their mothers watering them down with a hose so that they might ride out the intense heat.

It made her think more and more about her life back home. And she found herself missing it more than she'd imagined she would.

She'd started regular video chats with her family. Meaning she'd been able to see how truly well her parents were doing. How healthy. How happy. How crazy they were driving her brothers now she wasn't around for them to concentrate on.

After that first odd morning following The Conversation, things with Sean had found a new groove too. In between day trips to trade school to give guest lectures, phone calls with a couple of extremely famous movie stars whose Aspen chalet he was decking out with custom beams, of all things, he'd found ways to be with her.

Cinque Terre and Siena. A sunrise hot-air balloon over the Chianti region with views to San Gimignano and the Apennine Mountains. A midnight tour of the Crypt of Santa Reparata. Vespa rides and more museums and galleries and eateries than she could hope to remember.

She'd assured him if the whole famous furniture designer thing ever fell through, he could get a job with Contiki, no sweat. He'd not been impressed.

The days he couldn't get away he continued offering up

staff to "hang" with her, despite his promise to treat her just the same. Having met his beast of a heart she knew how hard it was for him not to be a protector.

She could not have faulted him. Truly. He'd even started telling more stories of his life back home. A childhood less warm than her own, but there'd been love there all the same.

And yet there was a teeny little voice in the back of her head telling her to pay attention.

She couldn't shake the sense that a new kind of tension rode him. Different from the one that had kept him in its thrall when they'd first met. Tighter, sharper, more immediate. As if the thing that worried him most now wasn't his past, or an email he didn't want to answer. It was her.

That, plus the fact she had no clean clothes and could rely on the hotel to do her laundry, and how she'd not felt a hundred per cent the past few days, meant Aubrey had spent the last couple of nights crashed out in her neglected hotel suite.

She woke from a nap on her hotel sofa, to the sound of someone knocking on her door.

With a groan she rolled out of bed, and hobbled to the door.

"Sean?" she said as she peered through the peephole to find an eye pressed up to the other side.

A voice call loudly from the other side, "No, darling, it's Vivian. So open up."

Viv? Here?

Aubrey blinked, taking what she would forevermore think of as a "Sean moment" to let things settle in her head, before she whipped open the door.

And sure as toast, there stood Vivian Ascot, billionaire and life-changer, looking resplendent in a draping grey ensemble pant suit, her silvery hair a gravity-defying coiffure, enough jewels bedecking her fingers to sink a ship.

A far cry from the pale, injured older woman Aubrey had first met two years before.

With a laugh, Aubrey threw herself into Viv's arms. "I

can't believe you're here! I have to call the others. Daisy and Jess. This will blow their sweet minds."

"Of course, dear, whatever pleases you. But first, I would very much appreciate an invitation inside. My feet do not take to plane travel as they used to."

"Oh, my gosh, of course. Come in! My room is your room. Literally. You own it, after all."

"Well, yes, that's true."

After Viv strode inside the room, Aubrey went to close the door only to squeal when she found the space filled by a man who looked as if he could eat Aubrey's brothers for breakfast.

"That's Frank," said Viv from somewhere inside the suite. "My security."

"Frank?" Aubrey asked, checking to make sure.

The mountain nodded.

"Well, then. Come in, I suppose."

Frank did; casing the joint before taking up position by the door, hands clasped in front, eyes constantly scanning, as if some deadly threat might materialise out of thin air.

"Who is this Sean?" Viv asked.

Aubrey turned to find Vivian sitting on the couch, watching her. *How did she...?* Ah, right, she'd called Sean's name at the door.

"He's a...friend."

Though as soon as she said the words they sounded ridiculous. To think she'd tried to talk herself into believing that was the goal. How things had tumbled since; Florentine Fling. now confidant, protector, a pair of warm arms, a listening ear, a lover...

Her head suddenly swam. Her insides felt fluttery. She walked her hands across the backs of the chairs till she found herself a seat.

It's not my heart, a voice said inside her head. *It's not.* She must have got up from her prone position too fast.

Though when had she last checked in? Closed her eyes, held a hand over her heart?

The last few days she'd found herself yawning by ten in the morning. Feeling starving hungry or not hungry at all, no in-betweens. Even Sean had noticed. Encouraging her to sleep in her own bed, claiming he needed "a night off from her incessant ravishing" if he was going to function as a human person.

Or she might not have been here to meet Viv at all.

She sat, reached out to take Viv's hand. "I can't believe you're here. I'm so happy you are, but this is surreal."

"Good surreal, I do hope."

"The best surreal!"

"Mmm." Viv's gaze moved to look out of the window, a view of the top of the Ponte Vecchio peeking over the balcony railing. "I haven't been to Florence since I was a girl. About your age, in fact. And it hit me when I last spoke to you that if I didn't come soon, I might miss my chance."

"Oh." Aubrey breathed through a sudden wave of nausea. "I know you insisted you were fine when I nudged, after Jessica mentioned you'd pulled out of the book deal citing ill health. But Daisy said you were a no-show at this year's Annual Ascot Music Festival too. Is everything okay?"

Viv's hand landed over Aubrey's. "I am very well. I've simply hit a point in my life where I no longer wish to do what people expect of me. I'd rather read a book than write one. I'd rather listen to music than present it. And I'd rather go to one of the most beautiful cities on earth to feel romance again, than go because I have some kind of business opportunity lined up there. Does that make any sense?"

Aubrey smiled. "It makes *all* the sense. No set plans. No expectations. That's exactly how I started this trip."

Viv's clever eyes narrowed. "And you've stayed here, in this one place, far longer than I'd imagined you would."

Aubrey sat up. "I know. Sorry. The hotel room—"

"Is yours. For ever if you want it. You do exactly as you

please. You needed space, to breathe, to be, so I gave you that. Beyond that, how you spend the money is entirely up to you." Vivian sighed. "I've so enjoyed living vicariously through you all. I never had daughters to spoil. But this has given me an inkling of what that might have been like."

Aubrey squeezed Viv's hand again.

"What I didn't expect was for you to show me what I needed as well."

"And what's that?" Aubrey asked.

"I'm retiring!"

"I'm sorry. Wait? What?"

"I'm retiring! I'm going to travel, as you have. Perhaps find a little holiday cottage of my own to do up." Viv's eyes looked a little wild as they landed on Aubrey's things around the room. Her dad's ancient fedora. Her phone with its scratched-up stained glass heart on the case. "I might even start carrying a backpack. Whereabouts might I find one like yours?"

Aubrey's head started to spin, for real. "Um, well, it's actually probably not the best choice. I mean, I love it. But it doesn't actually close properly. Sean, my friend Sean, it drives him crazy. He's constantly having to yank it shut. So there's a good chance your stuff will get pinched."

Aubrey put a hand to her forehead expecting it to be hot. But it felt fine. A little damp perhaps, but no fever.

Viv blinked. "No one will be pinching anything. I have Frank."

"There is that." Aubrey swallowed, her belly turning over on itself. When her phone buzzed she took the distraction gladly. It was Sean. "May I?"

Viv waved a hand and pushed herself to standing. "Answer away. I need Frank to help me call Max."

Max. Viv's adorable little sausage dog, and his bolt from her arms at a music festival in Denmark, were the reason they'd all met.

"Say hi from me!"

She read Sean's message.

Aspen job is coming along well, if you're bored and need company?

She sent him one back.

I've found another friend to keep me entertained. Vivian Ascot just turned up at the hotel!

Now you're definitely mocking me.

Aubrey took a quick selfie with Viv in the background and sent it to Sean. Then to the girls while she remembered. Her head had been so fuzzy and forgetful of late.

Sean's response?

Hallelujah. I was getting pretty sick of you.

Aubrey laughed out loud. The sound reverberating through her till she felt warm and fuzzy all over. For *that* was mocking. Mr Serious cracking jokes at her expense, smiling because she made him feel safe enough to do so, made her poor heart swell.

Aubrey's smile faded, her hand going to her mouth as her whole body seemed to revolt at once.

At which point she ran to the bathroom and threw up.

Aubrey sat in the big empty hotel bath—the only spot cool enough to take the edge off the hot flush that she couldn't seem to break—fully clothed, her phone to her ear, her other hand over her eyes, as she spoke to her cardiologist back in Sydney.

The pregnancy test Frank had managed to source from

goodness knew where, and its big blue positive cross, twirled over and over and over in her hand.

"It sounds like plain old morning sickness. You should be just fine," the doctor said. "Falling pregnant was the hard part. But, now you are, so long as you take care and are monitored closely, there is the possibility of a low-complication pregnancy."

Falling. Miracle. Possibility. Complication. Pregnancy.

"Okay," Aubrey said, squeezing her eyes tight to try to keep the words in the right order. "That's a big relief. But, the thing is… I'm travelling, remember? I'm in the first city in a whirlwind world tour."

Travelling because she *couldn't* fall pregnant. On a whirlwind tour in the hopes of finding her *new* normal. Her *new* dream. And she and Sean had taken care. Every time. Hadn't they? Sean *had* joked that the condoms in his beside drawer had been there for some time…

"Ah," said the doctor, "that's right. So I'm taking from that this was unplanned."

"Most unplanned. I'd thought my planning days were done."

"Yes. So did we all. Whereabouts are you?"

"Florence."

"Ah, Firenze. A most beautiful city. I bet you're having a wonderful time. Have you seen the David yet?"

"Of course. And, yes, I *was* having the best time imaginable, till I threw up this morning."

"Yes. Mmm… Look, I'll email you the name of a local specialist, a doctor I met at a conference a year or so ago. Very proficient. Make an appointment immediately. I would also stop taking your ACE inhibitors right away."

"My meds?"

"Yes. I would not recommend taking them while pregnant."

"Right." A beat then, "Might they have…damaged…" Aubrey couldn't even say it. For a woman who'd believed there would never be a baby to worry about, the thought of the tiny little peanut in her belly under stress made her feel faint. And ferocious.

"Let's get you along to the specialist, okay? They can check you out and make a plan from there."

Aubrey nodded, not sure she'd be able to form words.

So no heart meds. And pregnant. In a foreign city. Pregnant by a man to whom she'd promised to keep things easy, and light. A man who had made it all too clear a family was not on the cards for him. With very good, heartfelt reasons why.

She gulped, and looked up at the ceiling to stop gravity taking a hold of the tears brimming in her eyes. "Should I just go home?"

Even as she said it, she saw the irony. She was travelling to make peace with the life she'd left behind. So she could go home to a bright new future. Only now, the thought of leaving this place, leaving Sean... Sean. Her baby's father. Who didn't want children. It felt as though the future she'd been working towards had just slipped through her fingers. Again.

What a mess.

"Be honest about how you feel. Ms Trusedale, you alone know what you are capable of."

Aubrey pressed her thumbs to her eyes and nodded. When she remembered the doctor couldn't see her, she said, "Okay. Thanks, Doc."

Once they had disconnected, Aubrey looked at her phone's background pic: her brothers' kids, the manic brood of nieces and nephews.

Be honest about how you feel.

She knew her doctor meant healthwise. Cold sweats, overtired, fainting, that kind of thing. But the sentiment was far bigger. How did she *feel* about having a baby? A miracle baby? Especially if it might turn out to be her only chance.

Oh, the bittersweet tumble of feelings that swept through

her. Too shocked to dissemble, too raw to lie to herself, she knew how she felt.

She was utterly smitten with Sean Malone.

With his focus, his seriousness, his generosity. The thought of being with him, *really* being with him, as he worked, as he lived in this magical city, surrounded by so much art, beauty, food, friends, warmth, felt doable. Felt like a plan she could get behind.

Now adding a child to the mix. Their child… Aubrey imagined a wavy-haired toddler, playing chase in the orchard. The three of them lying on the grass, eating peaches, and watching the clouds drift by.

That wasn't a plan. It was the fairy tale.

The vision hovered a moment—so fragile yet so real, like blown glass before it started to cool. Then it fell in on itself till it was once more a formless blob.

How could she tell him? For just a second she considered not telling him at all. He was such a strong mix of stubborn and good, not telling him would save him from the guilt that would hound him for not being what she needed him to be. Perhaps she could disappear the way she'd always joked she would.

She could go home, and still probably find a nice, unassuming, indulgent, docile guy she'd imagined she'd end up with. The kind that would always buy her mother the same wine for family get-togethers, who would talk engine mounts with her dad, while she mucked about with their kids in the backyard pool.

Only now *that* life felt like the formless blob. A life here, with the people she'd grown so fond of, with Sean—it could be so shiny and sparkly and sophisticated and healthy and rich and inspiring and full.

If not for the soulful, deep, serious, stoic, damaged prince of a man who refused to believe he was worthy of happiness.

His problem was he thought he was done. Forged. Fully formed. As if *he* were the one made from marble.

Not over his sister's death. Refusing to forgive himself, or his parents, for the perceived roles they'd played in Carly's unhappiness. He could be an amazing father and partner, thoughtful, protective, witty, and good. If only he weren't so stubbornly resistant to believing in the true capacity of his beastly heart.

What was she going to do?

The hand holding the long white stick with the big blue plus symbol moved to hover over her belly. Where it landed.

She closed her eyes and checked in. But rather than reaching for her heart, she reached for the cells multiplying madly in her womb.

Hey there, little one, she thought. *You hear me, okay? I may be a bit flummoxed right now, but, believe you me, you were made from joy. And you are loved.*

Her phone buzzed. She glanced at it to find another message from the man of the hour. His fourth of the day.

Sean had sent her a photo of Elwood looking forlorn.

Big guy is missing you. Me? I'm great. Getting so much work done. Tell your famous friend not to rush off.

She laughed. Then choked on a sob.

Hormones? Probably.

Or, more likely, it was the fact that she had finally found a new life's dream. And was about to lose it all over again.

Once Aubrey had called the cardiologist in town, and an obstetrician recommended by her, she dragged her feet into the lounge to find Viv sitting, waiting, hands clasped in her lap. Frank the security guy still stood stiffly by the door.

"Report?" Viv said, all business.

"It went…better than expected."

"Do you know what you are going to do?"

"Right now I'm not sure if I want to sit or stand. Beyond that it's a blur." Aubrey leant her arms along the back of the sofa. "Have you ever been in love, Viv?" Then, "Sorry. That's so out of left field. And an incredibly private thing to ask."

Viv surprised her by saying, "Yes. I have been in love. But only the once. His name was Giuseppe. He was a beatnik, from Rome. We met one long hot summer I spent in Florence."

Oh. "Is that why you wanted me to come here first? You were pining?"

"Don't fret, my dear. I got plenty."

"Did you now?" Aubrey said on a choke of laughter.

Viv flapped a hand over her face. "I've had a fine life. No regrets. For what is the point? Life is a potato—you mash it, make gems, or beer-battered fries. All of which are delicious in their own way."

Viv had a point.

"Last I heard, Giuseppe moved to San Francisco. Became a used-car salesman. Married a good Italian girl. Had eight children. Has a comb-over."

"Oh, Viv," Aubrey said on a laugh. "Perhaps you dodged a bullet. And that's quite a lot of very specific info you have there."

"My private detective is very good. How do you think I kept such good track of you girls all these years?"

"Ah, social media?"

Viv patted Aubrey on the cheek. "So innocent. Now, back to you. When do you see the doctors?"

"Early next week."

It would give her time to take two, three, maybe several more home tests. And figure out how to tell Sean. When the time was right. There was no point concerning him unless it was real. Once the doctor checked to make sure everything was okay.

"Pfft. We'll have none of that." Viv motioned to Frank, who came over with a phone in his meaty outstretched hand. "I'll have you in to see them both this afternoon. What use is a rich fairy godmother unless she can wave her magic wand when it's most needed?"

This afternoon? That gave her *no* time to figure things out. But it would give her peanut the best chance at starting off on the right foot from this point on. So yes, a thousand times yes!

Aubrey hugged Viv hard. And did not let go till Viv destiffened, and hugged her back.

"Are you staying here?" Aubrey asked. "There's a spare room. A couch for Frank. Unless he bunks in with you—"

Viv's eyes nearly popped out of her head. "Frank? He's got to be half my age."

"So?"

The women both looked his way. Only the very slightest widening of his eyes made them both sure he'd heard.

"Point well made," said Viv, "but no. I've always preferred a more mature man. Besides, my Max is still in the jet. Customs wouldn't let him leave the Lear, wretched souls. He'll be fretting for sure. I will go get that sorted, have Frank message you about your doctor's appointments, organise a car to get you there. Unless your...friend might care to accompany you?"

Aubrey imagined sending *that* message.

Hey, Malone! Wanna pick me up? Gotta go see a cardiologist as I have to give up my meds asap. You'll never guess why! And I have to see a baby doctor! Oh, no, I gave the surprise away! You in?

"Ah, no. No point scaring the guy without actual professional back-up proof."

Viv nodded. Her expression all too understanding. "Then I'll see you in the morning. You can fill me in on your appointments and show me your favourite parts of this beautiful city."

"Would love nothing more."

Once Viv and Frank were out the door, Aubrey shuffled

into her bedroom and lay back on the bed, her hand on her belly, the other resting over her heart.

Giving them the chance, the quiet, to get to know one another. For if all went well, they'd be in cahoots the next few months.

Making a baby.

Aubrey caught sight of the cherubs floating about on her ceiling, she felt a kind of peace she hadn't felt in a very long time.

CHAPTER NINE

"THIS," SAID AUBREY as she and Viv—and Frank, with little Max in his arms—turned the corner into the laneway that had become one of her favourite places in the world, "is Via Alighieri."

"How charming. Named after Dante, no doubt." Viv had clearly decided to take her retirement decision to heart, forgoing her smart business suit for jeans, a T-shirt and hair in soft waves. As if she'd looked up *Helen Mirren street style*.

Aubrey wore a floaty halter dress. After the cardiologist had declared her *molto salutare*, in excellent health, the day before, and perfectly able to stop her meds, the OB/GYN had given her a heads-up that loose clothes might help with her unsettled tummy. Because she was most definitely pregnant.

She had a photo in her backpack. A video on her phone. A strong little heart beating away.

Her own heart picked up the pace as they neared the smoky glass window where the name Malone's was etched in gold in a heavy vintage-type font across the glass.

Sean was meant to meet them there in half an hour or so, giving her time to find her feet. Find some words. Let go of Viv.

Not enough time, she thought, her heart beginning to race. *Once he knows, time might be about to run out, for good.*

"So this is my Sean's joint," she said.

Viv noticed, for Viv noticed everything, but she kindly didn't make a big deal about the "my Sean". Her sophisticated eye took in the original inlaid mosaic floors, the minimalist smattering of heavy, sculpted chairs, made to look lush and touchable under perfectly angled spotlights. Elegant, modern, secure, with a nod to the old ways. So very, very Sean.

It had been nearly three days since she'd seen him. The longest amount of time apart since they'd met.

They'd messaged back and forth dozens of times. She'd sent him a picture of the sad little coffee she'd made in her room. Decaf now, alas. He'd sent her a photo of the mosaic on the floor of a fancy restaurant in which he was meeting a client.

She'd sent him a picture of Frank, labelled "Cheese!" Frank had not smiled at all. Sean had sent her a drawing of Elwood another client's four-year-old daughter had made for him in bright purple crayon. The caption, "Now this is art."

That one had cut. Deep. That he found that charming. That a little girl liked him enough to have made him a picture.

"What do you think?" she asked, her voice a little high.

Viv turned to Aubrey, silver brows raised. "I never saw you as the type who needed a beard, my dear."

"Sorry?"

"Am I to be a distraction for your young man when you tell him your news?"

"No! I just—" She lost her nerve pretty fast. And leant her head on Viv's shoulder. "No. But you can hold me upright till then."

Viv patted her hand. "Even the strongest of us are not strong all the time. There is no light without dark. No power without vulnerability. No—"

"Aubrey!" Enzo's voice called from down the way. "*Bella ragazza.* It has been days since you have graced my humble bistro. How are my Flora and Angelina? *Le mie belle figlie.* And how is—?"

Enzo stopped, his gaze alighting on something wondrous over Aubrey's shoulder.

Aubrey turned to find Viv walking towards her, her cheeks pink, eyes shining. She even lifted her hand to check her hair.

Frank, sensing changing strange currents in the air, stepped in.

Aubrey stilled him with a look. "It's okay. I'll vouch for the man. Give her a moment."

Frank frowned. Max panted. Enzo stopped, bowed from the waist and held out a hand. "Enzo Frenetti. At your service."

Viv took his hand. "Vivian Ascot."

Enzo smoothly tucked her hand into the held-out crook of his arm. "*Per favore, bella signore.* Do you care for *tiramisu*? Or *cassata Siciliana, panna cotta, babà, tartufo di Pizzo…*?"

They'd just eaten, yet Viv, a hand to her décolletage, said, "Surprise me."

Aubrey looked to Frank with an eyebrow raised. "Ever seen its like?" she asked.

Frank shook his head, then lumbered after his employer, her little sausage dog in tow.

Aubrey took her phone out of her backpack to check the time. To find a message from Sean. No photo this time, only a pin in a map.

She recognised the destination. It made her smile. Then her stomach lurched. Reminding her what she was walking into.

It would be a miracle if he took the news well, and she'd used up her one miracle already. She only wished they'd had more time. More time simply being them, before they were about to become something neither of them had gone into this thing prepared to be.

She sent a message to Frank to let him know she was heading off to meet Sean. She'd catch up with them later. Much later, if the look in Viv's eye was anything to go by.

Taking a quick sip of the lemon water from the bottle in her backpack, she wiped a little extra across the back of her hot neck, and set off.

Aubrey stood looking at the David.

He really was a marvel. All sinew and glorious musculature. She'd totally paint him on something one day. Maybe just his hand reaching for a door handle, looking as if it had torn through the metal.

But the urge to touch him was no longer there. Not when she'd already had the real thing.

A security guard walked by. Different from the one she'd befriended her first day in town. What was that, five weeks ago now? Six?

She gave him a smile. He gave her a nod. It was enough. She wasn't sure she had it in her to make new friends today.

She was too wired. And tired. And hot. And nauseous. And terrified to the bottoms of her sandals that Sean, for how far he'd come, would turn to stone the moment she said those life-changing words.

What if his demons were too great? His determination not to care much too entrenched? What if his feelings…? She gulped. What if his feelings simply weren't on a par with hers? Even considering his colossal heart and her busted one.

Feeling a little soft in the head, she moved to the edge of the room and leaned against the wall. Her forehead felt tight, as if it was trying to break out in a sweat.

It was hot out there today. And she'd not ambled. Her desire to see him, to hold him, to kiss him, to absorb him, greater than her fear about what came next.

"Aubrey?"

Aubrey spun, and the world kept spinning.

"Hey, stranger!" Her voice sounded odd to her ears. As if it were coming from far away.

But her joy at seeing Sean kept her upright.

Fresh from a meeting, he wore black suit pants, a pure white button-down shirt tucked in, tie tucked into the pocket, top buttons popped open, and sleeves rolled to his elbows. He looked healthy and blue-eyed and beautiful.

He had a small basket in hand and a picnic blanket under his arm. And she knew, she just knew, his plan was to set up a little spot in the middle of the floor for as long as they could before they were kicked out.

It was the single most romantic thing anyone had ever done for her.

She laughed, or at least she tried to. She no longer felt as if she had control over her mouth. Or her face. Then her vision started turning black at the edges.

She saw Sean's face, his beautiful face, come over anxious before he dropped everything and ran towards her. But only in slow motion. It was the weirdest thing.

The second last thing she noted, before the world turned black, was the wretched fear in his eyes. As if his world were crumbling before his eyes.

The last was how much she loved him for it.

Audrey woke with cold bright light shining through the backs of her eyelids. She opened them, slowly, to find herself looking at a utilitarian ceiling. No chubby cherubs. No David poster behind her bed. No chandelier.

But there was a woman in a lab coat writing on a chart, and another taking her pulse. An IV dripped into the back of her hand.

She was in a hospital. A language she couldn't catch murmuring around her. As situations went in Aubrey land, it was about as bad as it could be. The flashback to the months spent in a hospital in Copenhagen brought her out in an instant cold sweat.

"Aubrey?"

She blinked to focus on the woman in the lab coat. It was the cardiologist she'd seen the afternoon before. Her voice shook with relief as she said, "Dr Ricci."

"*Sì*. Hello, Aubrey. Do you know why you are here?" she asked.

And a brand-new panic set in. "I… I fainted. Near the David."

"I do not blame you; he is one fine specimen of man. I know, I'm a doctor." Dr Ricci smiled, then placed a hand on Aubrey's shoulder. "You are fine. Your heart is strong. The baby's heartbeat is pumping away beautifully. We need to make sure you are fit enough to walk out of here, but the signs point to it being dehydration. By the colour in your cheeks, on your shoulders, I'd suggest you were overheated. Were you out in the sun today? Walking?"

Walking fast. To get to the David. To get to Sean. *Sean*. The look on his face when she'd begun to fall. The full-blown terror. She had to let him know she was okay.

"Sean?" Aubrey tried to sit up but her head swam.

Dr Ricci pressed Aubrey back into the bed. "Stay. Rest. I'd like to keep you in here a few more hours, just for observation."

Aubrey slumped back onto the pillow and closed her eyes shut tight. Observation. That's what they'd said last time. When hours had become months.

Before panic took over, she inhaled deeply. Placed a hand over her heart, another over her belly. Checked in. Reminding herself they were both fine.

"Now," said Dr Ricci. "This Sean. He is the dashing gentleman who brought you in?"

Aubrey nodded.

"He claimed he was your friend. Or more than a friend, if I remember the nurses at reception speaking correctly. They were in quite the twitter."

"He is super hot," Aubrey managed, her head feeling a little swimmy again before she felt herself dragged under.

"Rest," Dr Ricci's voice came from a long way away. "I'll check on you again soon."

When Aubrey woke again she felt much better. The light had changed. She felt cool and clean and rested.

She opened her eyes and tipped her head to find Sean, seated upright in the chair by her bed, asleep. She wondered what he'd said or done to force his way in here. She wished she'd been awake to see it.

She watched him for a few moments, remembering the last thought she'd had, just before she'd blacked out. Knowing it hadn't been due to a lack of oxygen.

She loved this man.

She was in love with him.

He was a mile from the nice, docile guy she'd imagined she'd end up with. A man she now knew would have bored her silly.

She still wanted the same things she always had. Love. And family. And joy.

But the form it took? That wasn't something one could prescribe. Done right, it was organic and tempestuous and joyful and hard. It was a process. An awakening. It took work. And for two people to find one another at just the right time, when they were ready and raring to go on the same journey together.

She'd come on this trip with the burning desire to figure out her future. There was a strange relief in knowing it was something she'd could never have known till it happened.

She dragged herself to sitting. When the bed sheets rustled, Sean opened his eyes, and moved to her side in an instant, his hand wrapping around hers, his lips going to her forehead. She dragged her hand into his hair and held him there.

"I'm fine," she said eons later.

"I know." Sean's voice was rough. Raw. "Still, that was not fun. Seeing you collapse like that. I thought—"

"I know."

Ending up in hospital was right up there with Aubrey's worst nightmares. Seeing someone he cared about collapse was Sean's. And while he might not be in love with her, not the way she now knew she loved him, he did care.

Only now the time had come to see how much.

Aubrey let her hand fall to his chest, and said, "There's more."

He breathed in long and slow through his nose, the slight flare of his nostrils giving away the fact that he was still on edge.

"You might need to sit down for this one."

"I'd like to stay right here, if that's okay."

She nodded. Wished she'd figured out the exact right words to say this. Then in the end went with the simple, unadorned truth.

"I'm pregnant."

A shadow passed over Sean's face. "I know."

"How?" she asked, her throat tight. Her eyes darting over his face, trying to pick up any kind of sign as to what he might be thinking.

"I listened in when the doctor was talking to the nurse."

"How devious," she said.

But Sean didn't laugh. He didn't move a muscle.

"Uh oh," she said, her tone light, even as her insides twisted.

"What?" he said.

"You took a Sean moment."

"A—"

"You take a breath or blink before speaking, as if lining up your words just right before releasing them into the world. Especially when they are words you think I might not like."

This time a muscle twitched in his cheek. And she felt him pulling away from her.

No, no, no, no...

She gripped his hand tighter, using it to pull herself to sitting. "Look at me, Malone. We have to talk this through. *Sean.*"

His eyes snapped to hers and she held his gaze. Hoping he might see the feelings in her eyes, that she was too scared to say with her words.

"I'm pregnant. With your baby. It's inside me right now. Its tiny heart beating. I think it's miraculous, but you have every right to feel shock. Or fear. Or concern. Or delight. Happiness. Celebration."

Still nothing.

She looked around for her backpack. Her phone. "I have a photo. And a video—"

Sean stepped back as he made a sound, something like a hollow laugh. Or a groan. "No."

Her hand paused on the mouth of her backpack. Her voice reed thin as she said, "No? You don't want to see?"

His hand went over his mouth. His chin, his throat. His eyes beseeched her. "Aubrey, what the hell happened?"

If only she knew what those eyes were truly asking for. Comfort? Solidarity? Absolution? Without a map, without a clue, she swallowed and played to her strengths. Said, "When a man and a woman make love—"

He cut her off with a look. Okay, so he *wasn't* after comic relief.

But right now, humour was the only thing stopping her from breaking down completely. From *begging* him to stop moving away. To tell her how he was feeling. To yell at her, or cry with her. To just hold her. To know she was scared too. And to reciprocate her joy, her love. For ever, if he could. That would be fabulous.

"You said…" he began. "You told me you couldn't."

"I was told it would be nearby impossible. Clearly a huge amount of hanky-panky helps beat the odds."

There. Finally! A flicker of heat. Of understanding that she was doing her best here.

He *knew* her. He knew this was her way. If he could bend, just a little, rather than fall back on the stoic inability to let people in that had been his benchmark before she came along, they might find a way through this.

But then he rubbed his eyes and wiped all evidence of a connection away. "Look. Can you be serious, just for a second? Tell me, convince me, that all this has not put you in danger. Your heart."

A strange haze came over her then, some ancient mother instinct. *"All this?* If by that you mean the peanut growing inside of me—"

His eyes flared then. As if he'd been readying for the fight. Itching for it. To step back behind the ramparts, back inside his comfort zone. A place she didn't belong.

"If the doctors thought it was nearby impossible, can your body even handle this?"

"My cardiologist and OB/GYN have assured me everything looks as it should. No evidence of side effects from my meds. I stopped them immediately, which is fine as their levels were as near to a placebo as it was possible to get."

She hoped to see a measure of relief. Instead, even more barricades came crashing down.

"You've known about this long enough to see doctors? Plural?"

Aubrey swallowed, though it felt more like a gulp. "Not that long. It all happened so fast. The discovery. The checkups. I didn't want to concern you until I knew it was real. That it was possible. That it was all okay."

"All okay," he repeated, his tone incredulous, as if it was anything but.

Feeling too tender to control herself, she shot back, "As

for the rest, how it affects me as the months go on, I guess the only answer is *We'll see*."

It was the truth, but she'd chosen not to soften it. She'd wanted the reaction, wanted to shake him out of his stillness. The look he shot her was hard, hot, and dismayed. But dammit, *she* was scared too.

"I don't want your pity, Malone."

"I don't pity you. I'm…in shock. And concerned. And in a position I never planned to put myself in."

She was getting that. "This is all very new to me too, okay? I'm still trying to come to terms with it myself. I'm pregnant. After having been told it was not on the cards. You know how devastated I was. Yet here I am, with what might be my only chance to do this. But I believe, truly, it doesn't have to change anything between us. Unless… Unless we want it to."

"Aubrey," he said, rearing back. "You can't be serious."

Wow. Like a dagger to the chest. He couldn't have aimed more squarely if he'd tried.

"I am. I am serious. Can you honestly say, when we first met, that you had a single clue that the past few weeks were even possible?"

Something flickered behind his eyes then.

"No? Me neither. Yet it's been the time of my life. And not because of some fancy hotel, or a whole lot of amazing art. But because I met you."

Her voice broke at the last. Emotion uncoiling inside her till she could no longer control it.

But while she could feel his energy, the force of it, shaking to be set free, he remained unflinching in his determination not to yield.

"I just… I don't get it, Malone. Are you waiting for permission?"

"For what?"

"To love me!" she cried, her arms out wide.

The room was so quiet after, her words seemed to catch on the air-conditioning current and bounce about the room.

Aubrey felt tears streaming down her face and she swiped them away with a hard hand to each cheek. Then she felt the hospital gown fall off her shoulder. She yanked it back into place, feeling horribly exposed. "I didn't… I didn't mean that. I just meant… You know what. It doesn't matter—"

Sean spoke, his voice so husky she missed it.

"Sorry? What was that?"

His jaw worked as he looked at the ceiling. "I said, I can't."

"Can't…? Oh."

He couldn't *love her*.

Not enough, anyway. Not enough to leap. To take what they had and turn it into something more. Bigger. Whole. A family. For ever.

Tears still streaming down her face, she looked down at the sheet pooled at her waist. "I think I'd like you to leave."

"Not happening. I'm staying till they let you go."

"Malone, you're killing me here."

"You think this isn't hurting me too? I've been sitting here for hours, since I heard the news. After seeing you faint. Watching you lie there. Knowing that all that was keeping you alive was your damaged heart. You, and the baby. My baby."

He looked off into the distance, a hand rubbing over his mouth as he spoke. Aubrey bit her lip.

"I too imagined," he went on, "when I was younger, that one day I'd meet a girl, fall in love, have kids. But it was a concept. A determination that when it happened I'd do it differently from my own parents. I'd be gentler. Kinder. I'd choose to prioritise my kids. I'd love them so hard they never ever doubted me.

"Watching you lie there in that bed, a drip in your hand, suddenly I was my parents. With this tiny helpless creature in my care." As if he'd sensed her intake of breath, her readiness to speak, he cut her off. "And no, by that I did not mean you."

"Right. Sorry. Go on."

"What if something happened? What if you lost it? What if I—?"

Aubrey held her breath, absolutely sure he'd been about to say *What if I lost you?*

"My parents..." He stopped. Swallowed. "My parents raised us, brought us to adulthood, only to lose Carly. And then... And then I left. I left and they lost me too."

If Aubrey weren't attached to a drip and feeling as if she'd been hit by a truck, she'd have leapt out of her bed and into his arms, and held him tight till he held her right on back.

Instead, she had to watch as his eyes finally met hers again. Tortured. And apologetic. Decided.

"I may look like a living breathing human person, but I'm not, Aubrey. Not in the way you need. The way you deserve. The way a child—"

Aubrey's heart twisted and squeezed, riddled with her own pain. And his. "Malone, stop," she finally managed. "What happened with your sister, it wasn't your fault."

He threw his hands in the air and began to pace. "I promised I'd take her in hand. That I'd help her get her head sorted. And I failed. Of course it was my fault."

"It wasn't your fault."

The small private room seemed to shrink the more he paced. "I let myself become distracted. And she spiralled so fast. It broke all of us. And we couldn't... No matter how much we wanted it, we couldn't put each other back together again. I can't go through that again. I won't."

He was shouting now.

A nurse popped her head in the door.

Aubrey held up a hand, shook her head.

The nurse took a look at Sean and melted away.

Aubrey looked to the ceiling. She was good with words. Maybe even better than she was with a pencil. How was she messing this up so badly?

"I'm going to say this one more time. It wasn't your fault. You are that good a man, Malone. You've provided work, and respite, and opportunity, and comfort, and shelter, and friendship, and kindness to so many people in your sphere all while convincing yourself you were alone. You are a living, breathing human person, Malone, the livingest, breathingest I've ever known. With a big strong heart. Big enough for the both of us, if you'll just let it do its thing. No matter what the voices in your head are telling you."

They looked at one another across the room, both breathing heavily. At an impasse. Both at a loss as to what to do next. What else was there to say? To convince the other that they were right.

Then Sean pulled himself upright and she saw the architect, the boss, the good son, the island, and she braced herself for whatever might come next.

"I will contribute," he said. "Time, money. Whatever the baby needs."

Ready for it, still she flinched at the finality in his voice. "Contribute. Well, that sounds like fun."

"Fun? You think that's what we're arguing about here? How much fun we can make this…this…"

Aubrey's entire body cooled by a good degree. "This what? Disaster? This tragedy? It's a baby, Sean. A tiny cluster of cells hanging on dearly to life. That hustle, that desire to *live*, despite all the walls my body had put in its way, I respect the hell out of this kid of ours already. Malone—"

He cut her off. "It is a miracle. Life is a miracle. The fact that any of us are here, the things we survive, is utterly humbling. Yet, you make jokes, Aubrey. And I get that's your way of dealing with some pretty heavy stuff in your life. But you need to respect that my way of dealing is to retreat and collect my head. Whether that takes a moment, or years."

He was trying to appear as if he knew what he wanted, but he seemed so lost. She bit her lip and tried to wait him out. But, as was her way, she leapt. "Malone—"

"Enough." When his eyes met hers they were burning. Ferocious. Full. "I suggest you do the same. Take some time to really think. Because right now, I can't see how it would work. Especially when you still struggle to call me by my name."

Aubrey gaped. Readying to defend herself. Until she realised she had no defence. He was utterly, one hundred per cent, in the right.

She called him Malone as if it was cute. Banter. She was the one who'd made all the noise about them being finite.

We're friends. A summer fling. Let's promise to be light and easy. Till the day I decide to walk away.

She'd told herself she was doing him a favour. Giving him the illusion of space. When the truth was, she was the one who'd needed it. Used it to self-protect. To remain one step removed from true intimacy. From heartache. From loss.

On her next breath out she deflated. Completely. Falling back onto the bed, she pulled the sheets up to her chin. Feeling as if she could sleep for a hundred years.

"Aubrey," he said, his voice throaty, sounding as wrung out as she felt.

"Mm hmm."

"Will you stay? In Florence? I hope you do. The hospitals here are top-notch."

"Glad to hear it."

"Or will you go home? I need to know how to stay in touch."

Her subconscious screamed, *You are my home, you big lug!* But she closed her eyes so he wouldn't see it. She already felt foolish enough.

"Not yet sure," she said. She'd held onto a tiny thread of hope that he might have made the decision easy. "I might yet continue on with the trip. The doctors I saw— Viv has me hooked up with the best across Europe. Just in case. I put my foot down at taking the Lear jet… Oh, God! I was meant to check in with her. She has no idea I'm here."

"How can I contact her for you?"

"Her number is in my phone. And last I saw her she was with Enzo."

"Enzo?" he said, his voice barely curious, as if all the colour had leeched out. "Leave it to me. Let me do this for you."

This. Not love her. Not be with her. Not raise their baby together. Make a phone call.

She was too exhausted to fight it any more. She opened her eyes and found his. "So much for our deal. Where I was the one who got to walk away. To catch my foot on a sheet and make a right ruckus."

The humour was weak, but by that point it was all she had left.

"I'm not walking away from you, Aubrey. Or the baby. But us… It needs to stop here. Before things get confused." He came back to her then, took her hand, lifted her palm to his lips and kissed her. "I never want to regret you, Aubrey."

"I never want to regret you either," she said. Then, in a last-ditch effort at self-protection, added, "Malone."

He sniffed out a laugh, then let her go and walked to the door. He turned and asked, one last time, "Are you sure you're okay?"

"Not so much," she said, the first truly honest moment of her day. "But I will be. And so will you, Sean. I promise, so will you."

CHAPTER TEN

BAGS PACKED, AUBREY took one last look around her fancy hotel room, making sure she hadn't left anything behind.

Anything, that was, apart from her heart. Busted as it was, she'd miss it. It had served her well. It had led her to Sean, after all. The man who'd kick-started her dreams again. Dreams that weren't to be.

In their place, international co-parenting.

They'd find a way to make it work. Even while it would ache, seeing him. Unable to hold him. To kiss him. To lean into him when tired. To fall apart in seconds when he did that thing with his pinkie finger.

Till then…she'd decided it was best to go home.

Her parents would be so excited. Another grandchild in the mix.

Though they'd protest, she was doing this on her own. She'd find a cute little cottage with a yard. Room for a paddling pool. And maybe even a dog. A little smaller than Elwood. A lot more smarts.

Her life hadn't ended when her heart had stopped. It had been given a new start.

And she was still determined to follow her curiosity and see where it led.

But first, sitting on the edge of her bed, she nibbled on a cracker, sipped a little warm water, had a quick suck on a lemon to make sure she didn't throw up, then returned the call she'd missed the day before.

The first step towards filling in the rest of her world on what her new normal was about to become.

Daisy answered first. "Morning, sunshine!"

Who'd stolen Daisy and put this Daisy-shaped person in her place? "You're chipper."

"Yeah, I am!"

Jessica popped up. This time *she* was yawning. "We really need to line up our chat times better. Who called? Aubrey? Everything wonderful and brilliant wherever in the world you are today?"

"Still Florence."

"Huh, thought you'd have seen half of Italy by now."

"I'm actually leaving today."

"Perfect timing!" That was Daisy. "Guess what? We're doing a surprise gig in Copenhagen! The boys and I. An anniversary gig, though on a much smaller scale. Jay owns this club there. It's brilliant, like an old-fashioned speakeasy. And we're going to make a surprise appearance. It's three days from now and I want you guys to come."

A tiny spark lit inside the wasteland that was Aubrey's enthusiasm, as if the peanut were cheering, *Yes! Travel! I love to travel! Let's do it.*

"And bring Sean! I promise not to drool on him. And I'll make Jay promise the same. When he found out you guys were friends, he turned into a blushing schoolgirl. Apparently, Malone's chairs are like rock-star porn."

Aubrey shook her head, infinitesimally. It was too much. The talk of drool. And Sean's beautiful chairs. And, well, porn.

Jessica, being Jessica, noticed. "Aubs? You okay?"

"What? No. I'm fine. But it'll just be me."

"No hot wood guy?"

"No hot wood guy," she parroted back, her voice sounding clownish. She cleared her throat, settled herself down. And said, "Just me. Which is fine, because I have so much I want to catch you guys up on! But I'll save it till in person. Much better that way."

Besides, she needed to get off the phone. Her throat felt as if it was closing up. And the backs of her eyes were burning.

"No," said Daisy. "You don't look right. Tell us now."

Aubrey blinked and a single tear fell down her cheek.

And that opened the floodgates. She told her girls everything. Well, everything bar Sean's magical pinky-finger
move. That she saved just for her.

"A baby," said Jessica, her eyes round. And full of wonder. "Oh, Aubrey. That's wonderful. And when you thought
it wouldn't be possible."

While Daisy stared down the phone as if she wished
she could jump through the thing and hold Aubrey close.

"Daisy?" Aubrey said. "You okay?"

"What? Yes. I'm assuming Sean's the father?"

"Of course he's the father. Jeez!"

"I'm in London right now but I can get to you in a matter of hours. You know, if you need me to have a word."

"With Sean?" Aubrey felt laughter unexpectedly bubble
into her throat. "No! He's promised to 'contribute'. And I
fully believe him. He just…he just doesn't want me as part
of the bargain."

The girls all let that sit, like a dark foggy cloud making
it hard to breathe.

"How can that be? We saw the way he looked at you on
the phone that day, when he so kindly greeted us in nothing but a towel."

Aubrey rolled onto her back, holding the phone above
her face. A complete glutton for punishment, she asked,
"And how was that?"

"Like he couldn't believe his luck," Jessica said.

Aubrey let the phone fall to her chest for a moment, while
she collected herself.

"You're in love with him, aren't you?" Daisy's voice
hummed.

Aubrey lifted the phone, and nodded.

"But I'm guessing, by the way things turned out, you
never said so."

"Not in so many words. More like I made him promise
to keep things light and easy and fun. I rarely called him

by his first name. And any time things became serious, I cracked a joke."

"That's our girl," Jessica murmured.

"Look," said Daisy, glancing over her shoulder, "I really have to go. We're in final rehearsal for the gig before we fly out tonight. Tell me you'll be there."

"I'll be there," Aubrey promised. "So long as you have crackers and lemons on hand so I don't hurl."

"Done. I've just sent all the details. Time. Date. Name on the door. All you have to do for me is be far less maudlin."

"Done. A good sixty...sixty-five per cent less."

"Good girl. Jess?" Daisy asked.

"Yes! I'm in. I'll get someone to cover me at work for a few days. This is going to be brilliant. We can all finally debrief about the crazy last few months in person. And do the ring test on Aubrey to see if it's a girl or a boy. All good things."

When the girls looked to her, in the hopes of having cheered her up, Aubrey forced a smile. "First thing on the agenda? Viv's new boyfriend."

"What?" the girls said in unison, before Aubrey hung up.

She watched her friends disappear from their squares, one after the other. Then stared at the little pop-up that came up at the end of the call.

If you love this app, please review! Click here to rewatch.

After a beat, Aubrey clicked. Her heart racing, just a little, when she saw all her video chats had been saved into a folder.

Thumb racing now, she scrolled and scrolled and...there!

Her third morning in Florence. The conversation from Sean's bed.

She fast forwarded, through Daisy's frowns and Jessica's sighs, until...

She paused on a shot when Sean had walked into the room. The moment she knew he was coming up behind her.

She looked so happy. And relaxed. As if she had not a care in the world. When before meeting Sean, she'd been a right mess.

Whereas he…

Attempting to look beyond the towel slung low around his hips, the super muscles and tanned skin, his hair falling over his eye, she saw the smile. Honest. Sensual. And a little surprised. As if he didn't know what he was in for, but it was too late now. He was already on board.

She played it again, and paused on the moment his eyes met hers.

Her heart clutched. She rested a hand on her chest. And remembered back to how she'd felt in that moment. To think how much deeper her feelings now went. Now that she knew him. Now that she'd seen how he treated others. Now she knew how hard he was on himself.

Yet, in the hospital room, she'd pushed for an answer. Knowing he didn't respond to that kind of pressure. When what she ought to have done was be there. Beside him. Supporting him. Holding him. Giving him the chance to catch up to her much faster schedule in his own time. Then, when he came out of his cave, she'd be there. Loving him.

But it was done now. Over. She couldn't wait for ever. Not only because she'd finally given the hotel her notice of departure. But because she wasn't making decisions for only herself any more.

But she had an hour. Maybe a little more before she had to hand in her key.

And there was one more thing she had to do before she left.

Sean would have liked nothing more than to hole up in his workshop, alone, with a hunk of wood and a piece of sandpaper, for the next few months.

It used to soothe him when he was a kid. Finding some place quiet in his head to turn over his thoughts. Turning the rough to smooth. The rugged into something that made sense.

Only now there were people everywhere he looked. People he'd been stupid enough to hire.

He could feel Flora's angry gaze burning between his shoulder blades. Even Angelina couldn't look him in the eyes. Only Hans had said good morning, but likely because—hailing from a tiny village in Germany—he spoke little English and less Italian, so had no clue what was going on.

Sean had tried whacking on a set of headphones, pumping up the Puccini, grabbing a heavy-duty chisel and just hacking at a plank of Baltic pine in the hopes of finding inspiration.

Or a way through the heavy fugue that had draped over him ever since leaving Aubrey at the hospital. He was beginning to think that fugue might linger. That it might have a terribly long half-life. Because Aubrey had been an extinction event. She'd crashed into his life like a meteor. And when the first dust cleared, the landscape was not even close to recognisable.

Problem was, he was having a hard time remembering why that was a bad thing.

Ben cast a shadow over him, waited till he made eye contact, and asked, "How long you gonna keep that up, boss? Till you chisel that stump into a toothpick?"

Wishing for the good old days when they'd all been scared of him, Sean grabbed his laptop, left Elwood at the villa, and headed into town. He'd do some admin in the quiet privacy of the showroom.

In Via Alighieri, key in hand, he turned as Gia appeared in the doorway of her leather shop, murmuring, "Keep walking, Malone. Just keep walking."

But it was too late.

"Gian!" Enzo called, descending from his bistro, hands wringing a tea towel. "What is this I hear about our Aubrey? She is gone?"

Sean hung his head, breathed deep. He had a splitting headache, his ears felt as if they were full of cotton wool and he had some kind of constriction in his chest that just wouldn't ease no matter what he ate. He didn't want to play these games today.

But Enzo was a kind man, with a good heart, and didn't deserve his bad mood. He regrouped. Took a Sean moment, as Aubrey would call it. If she were here. At his back.

"So you're Aubrey's Sean; the one who called me the other day."

Sean turned to find a woman he'd never met—posh accent, expensive clothes—and something twigged. "Vivian Ascot."

"I am she. Where's my girl?"

Aubrey was pregnant. Off her medication. Fragile. And frustrated. And disappointed in him. And yet she was okay. Always would be.

While he… He already missed her with an ache he couldn't contain.

"Mr Malone?" Vivian Ascot chastised, using the voice that had built a business empire.

Sean's hand gripped his keys. Then he breathed out hard. "She's on her way to Copenhagen to catch up with her friends. Your friends. Jess and Daisy? She sent me a message this morning."

They were keeping in touch, as promised. It was all very civilised.

"Thank you."

Sean nodded, and moved inside, locking the door behind him.

Civilised. How had it come to that? From the very moment they'd met their relationship had been built on friction. His obstinate grip on the status quo. Her determined need for change. She was dauntless. Presumptuous. Meddlesome. And she'd won out, more often than not.

Except this last time. This time he'd won. Though it sure didn't feel like any kind of victory he'd care to choose.

Sean took a step, his foot slipping on a piece of paper on the floor.

He recognised the slanting script on the front as Aubrey's hand.

She'd taken to leaving notes around his workshop. On his bed. In the fridge—*'When life shuts a door...open it. It's a door—that's how they work'* and *'Always trust people who like big butts—they cannot lie'*—in case he ever wanted a tattoo.

It took him a moment longer to notice it wasn't a note, but an envelope. With only one word written on the front. His name.

Not Malone.

Sean.

His lungs tightened. He breathed through it. Told himself not to read into it.

He'd been reading into her expressions, her movements, her attention, her smiles, for weeks. Looking for signs that she might be feeling as he did. Falling deeper and deeper with each passing day. Each sublime night.

But he'd never been able to feel any assurance that she was all in. How could she be? She'd come to Florence to suck the marrow out of life; he'd come to Florence to hide.

Still, there had been moments when he'd seen past her humour, to a glimpse of something deeper. Some flash of desire. A wash of affection. A moment of true, rare connection in which he saw a vision of what a future, together, might look like.

Then she'd say, "Fun! Light! Easy! Casual!" And she'd call him Malone.

So he'd held back. Kept his feelings in check. Until he'd

walked into the Galleria to see her faint. Her face deathly pale. Her eyes rolling back in her head.

He'd never run so fast, getting to her just before she hit the floor.

The feel of her in his arms—limp, a rag doll—had been the single most terrifying moment of his life. His shout for the guard to call for an ambulance must have made every statue in that place flinch.

Hearing the doctors say that she was okay—that it was heat, not her heart, that had knocked her out—had made his legs near give way with relief. Promises had tripped over themselves in the back of his head. Promises to tell her how he felt the moment she woke up.

That he adored her, and that she had saved him, and that while he wanted her to travel, to see the world, he wanted her to know she could always come home to him.

And then to find out she was pregnant...

He knew it was possible to breeze through pregnancy. But he also knew a child could wreak havoc on even the healthiest body. His own mother had pulled that one out of the bag whenever Carly was acting ungrateful. That she'd nearly died on the table having her.

Their mother had wondered, out loud, just the once, in a rare moment of frailty, if that pressure was why Carly acted the way she did. Each of them burdened with their share of guilt.

When in the end, the truth was far more simple. Carly was an addict. She made many bad choices. One of which had ended her life.

Choices. Choices were hard enough for someone whose head was clear.

Love me! Aubrey had cried, while curled up on the hospital bed.

Seeing her in the hospital gown, so big it fell off her shoulder, her face pale, her eyes scared, he'd taken too long a moment and the moment had been lost. Any other day, if she'd looked him in the eye and said, *Love me,* he might have made the better choice. To grab her, hold her close and say, *Always.*

Sean looked down at the envelope in his hands. How long had it been there? Days? Weeks?

He couldn't open it. Not now when he still felt so raw. He went to put the envelope onto the bench but at the last second said, "Screw it," and tore the edge open.

What he found inside was no joke at all.

The very first thing he saw was a photograph. Black and white. A speckled grey mass, with a dark splodge in the middle.

A sonogram. Aubrey's name in one corner, Baby Malone written in the other. And in the centre, a peanut. Clear as day.

Sean moved to sit on one of the stools by the bench.

Why had she sent this to him? Was it a parting gift? Or a last-ditch plea?

Look what we did.
Look what we made.
Love me.

Aubrey never had been afraid to play dirty.

Adrenaline bucketing through him, Sean opened up the other papers inside the envelope. Stationery from her hotel. Each piece of paper branded with a sketch.

A hand holding a lathe. A finger—short nails, scarred—running across a pair of closed lips. A pair of eyes, looking directly at the artist. His eyes. His hands. His lips. His father's nose. His mother's dark hair. And Carly's stubborn jaw. A dozen drawings. Each with the fluidity he'd seen in her that first day. But it was the detail that had his lungs emptying in a rush. The study.

The *intimacy.*

He went back through them till he found the eyes.

He'd avoided mirrors for years; the pain he'd see in his face, the guilt, only piling on. But in the drawing, his eyes were clear. Laughing. Charmed. Was this how he looked when Aubrey was in the room? If so, there was no way she didn't know his feelings for her.

But for all her joy, her spirit, she'd been through the wringer too. Her faith in her own happiness was shaken. She might not trust all the good she saw. She'd needed to be told.

All people needed to be told. To hear the words. I want you. I can't live without you.

I forgive you.

Gathering the scattered papers in one hand, Sean dialled her number with the other, then tucked his phone beneath his chin. But it rang out. She was probably already on the plane to Copenhagen.

He hung up. Locked up.

Striding down the street, he called another number. His own.

"Sì," said Flora, the only one who ever answered the landline.

"Hey, it's me. Can you look after Elwood for a few days?"

"Of course. So long as it means I can stay here. And have full use of the bar. Papa has a new girlfriend, some rich English lady, and I can't watch. Do I need to guess where it is you might be going?"

"Yeah," he said, surprising himself. "I think maybe you do."

A little over thirty-six hours later, Sean's driver pulled up outside a Melbourne building covered in scaffolding. A man in a suit, and a black and white striped tie, president of the football club and old family friend, barrelled his way towards him the moment he got out of the car.

"Sean! So good to see you my boy," said George. "When I got your message, I was thrilled. Can't express how much. No luggage?"

"Not staying long."

George nodded. "Fair enough. Come on in so I can show you the space."

Sean followed. Taking a moment to breathe in his surroundings.

Midwinter and the weather in Melbourne was as per usual: chilly, with sunshine beaming through the grey clouds. It hadn't been the weather that had kept him away.

"He here?" Sean asked.

George looked over his shoulder, didn't have to ask who.

"He's inside. I didn't tell him you were coming. That was how you wanted it, right? I want you to know, it doesn't feel good not telling your mother."

"She knows. I went by home to see her first." Sean scratched the edge of his nose. "Was worried she might keel over from the surprise."

"And did she?"

"She took it well."

Better than well. Sean's mother had dragged him into her arms and not let go for a good five minutes. After which she'd made him a coffee, forced him to eat cake the cook had made, and held his hand tightly as he'd given her a rundown of the past five years of his life.

When he'd asked after her, she'd just shaken her head. Sniffed loudly. Looked at him fiercely. And said, "None of that matters. It all begins again from here."

And he'd believed her. Believed that they could overcome the mistakes they'd made in turning away from one another and not in. He'd seen it happen. A life beginning anew. Hinging on a single moment. Nothing that came after ever the same as what had gone before.

He'd not planned on telling her about Aubrey, but as if he'd needed to tell someone, to say the words out loud, it had all spilled out. How they'd met. How she'd infiltrated his life. How she'd shifted his perceptions of everything.

From time to forgiveness. To the limits he'd put on his life. His capacity to feel joy. To feel at all.

When he'd got to the ending, the ending as things stood now, a child, her grandchild, his mother had swallowed hard, a torrid mix of happiness and sadness behind her eyes. Then she'd hugged him hard, told him she was sure he would find a way to make things work out for the best. That it was his gift. And his burden. But if she had a say, she'd very much like to meet this young woman one day soon.

And Sean knew, more than he'd ever known anything his entire life, that if he had a say, he'd make that happen.

"Well," said George, tears welling, throat clearing. "Then you've made my day, boy. My year. Don't much care if you refuse to take my commission now. Actually, I do care. Would put us on the map, culturally speaking, so do consider it rightly."

The doors to the front of the building whispered open, a pair of famous footballers in black and white tracksuits shouldering their way past with polite nods.

And inside, standing by the front desk, in a hard hat and tweed jacket, Sean's father.

"Brian," Sean called. But his voice barely travelled past the tightness in his throat. He cleared it, took a breath, and called, "Dad."

He saw his father still. Breathe out.

And turn.

CHAPTER ELEVEN

AUBREY FELT AS if she was in a Daisy and Jessica sandwich, the girls hugged her so hard.

"Don't squish the baby," she managed between her smushed lips.

The girls both sprang away as if they'd been electrified.

"Kidding. Peanut is about the size of a raspberry right now."

Thinking about Peanut made her think of Sean. Which meant she was thinking about him a thousand times a day. The fact that he was no longer in her days. Or her nights. The wondering if he'd found her envelope. If it had sparked any kind of revelation. Or even if he was simply somewhere in the world thinking about her too.

She shook it off. She was with her best friends in the world. And if that didn't go some ways to cheering her up, nothing would. "Viv—in a bid to be actual godmother not merely fairy godmother—had me checked out by the best and brightest and so far so good."

Jessica slid a hand around her arm and leant her head on her shoulder. "Viv's not going to be the only godmother, right?"

"Of course not. Daisy too."

Jessica laughingly slapped her on the arm. Then swiped away a tear. "Sorry. It's all a little emotional. This has just been the best summer of my life. And finishing it up by seeing you guys…"

They fell into another group hug, only this time Jessica was in the middle.

To think they'd managed to build such a strong friendship from the other side of the world. International friendship. Now international parenting. It was a whole new world out there!

"Now what's this about Viv? And some new man in her life? So much to discuss," said Daisy, checking the time on her phone, "none of which you are allowed to even hint at without me. But I really have to head backstage."

Daisy dashed away.

While Aubrey took her chance to hitch the deep neckline of her fabulous black, bare-shouldered, all-in-one jumpsuit. It looked as if she were wearing a push-up bra when really she wore none at all. Ah, pregnancy. On that score, she snaffled a cracker from her backpack.

"Aubs?" said Jessica, a funny note in her voice.

Aubrey wiped cracker crumbs from her lips. "Mmm?"

"That dashing man over there, the one looking at you like he wants to kiss you and throttle you at the same time, is that who I think it is?"

Aubrey glanced over her shoulder. Took her half a second to spot him amidst the seething crowd. That dark swishy hair, the cool mien, those ridiculous blue eyes.

"Malone," she said on a sigh. He was so beautiful he practically glowed.

"I don't know about glowing," said Jessica, "but he is very handsome."

"Did I say that out loud?"

"Sure did. I'll leave you to it, shall I? Now where is my silver fox?"

Jessica faded into the crowd, leaving Aubrey feeling as if her feet were nailed to the ground.

Sean. Sean was here. Not holed up in his cave, licking his wounds. But out in the world. At a club, no less. And he was walking her way. Looking dark and broody and focussed and *fine*.

Once he was near enough to touch, he said, "Trusedale."

Aubrey went with, "Hello, *Sean*."

And, oh, the way his deep dark eyes lit up when she said his name.

Had it always been that easy? Yes, she thought, it really had. Which was why she'd struggled to go there. For all her determination to experience the heck out of life, Sean Malone had always been more than she knew what to do with.

Aubrey felt bumps from the left, and the right. But only vaguely. Every cell was stretching towards the man before her. There was more than shadow bristling his hard jaw. Smudges beneath his perfect blue eyes. He looked as if he hadn't slept in days.

Only one reason she could think of why he looked so messed up.

He missed her.

She took a moment, a Sean moment, to let that settle. To absorb it. And to let herself believe it. A sense of free fall had her catching her breath, before she trusted it, trusted herself, and let her heart flutter and flap and glide. And soar. Till it angled its way back to him.

"Fancy meeting you here," she said.

His gaze, shadowed in the low light, played over her face. Drinking her in as if he'd stumbled out of the desert and she were a pina colada. Or, you know, a glass of water. Either or.

"I'm a fan of the band, you know," he said.

Aubrey baulked. For a fraction of a second.

"Mocking," he said, his face slowly creasing into a grin. All flashing white teeth and eye crinkles and her heart filled so fast it nearly burst.

Only her heart didn't burst. It held strong. And true. Ready to take him on. For good. If he'd stop fighting it and let her.

The music changed, the dance floor filling fast. Aubrey was bumped again, and this time she used it as an excuse to step closer, her hand landing on Sean's chest. His arm slid around her waist, pulling her close. And they began to sway.

"I've been thinking," he said.

"First time for everything." *Really? With the jokes? Not now, you goof!*

Sean smiled down at her, his gaze hot. Hungry. "I've been considering your request."

"My request."

"To love you."

"Oh," she said on an outshot of breath.

That level of assertiveness was usually her move. It was quite the thing being on the receiving end.

Then his knee slid between hers as he turned her. And there it stayed. Till they were plastered up against one another. As close as two people could get with their clothes on.

"Here's the thing," he said, his voice clear. Calm. As if he'd come out the other end of a really big Sean moment. Ready.

While she trembled all over.

"When you made your request—for me to love you—"

"Yep. Got it."

"I need you to understand that kind of thing has never been a part of my vocabulary. I grew up in a home that was the epitome of sang-froid. We learnt young to distil our emotion. Keep it locked down tight. Use that pressure as fuel to succeed. Even after we all learned how destructive bottling it all up could be, I remained good at it. It was all I knew."

Someone walked past with glasses of beer overhead and Sean deftly moved Aubrey out of the way. Protecting. Always protecting. If she was lucky, he'd never stop.

Aubrey slid a hand into the back of Sean's hair, the slippery strands scraping through her fingers. And his gaze came back to her. Those stunning Le Mans blue eyes that she loved so very much.

"Talk to me," she said.

"So demanding," he said, pressing against her, all hard heat and promise.

She might even have swooned. Just a little. But still managed to quip, "It's part of my charm."

"That it is. So, where was I?"

"Poetically tragic hot guy, bottled emotions."

"Right," he said, clicking his fingers. "Could have had *that* as a tattoo. Until I met you."

His eyes found hers. His gaze tender. And steady. "Everything changed that day, Aubrey. Everything."

"For the better, I hope."

A smile. A dimple. A flutter in her heart.

"Better than better. My staff are happier. Walking down Via Alighieri is now like walking into a fair. Even Elwood is more spry. Though any time he hears my footsteps now only to find you're not with me, he snuffles and goes back to sleep. My whole world is not what it was. My whole world," he said once more, brushing a stray strand of hair from her cheek.

"Sean," she said, her voice cracking.

"Ask me again, Aubrey," he said, his voice deep, rough, intimate. "Ask me again to love you."

The words felt so big, her throat so full. If she said it, her life would never be the same again.

Aubrey ran a hand over his collar, untucking it from where it was endearingly hooked over on itself. Then, her voice steady, she said, "Love me, Sean Malone."

"Done."

And then he kissed her. Right there in the middle of the dance floor. It was lush and hot and delicious. It was sweet and tender and full of longing.

She loved this man with her whole entire heart. Every bit of gristle. Every life-affirming pump.

It occurred to her, in the haze of his kiss, that she hadn't told him so.

Aubrey pulled back so fast they stumbled. Sean righted the ship, which was his way.

"I love you, Sean. I love you. I'm in love with you and

have been for such a long time. Possibly even for ever. And it has nothing to do with the peanut you put inside of me. Though I do love you for that too. Our feisty little miracle."

Sean moved away, just enough to look down between them.

"Are you checking out my cleavage?"

"What?"

"Look," she said, puffed out her chest. "They're bigger already. One of the benefits of pregnancy. You're welcome."

His gaze, on her eyes, was indulgent. But heated. "I was preparing to say a private hello to the peanut."

"Right. Proceed."

Hand on her hip, Sean looked down once more and said, "Hello, Peanut. I love your mother. Just want you to know that right up front. I promise to protect her, and hear her, and lean on her, and never ask if she's okay for as long as she'll let me. I saw your picture the other day. And while you're a funny-looking kid, I'm smitten with you already too."

Aubrey laughed. And hiccupped as tears filled the back of her throat.

"You two," he said, his voice dropping as he moved to look down her top, past her heart tattoo, past her scar to the new cleavage below, "I'll talk to later."

Then he pulled her back in. And they swayed. No words. Just love. Aubrey could not remember ever feeling this wonderful. As if her blood were pure champagne.

She looked up at him, because she couldn't not. "You, Sean Malone, really are the gin to my tonic. Do you think maybe that is the tattoo meant for you?"

"I'm not getting a tattoo."

"Come on! Was everything you just said for nought?"

"Not everything," he said, laying a kiss on top of her head as they moved to the music. "For you, I am willing to try new things. Like barbecue."

"Turns out I prefer pasta."

"I can keep the workshop going. Promote Flora to project manager. Hire more cabinet makers. Then you and I can base ourselves in Sydney. I know how important your family is to you."

Aubrey's heart clutched. This man! "Or we could move to Melbourne. It doesn't suck there. It would give you the chance to reconnect with your family."

"I went home."

"You what?"

"A couple of days ago. I caught up with my mum. And my dad. I took the commission."

Aubrey hit him on the chest with a balled-up fist. "Oh, you good and wonderful man."

He caught her fist in his hand. Kissed her on the small flower ring she'd bought on the Ponte Vecchio. Unwrapped the fingers. Held them as he placed them over his heart. His glorious beast of a heart.

"Thing is, though, I love Florence," said Aubrey. "It might, in fact, be the most beautiful city on the entire planet. There are so many back streets I've yet to explore. Then there's the fact that I still haven't touched the David. Working up to that might take some planning. Might take some time. So I suggest we start there and see how we go."

"Florence it is. What about—?"

"Do we have to decide all of this tonight?"

"No, but—"

Aubrey kissed him to stop him talking.

It was the only way.

Like a hazy hum in the back of her head, Aubrey heard the crowd go wild as Daisy and Jay and the rest of Dept 135 burst onto the stage.

But Aubrey and Sean kept swaying. Kissing. Planning. Dreaming.

Three hearts, beating in perfect sync.

EPILOGUE

I'VE NEVER BEEN a fan of summer, preferring to follow more temperate climes as I travel the globe.

But this steaming hot summer's day in Sydney, in the bar jutting out over the rocky outcrop overlooking the sparkling harbour, watching our darling Aubrey marry her man Sean, well, it might well have been one of the best of my life.

And that's saying something. I am a zillionaire after all.

Yes, I have stepped back from running Ascot Industries, leaving my very able second in charge, the right woman to take the business fully into the next century. But I am still loaded. I could buy this famous little restaurant right now if I pleased.

Except, for the first time in my life, I have no urge to conquer.

"Vivian." I turn at the sound of the deep voice calling my name.

"Enzo, my dear, I was hoping you were near. Would you mind nabbing me a drink?"

Enzo takes me by the hand, turns it over and kisses my wrist, right upon my pulse. Such a charmer.

A wallflower now, content to watch the world rather than run it, I spy Jessica and Jamie, snuggled close together on the dance floor, her hand clutched in his, his lips resting on her knuckles.

I wonder if they know she is pregnant. It's so clear to me, my gift twanging like a bell.

There's Daisy, up on stage with her man Jay. The two of them sharing a microphone, his hand wrapped around hers. Their eyes on only each other.

Just quietly, the music isn't to my taste. A little too rock and roll, when I've always had a little thing for Barry Manilow. But the crowd don't share my sentiment. The joy in the room is palpable. No wonder they've done so well for themselves.

"Ladies and gents," calls Jay, and the crowd cheers so loud my new hearing aid buzzes. "The bride and groom!"

Aubrey—dear girl—bursts through the doors in her whisper of a dress; arms spread out, fingers beckoning the cheers to continue. Such a riot, that girl. If she'd come sliding in on her knees I'd not have been surprised.

Then through the doorway, cool as you please, comes her man. All brooding bone structure and broad shoulders, that one.

Aubrey turns to him with a smile. No, a grin. Then laughter lights her face up till she's pure sunshine. While he looks at her as if she is the moon and stars, all wrapped up in one pocket-sized package.

A woman who must be Sean's mother—same dark hair and intense blue eyes—comes in behind them, Aubrey and Sean's darling little girl in her arms. A button of a child with her mother's auburn curls and father's bright blue eyes. She'll be trouble when she grows up, no doubt. But the good kind. The kind that fosters *joie de vivre*.

The little one holds out a hand and Aubrey takes her to her hip, leaving the hand for her daddy to hold. And together they move to the dance floor. A threesome, swaying and laughing and hugging, while Daisy and Jay croon a song that puts a tear even in my tough old eye.

This, all this, is more than I ever could have hoped when I gave each of my girls the nudge to go after what they needed most—the opportunity to put their fears behind them and come into their own.

The crowd parts in that moment, and there he is. My Enzo. Drink in hand.

"Bless you, dear man," I say as I take a sip of the most excellent champagne I've had shipped over for the occasion.

Apparently, the groom's family are old money, but one must never leave such things to chance!

Enzo draws me close. The look in his eye makes me feel twenty-one again. The world at my feet.

"Dance with me," he croons.

"I shall," I promise. "Till I can dance no more."

And so the night goes on. A night of laughter and song and love and hope and friendship and family. Of more happily-ever-afters than even I could have imagined.

It seems fairy tales do come true.

* * * * *

THE MAVERICK'S
BABY ARRANGEMENT

KATHY DOUGLASS

This book is dedicated with love
to my wonderful husband and sons.
Each day with you is better than the one before.

Chapter One

Brittany Brandt double-checked the contents of her tan leather satchel, making sure she had everything she needed before snapping it shut. She closed her eyes, inhaled deeply then slowly blew out her breath, envisioning a successful outcome to her meeting with Daniel Dubois. Other planners at Bronco Hills Elite Parties, the event-planning firm where she'd been employed for the past several months, had been reluctant to take him on when he'd hired the firm to plan an important dinner party. While the others had cowered in fear, Brittany had stepped forward. She wasn't afraid of a challenge—or of a man rumored to be impossible to please.

Besides, organizing his party was part of her master plan to advance her career and earn a promotion to partner. Shying away from hard situations and difficult clients wasn't going to help her accomplish that goal. Showing her bosses and the upper crust of Bronco, Montana, what she was capable of doing would.

She'd been fully aware that Mr. Dubois wouldn't be the easiest person to work with before she'd volunteered to take on the job. The trail of other event planners who'd scurried away from Bronco with their tails between their legs made that abundantly clear. Everybody knew that BHE wasn't his first event planner. Or second, for that matter. Originally, he'd hired a firm from L.A. with a reputation of catering to celebrities. They hadn't lasted long. Next, he'd hired a big-name firm out of Chicago. They'd come and gone even more quickly. There'd also been some firm from New York, but their tenure had been so short they were hardly worth mentioning. He'd finally decided to toss the local firm a bone as if doing BHE a favor.

Others might be offended by being a last choice, but not Brittany. In fact, to her, the failure of the other firms was a good thing. Once she pulled off the event—and she had no doubt she *would* pull it off in spectacular fashion—the Who's Who in town would take notice of her and beat a path to her firm, requesting to work with her specifically. Cornelius

Taylor, the patriarch of the richest family in Bronco, would certainly be impressed enough to hire her. She'd pitched her idea of the Denim and Diamonds fundraiser to raise money for programs to aid low-income families in Bronco to him, but so far he hadn't been persuaded. Although she'd put the idea on the back burner temporarily, she wouldn't give up on it. But right now, she needed to focus on creating a memorable dinner party for Mr. Dubois.

Opening her eyes, she grabbed her satchel and purse, strode from her office and into the main area of the firm. Rachel, the assistant Brittany shared with two other planners, looked up from her desk and smiled. "Heading off to your meeting with Mr. Dubois?"

"Yes."

Rachel pretended to shiver in fear. "You're braver than I am."

"He's just a man."

"A man who has chased off three firms already."

Brittany waved a hand in dismissal. "I'm made of sterner stuff. Plus, they weren't as creative as I am. Or as determined. There's no way I'm going to run away in fear from any man."

"Knowing you, you'll have him eating out of your hand before the meeting is over."

"I won't go that far. I know he's no pushover. But remember, I'm the oldest of five children. I have experience dealing with stubborn and demanding people. Trust me, nobody is more unreasonable than a two-year-old hopped up on sugar at bedtime."

Rachel laughed. "I've seen the man, albeit from a distance. There's nothing childish about his looks."

Brittany already knew that. Although she had yet to meet Daniel in person, she'd seen pictures of him in gossip rags and business magazines. The creativity she used in her job failed her when it came to describing Daniel Dubois. The best she could do was *tall, dark and handsome.* Cliché as it was, the saying fit him to a T. He had a face designed to make a woman's heart beat faster and a muscular body that had Brittany imagining things she shouldn't if she wanted him as a client. In short, he was six feet of deliciousness.

"No, there isn't. But since his personality isn't nearly as appealing as his looks, I'd better get going. The last thing I want to do is get on his bad side by being late."

"From what I can see, the man doesn't have a bad side," Rachel quipped.

Brittany laughed then left.

Daniel Dubois was a very wealthy horse rancher and his lifestyle reflected that. He owned a magnificent property in the exclusive section of Bronco Heights.

Two hours north of Billings, Bronco was actually two cities: Bronco Heights where the incredibly rich people resided and Bronco Valley where the regular folks lived. Bronco Heights was consistently included on lists of the country's best places to live while Bronco Valley's claim to fame was as a popular tourist destination.

As Brittany drove through the town, she passed by the business district. Exclusive boutiques, a high-end jewelry store and DJ's Deluxe upscale barbecue restaurant lined the pristine streets. Shoppers strolled down the wide walks, enjoying the beautiful late-summer day.

After a relaxing ride, Brittany reached the winding road that lead to the Dubois mansion. Signaling, although there was no traffic behind her, she drove the nearly mile-long private road to his estate. The sprawling property was nothing short of magnificent and she slowed to take it all in.

The ranch had an air of serenity that only nature could provide. She was slightly nervous about her upcoming meeting and, with each breath she took, she felt more tranquil. In the distance, deer and elk meandered between the trees as if they, too, were at peace. Mountains soared in the background, reaching toward the wide sky. Given the amount of money Dubois had, she wasn't surprised by the grandeur. What was surprising were the numerous small cabins she spotted in the distance. She briefly wondered what they were for and then dismissed the thought as unimportant. She was here to plan his dinner. Nothing else about Daniel Dubois was her concern.

Brittany parked her car at the end of the long circular drive, using the walk to the portico to prepare herself mentally for the meeting.

As she neared the covered walkway, she spotted Malone, the cook for one of Bronco's established families—the Abernathys—coming out the front door. Although she didn't know him very well, she liked the older man and called out a greeting to him. He spun around and looked at her. His face flushed momentarily before the color drained from it, leaving him pasty white. He appeared guilty, although she couldn't imagine why.

"Hi. Funny seeing you here," she said with a smile.

"Yes. Well." Clearly flustered, he took a deep breath. "I've been working for the Abernathys for more than twenty years. And I like my job and am very loyal to them."

"Of course." Where was all this going? She'd only been making small talk. She certainly didn't expect an accounting of the man's time or an explanation of his presence.

"I didn't know that Mr. Dubois had invited me out here to try and hire me away from the Abernathys. Had I known that, I would have saved both his time and mine."

Brittany nodded as the older man continued on his way. Apparently, loyalty didn't mean anything to Daniel Dubois. If he didn't expect people to be loyal to their employers, he surely wouldn't regard loyalty to his employees as something that he owed. She briefly wondered if he applied that same attitude to personal relationships then brushed the ridiculous thought aside. The only relationship she wanted with him was a business one. One where contracts would be signed and expectations clearly spelled out, not one where her heart was on the line.

Not that she was at risk of losing her heart to him—or anyone else, for that matter. She was a career woman through and through. Marriage and kids weren't part of her five-year plan.

Brittany reached the front door and rang the bell. The sound of chimes filtered through the open windows and continued for several seconds until the melody finished. A moment later, the door swung open, revealing a uniformed woman who appeared a few years older than Brittany's own thirty-three. The woman introduced herself as Marta, Daniels's housekeeper, then she ushered Brittany inside and closed the heavy wooden door behind them.

"I'm Brittany Brandt."

Marta smiled. "Welcome. You're right on time, which will please Mr. Dubois. He'll be right with you. He'll meet with you in the study."

Brittany followed the woman through the entry, through an impressive living room and several equally large rooms, before coming to a closed carved-mahogany door. Marta opened the door and waved Brittany inside. "Would you like a drink? The cook just made fresh lemonade."

"Thank you, no. I'll just wait for Mr. Dubois."

"Okay." Marta left, closing the door behind her.

Alone, Brittany took the opportunity to look around, trying to get a feel of Daniel's style. In her experience, clients often could not put their likes or dislikes into words. She couldn't count the number of times someone had told her they knew what they liked when they saw it. Which was fine when it came to deciding which dress to buy. It wasn't as helpful when putting together a special event.

Though she'd only glimpsed the other rooms, adding that bit of knowledge to her quick study of this room revealed that his taste ran toward the masculine and Western. And exceedingly expensive. She ran her hand across a carved horse and rider sitting on the corner of his massive desk then crossed the room to the far wall where a built-in cabinet was filled with trophies for horse breeding. Several awards and commendations from civic organizations were there, as well. Beside the trophy case was a prominently displayed framed letter thanking Mr. Dubois for his ongoing generous contributions to their organization supporting mental health. Another letter thanked him for funding the Francine Dubois scholarship. She briefly wondered whether the woman was his mother.

Apparently, he was a charitable man, which was

a mark in his favor. He might be demanding, but clearly he cared about those who were less fortunate than he was. A believer in giving to others whenever she could, Brittany's opinion of Daniel Dubois rose several notches. Not enough to put up with any nonsense from him, but enough to give him the benefit of the doubt when necessary.

But something was missing in the room. There were no personal items. No photos of people he loved. People who were important to him. She thought it best to keep business and personal lives separate, but this was his *home* office. Surely, a personal item here or there would be acceptable. Come to think of it, she hadn't glimpsed anything personal in the other rooms, either. Curiouser and curiouser.

She heard the door open and she turned. Daniel Dubois stepped into the room. Brittany took one look at him and barely managed to stifle a gasp. The magazines hadn't done him justice. They'd completely failed at capturing his good looks. Daniel Dubois was absolutely stunning.

He had the kind of chiseled features that could make women swoon. Even her knees weakened for a moment before she forced herself to stay upright. His light brown skin was unmarred by the slightest blemish and his dark brown eyes, rimmed by thick soot eyelashes, were filled with intelligence. With his looks, he could make a fortune as a male model.

More than great looks, he had a commanding

presence. No doubt he'd dominate any room he entered. He smiled as he crossed the room to shake her hand and her stomach took a foolish tumble. *No way.* He was a client. She couldn't allow herself to feel the slightest attraction to him.

"Thank you for waiting."

"No problem." As she shook his hand, she felt the calluses on his palm. Daniel Dubois wasn't some rich guy dabbling in ranching until something else drew his attention. He worked his ranch. Impressive.

After declining his offer of a beverage, she let him lead her to a seating area in front of a wall of floor-to-ceiling windows. The drapes had been pulled back, revealing a view of the ranch that went on forever. From this vantage point, she could see all the way to a babbling brook about twenty yards away. Shrubs and purple-and-yellow wildflowers billowed in the breeze and a few deer drank from the water As dedicated as she was to her work, she'd have to use all of her discipline to not be distracted by the beauty the windows revealed.

Once they were seated, her on the brown leather sofa and him on a coordinating chair beside her, she opened her notebook and took out a pen. She preferred the old-fashioned method of taking notes when meeting with clients. It was more personal and didn't create the artificial distance a computer did.

"So, tell me about your event. What do you envision? What are your goals?"

He leaned against the back of his chair, stretched his long legs in front of him and crossed his ankles. Dressed in comfortable jeans that had been faded over time and a chambray shirt that stretched across his muscular chest and shoulders, he looked at ease. But given his reputation, she knew his mind was sharp and that he wouldn't miss a trick.

"Did you notice the cabins in the distance while you were driving in?"

"Yes. They're lovely."

"Those are guest cabins. I plan to turn a part of my ranch into a dude ranch. A top-of-the-line resort worthy of Bronco Heights and serving an exclusive clientele. I've been in business long enough to know that community buy-in is important to any business. Although there is a lot of land between me and my neighbors, I want them to feel comfortable with what I'm about to do with my property."

"That's a good idea."

"That's where you come in. I want to have a dinner for the leading families and community leaders in Bronco to inform them about the resort. I'll distribute information packets as well as answer any questions they may have."

Brittany nodded. She admired the way he planned to take the proverbial bull by the horn. As a newcomer to town, he would be subject to a lot of suspicion by the old-moneyed folk who at times could be a bit insular. He struck her as someone who wouldn't be cowed and who'd soon earn everyone's respect.

He glanced at her and his beautiful smile faded. "Why do you think you're qualified for a job that other firms were incapable of handling?"

Brittany was momentarily stunned by the abrupt change from charming man to cold businessman, but she shifted gears, as well. Now that the pleasantries were over, it was down to business. "I can't say why the others failed, because I'm not acquainted with them. What I can tell you is that I'm good at my job. Very good. You strike me as someone who knows what he's doing, so I'm sure you've already asked about me."

"I have."

"Then you know I have an excellent reputation."

"I've heard good things. But I also know that you've only been with Bronco Heights Elite Parties for a few months. Before that you worked at that ghost-hunting company." He shook his head, making it obvious what he thought of *that* business. "All told, you don't have very much experience."

"I can see how you would believe that."

"It's not a belief. It's a fact."

She'd give him that. "The people you hired before had experience, right?"

"Yes."

"How'd that work out for you?"

His eyes narrowed. Obviously, he didn't like being challenged.

Smiling internally, she continued. "They weren't able to deliver. Clearly, a long résumé doesn't guarantee ability or a successful outcome. You should consider my natural assets." He raised an eyebrow and she realized how suggestive that comment sounded. Rather than try to clean it up and thereby prolong the uncomfortable moment, she soldiered on. "I have skills that can't be taught. I can arrange a dinner party that your guests will be buzzing about for months. And I guarantee they'll be lining up for invitations to your next dinner party while those unfortunate enough to have been left off the guest list try to wrangle invitations to your next event. More than that, it'll drum up interest and support for your resort."

"You're pretty sure of yourself."

"I know what I can do."

He nodded, as if impressed. "Do you have time to see the ranch? If you're going to be organizing this function, it would be helpful for you to have a look around."

"I have time." She'd cleared the afternoon for the express purpose of getting to know him.

"Okay. There are a few places we can only reach by horseback, so I'll have to settle with describing them to you."

"Why? I can ride."

One side of his lips lifted in a sexy half smile that had her toes curling in her boots. She forced them straight. She didn't get involved with clients.

"Really? In that case, let's take the horses."

"Yes. Let's."

He stood and held out his hand to her. Pleasantly surprised by the gesture, she placed her hand in his and rose. He led her from his office and through the magnificent house. The rooms were spacious, airy and exquisitely decorated, if a little masculine for her taste. But then there wasn't a Mrs. Dubois in the picture to soften the décor. Or the man.

They walked through a long hallway where gorgeous paintings hung from the dark-paneled wall. She would have liked to slow down to get a better look at the artwork, but he was on a mission. Nearly half a foot shorter, she couldn't keep up with his long strides.

They exited through a door and stepped into the warm air. She inhaled the scent of wildflowers and freshly mowed grass. The view from here was even better than the one from his office, showing a property more expansive than she'd thought. A paved path led from the door into two directions. One led to a small pond. The other—the one they took—led to the stables.

A man approached them as they stepped inside, pulling his cowboy hat from his head when he saw her. "Good afternoon, Mr. Dubois. Ma'am."

"Hi," Brittany said.

"I'm going to take Ms. Brandt on a ride around the ranch, Jerry. Would you saddle Sugar Cookie for her?"

"Right away," he said and then ambled away.

"Sugar Cookie?" Brittany asked. He didn't strike her as the kind of man who'd give a horse such a fanciful name.

"I didn't choose it," he said quickly, as if his man card was in danger of being revoked. "The previous owner's daughter named her that."

"I think it's sweet."

He snorted and strode to a stall where a gorgeous stallion waited. In under a minute, he'd saddled the horse and led it to where Brittany waited. The groom returned with Sugar Cookie and stepped up beside Brittany to help her mount.

"I'll do that," Daniel said.

"Okay," Jerry said and walked away.

Before Brittany could tell Daniel that she was perfectly capable of mounting the horse on her own, he was beside her. When he gently put his hands on her waist and, her voice abandoned her as he lifted her into the saddle. She inhaled and she was instantly surrounded by his masculine scent. Her heart beat a little faster and the blood raced through her veins. Then he adjusted her stirrups. When he turned his back and returned to his own horse she blew out a shaky breath and wiped her hand across her suddenly damp brow.

How many times did she have to remind herself that she didn't get involved with clients? She'd never struggled this hard to keep business and personal separate. Hopefully, this was a temporary problem.

She twisted in her seat, getting comfortable in the saddle. If she'd known ahead of time that she'd be riding a horse, she would have worn jeans and a T-shirt instead of the high-waisted black pants and pink-and-white chiffon blouse. But since this was the opportunity to get to know Daniel better, she wouldn't complain. Besides, her parents owned a large dry-cleaning business, so getting her clothes cleaned wouldn't be a hassle.

Daniel swung up onto his stallion and led them out of the stable and into the pasture. Without the slightest hesitation, he started off across the large expanse of grass. He went slowly at first, as if not believing she could really ride. She'd grown up in Montana. Of course she could ride.

Apparently satisfied that she knew what she was doing, he sped up. She tried to keep her eyes on the beautiful scenery, but they kept drifting to Daniel's muscular body. He looked so fine riding on his stallion that her mouth began to water.

She was in unchartered territory here. Normally she had laser focus on work. Now the dinner was the farthest thing on her mind. The only thing she could concentrate on was the very sexy Daniel Dubois. If she didn't get her wayward mind under control and tamp down on her attraction, she was going to be in deep trouble.

Chapter Two

Daniel glanced at Brittany. She was smiling broadly, her beautiful brown eyes gleaming with excitement, her cheeks glowing. What in the world had possessed him to invite her to go riding with him? It certainly hadn't been part of the plan when he'd set up the meeting. If he had stuck to his agenda, she would be on her way back to her office and he would be repairing fences or one of the many other tasks he'd scheduled for today. Yet, here they were.

He had to admit that he'd enjoyed sparring with her. She wasn't afraid to voice her opinion, something he admired. The last thing he wanted was to do business with someone who didn't stand up to him. Weak people generally made bad employees and even worse partners. And if she was going to work with him on this party, they'd be partners, so it made sense to get to know each other better.

After they'd accomplished everything they'd needed to in his office, he'd been about to bring the meeting to a close. Then she'd crossed her legs and his mind had begun to wander to places that had nothing to do with business. Her sweet scent had wafted over to him, tying him up in knots, and his good sense had deserted him.

So instead of saying goodbye, he'd invited her for a tour. Now they were galloping across the ranch to one of his favorite spots. An argument could be made that it would help if she saw more of his land and got the complete picture of what he planned to do. But it wasn't essential to her role as party planner. Besides, the waterfall wouldn't be accessible to the resort guests, so there'd been no real reason to bring her here. But still, he'd wanted to share this spot with her. To see her reaction. If her quiet gasp was anything to go by, she was getting just as much pleasure from her surroundings as he always did.

Bringing his horse to a stop, he dismounted. He was about to help Brittany when she expertly got off her horse on her own. They looped the horses' reins around a tree branch then stood side by side.

"This is beautiful. How many acres do you own?"

"Two hundred and sixty."

"Wow." She turned in a slow circle and, when her back was to him, his eyes strayed to her round bottom. He'd tried not to notice the way her pants fit, but he was still a man. Ignoring such an enticing sight was something he wasn't equipped to do.

"That's what I thought when I found this spread. I rode over every acre before deciding that this was the perfect place for my horse ranch. Then I had to find the right place to build my house. I wanted easy access to my home from the road, but I want privacy from the guests. It's a balancing act."

"One that you've handled very well." She gave him the once-over, taking him in from boots to hat before her eyes met his. "So why did you bring me out here on this ride? You could have told me about your ranch just as easily while we were sitting in your office."

The way her eyes held his was impressive. Most people avoided prolonged eye contact. And they certainly didn't challenge him. "Seeing it for yourself is better than any description I could have given."

"So you're admitting to a weakness?"

"I wouldn't exactly call it that. As the saying goes, a picture is worth a thousand words."

She grinned and the picture she presented would need more than a thousand words to describe. Or perhaps not. Maybe only one was necessary. *Stunning.*

Brittany Brandt was absolutely stunning. He frowned. Her appearance was the last thing he should be thinking about. His plate was already overflowing without adding a woman to the mix. Not that he was considering doing that. Admiring Brittany's beauty and spunk was miles away from becoming romantically involved with her. But with that smile lighting her face and the joy radiating from her every pore, given the right motivation and opportunity, he would cross that distance in a heartbeat.

"Another reason I brought you out here," he continued, pulling his mind back to business, "is so you can get the feel of the land. Smell the fresh air. Soak in the atmosphere."

She stared at him for a long moment and he wondered if he'd waxed too poetic. He frowned. Since when did he doubt himself? Brittany's presence was definitely affecting him—and not in a good way. She had managed to knock him off-kilter. He didn't like the feeling.

"I'll be able to use this experience to bring the party to life."

"Then I succeeded."

"Trust me, this party is going to achieve each of your goals."

He blew out a breath. "I hope so. I'm new to Bronco. I've only been here a year and people have been slow to warm up to me. Not that it was entirely unexpected. I bought one of the biggest ranches in the area. This is prime real estate that no doubt one of the old-timers wanted for one of his kids. That I own a horse ranch in the middle of cattle country didn't help. I don't want to be enemies with my neighbors. I would like to have cordial relationships with all of them if possible."

Brittany smirked. "Quiet as it's kept, not all of your neighbors get along with each other. There's a new money versus old money dynamic in Bronco Heights. Then there's the wealthy Bronco Heights versus the middle-class Bronco Valley divide. City council meetings are boisterous, to say the least. I predict that one day the fights won't stop with words."

"I hope it doesn't come to that."

"My point is twofold. First, getting along with all of your neighbors might be a pipe dream. Honestly, I'm not sure it's wise to have some of them in a room at the same time. Second, you're not the only one on the receiving end of the cold shoulder."

"I don't know if that's better or worse," he said with a laugh.

She laughed with him. "Of course, with an expert like me on your side, someone local who knows all the players, the impossible will be made possible."

"Is that right?" Daniel took a step closer to her and, although her eyes widened, she didn't back away. He wasn't sure whether that was good or bad. Did she feel the attraction between them? Did she share the same yearning to close the distance separating them? To touch? She nibbled on her full bottom lip, mesmerizing him.

Suddenly a bird squawked overhead, breaking the spell, and Daniel's senses returned.

What was wrong with him? This was a business meeting, not a date. He pointed to several boulders shaded by a large oak tree, where they could sit and talk.

She walked beside him. After they sat, she turned to him. "Just tell me what you envision. I know what you *want*. You want the support of the community. Tell me what you *see*. What do you visualize this dinner looking like? Paint a picture for me."

Art was never his strong suit. In fact, he didn't have a gift for any of the softer subjects like music, literature or the like. Math. Science. That's where he'd excelled. After earning a Ph.D. in mechanical engineering from MIT, he and his best friend, who'd gotten an MBA from Harvard, had started a bioengineering company that was a leader in genetic testing. They'd taken the company public six years ago and made more money than either of them had ever dared to dream. Two years ago, Daniel had resigned as CEO. He still owned stock in the company and was on the board of directors, but he was no longer involved in day-to-day operations. Last year, he'd moved from Texas to Montana to live his dream of ranching and owning an exclusive dude ranch. His background in genetics came in handy when it came

to breeding horses and he was becoming successful and making a name for himself in the industry.

Stephanos Dimitry, his former partner, hadn't understood why Daniel had wanted to leave, but as a
good friend, had wished him well. He'd also promised to be Daniel's first guest once the resort was
up and running.

"Well?" she prompted when he just sat there like
a bump on a log.

"I want my dinner guests to see the good in what
I'm doing. I want them to see the positive impact
the resort will have on the entire community. I want
them to feel invested in the success of the business."

"I can do all of that for you. And more. Believe
me when I tell you that I'm not simply the best person for the job. I'm the only person."

His phone rang before he could comment. He
glanced at the screen then answered the call. "Mr.
Dubois?" The woman's voice trembled, striking fear
in Daniel's heart.

"Yes? Is everything okay?" Worry made his voice
sharp. Brittany raised an eyebrow but remained silent.

"No. I have to leave. I have a family emergency."

"Leave? When?" He jumped to his feet.

"Now."

He ran across the grass. Brittany, as if sensing
something was wrong, was right behind him. "I'm

on my way back to the house. I'll be there in twenty minutes. I expect to see you when I get there."

"I—" She sputtered as he ended the call. He didn't want to waste time having a phone conversation; they needed to speak in person.

He grabbed Lightning's reins and hopped on his back. "I need to get home."

"Of course." Brittany mounted Sugar Cookie in an easy motion and galloped beside him as he sped toward the mansion.

When they reached the stables, he jumped from Lightning's back and then looked over his shoulder at Brittany. She slid from Sugar Cookie's saddle then rubbed the mare's neck. Jerry jogged over and took the horses. Daniel knew his groom would take care of cooling them down, so he didn't bother issuing the order. He had a more important matter to attend to.

He strode down the path, over the brick patio and into the house, not stopping until he reached the living room where Emma was pacing. A large red-plaid suitcase leaned against the sofa. When Emma heard his footsteps on the hardwood floor, she turned to look at him. Even through his worry and anger, he recognized the grief in her eyes.

"Where do you think you're going?" he demanded. "We have a contract. Remember? One that I fully intend to enforce."

"I'm sorry, Mr. Dubois, but my father had a heart

attack. I have to go home today. Now. I have to leave right now."

Daniel ran a frustrated hand over his face. He knew it was irrational to demand that she stay given the circumstances. He'd lost his parents three years ago, barely five months apart. They'd married when they were both twenty-one and Daniel's father hadn't been able to live without the love of his life. Though Daniel's mother had succumbed to breast cancer, his father had died of a broken heart.

Despite knowing how he should behave, Daniel struggled to find the compassion inside himself.

"I'm sorry, Mr. Dubois. You can sue me for everything I have, if that's what you want to do. But my father needs me and I'm going to be there for him."

As Daniel and Emma faced off, he became aware that Brittany was staring at the two of them in confusion. Clearly, she was trying to make sense of the conversation. Not that any of this was her business. His private life was his own, a concept he would obviously need to reinforce once—*if*—they began working together.

"Then go." What else could he say? He couldn't imprison her. If she wanted to leave, she would.

Emma grabbed her suitcase and darted from the room without looking back.

A cry cut through the tense silence. Without a word to Brittany, Daniel sprinted from the room and up the stairs to the nursery. Hailey was sitting, gnawing on a rail of her crib. When she saw him, she wiggled on her bottom and gave him a four-tooth grin Smiling, he picked her up and held her warm body against his chest.

He really loved his little girl. Why was it so hard to get the day-to-day right?

Hailey babbled something to him in a language only she understood. When he didn't respond, she slapped her hand against his cheek as if demanding he snap out of it. Right. She needed a new diaper. She might be chatting happily right now, but experience had taught him that if he didn't get her into a dry diaper soon, she'd be howling like a wolf.

Carrying her to the changing table, he laid her down and put a hand on her stomach, holding her in place. She gurgled and wiggled her chubby little body. He grabbed a wipe and a diaper and expertly changed Hailey. Her clothes had gotten wet during her nap, so he swiftly changed those, as well. Then he took her back downstairs for a snack.

He was on his way to the kitchen when he remembered that Brittany was still there. Making a U-turn, he went back to the front room.

Brittany, who'd been staring out the window, looked around as he stepped into the room. Her eyes widened in surprise when she saw the baby, but she merely smiled.

"Who have we here?" Brittany said,

"This is Hailey."

Brittany's her mouth dropped open, her full lips forming a perfect "O". She blinked then regained her composure. "I see." She leaned closer to look straight at the baby. "Hello, cutie pie."

Hailey chattered a greeting and then reached out her arms to Brittany.

That was different. Hailey generally didn't take to strangers. That's why he'd tried so hard to hold on to Emma. She and Hailey had bonded. Before Emma, Hailey had spent most of the day crying. After Emma, Hailey had gradually become happy. She'd even begun going down for naps without a fight and Daniel had been able to get some work done. He would have his work cut out for him until he found another nanny.

Emma's quitting couldn't have come at a worse time. Still, he'd adapt the same as he had when Hailey had unexpectedly come into his life.

Brittany touched Hailey's dimpled finger then looked at him. "I didn't know you were married."

"I'm not."

"Okay…"

This wasn't going well. Brittany was clearly confused and slightly put out, not that he blamed her. There had been some low-key flirting between them and now he was standing there with a baby in his arms. Although there wasn't anything between them—and given that his life was in a shambles and he wouldn't be involved with her or anyone else in the future—he didn't want her to get the wrong impression of him. His reputation meant everything to him. But he couldn't worry about her feelings or her opinion of him now. He had to take care of Hailey, who was squirming in his arms. He set her down and she immediately giggled.

"We're going to have to end our meeting now. Obviously. Since I no longer have a nanny, I have to take care of the baby. We'll have to reschedule."

"That's not necessary. I have enough information to get started."

"You do?"

"Yes. I'll work up a few options and get back to you in a few days with my suggestions."

Hailey crawled over to Brittany and yanked on her pant leg. Daniel reached down to grab Hailey at the same time Brittany bent and scooped her up. Immediately, Hailey grabbed Brittany's hair and gave it a hard tug. Without missing a beat, Brittany pulled her curls from the baby's hand.

He took Hailey into his arms again.

"It looks like you're going to need a new nanny. I can ask around if you want."

"Absolutely not." His voice was louder than he'd intended and Brittany jumped. He didn't apologize, though. He needed to make himself perfectly clear. "You are not to tell anyone about Hailey, is that clear? Your job depends on it. If you breathe one word to anyone about Hailey's existence, I'll make your life a living hell."

She slammed her hands on her hips. "There's no need to be nasty. And threats don't work with me. All you had to do was ask me to keep your secret and I would have agreed. Gossiping about you is the last thing I plan on doing."

"Fine."

"Fine."

They stared at one another, each breathing hard and neither speaking. He had to give it to her. She wasn't one to back down.

Hailey let out a whimper, ending the senseless standoff. Brittany stalked into his office then returned with her satchel and purse. "You've got your hands full, literally and figuratively, so I'll leave. I'll contact you when I have something to share so we can discuss our next steps."

"You're assuming you have the job. I haven't seen your plans yet. I might not like them."

She frowned. "Fair enough. I'll work up preliminary plans and get them to you. Then you can decide what you want to do next."

Daniel walked her to the door and watched as she made her way to her car. When he caught himself admiring the gentle sway of her hips, he shut the door. There wasn't even enough space in his life for the no-strings relationships he preferred. Not that it mattered. Brittany was going to be working for him, setting her on the other side of a line he would never cross. Business and personal were never allowed to mingle. Too bad, he thought as he returned to the living room, the baby in his arms. Too, too bad. Because this was one time he wouldn't be opposed to them mixing.

Chapter Three

Brittany felt Daniel's eyes on her as she walked to her car. That had to have been the most bizarre meeting she'd ever had. And she'd had some doozies in her time. She'd been challenged, flirted with, insulted and threatened all in the space of a few hours. Flustering her was difficult, but he'd come close to knocking her off her game.

Daniel's reputation as a hard-nosed businessman was well established throughout Bronco, although, other than that he was single, very little was known about his personal life. But not from lack of trying. She'd scoured the internet for information about him to prepare for this meeting. Apart from the pictures of him with various women at public functions and the information provided by his company, there was nothing about his private life. Certainly there had been no hint of a baby.

The busybodies in town had worked overtime trying to dig up tidbits about the man's personal life. She had no intention of sharing what she'd learned with them. Or anyone.

Not that she was afraid of him or his threats. She wasn't. But she wasn't a gossip, either. Though she'd never been the victim of wagging tongues, she knew the harm that could result from loose talk. And, really, was the fact that he had a baby anyone's business? Still, the fact that he was a father had come as a shock.

As she drove back to her office, she forced all thoughts of Daniel's status as a parent from her mind and began to work out plans for his event. The ideas were coming fast and furious, but since she was driving, she couldn't write them down. So she began to sing them aloud. Long ago she'd discovered that creating lyrics for important information and singing them over and over helped her remember. That's how she'd helped her youngest sister pass eighth-grade science. Even now they still laughed at the esophagus-liver-stomach song whenever they got together.

Singing to herself about color schemes and centerpieces, she parked and went to her office where she booted up her computer then furiously typed her ideas for the party. Once that was done, she printed out a copy to take home to review later then turned off her computer.

It was the end of the workday and she could hear her coworkers bustling about as they prepared to leave. There was a knock on her door. Before Brittany could say a word, Julia, another event planner and one of Brittany's closest friends, opened the door and poked her head inside. "We're going out for drinks at BB&G. You want to come?"

Brittany often joined her friends for drinks and dinner after work, but today she turned them down. There was so much she needed to do for Daniel's event. Besides, she was distracted with thoughts of him and knew if she was questioned about it, she would probably blurt out something she shouldn't.

"Not tonight. It's been a busy day and I think I'll just go on home. You guys have fun."

"We'll miss you. See you tomorrow."

"Bye." Brittany grabbed her purse and satchel and headed out of the office, to the building's private parking lot and her car. In a few minutes she'd left downtown behind and was on her way to Bronco Heights and the condo she shared with her roommate, Amanda Jenkins.

Amanda was home when Brittany arrived, which was a pleasant surprise. Now that Amanda was engaged, she spent a lot of time with her fiancé, Holt Dalton. Even though Brittany didn't want to get married, she wasn't opposed to the institution. She was happy that her shy friend had found the love of her life.

"Hey," Brittany said, slipping off her shoes.

"Hi." Amanda looked up from the bridal magazine she was skimming, a smile on her face. She brushed her long brown hair over her shoulder.

A pile of other bridal magazines sat on Brittany's favorite chair, so she gathered them up and set them on the coffee table before sitting down. "How goes the dress hunt?"

"Oh, I'm still just getting ideas. I'm trying to figure out what I like and what I wouldn't be caught dead in."

Brittany laughed. Amanda was petite and quite pretty, something she didn't seem to know. "You're gorgeous and have a great figure. You'll look great in any style. You'd just better not make us bridesmaids wear some strange, never-worn-anywhere-in-the-real-world-created-by-a-design-school-dropout dress."

"Not to worry. You'll be able to pick your own dress."

"Really? Thank goodness. I have a closet full of horrible bridesmaids' dresses that I will never wear. Those things are so ugly, I can't even give them away."

Amanda set aside the magazine. "Enough about

the wedding. How was your meeting with Daniel Dubois?"

Brittany curled her feet underneath her. "Interesting."

"Come on. That tells me exactly nothing."

"He wasn't what I expected. And at the same time, he's exactly what I expected."

Amanda laughed. "Mud would be clearer."

"I guess that didn't make sense. Here's the thing. Everybody knows that Daniel Dubois is a hard-nosed businessman. He demands to have things his way. And because he's extremely rich, people usually give in to him."

"Sounds about right."

"But there's more to him than that. When we were riding horses, he was friendly. Funny. Charming." He'd looked so rugged and handsome sitting on that magnificent stallion—like an ad for outdoor living at its finest. He would be the perfect model for any brochures advertising his dude ranch. Of course, she knew without asking that he'd never agree to such a thing. That was too bad. Beauty like his should be shared with the masses.

Amanda made the timeout signal with her hands. "Hold on. When were the two of you riding horses? I thought you had a business meeting."

"We did. Afterward he wanted to show me his property. He owns a horse ranch, and I ride, so it only made sense to see his place on horseback."

"Really? That sounds like a date to me."

"It wasn't. It was business."

"So you say. But why did you need to see his ranch? It's certainly isn't necessary in order to organize his party."

"Who am I to question him? He's the client. He wanted to show me the ranch, so I went." And she'd enjoyed herself immensely. Those quiet moments they'd shared admiring the beauty of the waterfall far surpassed any of her recent dates.

"Mmm-hmm."

"What does that mean?"

"It means that you went from really disliking that man and only working with him as a means to an end, to describing him as charming. Your interest in him sounds more than professional."

"Being in love has addled your brain. You're seeing love and romance when there isn't any."

Amanda's brown eyes sparkled with amusement. "Oh ho, who said anything about love or romance? I just said that you're interested in him."

"I'm not." Brittany was definite about that. Sure, the man had an undeniable magnetism. What woman wouldn't feel a tug on everything that was feminine in his presence? But that perfectly human reaction didn't alter her life plans. The only thing she wanted from Daniel Dubois was his business. She wasn't interested in becoming involved with him—or any man for that matter.

Not that she didn't date. She did. But much to her parents' dismay, she wasn't looking for a serious relationship. A husband and kids were the furthest thing from her mind. Perhaps her lack of interest stemmed from the memories of caring for her siblings. Or maybe it came from seeing how exhausted her mother had been. Her mother had worked almost as many hours at the cleaners as Brittany's father had. Then she'd come home and take care of her kids. She'd never had a minute to herself.

Brittany was determined to take a different path, which was why marriage wasn't on her agenda. And kids were out of the question. Other thirty-three-year-old women might hear a ticking biological clock, but not her. She didn't hear a thing. In fact, her clock might not even be plugged in.

Her mother insisted that when she met *the one*, whoever that mythical man might be, she'd be ready to settle down and have babies. Not likely. Brittany had big plans that didn't include becoming Mrs. Anybody and raising kids. Besides, Daniel's life was complicated. He had an infant. Even if Brittany was willing to consider a relationship with him—which she wasn't—his daughter was a deal breaker. Brittany liked kids, but she didn't want any of her own. She'd seen the toll being a working mother had taken on her mother. Mallory Brandt had been exhausted most of Brittany's life. And since Brittany had no plans to give up her career, kids were out.

She wasn't cut out to be a mother with the full-time responsibility that came along with having kids. That wasn't the life for her. She'd be the favorite aunt to her siblings' and friends' kids, taking them on fun outings, letting them have sleepovers at her house, and buying them ridiculously expensive gifts, but that was it.

Despite all the reasons he was wrong for her, there was something about Daniel that had reached out to her on an elemental level. Though she might not want to admit it, something in her had reached back.

"Deny all you want, if that makes you happy. But remember, when you and Daniel do get together, I reserve the right to say I told you so. Oh, and I expect all of the details."

Brittany laughed as she stood. "You'll be the first to know. On that note, I'm going to say good-night and leave you to your dress hunt. See you in the morning."

After heating up leftover meatloaf she'd brought home from dinner with her parents earlier in the week, Brittany went into her room. She loved the condo she and Amanda shared, but her bedroom suite was her sanctuary. She'd decorated it in soothing creams, whites and pale blues. Personal pictures were scattered across her dresser and bedside tables. Her desk was situated beneath the windows, where she was able to enjoy a view of nature whenever she worked there.

She took out her notes with the intention of add-ing contacts so she could hit the ground running tomorrow morning. She'd pull out all the stops and call in every favor she'd earned to make this dinner the talk of the town.

But rather than work, she sat there, pen in hand and stared out her window. Instead of her normal view of trees, a manicured lawn, with perfectly spaced flowers, she saw Daniel astride his magnifi-cent horse, galloping across the untouched beauty of his ranch. To her. When he reached her, he jumped from his stallion and closed the distance between them. Smiling, he held out a hand to touch her face. Then he lowered his head as she raised hers to re-ceive his kiss. Just as their lips were about to meet, an owl hooted, and Brittany jerked. Blinking, she tried to clear her head.

What in the world was she doing? Why was she daydreaming about Daniel? He was her client. And he had a child. Either one of those things alone should have given her pause. Both together should have made her stop and then run in the other direc-tion. The fact that she was fantasizing about him scared her witless.

"I'm coming," Daniel said more to himself than to Hailey. For the past few days, he'd been caring for the baby on his own as well as trying to get his busi-ness up and running. Caring for Hailey took priority, so he generally didn't get much work done during the day. By the time she was asleep at night, he was all but worn out. In the past, he'd put in long hours, rising with the sun and working well into the night without a problem. But in those days, he hadn't been caring for a child.

Who knew someone so small could be so draining?

Hailey was screaming at the top of her lungs by the time he reached the nursery. It was only four in the morning and, hoping she'd fall back to sleep, he didn't turn on the light. A quick check revealed that her diaper was still dry, so that wasn't the source of her displeasure. Holding her against his chest, he sat in the glider and began to rock back and forth. Though she was no longer screeching, Hailey still cried. She didn't feel warm, so he had no clue about what was wrong.

"Did you have a nightmare?" he asked, rubbing his hand up and down her back in a soothing motion. "Or are you missing your mommy?"

Daniel knew he did. He still couldn't believe Jane was gone. If only he could go back in time and change things, he would. Instead he was forced to live with the reality that the past couldn't be altered. He wanted Hailey to know about her mother. And when she was older, he would tell her. At least he'd tell her the positive things he remembered about his sweet little sister. After all, he wanted Hailey to have a positive image of her mother.

Daniel would have liked to tell her about her father, too, but other than the man's name—Craig Larimar—Daniel didn't know anything. He'd never met the man who'd fathered his sister's child. And since he'd died in the same accident that had claimed Jane, Daniel never would. He'd have to be satisfied with telling Hailey that her father had loved her.

"Your mother would be so proud of you," he said to Hailey, whose sobs had finally stopped. "She loved you very much. She wanted me to raise you as my own child and that's what I'm going to do. I love you, too. Very much."

"Badanappa."

"Why, yes, it would be nice if you would go back to sleep."

She laughed and clapped her hands.

He laughed softly. "I hope that means you agree with my suggestion."

"Batba ooh ooh."

Daniel didn't reply, not wanting to prolong the conversation. Instead he rocked slowly until Hailey fell back to sleep. Rising carefully, he put her into her crib and covered her with the light blanket. With any luck, she would sleep for the rest of the night.

One thing was certain. He couldn't go on like this much longer. He needed help. Perhaps he should have taken Brittany up on her offer to help him find a new nanny. But that would mean letting the people in Bronco learn about Hailey. So far, he'd been able to keep her existence a secret and wanted to keep it that way.

He'd learned at a young age to guard his private life. Although he'd prefer not to be mentioned in the press, it had been part and parcel of starting a successful company in his twenties. He'd had to do interviews and make himself available to be photographed. But even then, he'd avoided answering questions about his family and personal life.

Protecting his privacy had been important before, but it was essential now that he had Hailey. She deserved to have as normal a childhood as he could give her. Being followed by press and having her picture splashed all over the internet so people he didn't know and who didn't know them could get a glimpse of her made his stomach twist in knots. Still, he had to do something.

He kissed her soft cheek. "Sleep well, little one."

Daniel didn't return to his room, going instead to his office. There would be no more sleep for him tonight, so he may as well get some work done. Hopefully, he'd hear from Brittany soon with her ideas for the party. He really was looking forward to talking to her, and not just about her ideas. She was an attractive woman with a lot of spunk. Under other circumstances, he might have pursued her.

Sadly, these weren't other circumstances. And if he liked her proposal, she would be working for him. Their relationship needed to remain strictly professional.

Now he just had to figure out a way to keep her from invading his thoughts night and day.

Chapter Four

Brittany took the last paper from the printer, stacked all of the pages neatly, then inserted them into a folder. She'd outdone herself and was pleased with the results. Every vendor she'd sought out had been available and had given her reasonable quotes. She never liked to skimp on cost, believing you ultimately paid if you tried to nickel-and-dime people, but she didn't like to overpay, either, no matter how wealthy her client. She preferred to have win-win deals. That way, vendors would want to work with her again as well as accommodate special requests.

She hadn't heard from Daniel in the past few days, which gave her pause. She'd left two messages for him, but he hadn't responded. As far as she knew, he hadn't hired another firm and she was still working for him, so she needed to update him on her plans and get his go-ahead to proceed. If he wanted to make changes, now was the time.

Since he also wanted this event to occur as soon as possible, she needed his approval now. Leaving messages had been futile, so she had to try a different tact. She'd drop by his house. Stopping by without an appointment was a gamble, but it was a risk she was willing to take. If he wasn't available, she'd leave a copy of her plans with a member of his staff.

After letting Rachel know she'd be out of the office for a few hours, Brittany drove to the Dubois ranch. As before, she was struck by the beauty of his property. It was nature at its absolute most stunning. She could only dream of waking up to this beauty every morning; of walking through the grass to the lake every day. But since she was only here for business and not to move in, imagining was as close as she would get.

She parked in the driveway and headed to his front door. The closer she got to the house, the harder her heart began to thump. She inhaled deeply, trying to calm her suddenly jittery nerves. She didn't understand the reaction. She had follow-up meetings with clients all the time and never got nervous. In fact, meeting with clients generally energized her.

Blowing out the breath, she forced herself to admit

the truth. Her blood wasn't racing through her veins because she was concerned about the meeting. She was reacting this way in anticipation of seeing Daniel again. Though she was loathe to admit it, she'd been thinking of him quite a bit these past few days. He'd invaded her thoughts at the most inopportune times, not that any time would be good. But no matter how many lectures she gave herself, she'd found herself daydreaming about him.

Well, that wouldn't do. He was her client and she had her rules. Straightening her shoulders, she rang the door-bell. Before it stopped ringing, the door swung open.

"Hello, Ms. Brandt."

"Hi, Marta," Brittany replied, grateful for the warm greeting. "I realize I've dropped by unannounced, but I'm wondering if Mr. Dubois is available to meet."

"I'll check. Come inside."

Brittany waited in the foyer for a minute or two. She was reconsidering the wisdom of her impulsive trip out here when Marta returned. "Mr. Dubois is available. Follow me, please."

Brittany expected to be shown into Daniel's office, but instead she was led deep into yet another wing of the house to an enormous family room. Daniel was sitting on a comfy-looking couch, Hailey on his lap. Whereas his clothes had been neat, if not immaculate when she'd last seen him, he now looked slightly disheveled. Orange specks of what was probably strained peaches dotted the front of his wrinkled shirt. He didn't seem to notice. Or maybe he was just past caring.

The look on his face gave away his exhaustion. His deep brown eyes were red-rimmed and puffy. And it looked like he hadn't shaved in a couple of days. He stifled a yawn, confirming what she'd already surmised. He needed rest.

He glanced at her ruefully, rubbing the stubble on his chin. "Sorry I haven't called you back. I intended to, but Hailey has been fussy lately and not in the mood to cooperate with me."

"I take it you haven't found a nanny yet."

"No." He heaved a deep sigh. "My staff have pitched in when they could, but Hailey hasn't warmed up to them. Besides, she's my responsibility, not theirs."

Brittany resisted the urge to repeat her offer to help him find another nanny. The last time she'd made the suggestion, he'd bitten off her head and threatened her. If he wanted her help, he was going to have to ask for it. Yet a piece of her heart ached for him. She remembered how worn out her mother had been when Brittany's siblings had been little. Babies might be adorable, but they were exhausting.

At the sound of Brittany's voice, Hailey turned and gave a bright smile, showing off her four teeth. She might be the cutest baby Brittany had ever seen, but she wasn't fooled. She knew Hailey would give her a run for her money in a minute.

"I stopped by to go over my proposal with you, but I can tell you're busy. I'll just leave a copy of it with you, so you can read it at your leisure."

"Leisure. That's a distant memory. Kind of like a good night's sleep. If you don't mind, I'd like to go over the proposal with you now."

Hailey rattled off a few nonsensical words then stretched out her arms in Brittany's direction.

Daniel covered another yawn. "I know I rejected your offer to help me find a nanny, but if it still stands, I'd like to take you up on it."

"Sure. I can ask around. I won't let anyone know it's for you. I'll just say a friend is looking for help. How's that?"

His bleary eyes widened in surprise. What? Did he think she didn't recall how he'd freaked out at the idea of anyone knowing about Hailey? She didn't know why he felt that way, but it wasn't her business. She could help him and allow him to maintain his privacy.

"That sounds perfect. Thank you. And let me take this time to apologize for being a jerk. I was a bit stressed the other day, but that's no excuse for how I treated you. I'm sorry."

Brittany hoped she covered her surprise better than he had. "You're forgiven."

"Thanks."

They shared a smile and Brittany's heart went pitter-patter. It was foolish and a bit dangerous to give her attraction to this man even a breath of air, but apparently she wasn't as smart as she'd liked to believe. Luckily, they weren't going to be in each other's lives for much longer. If he approved her proposal, she would set her plan into action and not see him again until a day or two before the dinner. Once the event was over, they would go back to their regularly scheduled lives. Since their social circles didn't overlap—he was a wealthy rancher and she was a middle-class working girl—it was unlikely their paths would cross again.

Mr. Rogers, Daniel's butler, entered the room. "Sorry to interrupt, but you have an important call from Dallas."

"I'm in the middle of a meeting," Daniel said. "Take a message and I'll call back."

"You'll want to take this call."

"Who is it?"

"A man with the last name of Larimar."

Daniel stiffened. "Right."

Brittany looked from Daniel to Mr. Rogers, who wore a somber expression.

"Would you mind watching Hailey for me while I take this call?" Daniel asked.

"Uh," Brittany uttered as words failed her. Daniel must have taken that sound as a yes because he stood and handed over Hailey, who immediately grabbed the front of Brittany's shirt in her tiny hands. For someone so small, Hailey had quite the grip.

Mr. Rogers followed Daniel from the room, leaving Brittany alone with the baby. Hailey blew spit bubbles and giggled at her accomplishment. After a moment, she pushed away and tried to slide down Brittany's body.

"I take it you want to get down," Brittany said, bending to set the baby on the floor. Hailey bounced her bottom on the thick rug centered on the dark hardwood. A few seconds later, she got on all fours and crawled with amazing speed across the floor. When she reached a leather ottoman in front of an oversize chair near the unlit fireplace, she tried to pull herself up. Brittany crossed the room and sat on the floor beside her. "Well, let's see what you can do."

Hailey stopped moving long enough to string together a bunch of syllables before returning to her chosen task. When she was standing, Hailey looked at Brittany, let go of the furniture and wobbled for a moment before plopping back down on her bottom. Undaunted, she grabbed hold of the ottoman and began to climb again. Within seconds, she was on her feet. Chortling happily, she began bouncing up and down in what Brittany surmised was the baby version of the happy dance.

Brittany heard footsteps and placed a hand on the baby's back before turning around. Daniel was standing there. The color had drained from his face and he looked distraught. Shaken.

"Is everything okay?" Brittany asked.

He shook his head. "Look, I need a favor. I know this is an unusual request in a business meeting, but would you mind keeping an eye on Hailey for a while longer? I have no idea how long I'll be. I need to call my lawyer. I would ask one of my staff, but to be honest, she hasn't bonded with them the way she has with you. She cries when she's left with any of them. I'll pay you for your time, of course."

"Oh. Sure."

"I know this wasn't how you expected to spend your time and I appreciate your help."

"I'm a full-service event planner." Brittany smiled, but it wasn't returned.

"Thanks. I'll just be in my office. I'll be back as soon as I can."

Daniel was out of the room before Brittany could even nod.

"Intense. Your daddy is intense," Brittany said to Hailey.

"Bah," Hailey replied.

Brittany laughed. Although she hadn't planned on babysitting, spending time with Hailey was actually kind of fun. None of Brittany's siblings or close friends had infants, so she didn't spend much time with babies. Though she'd thought she'd gotten her fill of little ones when she'd been tasked with taking care of her siblings, she'd been wrong. Being with Hailey was a nice change of pace. Being responsible for Hailey wasn't something Brittany would choose to do every day, but today was novel and enjoyable.

Hailey let go of the ottoman, teetered on her feet then landed on her diapered bottom. Her lip quivered as if she was about to cry.

"Oh no you don't." Brittany scooped Hailey onto her lap then buried her face in her neck, kissing her sweet baby skin.

Hailey giggled, so Brittany did it again. Then she moved on to Hailey's chubby belly and planted kisses there, making Hailey laugh loud and long. They were still playing when Daniel returned. One look at the strained expression on his face and Brittany knew that the conversation with his lawyer hadn't gone the way he'd hoped.

Brittany stood, Hailey in her arms. "You don't look so good. Is there anything I can do to help?"

Daniel didn't say anything, but any number of emotions raced across his face, ranging from despair to hope before finally settling on determination.

"Actually, there is something you can do to help me."

"Name it."

"You can marry me."

"Say what now?"

"You can marry me," he said. Initially when he'd

blurted out the words, the idea was still forming in his mind and he'd been speaking out of desperation. But now that he'd said it, the idea was starting to take hold.

The first call he'd received had been from Craig Larimar's parents. Hailey's paternal grandparents. They'd only just learned that their son was dead and that their granddaughter was, in their words, living with a stranger in Montana. They demanded immediate custody of Hailey.

A few weeks ago, he might have been relieved that someone else wanted the responsibility of caring for Hailey. Back then, he would have been glad to be relegated to the role of doting uncle. He would have happily kept his bachelor lifestyle while making frequent visits to his niece. But that was then. This was now. It might not be official yet—something he intended to remedy immediately—but he loved Hailey as if she were his biological child. There was no way he would give her up without a fight. Besides, it was Jane's dying wish that he raise her child. He might have failed his sister in life, but there was no way he was going to fail her in death.

Unfortunately, since there was nothing in writing, his case wasn't as strong as he would have liked. As the Larimars astutely pointed out, they were a married couple while he was a bachelor with a reputation as a ladies' man.

Though his lawyer, John Kirkland, had told him

there was a good chance he would prevail in court, that wasn't good enough. Even the slightest possibility of losing Hailey was too great a risk. He needed to improve the odds so there was no doubt that the judge would grant him custody. John had mentioned that it was too bad Daniel wasn't married, planting an idea in Daniel's mind.

If he was going to compete with a married couple, he needed to have a wife by his side to balance the scales. And not just any woman. He needed someone who would impress the judge. Someone with an impeccable character. Most importantly, he needed someone who'd bonded with Hailey. Someone who Hailey responded to. He'd thought it was a fluke that first day when Hailey had seemed to like Brittany enough to let her pick her up. But after seeing them playing right now, he knew that Brittany would be the perfect person to bring into their lives until the custody battle with the Larimars was resolved.

He needed Brittany to marry him.

Brittany reared back and a confused expression crossed her beautiful face. Then she laughed. "Good one. And clever. You say something outrageous so I'll be more inclined to agree to what you really want. So now that you've shocked me, why don't you tell me what you actually want?"

"I want you to marry me."

She shook her head, handed Hailey to him and took a step back. "I think I need to leave."

He stepped in front of her and put a hand on her arm. "Wait. Please. I'm not doing a good job of explaining. I'm still trying to figure it all out. Give me a minute, okay?"

"A minute to what? What do you think is going to change in a minute? Or ten minutes?"

"Your mind?"

She stepped around him.

If he had a chance of convincing her to agree, he had to tell her everything about Jane and Hailey. "Hailey isn't my daughter. She's my niece, and I'm about to be engaged in a custody battle."

"Say what?"

"Can we sit down and talk?"

She hesitated for the longest seconds of his life. "Fine."

He put an arm around her waist and guided her toward the sofa. When they reached it, she perched on the edge, as if poised to flee if he made one false move. He'd made a mess of things. Rather than lead with a proposal, he should have given her the backstory and gained her sympathy. Heck, if he'd said it right, she might have been the one to bring up marriage. Well, it was too late to start over. He'd just have to plow through.

Daniel settled Hailey into her baby saucer. Once she was contentedly swatting at a purple star that bounced up and down, Daniel turned back to Brittany. "It's a long story."

"I have time. And if you plan on convincing me, I suggest you don't leave anything out."

"I'll start at the beginning."

"That's always the best place."

She still sounded shocked, but given the circumstances, that was to be expected. And she hadn't left, which gave him hope that she'd actually listen to what he had to say, and his fear subsided.

"Like I said, Hailey is my niece. She was my younger sister's daughter. Jane was wonderful. So pretty." He paused, letting the past wash over him.

"I remember the day my mom and dad brought her home from the hospital. She was so tiny. Even though I was only five, I knew she was special. I promised to be the best big brother in the world.

"I adored Jane and she loved me, too. She liked to follow me around when we were kids." He'd included her as much as he could when he'd played with his friends.

He looked at Brittany. She was following his story intently.

"As I got older, I focused more on my studies. Actually, school was kind of easy for me. I skipped second and fifth grades. I earned my high school diploma in three years and started college at sixteen. But I went to school out east, so it was too far away for me to visit a lot. When I did come home for summer vacations, I worked construction and spent time with my friends, and it didn't leave me a lot of time for Jane. Because I'd been distracted by my life, I hadn't noticed the changes in hers."

But he should have. And he would have if he'd bothered to look.

"What kind of changes?"

"Jane had struggled with depression and an eating disorder. Bulimia. She'd always been what our mother had referred to as 'pleasingly plump.' Jane hadn't seen her body that way. Neither had the bullies in her high school, whose taunts only echoed the dark emotions that plagued her, feelings she'd been powerless to control.

"Our parents were big believers in higher education, and they'd wanted her to go to college. But she'd hated school and couldn't wait to be done. When she graduated from high school, she got a job as a waitress and moved out of our parents' house. After that, she barely kept in touch with them. Or me."

That had hurt. He and Jane had been so close as children. He'd recognized his own responsibility in letting the relationship fade when he went away to school, and tried to keep in touch with her, but she'd grown distant, too. She hadn't wanted him in her life in any significant way.

"It was obvious that she was floundering. Our parents tried everything they could to help her, offering to go with her to therapy, but all of their efforts failed. They just hadn't been able to reach her."

Daniel, too, had done his best to help Jane, offering to help with her bills or help her find a therapist she would trust, but nothing seemed to work. Time and distance had severed the bonds that once had seemed unbreakable.

Once their parents were gone, Jane hadn't seen the need to maintain even minimal contact with him. May God forgive him, Daniel hadn't forced the issue. He hadn't tried as hard as he should have to remain a part of Jane's life. Her repeated rejections had torn him apart. He'd loved her and thought eventually she'd recognize that and come back around.

"Then one day she was gone without a trace. I searched for her, but she'd vanished. It was as if she'd dropped off the face of the earth. When I couldn't find her, I hired a private investigator. She tracked her to a house in a Dallas suburb. At the time, I was still living in Texas while this house was being built. She didn't look good, so I asked her to move in with me. Not for forever. Just long enough for her to get well. She said no."

He hadn't been trying to run her life as Jane had accused. All he'd wanted to do was help her get healthy. She'd been so distant. So aloof. It was as if she was no longer the little sister he'd adored. No, that sweet young woman had been replaced by a stranger. She'd claimed she needed to stay where she was. She hadn't elaborated. Nor had she mentioned being pregnant.

"I tried to keep in touch, asking her to meet for

lunch or dinner or just to talk on the phone, but Jane kept rejecting me. One day I showed up at her house only to discover that she'd moved out. She hadn't left a forwarding address. And she'd changed her cell phone number. She was gone."

He looked at Brittany and saw the sympathy in her eyes. He'd never revealed just how devastating Jane's rejection had been. He hadn't said the words, but he knew Brittany understood.

He tried to tell the story unemotionally, but his voice cracked on the last word. He cleared his throat and soldiered on. "I could have tracked her down again, but I didn't. What would have been the point? I decided to give her space, since that was apparently what she wanted. That was a horrible mistake." One he'd yet to get over.

"The next time I heard Jane's name was a little over a month ago from a police detective. She was dead."

"Oh, Daniel. I'm so sorry."

So was he. But that didn't change a thing. The little sister he'd adored was gone. He'd failed her and now he'd never get a chance to make it up to her.

While grief and sorrow had pounded Daniel's heart like a fist, the officer had continued talking. Jane had had a daughter. Daniel was her next of kin. Would he be willing to take care of his niece?

"That's when I found out about Hailey. Jane and the baby's father, Craig Larimar, had been in a car accident. Hailey had been strapped in her car seat, so she hadn't been harmed at all. Craig died at the scene. Jane…" He swallowed "They rushed Jane to the hospital, where she survived for a few hours. While she was there, she gave one of the nurses my name and told the nurse that she wanted me to raise Hailey."

Heartbroken over the loss of his sister, and grateful to have her child in his life, he'd brought Hailey home with him that day.

"Despite all my money, I couldn't help Jane. I couldn't make things better for her. Couldn't protect her from the world. I may have failed my sister, but I won't fail her child."

Brittany placed her hand over his. The warmth from her skin soothed some of the hurt in deep places he hadn't had a hope would ever stop aching.

"Looks to me like you're doing a great job. Hailey is happy and loved."

"That might not be enough now."

"Why not?"

"The phone call I just received was from Craig Larimar's parents. Apparently, they plan to sue me for custody of Hailey."

"I don't see what the problem is. Your sister wanted you to raise Hailey. Therefore you should win the case easily."

"I have no written proof of that. She didn't have a will. And she'd never even mentioned me to any of her friends. Not only that, they're a couple. I'm a single man. And before I had Hailey to think about, I lived like a single man. I dated. A lot."

"So? That doesn't make you a bad person."

"But it doesn't make me father material, either."

"Says who? Single men can be great dads."

"I'll have a better chance of winning if I have a wife. Then it will be one married couple versus another. And we're younger, so that should give us the advantage."

"We?"

"Yes. We." He infused his voice with more confidence than he felt.

"I didn't agree to marry you." Her voice quivered, but he didn't know her well enough to tell if it was from nerves or irritation. Neither was welcome.

He tapped the tips of his fingers together, trying to cover his concern. Desperation was growing within him, but he didn't want her to see his weakness. This argument wasn't working. He needed to find a different way to convince her.

"What do you want, Brittany?"

"What do you mean what do I want?"

"I want to raise Hailey. Not just to honor my sister's wishes, but because I love her." He paused. "You're smart. Ambitious. Too smart and ambitious to work for someone else for the rest of your life."

"So?" She sounded cautious, but she hadn't gotten up and left.

"You'll want to open your own event planning business one day. I can help you do that. If you marry me, I'll give you all the money you need to start your business. Not only that, I'll introduce you to my friends and business associates, and suggest that they hire you to plan their events. With my help, your business will become a nationally recognized event planning company in no time."

"And all I have to do is marry you."

The flat tone of her voice worried him, but still he nodded. "Yes."

She slowly rose and straightened her shoulders, standing as erect as a queen. Luscious lips pinched and eyes narrowed, she glared at him. "I'm not for sale. Not to you or to anyone. I can't speak for Bronco Elite, but as for me, I will no longer be working on your party." She picked up the folder she'd brought him. "And you, Daniel Dubois, can go straight to hell."

"Wait." He reached for her to try to explain, but she brushed by him and out of the room. He hadn't meant to offend her. He'd only wanted to show her how marrying him could benefit both of them. Usually he was so much more eloquent than this. The fear of losing Hailey had turned him into a bumbling idiot.

Sagging back onto the couch, he decided that it was best to retreat and regroup. He'd shocked her. That was clear now. Given time, she would see the benefit of the deal he was offering and come around. A marriage between them would be a win-win situation.

Now he just had to come up with a plan to convince her.

Chapter Five

Brittany stormed down the walk, jumped into her car and sped down the driveway. Inhaling deeply, she tried to center herself, but she couldn't. She was too furious. Had that man really tried to buy her like a piece of meat? She wanted to own her own company, but selling herself wasn't part of the plan. She'd go back to working for that money-hungry Evan Cruise and that ghost tours company first. She couldn't believe Daniel Dubois thought so poorly of her that he believed she would sell herself. True, they'd only known each other for a short time, so he didn't know her character, but she'd thought he'd respected her as a person. Boy, had she been wrong.

As Brittany neared her office, she began to calm down. The conversation with Daniel, though insulting, was now in the past. Since she'd let him know in no uncertain terms that she was not for sale, she didn't expect to repeat the conversation anytime soon. But as she stepped into the building, worry began to gnaw at her insides.

Daniel Dubois was a powerful man who clearly thought he was entitled to whatever he believed his money could buy. What if he'd called her boss to complain? What if he'd insisted that she be fired, thinking that putting financial pressure on her might force her to give in to his demand? She wouldn't have suspected him of being that low before, but now? Now, she wouldn't put anything past him.

Stepping inside the office, she looked around. Linnea, her boss, smiled as she came toward Brittany. "How did your meeting go?"

Brittany wasn't sure how to answer that. Mentioning that she'd told a client to go to hell didn't seem the way to go if she wanted to advance her career. Even if Linnea was willing to listen to Brittany's explanation, what could she say? That Daniel wanted to marry her so he'd have a better chance of keeping custody of his niece? That might convince Linnea not to fire her, but Brittany knew Daniel didn't want anyone to know about Hailey. Even as hurt and angry—and yes, disappointed—as she was, she wouldn't betray his confidence. She had integrity even if he didn't.

Brittany opened her mouth to answer Linnea's question as honestly as possible when Reese, another one of the event planners, approached. "Sorry to interrupt. Linnea, do you have a minute?"

Linnea looked at Brittany, who nodded. "We can catch up later. I don't have anything new to tell you at this point."

"Good enough," Linnea said as she and Reese walked away.

Brittany sighed with relief as she went to her office and closed the door. She didn't know how such a perfectly planned day had gone awry, but it had. Now she had to figure out how to get the proverbial train back on the tracks.

She managed to keep her mind focused on work for the rest of the day. Since she hadn't been summoned to her boss's office and read the riot act, she surmised that Daniel hadn't called to complain. And since she didn't want to mention to her boss that she'd told a client to go to hell, there was no way around it. She was going to have to plan the event. That meant she was going to have to meet with him again. They hadn't discussed the details of the party today and she still needed him to sign off on her ideas and menu suggestions.

Given his home situation, she didn't expect him to come to her office. She doubted he'd be leaving his ranch in the next few days. So she had no choice but to meet with him at his house again. Fine. She was a professional. She could handle that. She'd do whatever was necessary to get this project over and done with as soon as possible so she wouldn't have to see him again.

But she wouldn't mind seeing that cutie pie Hailey again. Not that she was becoming attached to that sweet baby. She wasn't. Brittany had just enjoyed spending time with her, that was all.

Amanda wasn't home when Brittany got there, so she decided to make an early night of it. After soaking in the tub long enough for her fingers to prune, she smoothed on lotion, put on her favorite silk pajamas, wrapped her hair and then got into bed. Closing her eyes, Brittany instantly fell asleep. But instead of her normal peaceful rest, she dreamed she was alone in her apartment. There was a baby crying, but no matter where Brittany looked, she couldn't find the baby. The crying grew louder and more despondent, and Brittany became more frantic in her futile search. She called out to the baby that she was coming, but she never did find the child and the crying never stopped.

Brittany awoke with a jerk, tangled in her sheets. Sitting up, she wiped a palm across her sweaty forehead. She leaned against the headboard and then checked the clock on her bedside table. Four thirty. Way too early to get up, yet she didn't think she'd be able to fall asleep again. She wasn't sure she wanted to. She might not be a psychiatrist, but even she could interpret this dream. She was worried about Hailey. What would happen to her if she was taken from Daniel and placed with her grandparents? Would the older couple love her the way Daniel obviously did? Would all of the upheaval at such a young age affect her ability to bond with people in the future?

Brittany frowned. Why was she so worried about it? This wasn't her problem. She'd only just met Daniel and Hailey. Besides, Daniel had money and could afford the best lawyers. He could solve this problem without her help.

Brittany grabbed the mystery she'd been reading, determined to distract herself from a problem that wasn't hers. When, after finishing a few chapters, she still was on edge, she rose and took extra care getting ready for work. She wouldn't be able to function until she had clarified her status with Daniel. If they were going to move ahead with the party, she needed his approval. If not, she needed to know that, too.

She decided to stop by his ranch before going to the office to leave the information with Marta or Mr. Rogers.

Pulling into the driveway, she thought of one of her favorite movies, *Groundhog Day,* where the main character kept living the same day over and over. This wasn't quite the same, but she was spending quite a bit of time at the Dubois ranch trying to get Daniel to look at her work. Maybe today he actually would.

When the front door swung open, she was once again greeted by his smiling housekeeper. Despite Brittany's protests, Marta insisted on ushering her inside, through a different wing than she'd used before, and into an enormous kitchen. There were oceans of marble countertops, professional-grade appliances and cabinets that reached the high ceiling. The feature she liked the most was the wall of glass doors with its gorgeous view of nature. If she'd had even the slightest interest in cooking, this would be her dream kitchen.

Daniel was seated at the table, feeding Hailey, who was sitting in her high chair. The remains of a smashed banana and baby cereal were smeared in a plastic bowl. Bits of food were in Hailey's hair and on her face and scattered on the stone floor.

Daniel was so focused on getting Hailey to eat that he hadn't noticed Brittany enter the room, so she took a moment to study him. His broad shoulders moved beneath his shirt as he lifted the spoon to Hailey's mouth. The baby turned her head away from him and spotted Brittany. She babbled a few excited syllables while reaching out to Brittany.

Daniel turned his head and, when he saw Brittany, jumped to his feet. He brushed a hand over his shirt then flicked a gray lump of dried baby food onto the table. "I didn't think I would see you again."

He didn't sound particularly aggravated. Actually he sounded relieved, which made her heartrate slow down.

"We never did discuss my ideas for the party. So, if you still want to work with my firm, I'm hoping you have time now."

"Of course I want to work with your firm, and you specifically. If I made you believe otherwise, I apologize. I really want to hear your ideas." He looked over at Hailey, who'd eaten all the breakfast she intended to eat and was straining against the belt securing her in the chair.

"I guess I should have called first."

"It wouldn't have made a difference. As you can see, we're already awake."

Brittany nodded. She knew from experience that there was no such thing as sleeping late with a baby in the house.

"And since my nanny search is going nowhere, I'm pretty much held captive in this house." He blew out a breath. "I have a few more agencies to call, but I'm not holding out hope. Until I find the right nanny, I'll be taking care of Hailey on my own." He removed the bowl from the tray and started to take Hailey from the high chair.

"You might want to wipe off her hands and face first. It'll save your clothes. And walls."

"Thanks. I should have thought of that." He dampened a dish towel and then cleaned the food from Hailey's hands and face. She protested a bit but didn't cry. When he was finished, he freed the baby and held her against his chest. "Let's go to the family room. She has toys there and we can go over everything."

Once Hailey was settled on the play mat, surrounded by toys, Daniel and Brittany sat on the couch. Brittany reached for her satchel, but Daniel put a hand on her wrist, stopping her. Electricity shot out from where their skin connected and raced through her body. *Darn it. Why was this still happening?*

"Before we start, I want to apologize to you. Again. I realize now how offensive my proposal must have sounded. I wasn't as eloquent as I would have liked to have been."

"Forget about it. I have." That wasn't exactly true. She'd thought about his crazy proposal more than she should have. In fact, it was all she could think of. But he didn't need to know that.

"I can't. I still think that having a wife will be the equalizer I need in the custody case. I'm a single man. It's no secret that I'm busy. Even though I work from home, I still put in long hours. A wife will help me prove that I can give Hailey a stable home."

"And you think a quickie marriage to your event planner will give you some sort of advantage?"

"I know you think it sounds outrageous, but hear me out." He leaned forward, his elbows on his knees. His voice was intent yet earnest. "We can make it work. I've seen you in action. You can easily accomplish anything you set your mind to. I believe you can play the role of wife and mother well enough to convince any social worker or judge that Hailey belongs here with me."

Brittany laughed. "I'm not some Mary Poppins or Suzie Homemaker. In case you haven't noticed, I'm not exactly maternal. I'm focused on my career. You were right. I do want to own my own business. All the social worker will have to do is ask a few people about me and your plan will crumble."

"So, you'll be a working mother. That's not so unusual."

She sputtered. "And I'm not much of a cook."

"You don't need to be. In case you haven't noticed, I employ a cook. And a housekeeper. All I need is for someone to play the role of wife and mother for the judge. I can take care of the rest."

She cleared her throat. "That's all?"

"What else would there be?"

She simply looked at him.

After a moment, his eyes narrowed as he understood her meaning. "I don't need to pay for female companionship. Not to be arrogant, but I have women throwing themselves at me all the time. I don't have to coerce a woman to get her into my bed."

Brittany fought off the twinge of something that felt suspiciously like jealousy at the idea of another woman being in Daniel's bed. She brushed the idiotic thought aside. "Well, if you're so popular with the ladies, why don't you simply catch one of the ones throwing themselves at you?"

His mouth compressed as if he was suppressing a grin. When he spoke, there wasn't the least bit of mirth in his tone, so maybe she'd imagined the reaction. "Because Hailey has already bonded with you. That's rare for her. I won't be able to convince the judge that Hailey and my new wife have a loving mother/daughter relationship if Hailey fusses every time my wife comes within six feet of her. You might not think you're the maternal type, but you do a good imitation. I'm convinced that you care about Hailey enough to fool the judge or social worker.

"As I said a minute ago, ours would be a marriage of convenience. I'm willing to put that in writing, if that will make you feel better about our arrangement. Once a judge grants me full custody of Hailey, we can get an annulment. Then I'll give you any amount of money you want to finance your company. And I'll recommend you far and wide. I can have my attorney draw up everything. Or you can hire your own lawyer to represent your interests."

Her interests. He made it sound cut and dried— like a simple business deal. And to him, it was. But marriage was so much more than a business arrangement to advance one's cause, no matter how noble that cause might be. Her parents had been married for thirty-five years. Though Brittany had never liked the distribution of duties—she thought her mother did more than her share of the housework and caring for the kids—she never once doubted her parents' devotion to one another. Her biological clock might not be ticking now, but she did want to get married one day and have the kind of marriage her parents had. Minus the kids.

"I'm sorry, Daniel. I just can't say yes. I hope my decision doesn't interfere with our working relationship. I know I can help you get your resort off to a great start."

He seemed to deflate with every word she spoke. Still, he didn't press her. "I'm sure you can."

She was under no obligation to marry him—in fact, she'd been clear from the beginning that she wouldn't. So why did guilt prick her conscience as if she'd done something wrong?

His cell phone rang. He checked the Caller ID and glanced at her. "Excuse me. I need to take this call."

"Of course."

Brittany didn't want to eavesdrop, so she went over to where Hailey was playing with brightly colored stackable plastic doughnuts and sat. Brittany's younger brothers had also had this toy and had played with it for hours on end. Hailey was chewing on the orange ring. She pulled the plastic from her mouth and, grinning, offered it to Brittany.

"No thanks. I only eat the yellow ones."

Hailey chortled as if she understood Brittany's joke.

Though she tried not to listen, she could hear Daniel's conversation. It was clear from his words that he wasn't succeeding in finding a nanny for Hailey. Would that hurt him in the custody case? If so, what would happen to the little tyke?

Finally, he ended the call and she returned to her seat.

"I guess you heard all that."

"Yes. I couldn't help but overhear."

"You must think I'm a manipulative jerk, but I'm not. I'm just desperate. Jane wanted me to raise Hailey. I have to fight for her. And win. That means that no tactic is off the table. I failed my sister when she was alive. I should have known something was seriously wrong, but I didn't. I was so wrapped up in my own life and my own hurt feelings."

"It's not your fault. You didn't see her problems because she hid them from you. She shut you out of her life because she didn't want you to know about her troubles."

"I should have been there for her. Tried harder. I can't go back and fight for her. She's gone. But Hailey's here and I'm not going to give up on her. It's just the two of us. I can't lose her, too.

"I'm sorry for suggesting that you marry me. You're trying to do your job and I put you in an awkward position. It didn't help that in my frantic state I let you believe I was trying to force you."

"I understand. I know your heart was in the right place." The sorrow in Daniel's voice touched Brittany's heart. She came from a big family and couldn't imagine losing any of them, much less all but one of them. Holding on to that lone remaining family member might make her a little desperate, too. Who knew what crazy scheme she'd come up with if their positions were reversed? Maybe she would propose the same thing.

Brittany was no lawyer, so she didn't know the legal ins and outs of a custody case. Nor did she know what judges thought was important when making a decision. This judge might believe that a little girl needed a woman's influence. Right or wrong, wasn't that something most of society believed? Would a judge be any different? It hit her then. Though she didn't think he should lose the court case, there was a real chance that Daniel could lose the custody battle.

His voice broke into her thoughts. "Well, enough of my woes. I'll think of something. Let's look at what you have in mind for my dinner."

They tried to discuss Brittany's plans, but his heart didn't appear to be into it any more than hers was. Only Hailey, who was oblivious to the adult worries, was unbothered. She babbled happily to herself, setting the plastic rings on top of her head and then bending over and letting them slide off. When it became clear that they were each too distracted to focus, Brittany decided to leave the plans with him and suggested that they meet another day.

Daniel agreed and she gathered her belongings. Brittany went over to Hailey and scooped the little girl into her arms, giving her a long hug before handing her to Daniel. Since Brittany was leaving the material for Daniel to review, she wouldn't need to show up on his doorstep tomorrow morning. She might have only spent a little bit of time with Hailey, but the little girl had wiggled her way into Brittany's heart. She was going to miss her. And though she would definitely never say it out loud, Brittany was going to miss Daniel, too.

The rest of the day passed by in a blur and Brittany was glad to get home. She'd gotten a few questioning looks and more than one raised eyebrow when she'd told her coworkers she'd be skipping happy hour, but nobody pressed her for a reason. She was the furthest thing from happy and didn't think she could fake it. Daniel might believe she was a great actress, but she knew better. Her feelings always showed on her face.

She changed from her work clothes into a pair of shorts and a T-shirt before pouring a glass of wine and going outside to sit on her balcony. The weather was just perfect. Although her view was nowhere near as beautiful as Daniel's, it was still pleasant. Normally sitting out here and letting the cool evening breeze wash over her soothed her. Today the magic was lacking. After twenty minutes, she was still troubled. Still confused.

If she didn't know better, she'd think Daniel was trying to trick her into agreeing to marry him by appearing to back off. But she did know better. He took the direct approach. Besides, no one could fake that kind of agony. His heart was aching at the possibility of losing his little girl. Brittany had seen the way he was with Hailey. He adored her. And Hailey adored him right back. They belonged together.

So what was she going to do about it? Could she really live with herself if Hailey and Daniel were torn apart when she'd had the ability to prevent it? Hailey had already lost her parents before she was old enough to know them. She didn't deserve to lose Daniel, too. And Daniel didn't deserve to lose his only remaining family member.

Muttering to herself that she was out of her mind, Brittany picked up her phone and dialed Daniel's number. When he answered, she didn't waste time with a greeting.

"I'll do it. I'll marry you."

Chapter Six

"Would you say that again?" Daniel asked. He needed confirmation that he hadn't imagined Brittany's words.

Her voice came over the phone loud and clear. "I said I'll marry you."

Relief surged through him, momentarily making him weak, and he sagged against his desk. "What changed your mind?"

"You and Hailey belong together. Anyone can see that. I want to do my part to even the odds. I would never forgive myself if you lost Hailey and I hadn't tried to help you."

His chest tightened and, for a minute, he couldn't

speak. He knew Brittany was a kind woman, but he'd begun to believe that marrying him so he could keep custody of Hailey had been too much of a sacrifice even for her. A part of him knew that his request was out of bounds. He wasn't going to retract it, though. Not if it meant losing Hailey.

"But I do have a condition."

"Name it. Anything you want is yours." He'd sign over his fortune if that's what she wanted.

"I'm renting a condo with a good friend. When I move, I want you to cover my share of the rent until our lease expires. I don't want to leave Amanda in the lurch."

"No problem. I'll give you a check for the balance of the rent immediately."

"What exactly are we going to tell people?" she asked.

"It's nobody's business."

"That may be true, but we have to tell them something. Otherwise they'll make up a story we might not want getting around."

"We'll tell people whatever you want."

She sighed. "Fine. We'll say it was a whirlwind courtship."

"Sounds good. How long will it take you to plan the wedding?"

"That depends on what you're looking for."

"You're the event planner, not me. Money is no object. I just want to get it over and done with."

Silence was her only reply and Daniel knew he'd made a mistake. Brittany understood that time was of the essence, but still, he could have been more tactful. "I didn't mean that the way it sounded."

She laughed, but it wasn't the joyous sound he'd heard on other occasions. "Of course you did. But it's fine. You're right. We do need to do this quickly. But since it's not going to be a real marriage, there's no need for an elaborate wedding. We can just get a license and get married at city hall."

She'd said all the right words, but he didn't get the sense that they'd come from her heart. Even though this was going to be a fake marriage, she was going to be a real bride. In the eyes of the law and everyone she knew, she was going to be his wife. As such, she deserved more than saying a few bland words in front of an indifferent judge.

"I think we can do better than that. What about a small party at DJ's Deluxe? We'll invite your family and our closest friends. How does that sound?"

"It sounds good. And speaking of family, you're going to have to meet mine. There's no way I can simply tell my parents I'm getting married to someone they've never met, no matter what kind of wedding we have. But if we have a ceremony, they have to be there. I can't get married without them."

"Of course not. Just name the time and the place."

"How about my parents' home on Sunday? The entire family gathers for dinner after church."

"The whole family? Just how many are we talking about?"

"My parents and my two brothers and two sisters. Sometimes a few aunts, uncles and cousins come by. But I'll ask my parents to limit it to just immediate family."

"I'd appreciate that." Brittany's family was a complication he hadn't considered. But if they were going to be convincing as a couple, he'd have to meet the in-laws.

"You can move in here after the ceremony. And although I've said it before, I'll say it anyway. There won't be a honeymoon or romantic wedding night. I hope that puts your mind at ease." Though he knew the marriage wouldn't be real, part of him regretted the fact that he wouldn't be sharing a bed with Brittany. She was a beautiful, sexy woman with a loving heart; the type of woman he'd want to marry if he ever chose to get married.

"It does."

The relief in her voice was proof her thoughts were miles away from his. He might find her desirable, but she was only marrying him to help him win the custody suit and to get seed money and recommendations for her business venture. This was a business arrangement. Sleeping together was the last thing on her mind. That was good. They didn't need the complications a sexual relationship would bring.

Once he won the custody battle, they'd get an annulment and put the marriage behind them.

"Have you contacted a lawyer yet?" Daniel asked her. "We need to iron out the prenup. In my experience, having everything spelled out and in writing saves trouble down the line."

"I'm not after your money."

"I know that. But I still intend to uphold my end of the bargain. I offered you money to start your business and I intend to provide it. That's not negotiable. We both need to benefit from this deal."

"Okay. I'll hire someone to represent me."

"Thank you. What are you doing tomorrow?"

"Wednesday is my day off." She paused. "I have some errands to run, but nothing pressing. Why?"

"Can you meet me in town for lunch? We need to iron out the details."

"Isn't that what we're doing now?"

"Humor me," he quipped.

"Okay. I can always come by your ranch, if it's easier."

"No. We need to meet in Bronco."

"What about Hailey?" she asked. "You don't want people finding out about her."

"That can't be helped now. She's obviously going to be at the wedding. Besides, if we want to convince people our relationship is real, we need to be seen around town together. We might as well start now."

* * *

The doorbell pealed and Brittany jumped, which was a ridiculous reaction. Daniel had told her he'd be here at eleven thirty and it was eleven thirty on the nose. Telling herself to stop being foolish, she crossed the room and opened the door so Daniel, Hailey in his arms, could enter.

Despite telling herself that she wasn't interested in him romantically, her heart jumped at the sight of him. Dressed in a heather-gray shirt and black jeans, he looked ready to star in a romantic movie. His eyes lit up when he saw her and warmth flowed through her body in return.

Reminding herself that this was only make-believe, she stepped aside. "Come on in. I just need to grab my purse."

"Sure."

Daniel stepped inside and looked around. "Nice place."

"Thanks. I've been happy living here. Of course, the views from my balcony can't compete with those on your ranch."

"That's good to hear. Otherwise I would feel bad for pulling you away from your home and moving you to a ranch in the middle of nowhere."

Her home. Only now did she realize that she might not return to this condo after their marriage was annulled. Amanda could be married by then and living with Holt. Unless Brittany found a new roommate, she'd need to find a new place to live. But she'd made her decision and wasn't going to back out now. She'd worry about tomorrow's problems tomorrow.

She draped her purse strap over her shoulder then led them out the door.

When they were in his car, she turned to him. "So you said we had a stop to make before lunch. Where are we going?"

"The jewelry store."

"What? Why?"

"To get your engagement ring, of course."

"I don't need an engagement ring. A simple wedding band is more than enough."

"No way. There is absolutely no way we can convince anyone that our engagement is real if you aren't wearing a diamond. Anyone who knows me knows that I would give my fiancée an engagement ring."

"Maybe. But anyone who knows me knows I'm not a gold-digger."

"It's simply a ring. A tradition. No one will think anything bad about you for wearing it."

"Okay. But I don't want you to think that, either."

Daniel laughed. "Trust me, Brittany. As hard as I had to work to convince you to marry me, the thought never crossed my mind."

"Just so you know."

"I do. Consider the point made. Now let's get this show on the road."

Although Bronco wasn't the biggest town in Montana, it was quite wealthy. With affluent ranchers living nearby, and tourism that catered to the rich and famous, the town had several businesses that served those for whom money was no object. One such store was Beaumont and Rossi's Fine Jewels. The items sold there were exquisite and one of a kind, often personally designed. Brittany had saved up for months to purchase a pair of teardrop diamond earrings. Other than that one visit, she hadn't stepped foot inside the store.

When Daniel parked, she put a hand on his wrist, stopping him. "Are we really going to buy a ring here?"

"Of course."

"Do you know how much they cost?"

"I have an idea, yes."

Before she could protest, he was out of the car and unstrapping Hailey from her car seat. With no choice but to follow, Brittany got out of the car then walked beside him. Acutely aware of the attention they were drawing, she pasted on a smile and tried not to think about the conversations that would be burning up the phone lines over the next hours. Though she would figure in them prominently, she knew most of the attention would be devoted to Daniel and the sweet baby in his arms.

The good citizens of Bronco had done their best to find out about Daniel, but the only knowledge anyone had gleaned had come from old media accounts.

He'd done a spectacular job of keeping his personal life private. Now he was strolling down Bronco's Main Street with a baby in one arm and Brittany on the other. From the carefree way he smiled as they entered the jewelry store, he wasn't bothered by the scrutiny. Or perhaps that was part of his plan. The more people who saw the three of them together, the more believable their story would be. This was one scene in the play he was writing and Brittany was simply a bit actor.

A well-dressed gentleman approached them. "How may I help you?"

There were several other patrons admiring the jeweled creations, but other than glancing up to see who'd entered, they paid little attention to the newcomers.

"I have an appointment with Angelique. The name is Daniel Dubois."

"Of course. Follow me."

"An appointment?" Brittany whispered as they were whisked behind a curtain and into a private room.

"Yes. I've hired Angelique to design your ring. From what I've been told, she's one of the most talented designers in the country."

"Would you like a beverage?" the gentleman said in a cultured voice. "Juice for the baby?"

"No, thank you," Brittany said, replying for all of them. She took a seat on the plush sofa.

"Very good. Angelique will be right in." The man exited quietly.

Brittany looked around the elegant room. Gray silk curtains flanked the floor-to-ceiling windows and a gray-and-blue-patterned tapestry hung from the ceiling behind the enormous desk at the far end of the room. Vases of fresh flowers subtly perfumed the air.

A door opened and a willowy woman dressed in a black silk blouse and a black pencil skirt crossed the thick carpet until she stood in front of them. Her natural hair was styled in a massive curly afro. Silver earrings dangled from her ears. "How do you do? I'm Angelique. I'm pleased to be designing your wedding rings."

Brittany and Daniel introduced themselves. Daniel had brought a play mat for Hailey and he spread it on the floor while Brittany pulled several toys from the diaper bag. Hailey was content to play while the adults chatted.

"What kind of ring do you have in mind?"

Brittany glanced at Daniel. This was his show. He'd nixed her idea of a plain gold band, so she was going to let him take charge.

"Something original without being too showy. Something beautiful and classy that demands attention without being ostentatious. Like my fiancée."

Daniel sounded so smitten that Brittany herself could almost believe he loved her.

"Are you looking for a diamond or another jewel?" Angelique asked. "Or a combination?"

Brittany shrugged. "I've never given thought to anything other than the traditional solitaire."

"Are we going with platinum?"

"Yes," Daniel replied before Brittany could say that gold would do.

"I'd like to ask a couple of questions about your relationship to get a sense of you as a couple. I'll design while we talk."

"You're going to come up with a ring just by listening to me?" Brittany was skeptical for a minute but then decided to give it a try. It wasn't too different from what she did as an event planner. From mere conversations with her client, she'd designed the most perfect parties. And if Angelique created something Brittany didn't like, would it really matter? It wasn't as if Brittany planned to keep the ring. It was a prop in the play she and Daniel were producing and she planned to return it when their marriage was annulled.

"Yes." Angelique grabbed a sketchpad and pencils then smiled. "I'm ready when you are."

Brittany inhaled, then looked at Daniel. Suddenly she felt vulnerable, knowing she was about to reveal herself in front of him. She could lie, but why bother? It wasn't as if Daniel actually cared about the real her. She just fit the role of wife and mother he needed filled.

"Ask away," Brittany said.

"I'll start with something easy. What first attracted you to Daniel?"

"His body," Brittany replied without thinking. When she realized what she'd just said, her face heated and she made sure not to look in his direction.

"I see," Angelique said as she drew on the paper.

"But it was more than the way he looked. It was his presence. His confidence. His essence. He has a way of taking over a room, commanding attention without even trying."

"So does that makes you the power behind the throne?" Angelique asked, looking up.

"No."

"Yes," Daniel said instantly.

"Interesting," Angelique said with a knowing smile.

Just what was that supposed to mean?

"What is your relationship like?"

Whew. Brittany had no idea the questions were going to be like *this.* What ever happened to asking about her favorite color?

"It's fine," Brittany said and then winced. A generic store brand fake fiancée could do better than that. She took a breath and tried again. What would her perfect relationship with her imaginary fiancé be like? "It's good because we respect each other. We each have a strong personality, so that makes discussions interesting. But we respect each other, so our conversations are always fair."

"What is your dream for your life together?"

"To always be in love. To spend each day doing something to make the other happy and fulfilled. To work to make each other's dream a reality."

Brittany glanced over at Daniel. He was staring at her as if he'd never seen her before. Had she revealed too much? She certainly hoped not. This marriage was going to be in name only and she intended to keep each of her emotions to herself.

Angelique made a couple of marks on the pad and, with a flourish, turned it around to reveal the sketch.

Brittany took one look at the drawing and gasped in amazement. The ring was nothing short of spectacular. It was a beautiful sapphire surrounded by numerous diamonds. "It's perfect. Exactly what I would have pictured if I could have imagined it. Can you really make that?"

Angelique clapped her hands in obvious glee. "I don't make the rings, but yes, the jeweler can make this for you."

"It is perfect," Daniel chimed in.

Angelique explained her design. "Listening to you talk, I knew that a simple elegant diamond, while beautiful, wouldn't capture your essence or that of your relationship with your fiancé. For you, I chose an oval-cut blue sapphire surrounded by round and marquis-cut diamonds. The design is inspired by the blue jasmine flower, which is a symbol of honesty and trust. The same qualities that are evident between the two of you. The blue jasmine also symbolizes that a woman is ready to give her heart to that special someone, as you clearly are."

Brittany suddenly felt uneasy. Apparently, she'd played the role of devoted fiancée a little too well. And now she was going to be stuck wearing a ring that symbolized a lie.

She knew she should have gotten a basic diamond that didn't stand for anything. Or better yet, she should have stuck to her guns and insisted on a plain gold band. It was too late now. There was no turning back.

"When can the ring be ready?" Daniel asked.

"It can take between two and four weeks."

"No. That's too long. We'd like to be married before then, so we need to expedite the process. Money is no object, so your store will be generously compensated."

Angelique's eyes darted to Brittany's flat stomach before returning to Daniel's eyes. "Of course. I'll speak with the jeweler right away. I shouldn't be more than a moment."

"She thinks I'm pregnant," Brittany said when the woman left.

"Does it matter?"

"It will when word reaches my parents."

"We're having dinner with them this Sunday. Surely the gossips won't beat us there. Besides, I can't imagine she'd risk losing our business by spreading baseless gossip."

"You could be right."

"I am."

The conversation ended with the arrival of the jeweler. He introduced himself as Amos Rossi and he immediately assured Daniel that the ring would be made in record time without sacrificing quality.

"If you want to sign off on the design now, I can put together a selection of sapphires and diamonds for you to choose from. They'll be ready for your review in two hours, if that suits you. You can choose the ones you like and I can begin work on your ring immediately."

"That works for us," Daniel said.

Apparently, they were doing this.

Brittany put Hailey's toys into the diaper bag as the baby began to fuss.

"Hailey and I will go for a little walk outside while you wrap up the details," Brittany told Daniel then looked at Angelique and Mr. Rossi. "It was very nice meeting both of you."

She hurried through the store, hoping to make it outside without attracting too much attention. Hailey liked the faster pace and her fussing turned into giggles.

There was a wrought-iron bench a short distance from the jewelry store, so Brittany headed there. She sat then stood Hailey on her lap. Gurgling happily, the baby bounced up and down.

Ten minutes later, Daniel joined them, sitting beside Brittany. "Would you like to get something to eat or would you rather do more shopping?"

"Shopping for what?" What else did he think she needed?

"Your wedding dress, of course."

"I'm not the superstitious type, but I believe it's bad luck for the groom to see the bride in the wedding dress ahead of time. Besides, I'm perfectly capable of picking out my own dress."

"I'll pay for it."

"No, you won't. I have money of my own."

"I'm sure you do. But I don't see why you should bear that burden when you're doing me the favor."

"It's not a favor." Calling it a favor gave the appearance that they were friends instead of business associates. There was nothing personal between them and she'd better not forget it. "We have a deal, remember? I get my business out of this. I consider the dress as one of my expenses." Her voice came out sharper than she'd intended, and Daniel winced.

"What's wrong?"

"Nothing." Nothing other than the fact that for a brief moment she'd lost control of her feelings and revealed more than she'd wanted. To him and to herself.

"You seem upset."

"I'm not." How could she explain that designing the wedding ring had been something she could only fantasize about? This whole fake marriage was becoming more confusing by the minute. And they hadn't even spoken their vows yet.

She'd gotten swept up in the emotional moment, forgetting that the ring didn't symbolize their promise of love. It had been all too easy to pretend that the romance they were perpetrating was real. But it wasn't. If Brittany wasn't careful, she would end up with hurt feelings at best and a broken heart at worst.

Chapter Seven

Brittany paced her apartment all the while telling herself to relax. Taking a deep breath, she counted to three and then slowly blew it out, then checked her appearance in the mirror. It wouldn't do to look stressed today of all days. She was taking Daniel to meet her family in a few minutes. Not only were her parents living lie detectors, but her siblings would also be able to pick up on her stress. The last thing she needed was to make any of them suspicious.

She'd chosen to wear a simple pink-and-orange sleeveless cotton floral dress with an orange short-sleeved cropped sweater. Although dinners at her parents' house was always casual, she'd felt the need to be a little dressier today. After all, she was arriving with her fiancé.

Her doorbell rang and she squared her shoulders. She could do this.

She opened the door and Daniel stood there, holding Hailey in his arms. When the baby saw Brittany, she babbled a few syllables and reached out to her. Though Brittany had no intention of having children of her own, there was something about Hailey's joy at seeing her that warmed Brittany's heart and made her smile. Taking the tyke from Daniel, she led them into her living room. Hailey strained to get down, so Brittany set her on the floor.

"I'm ready to go. I just need to get my purse," Brittany said.

"Actually, let's sit down a minute." His voice didn't sound as confident as it usually did, and a sliver of worry crawled down her spine.

"Okay." She sat on the sofa and Daniel sat beside her. Unbothered, Hailey sat at their feet and pushed buttons on her musical toy turtle. "What's up?"

Daniel tapped his foot three times. He sucked in a breath and patted his knee. She didn't know why he was suddenly nervous, but he was stressing her out.

"Okay," he said softly, and she wondered whether he was talking to her or his invisible friend. He cleared his throat, then stood. A heartbeat later he knelt in front of her and took her hand in his.

Wait. Was he? *Oh my goodness.* He was. Her heart skipped a beat, then began to race.

"Brittany, I know that we have not known each other long and that this isn't going to be a traditional marriage, but I promise to be the best husband that I know how. I'll always respect you and support your dreams. I'll help you to become your best self." He inhaled and his shirt tightened over his muscular chest. "Will you do me the honor of becoming my wife?"

Her heart stuttered and suddenly she was just as tongue-tied as he'd been only moments ago. Sure, he was really proposing, but it was for a fake marriage. One with an expiration date. But when he looked into her eyes, the sincerity there touched her heart. This wasn't real, so why was her vision suddenly blurry?

She realized he was waiting for an answer. "Yes." Her voice was barely audible, so she cleared her throat and tried again. "Yes. Yes, I'll marry you."

Daniel pulled the ring from his pocket and slid it onto her ring finger. It fit perfectly. Although it didn't weigh much, wearing it she suddenly felt the gravity of the situation.

She and Daniel were engaged.

Daniel stood and scooped Hailey into his arms. "Ready to go?"

Brittany blinked at the quick change in his attitude. It was as if they'd been filming a movie and someone had yelled "cut." The emotional atmosphere had dissipated, and he was on to the next thing, leaving her off balance.

But why was she suddenly so disconcerted? She'd known all along this was a business-arrangement marriage. She shouldn't expect love or romance, even with the marriage proposal. Besides, she hadn't been expecting one until he'd gotten down on his knee.

Telling herself to snap out of it, she rose, grabbed her purse and then pasted on a smile. "I'm ready. Let's go."

Brittany twisted the engagement ring on her finger, turning the stone to the inside against her palm before turning it back the right way with the sapphire back on top. She'd been fiddling with her ring the entire ride to her parents' home. From the way she was behaving, you would think she was the one about to try to convince her soon-to-be in-laws that she was good enough to marry their child and not the other way around.

"You want to stop that? You're making me nervous." Daniel had been doing his best to maintain a calm facade, but his stomach, which had been bubbling since this morning, had started churning wildly as the day passed. Now it felt as if he had a volcano inside him. But since Brittany was clearly stressed about the meeting, he'd done his best to appear confident.

When she looked at him, a question on her face,

he was struck once again by her beauty. With clear, light brown skin and large brown eyes and kissable lips, she could easily be on the cover of a fashion magazine. When they'd initially met, he'd tried to ignore her sexy, willowy body and her stunning good looks, but hadn't been successful. He had even less chance of ignoring her beauty now that he'd trashed his policy of not becoming personally involved with women he did business with. They were going to be married even if in name only.

"What am I doing?"

"You're playing with your ring."

"Sorry." She placed her hands in her lap and spread her fingers. "This entire situation feels a little bit surreal. I can't believe that we're actually pretending to be engaged."

"Stop right there. We aren't *pretending* to be engaged. We *are* engaged. And we're going to be getting married in two weeks."

They'd managed to snag DJ's Deluxe's private party room for that date. Ordinarily, getting reservations on such short notice was nearly impossible, but Daniel had money and money opened otherwise closed doors. The wedding would be lavish yet intimate. Daniel had wanted to leave the details to Brittany, but she'd insisted on his involvement, pointing out that he was the one who wanted to get married.

"You know what I mean," she said.

"I do. But you can't slip up like that. If anyone

ever suspects that we aren't really in love, it could be detrimental to my case."

"I know. You're right."

"Do you like the ring?" he asked.

She sighed and held her left hand in front of her. "Too much. It is so beautiful."

Knowing she was pleased made it worth every penny. Not that he cared about the money. "They did a good job."

"I still can't believe he made it in a few days."

Brittany and Daniel had returned to the jewelry store at the appointed time to select the jewels for the ring.

Mr. Rossi had showed them a selection of sapphires ranging in size from one to six carats. Brittany had looked longingly at the stones before asking if he had any smaller ones. The shocked look on the jeweler's face would have been comical if Daniel hadn't known he was wearing a similar one. He'd told the other man that while his fiancée was reluctant to spend his money, he didn't share her reticence.

Daniel had chosen a four-and-a-half-carat sapphire and another two carats in diamonds to complete the design. He'd picked up the ring that morning— by himself. He hadn't wanted her to know it cost six figures. Besides, he'd wanted her to be surprised when she saw it.

He'd been unexpectedly jittery when he'd arrived at her condo earlier that afternoon. Even Hailey's happy chatter in the car hadn't been enough to calm his nerves. When the door had swung open and Hailey had seen Brittany, she'd squealed with delight and lunged for her. Brittany had scooped the baby into her arms and kissed her chubby cheeks then smiled at him. His heart had leaped with joy at the sight of the two of them together. After he'd stepped inside, Brittany had settled Hailey on the floor with her toys.

He'd taken Brittany gently by the arm and led her to the couch. Then he'd taken her hand into his. Her fingers had trembled and, admitting to feeling a bit more emotional that he'd expected as he'd proposed, told himself, *This isn't real.*

The ring had fit perfectly. She'd gasped audibly before pulling her hand away from his. He hadn't wanted to release her and had struggled not to reach out and take hold of her hand again. The longing he'd felt to renew the contact had surprised him and was enough to have him jumping to his feet.

They'd left her condo shortly thereafter to go to her parents' house.

Now he couldn't stop thinking about the Brandt relatives he was about to meet. "Tell me about your family."

"What do you want to know?"

"Anything. Pretend like we were dating and you're sharing stories about how you grew up. Tell me things you would tell your fiancé. The last thing I want is for your family to have doubts about our relationship. I want them to believe we're in love. Or have you changed your mind about letting them in on our secret?"

"No. My parents are traditional. They believe in the sanctity of marriage. They were high school sweethearts and got married when they were twenty-one. If I tell them this marriage is only pretend, they wouldn't approve."

She clasped her hands and shifted toward him in her seat. "My father is the superintendent of the Sunday school and my mother sings in the choir. They're very close."

"Yeah, I'm picking up on that."

"They work together, so they spend just about every minute of every day with each other. They own a dry-cleaning business. They started out with one and now own fifteen locations throughout Montana."

"That had to take a lot of work."

"Yes. And while they were building the business, I was tasked with caring for my four younger brothers and sisters."

Her voice was dry and he might have heard a hint of bitterness. Did she resent her siblings? He'd give anything to have Jane back in his life. Taking care of her daughter was a joy and privilege. Clearly, Brittany didn't look at family the same way he did. Maybe he didn't know her as well as he'd thought. For that reason alone, he needed to remember that this was a fake relationship and that he had to take control of his physical attraction to her.

Brittany directed him to turn at the next corner and then into the third driveway on the left. The house was well kept and the lawn immaculate. Once they were out of the car, Brittany turned to him. "Thanks for doing this. I know meeting my family isn't part of our deal, but it's important to me."

"If it's important to you, then it's important to me." She smiled at him and the pleasure in her expression made his blood race. Hadn't he just told himself to keep a tight rein on his desire? "Besides, whirlwind romance or not, it would look really strange if I didn't meet your family before the wedding."

Her smile vanished. "You're right. We don't want to do anything that would make the judge suspicious."

He replayed his words in his mind and couldn't think of anything he'd said that would account for the change in her attitude. Perhaps she was just nervous. He was.

They climbed the stairs together and then Brittany rang the doorbell. She didn't wait for anyone to answer the bell, but opened the door and stepped inside. Deciding that it would be odd not to follow suit, he stepped inside, too.

The delicious aroma of greens and candied yams filled the air and his mouth began to water. He couldn't remember the last time he'd had authentic soul food. Definitely not since he'd moved to Montana. His cook had received training at the best school in the country and had studied in France, but the man couldn't make spaghetti casserole to save his life. As much as Daniel enjoyed fancy food, there was nothing like fried turkey and baked macaroni and cheese to make a man feel good.

"We're here," Brittany called.

"Hi. Did Amanda come with you?" a woman asked, stepping into the room. It only took one look for Daniel to identify her as Brittany's mother.

"No. I brought someone else. Two 'someones' actually." Brittany sounded a bit nervous and he reached out and grabbed her hand, giving it a gentle squeeze. She smiled at him and his heart squeezed in response.

"I see." Brittany's mother looked at Daniel, who was holding Hailey in his arms, and then back to Brittany. "And who have we here?"

"Mom, this is Daniel Dubois and this little sweetheart is Hailey."

"It's a pleasure to meet you, Mrs. Brandt."

"Call me Mallory."

Before Daniel could respond, two black Labs bounded into the room and Brittany bent to greet each of them.

"Baba," Hailey exclaimed, kicking her legs in an attempt to get down.

"Are they friendly?" Daniel asked Mallory.

"Yes."

Daniel was considering the best way to deal with the Labs when an enormous dog thundered into the room, knocking into a floor lamp, which teetered momentarily.

"Do not tell me Lucas brought that gigantic mutt of his," Brittany said.

"Hey, don't insult my baby," a man said, coming into the room. "You'll hurt his feelings."

"I'll hurt more than that if he drools on me. I still can't believe Daphne let you rescue a mastiff, of all things. She should have given you a cat." Brittany made a mental note to speak to her friend, who ran the Happy Hearts Animal Rescue shelter, the next time she saw her.

"I'm a dog man. Besides, Flash is my baby, aren't you, girl?"

"You're a mess," Brittany said, but with great affection.

"Hi. I'm Lucas, Brittany's brother," he said, offering his hand to Daniel.

"Daniel."

They shook and Lucas turned around and yelled over his shoulder, "Brittany brought a man with her. And a baby."

"What are you, the town crier?" Brittany grumbled, and her brother only laughed.

In the blink of an eye, the rest of Brittany's family filled the room. An older gentleman elbowed his way to the front. "Give the man some space. You'll likely scare him off crowding around him like that." When he reached Daniel, he smiled and held out his hand. "I'm Phillip Brandt, Brittany's father. And father to the rest of this unruly bunch."

Daniel introduced himself and Hailey, who was clinging to him, her interest in the dogs a thing of the past. Apparently, six additional people was more than she wanted to deal with.

"These are my sisters, Stephanie and Tiffany, and my other brother, Ethan," Brittany said. As she introduced her siblings, they smiled or nodded at him. Brittany's sisters shared her slender build, hair and eye color as well as her skin tone. They were quite pretty, but in his estimation, Brittany was by far the most beautiful of the three.

"You're right on time. We were about to put dinner on the table," her mother said. "And, Lucas, put the dogs outside. Can't you see that horse of yours is scaring the baby?"

Hailey looked around at the word "horse." She might not know how to talk, but she was beginning to understand the meaning of words. *Horse* was one she was clued up on.

Brittany led him into the dining room where Phillip was setting up a high chair. Brittany must have sensed Daniel's confusion because she replied to his unasked question. "A couple of my cousins have kids. Since they come over for dinner quite often, my mother has a high chair."

Once the chair was set up, Brittany took Hailey from his arms and placed her in the chair. When she was securely strapped in, Brittany dropped a kiss onto her forehead.

There were two minutes of absolute chaos as food was carried into the room and set on the table. Brittany's family bumped into each other, and there was some good-natured grumbling and fussing until the table was so full he doubted another serving bowl would fit. When everyone was seated, they joined hands for a quick grace. Once finished, they began to pass platters of food. He scooped macaroni and cheese onto his plate then turned to pass the dish to Brittany's brother, who was seated beside him. A shriek had him pausing in the action, holding the casserole in the air.

"What is that on your finger?" Stephanie asked, grabbing Brittany's hand and holding it out so everyone could see. He felt Brittany stiffen beside him.

The moment of truth had arrived.

Chapter Eight

Brittany gave him a rueful look, then turned to face her sister. "It's a ring. Why, what does it look like?"

"It's on your *left* hand."

"Your powers of observation are nothing short of astounding."

"Brittany." Stephanie's voice was part whine and part excitement.

"Okay. Daniel and I are engaged."

There was a moment of silence before the women all screamed. Then everyone began to talk at once. Her mother jumped up and ran around the table, giving Brittany a big hug. She then did the same to Daniel. After the commotion died down, people once more began to fill their plates.

"That wasn't too bad," Daniel whispered. "I thought there would be a lot more questions than that."

Brittany smiled internally. He was so wrong. He really had no idea what was about to hit them. Still, Brittany hoped the questions wouldn't come until after dessert.

"So how did the two of you meet and when did all of this happen?" her mother asked.

Brittany sighed as that hope went sailing out the window. She glanced at Daniel, who shrugged. She hated lying to her family, but it was the better of two bad options. She didn't want to make them accomplices to her deception. Especially when she knew how much they disliked lies.

Her parents had drilled the importance of honesty into her at a young age. Her father had emphasized that you only got one name. One reputation. If you ruined it by lies or other bad behavior, you had to live with the consequences. He'd given each of his kids a good name and would appreciate if they kept it that way.

She couldn't count the number of times her mother had reminded her that if you told the truth, you didn't have to worry about keeping your story straight. Those words had never rung truer. The plan she and Daniel had agreed upon was to stick to the truth when possible, limiting the risk of being tripped up.

"We met when Daniel hired me to plan an event for him. I took one look at him and wham. The feelings knocked me right between the eyes. It was kismet."

"I'm not surprised," her mother said. "I knew it would be that way for you. You were always so certain that you didn't want to get married and have kids. So focused on your career. And look at you now." She glanced at Hailey, who was feeding herself smashed macaroni and cheese and mixed greens. Just as much was ending up on her face and in her hair as in her mouth, but Brittany was still proud of the little girl.

"So when is the date?" Stephanie asked.

Brittany blew out a breath. "Actually, we're planning to get married soon."

"Vague much?" Tiffany said.

Brittany nudged Daniel with her shoulder. A little help would be nice. He must have gotten the message, because he chimed in. "I convinced Brittany to set the date for the Saturday after next."

"What? That soon?" Her mom's shriek was nearly drowned out by the rest of the family. Used to the commotion, Brittany kept eating as they talked over each other. She looked at Daniel, concerned that he was rattled by the racket, but he appeared unfazed as he took a second helping of macaroni and cheese. Pleased by his reaction, Brittany smiled.

When the conversation ended, Daniel looked at

Brittany's family. "I guess I'm a little bit impatient. But when you meet the right one, you don't want to wait."

"What about Hailey's mother?" Mallory asked.

"She died." Daniel's voice was ragged, and Brittany heard the pain there. She placed her hand on his and gave it a gentle squeeze.

"I'm so sorry to hear that." Her mother's voice was filled with genuine sorrow, as was everyone else's who echoed her comments. "Were you married long?"

"We weren't married at all."

"Oh." Brittany's parents exchanged a look.

This was just as hard as Brittany had expected.

"Jane, Hailey's mother, was my younger sister," Daniel said quietly. "She died in a car accident recently. She asked that I raise Hailey as my daughter and that's what I intend to do."

"I see," Mallory said quietly. Brittany could only wonder what it was her mother saw. Did she suspect that Brittany and Daniel weren't being entirely truthful? Was she now having doubts about whether the upcoming marriage was a good idea?

"It takes a good man to take on the responsibility of a baby." Phillip's voice was filled with approval.

"I love Hailey. It might not be legal yet, but she's my daughter now, in my heart."

"Of course she is," Mallory said before turning

to Brittany. "So what kind of dress are you going to wear?"

That was it? No talk about Brittany's new role as stepmother?

"Can we not talk about the wedding until after we eat?" Lucas pleaded.

"I second that motion," Ethan said. "Just hearing the word is making my stomach turn and I won't be able to do justice to this great food. Everything tastes delicious, Mom, by the way."

Mallory blew her youngest child a kiss.

"We'll stop talking about the wedding if you guys agree to clean up the kitchen," Tiffany said.

"Fine," Lucas said as Ethan nodded. "Anything not to have to talk about lace and beads."

After that, conversation switched to other topics. Brittany was pleased by the way her siblings included Daniel and even ribbed him good-naturedly. He seemed to enjoy the banter and gave as good as he got. If ever she found Mr. Right, she'd want him to fit in with her family just as well as Daniel did.

When dinner was done, Lucas and Ethan kept their word and cleared the dishes. The women teased them before they went into the living room to continue discussing the wedding.

"Let's talk in my office," Phillip said, clapping a hand on Daniel's shoulder.

"Sure." Daniel looked at Hailey, who was now lying across Mallory's lap. As the dinner had progressed, Hailey had grown tired of sitting in her high chair and had started to fuss. Daniel had taken her out of the chair, ready to hold her, but Mallory had taken her, saying that Hailey needed to become familiar with the rest of her family. Throughout the meal, Hailey had spent time on everyone's lap. Brittany had no doubt that the little girl was going to be spoiled in no time.

"Go. She'll be fine," Mallory said. "I've raised five of my own, so I know a thing or two about babies. Besides, Brittany is here if Hailey needs to see a familiar face."

Brittany watched as Daniel followed her father out of the room. Her mother patted her hand. "He'll be fine."

"I know," Brittany replied. Phillip was a gentle man who loved his family. As long as Brittany was happy, he would be happy.

"This is kind of sudden," her mother said softly so that her words reached Brittany's ears alone. She should have known her mother wouldn't let the timing issue drop easily.

"I know. But it feels right to me."

"I raised you to know your own mind and make your own decisions. You've done a good job to date. I'm not going to try to run your life now, so stop frowning at me before your face freezes that way. If you think getting married this soon is right for you, then it's fine by me. Now, let's talk about colors."

After that, Brittany was able to completely relax. Unlike most teenagers or women in their twenties, she'd never imagined her dream wedding. And, oddly enough for an event planner, she was stumped when it came to planning her own wedding. Perhaps it was because she didn't want to be surrounded by the symbols of love and devotion when she and Daniel weren't devoted to each other. And they certainly weren't in love. Heck, a week ago, she wasn't even sure she liked him. She'd grown to admire him, but admiration was a long way away from being in love.

Could she really go with pink hyacinths when they symbolized happiness and love? Or pink peonies, which meant romance and a happy marriage? Not a chance. And she certainly couldn't use dahlias knowing they symbolized commitment and honesty. Nothing about this wedding was honest.

"How about tulips?" Tiffany suggested.

"Yes, you love tulips," her mother added.

She did. But tulips were a symbol of perfect love. She wanted to say no as she had to magenta lilacs and their love and passion, but she didn't want to raise suspicions by being difficult. And, really, who else knew the symbolism behind the flowers? Definitely not her sisters.

"Okay. I like that idea."

"What about bridesmaids?" Stephanie asked.

"I want each of you to stand up with me, of course. And Amanda."

"Yes." Stephanie cheered, clapping her hands.

"I was hoping you were going to say that," Tiffany said. "What color dresses are we going to wear?"

"What color would you like?"

The sisters talked excitedly to each other, coming up with and then discarding several colors as too bold, too boring, too…something.

"Well?" Brittany asked when they'd finally stopped talking.

They grinned at each other before speaking in unison. "Pink."

Brittany laughed. Her sisters knew pink was her favorite color. Not because she was a froufrou girl. She'd just always liked it. And each of her sisters looked fantastic in pink. Of course, they looked good in everything.

All the laughter and chatting had Hailey stirring and she sat up and looked around. At that moment, Lucas and Ethan returned to the room. Hailey took one look at Lucas and began to bounce on Mallory's lap and clap her hands. Then she raised her arms and stretched her little body as she tried to reach him. With rich brown skin and pretty-boy good looks, Lucas appealed to females from eight to eighty-eight. Apparently, that number should be lowered to eight months since Hailey wasn't immune to his charm, either.

"Hey, sweetie. Want to hang out with Uncle Lucas?" He reached out and swept her into his arms then settled her on his shoulders. Hailey squealed in delight and grabbed his locs. Laughing, he went down on his hands and knees to give her a horsey ride. Hailey bellowed with laughter and kicked her legs as if urging him to go faster, so he did.

"You'd better slow down," Brittany warned.

"Why? She likes it." Lucas began bucking like bronco, which delighted Hailey even more and she laughed raucously. "See? I'm totally going to be her favorite uncle."

"When she spits up all over your head, don't say anything."

"What's a little spit between friends?" he asked. He did, however, get to his feet and lower Hailey from his shoulders. He held her against his chest and looked into her eyes. "You wouldn't spit up on Uncle Lucas now, would you?"

Hailey just laughed.

"Looks like she isn't making any promises. Smart girl," Stephanie said.

Lucas winked. "We have a bond that doesn't require words."

Brittany watched the interaction between her siblings then glanced at her watch. She nibbled on her bottom lip.

"Why do you look so worried all of a sudden?" Stephanie asked.

"I'm just wondering what Dad and Daniel have been talking about all this time."

"Dad is probably threatening him within an inch of his life," Ethan said, cleaning his glasses on his pressed button-down shirt before returning them to his face. "You know, telling him how you're his precious daughter and that he'd better treat you like gold or else."

"No way. Dad is probably telling him to run while he can," Lucas joked. "Brittany has been known to be bossy."

"Good thing you're holding the baby, or you would be toast," Brittany said.

"Would you two stop?" her mother said, clearly exasperated. "Your father and Daniel are just getting to know each other."

"Get away while you still can," Lucas said, laughing.

"Brat." But Brittany laughed. Her mother was probably right. So why couldn't she shake the mental image of her father chasing her fake fiancé?

Daniel fought back the ridiculous nerves churning his stomach. He and Phillip were going to have a simple talk. Daniel talked to people all of the time. This shouldn't be any different. But it was. Because this wasn't a talk between friends or business associates. This was a man-to-man talk between a man and his future father-in-law. True, the marriage between Daniel and Brittany wasn't going to be a real one, and Daniel didn't expect it to last long. But Phillip didn't know that. He believed Daniel and Brittany were going to be together for the rest of their lives.

Now that he'd met the Brandts and he and Hailey had been enveloped into her family, Daniel understood why Brittany hadn't wanted to tell them the truth. They were honest and open people who wouldn't be comfortable with the deceit. Though she'd tried to hide it, Daniel could tell that Brittany wasn't at ease with the deception, either. But because she wanted to help him, she was willing to compromise her morals.

"Don't look so nervous," Phillip said with a grin. "This won't be painful. I just want to get to know you better. It's easier to talk privately. You and Brittany are going to be getting married in a couple of weeks, so that doesn't give us much time."

"True. What do you want to know about me?"

Phillip laughed. "This isn't a job interview. I don't have a list of questions to ask you. Truth be told, I wasn't expecting to meet you today. When Brittany said she was bringing a guest to dinner, I thought she meant Amanda. It turns out she meant her fiancé and her future daughter."

"You didn't refer to Hailey as Brittany's future stepdaughter."

Leaning back in his leather chair, Phillip crossed his arms over his stomach and raised an eyebrow. "You didn't refer to her as your niece, either."

"True. I don't think of her that way. I think of her as my daughter."

"There you have it." Phillip nodded his head, as if that explained everything. And in a way it did. To the Brandts, family was family. That was why they'd opened their arms and their hearts to him and Hailey.

A lump sprouted in Daniel's throat and he had to swallow before speaking. This was what he wanted for Hailey. He wanted to raise her as his daughter, like he'd sworn he would. But more than that, he wanted to give her a loving family. Of course, this family would disappear once he gained legal custody of Hailey and he and Brittany split, but in the meantime, she would be loved beyond his greatest imagining.

Phillip crossed his legs. He fired off a few questions to get the conversation rolling but, true to his word, the talk was genial, relaxed. "So you want to open a guest ranch?" he finally asked.

"Yes. That's actually how Brittany and I met. I hired her firm to plan a dinner for me. Needless to say, she made quite the impression on me."

"That's Brittany. I was beginning to think she was so focused on her career that she wouldn't ever consider getting married and having a family. It turns out she was waiting for the right man." After a moment, Phillip stood and extended a hand. "I'm glad to know you. Welcome to the family."

Inexplicably, the lump returned to Daniel's throat.

He wasn't normally sentimental, but over the past few hours at the Brandts', he'd found himself growing emotional. The last few years had been rough on him. He'd lost his parents and sister, leaving him with only Hailey as his family. His family might not have been as big or affectionate as this one, but they'd loved each other in their own way. He hadn't realized just how alone he'd been before Hailey had come into his life. Now he had the Brandts, too. At least for the duration of his marriage to Brittany.

"Thank you. You have a great family."

"I think so, but then I'm biased. They'll be your family soon, too. Now, let's get out of here. I'd like to spend a little bit more time spoiling my new granddaughter. And another piece of German chocolate cake wouldn't hurt."

Daniel followed his future father-in-law into the living room. The sight that greeted him made him smile. Brittany and her sisters were sitting on the sofa, their heads together as they talked a mile a minute. Mallory was sitting in a chair beside them, nodding as she typed into her laptop. Wedding planning was apparently in full swing.

Brittany glanced up at him and smiled. He felt the strangest twinge in his chest as his breath caught. She was so beautiful; he could have looked at her all night. But her beauty wasn't limited to the physical. She had the most gorgeous heart of anyone he'd ever met.

Hailey was sitting on a blanket, banging on a metal bowl with a wooden spoon and "singing" along. He scooped her up and gave her a big kiss. "That's a bit noisy. How about we give it a rest?"

The women just laughed. Clearly, they hadn't been bothered by the noise.

"The guys are in the kitchen getting more dessert, if you want to join them," Brittany said. "Or you could help us with the planning. It's your wedding, too."

"Whatever you decide is fine with me."

"Besides, there's cake and coffee in the kitchen," Tiffany teased.

"Yep."

"We'll be done soon," Brittany promised.

"Take your time," Daniel said, stepping out and joining the male members of the Brandt family. The day was turning out better than he'd expected, and he was actually having fun. He didn't have a problem with enjoying himself a little while longer. After all, he knew it was going to end soon.

Perhaps too soon?

Chapter Nine

"I really enjoyed myself today," Daniel said. "I'm glad I got to meet your family."

"They loved you," Brittany said honestly. Though she'd been the one who'd wanted them to meet, she'd been worried about their reaction to him and news of her upcoming wedding. She should have known her family would welcome him and Hailey with open arms. He'd fit right in and had become fast friends with her brothers. When she and mother had hugged at the door before they'd left, Mallory had whispered in her ear, "Daniel's a good man. You've chosen well." Her mother's words had filled Brittany with unexpected pride and warmth. Her mother had always wanted Brittany to find the same joy in marriage that she herself had found. Brittany didn't want to think about how disappointed her mother would be when she found out the truth. But since Brittany had gone into this with her open eyes she would deal with her mother's reaction when the time came.

"I loved them, too."

They'd finally gotten Hailey down for the night. After her busy day, she'd splashed for a long time in her bath before calming down enough to let Brittany wash her, then dress her in footed pajamas and rock her to sleep. Brittany had been surprised by how natural it had felt to hold the little girl and sing her a lullaby. But considering that Hailey was about to become her temporary daughter, it was a good development.

Daniel and Brittany were sitting in his very masculine living room. The curtains were open and moonlight streamed through the windows, making the large room feel intimate.

She shifted, brushing against Daniel's shoulder. They both froze. Until this moment she hadn't realized how close they were sitting. Suddenly there was a shift in the atmosphere and Brittany felt a oneness with Daniel that she'd never felt with anyone else. She certainly hadn't expected to feel it with him. The bond that she'd been pretending to share with him was starting to feel real. That was a problem.

She needed to draw a bright line between what was real and what was fake.

She took a reluctant breath. "I guess I should be getting home."

"So soon?" He sounded shocked and maybe a little bit disappointed. No, she had to be imagining that. Why would he be disappointed? "I was hoping you could stay awhile. I could make some coffee to go with the cake."

Brittany laughed. Mallory had sent home two large pieces of cake, along with a plate of leftovers. "I'll just take the coffee. You can keep my piece of cake."

"You sure?"

She nodded.

He placed a hand over his heart and stared into her eyes. "You're the best."

Brittany's heart did a silly little lurch and she cautioned herself to calm down. His words didn't mean anything. He was just glad to have an extra dessert. Still, it was foolish to deny the way she'd reacted. Not one for lying—present situation excepted—she forced herself to acknowledge her attraction to him while simultaneously making up her mind not to let it grow.

How pitiful would it be to allow herself to fall for someone she knew had no intention of returning the feeling? Daniel had made it clear that theirs was now and always would be a business relationship.

And since she wasn't really the maternal type and wasn't looking to marry anytime in the near future, why was she so bothered?

Daniel was back in a minute, holding two mugs, one with a plate balanced on top. He offered her the solitary mug and then set the other on the table.

She took a sip of her coffee. "Delicious."

"Thanks." He settled back on the sofa beside her, grabbed the plate and fork, and then took a bite of cake. Leaning back, he closed his eyes, savoring the treat. She had never found the way a man chewed especially sexy, but she was slightly turned on by watching Daniel devour his cake. She licked her lips as she imagined his lips on hers and the pleasure they would both get from kissing.

"So, do you want to talk more about the wedding?" she said, suddenly warm. She needed to focus on something other than how sexy his lips were and how badly she wanted to feel them on hers.

"Sure. What did you guys come up with?"

"My sisters will be my bridesmaids. And I'm going to ask Amanda to be my maid of honor. Do you have three close friends who can stand up for you?"

"Yes. I'll ask my friends Sam and Dominick to be groomsmen and my best friend, Stephanos, to be my best man."

"Are you going to have a bachelor party? If so, I can keep Hailey for you."

"I don't think so. The four of us will probably just

get together the night they arrive and go to dinner or something. Of course, I have to tell them I'm getting married first."

She grinned. "What are you waiting for? Scared of what they'll say? Or has reality hit you? Are you scared of turning in your bachelor card?"

"Not hardly."

"I did a little checking on you. Before you moved here, you were considered one of the Southwest's most eligible bachelors. There were dozens of pictures of you with beautiful women. Emphasis on the word *women*. You were frequently photographed with a beautiful woman on your arm, but rarely the same woman twice. Maybe your friends won't believe you're ready to settle down with one woman. Especially with someone like me."

He turned and she felt the full force of his gaze. "Someone like you? Just what does that mean?"

"I live in Bronco, Montana. That's hardly a bustling metropolis. I'm an event planner, not a fashion model or actress—the type of woman you normally date. I'm a regular person with a regular job."

"You could be a model if you wanted to. You're just as beautiful as any of them."

She smiled. He thought she was beautiful? She'd never given much thought to her looks. Genes were inherited and thus not something that one could claim as an accomplishment. From a young age, she had been taught a person wasn't beautiful because of how they looked, but rather because of how he or she behaved. Brittany believed that and always tried to be kind. Still... *Daniel thought she was beautiful.*

"Thank you," she managed to say. "But that's not my point. I don't live a jet-set life. I don't mingle with celebrities and millionaires. My nights out are spent with friends at a local restaurant. And I'm all right with that."

"So am I." He leaned forward. "If I wanted to live life in the fast lane, I wouldn't have moved to Bronco. Although I enjoyed the life I had, I want to live a slower life now. I want to have a horse ranch and resort. That's why I moved here."

She nodded. It sounded believable when he said it.

"And if I wanted to, I could have married one of those women. But I don't want them. I want you."

A tingle raced down her spine and once more she was in danger of being swept away by his words. Her heart sped up as she thought of how great it would be if he'd really meant them. How fabulous it would be for him to want *her*, not just a woman who would fool a judge. What would it be like to be the woman Daniel actually chose to marry because he loved her? She cleared her throat and focused. Daydreaming was dangerous to her heart. And her goals. "Speaking of the wedding..."

"I told you. I'm happy with whatever you come up with."

"I know. But we haven't talked specifically about the marriage."

"Okay." He looked at her expectantly, waiting for her to continue.

"I want to clarify the details."

"Okay. You're going to move in here."

She nodded. "And just where will I be sleeping?"

One side of his mouth lifted in the sexiest grin she'd ever seen, and her stomach flip-flopped. His dark eyes bore into hers. "Wherever you want."

She immediately pictured being wrapped in Daniel's arms in a shared bed. She had no doubt making love with him would be heavenly. That was why they couldn't be intimate even once.

"Relax, Brittany," he continued. "Our marriage will be in name only, just as we agreed. You'll sleep in a guest room and I'll sleep in my room. Unless you choose for it to be otherwise. My door will always be open."

She forced her longings down. There was no way she could walk through his bedroom door. Not when one day she'd have to walk out the front door and out of his life. "I'll take the guest room."

"I thought you would. Remember, I have no expectations of a wedding night or a honeymoon. Does that put you at ease?"

She nodded. But why did she suddenly wish he wasn't so honorable? "I know our marriage will be in name only, but I won't feel comfortable with you dating anyone else."

"No problem with that."

"Really?"

"Yes. I don't want to see a different woman every night, like before. My life is different now. I have Hailey and she has to come first. I haven't dated since she's come to live with me. And I'm happy with that. I'd choose my daughter over a bunch of women any day of the week and twice on Sunday."

"Really?" She couldn't quite keep the skepticism from her voice. If he noticed, he chose to ignore it.

"Yes."

She'd expected a more detailed answer, but one wasn't forthcoming. Instead they sat in silence as they finished their drinks, looking out the windows. She would never tire of looking at the Montana sky, especially here on the ranch where there was no light to compete with the stars. Despite the fact that she was comfortable here with him—or maybe because of it—she stood. "It's getting late. I need to get going."

He stood slowly. "If you have to."

"I do. I have to go to work in the morning." Work. Where she was going to have to announce her engagement. She knew her coworkers would be happy for her. They'd no doubt want to talk about her engagement all day. She didn't know how she would manage to fake it for the next two weeks.

They walked to the door. She turned to say good-night as he reached for the doorknob bringing their lips within mere centimeters of touching. The heat from his body encircled her, tempting her to lean in closer. As her eyes started to drift shut, she jerked back, opened the door and darted down the stairs before she did something stupid like kiss him.

By the time she'd gotten into her car she was breathing hard. That was close. Being around Daniel was awakening desires and emotions that needed to stay dormant. She needed to get a grip on that. More than that, she needed someone she could confide in. Someone who wouldn't judge her or be disappointed in her. Amanda.

Amanda was not only her roommate. She was her best friend. Brittany knew she could tell her the truth and trust her to keep it to herself. Besides, she lived with Brittany and knew there hadn't been a whirlwind romance or a romance of any kind. Brittany might be able to fool people who didn't know she'd spent most nights at home alone, but she couldn't fool Amanda even if she wanted to. That meant she could tell Amanda the truth. And Brittany really did need to talk.

Luckily, Amanda was home when Brittany arrived.

"Hey," Amanda said.

"Hey, yourself. Got a minute?"

Amanda put down the laundry she was folding at the kitchen table. "As a matter of fact, I do."

"Good. I need a favor."

"Name it."

Brittany blew out a breath. "I need you to be my maid of honor."

Amanda laughed. "Good one. The Brittany Brandt I know is not even thinking about marriage. In fact, she's not even dating anyone seriously."

Brittany held out her left hand, revealing the gorgeous engagement ring. She still couldn't believe she was wearing it, but couldn't imagine taking it off.

Amanda's eyes grew wide and her mouth fell open. She raced over and grabbed Brittany's hand. "Is that real?"

"Yes. And no."

"Yes *and* no?"

Brittany nodded. "The sapphire and the diamonds are real. The ring is real."

"Is it …an engagement ring?"

"Yes. And the engagement is real. Sorta."

Amanda blinked a few times and put her hand to her head. "You're going to have to spell it out a little bit more for me. Like whom you're engaged to, for starters."

"Okay. But first you have to swear on all that you love to keep what I'm about to say a secret."

Amanda drew an X across her heart. "I swear

on all that I love to keep what you're about to say a secret."

"Thanks."

"Now, tell me what is going on."

"You might want to sit down for this. And I know I need to."

Brittany pulled out a chair and dropped into it and Amanda did the same. Amanda stared at Brittany. "Tell me."

"Daniel Dubois asked me to marry him and I said yes."

"Excuse me, what?"

"You heard me."

"You and Daniel Dubois? The same Daniel Dubois that you called a rich guy who thought he was entitled to have whatever he wanted whenever he wanted. That Daniel Dubois?"

"That would be the one."

"And you're going to marry him. Why? Did he decide he wants you?"

"Sort of." Brittany closed her eyes for a second. "He's in a custody battle and needs a wife to improve his chances of winning."

"Custody? Of whom?"

"His daughter. Actually, she's his niece." Brittany explained about Daniel's sister's death and the lawsuit brought by Hailey's paternal grandparents. "He really loves Hailey and wants to honor his sister's wish that he raise her."

"And you've met Hailey?"

"I have. She's the sweetest little thing. Cute as a button."

"Does your family know?"

"Only about the wedding, not the reason behind it. They met Daniel and Hailey today. They liked them."

"Of course they did. Your family likes everybody."

"True."

Amanda tapped her lips with a finger but didn't say anything else.

"You're thinking about something. Go ahead and say it."

"I can see what Daniel and Hailey get out of this. He gets to raise her and she gets to stay with the person she knows. But what do you get? The way I see it, you have a lot to lose and nothing to gain."

"What am I losing?"

"Possibly your heart. I know you say you don't want kids, but I've seen you with them. You're great. What if you fall in love with Hailey and then have to say goodbye to her when this marriage ends?"

"We're not going to be married that long, so I don't have to worry about getting too attached. Not only that, Daniel and I aren't emotionally involved, so we aren't going to have a bitter breakup when we end our marriage. I'm sure he'll let me see Hailey from time to time if I want."

"And what happens if you become emotionally

involved with him? What if you fall in love with Daniel Dubois?"

"That's not going to happen. He's not my type." Brittany mentally crossed her fingers, as if that childish gesture would somehow make the lie the truth. Because Daniel Dubois might not have started out as her type, but he was definitely becoming her type. The better she got to know him, the more she liked him. "And as far as not getting anything out of this, Daniel is going to give me enough money to start my own event planning business."

"That's something, I suppose."

"I can tell you aren't totally on board with this."

"I didn't say that. I admit the plan is a little crazy—well, a lot crazy—but I understand why you agreed. And it's not for the money. You've always helped anyone in need. You've never gone this far before, but it's completely in character."

"So, does that mean you'll stand up for me?"

"I guess it does. Just tell me when."

"Two weeks from now."

"Wow. That's fast."

"Yes. It can't be helped."

Amanda smiled and grabbed the ever-growing stack of bridal magazines from the table. "I guess we'd better start looking at wedding dresses for you, too."

"So, tomorrow's the big day."

Daniel turned to look at his best friend, Stephanos

Dimitry. Daniel's friends had arrived last night, and they'd had dinner out. Tonight they were hanging out together at his house. It had been just like old times. The four of them had spent hours recalling the past and embellishing stories that they'd all known were exaggerations of the truth.

Daniel then glanced briefly through the glass door at Rodney and William inside. He had missed his college friends—especially Stephanos. He'd missed the time the two of them had spent working to make their company a success. They'd filled long hours together at work, building their bioengineering company, and even more hours at play, dating some of the hottest women in Texas and then jetting off to Greece, where Stephanos's father lived, for long weekends. Despite the good times, Daniel didn't regret leaving the company and moving to Montana. But having the three of them here made him realize that no matter how many new friends he made, he still needed his old ones. He vowed not to lose touch with them like he had with Jane.

Looking back at Stephanos, who'd walked outside with him onto the patio, he said, "Yes, it is." Excitement had been building over the past few days.

"It's not too late to call the whole thing off."

"Why would I do something like that?"

"Because," Stephanos pointed out, "you're treating marriage like a business deal instead of a sacred institution."

"A sacred institution?"

"You know what I mean. Marriage isn't something to be used to win a lawsuit. Or to get seed money for your business."

"I shouldn't have told you. If I had known you were going to judge me, I wouldn't have. And you haven't met Brittany yet, so don't base your opinion of her on this deal. She's marrying me to help me keep Hailey."

Only yesterday his lawyer had informed him that the Larimar's attorney had demanded custody once more. And that they were insisting on weekend visitation—at their home—as if he would ever agree to let them take Hailey anywhere. Daniel had also been informed that a social worker would be making a visit in the coming weeks. No, there would be no backing out. Everything depended on this wedding taking place as scheduled.

"And for the money you're giving her," Stephanos pointed out.

"That was my idea. She never asked for a cent."

"But she's still taking it."

"Stephanos." Daniel's voice was steely, designed to stop Stephanos in his tracks. Nobody, and that included his best friend, was going to malign Brittany in Daniel's presence.

Stephanos held up his hands in surrender. "Okay. So she's not a gold digger. My point is still valid. Marriage is special and should be treated that way."

"I know. But this is an extraordinary situation." Daniel looked at his friend. "I'm sorry for putting you in this position. I shouldn't have confided in you and asked you to keep it from Rodney and William."

"I'm your best friend." Stephanos heaved out a sigh. "I understand why you're doing this. It's not the way that I would have handled things, but I get it."

"I just can't lose Hailey."

"You won't. Now, come on back inside. We're getting ready to call it a night and head to the hotel."

"You guys know you could have stayed here. I have plenty of room."

"And a baby who needs her sleep."

Daniel followed his friend back into the house. William and Rodney stood when he entered. "Thanks again for coming, guys. I'll see you in the morning."

Daniel watched as his friends climbed into their rental car and drove away. Stephanos's words haunted him as he turned out the lights and headed upstairs. Was he doing the right thing by marrying Brittany? Or was he making a huge mistake? Whatever, it was too late to back out now. He would just say his vows tomorrow and hope for the best.

Chapter Ten

Brittany's heart was thudding so hard she wouldn't be surprised if it forced a way out of her chest. In exactly twenty minutes, she would be walking down the aisle to marry Daniel Dubois. The doubts that she'd shoved down over the past two weeks suddenly surfaced and threatened to overwhelm her.

What in the world was she doing? Why had she agreed to marry Daniel? Sure, she believed that he and Hailey belonged together, but did that mean Brittany had to marry him? It had seemed like a good idea at the time, but now that the seconds were ticking down, Brittany's feet were beginning to feel a slight chill.

Guests were arriving. Though they'd put the wedding together rather quickly, she'd done everything in her power to make it elegant. DJ's Deluxe might not be the Ritz, but she and Reese, who was acting as her wedding coordinator, her sisters and Amanda had transformed it. They'd covered the walls with silk fabric and added pedestals wrapped with greenery and flowers. The entire place looked like a fairy-tale wedding was about to take place. In a way, it was. Not in the romantic sense where the couple would live happily ever after, but rather in the sense that nothing about it was real. It was all make-believe.

A string quintet was playing chamber music and it floated into the makeshift dressing room. Every detail had been seen to, down to the order of the musical selections. Only three more songs before the wedding would start.

Stephanie finished Brittany's makeup and Tiffany adjusted her veil.

"You look really beautiful," Tiffany said, clasping her hands against her chest. "Daniel won't be able to keep his eyes off you."

"Thank you." Brittany's voice caught in her throat. Turning to look at herself in the mirror, she couldn't believe that the glamorous reflection was her. Suddenly she felt like a bride. Though Brittany had chosen a white dress that stopped at the knee, the bodice had an elaborate lace-and-bead design. Her veil, though simple, reached the hem of her dress.

"You three look beautiful, too," Brittany said, rising from her chair. "Thanks so much for being a part of my special day." She hugged her sisters and Amanda. "I have gifts for you."

"You didn't need to do that," Amanda said. Brittany's sisters echoed the sentiment.

"Of course I did. It's tradition. More than that, you all mean so much to me." She'd found silver bracelets and earrings that would look lovely with their dresses. They'd selected elegant pink silk that fit at the waist, skimmed their hips and floated around their knees. Their silver shoes matched the color of the groomsmen's ties.

They opened their gifts, then quickly removed their earrings and put on the new jewelry.

A knock sounded on the door and her father poked his head in. "Are you ready?"

"Yes."

"Good." He stepped inside and then kissed her cheek. "You look positively radiant."

"Thanks, Dad."

"Daniel is a fine man. I know you'll be happy with him."

Brittany, Daniel and Hailey had gone to visit her parents three more times over the past two weeks. It had been Daniel's idea. He'd wanted her parents to know him better. She'd teased him that he'd only wanted to eat more of her mother's cooking, but inside Brittany had been pleased. Though their marriage was a sham, Daniel had behaved like a real fiancé, which had put her parents at ease. Unfortunately, it had had the opposite effect on her.

Reese stepped inside. "It's time to start."

Brittany's breath caught in her throat. She might be entering into a marriage of convenience, but it was still a marriage. *Her* marriage. It might not be a permanent union, but she was going to do her best to make Daniel happy.

Brittany and her bridesmaids filed into the back of the dining room. A curtain hung from the ceiling, so they were out of sight of the guests. The chairs had been arranged in two sections with a wide aisle down the center. Though they'd planned to have a small wedding with only immediate family, the guest list had ballooned to seventy-five, which included their closest friends as well as the Bronco elite.

Her cousin's three-year-old twins, Leo and Natalia, were serving as ring bearer and flower girl. Leo kept checking himself out in his tiny tuxedo and grinning. Natalia spun in a circle, making the skirt on her pink dress fly into the air.

All at once the quiet talk stopped and the quintet began to play the song Brittany had selected for the entrance of the bridal party. Tiffany walked down the aisle beside Rodney, followed by Stephanie and William. Amanda walked down next, followed by Leo and Natalia.

And then it was time for Brittany and her father

to enter. As she took his arm, she began to tremble. He covered her hand with his and gave it a gentle squeeze. She glanced up and saw Daniel standing at the end of the aisle. Dressed in a perfectly tailored black tuxedo that emphasized his broad shoulders and trim waist, he looked like every dream she'd ever had come to life. His eyes were riveted to her as if he'd never seen her before. He smiled and she smiled in return. Just looking at him soothed her. What had she been so worried about? This was *Daniel*.

She and her father had reached the middle of the aisle when Daniel took a step in her direction. And then another one. What was he doing? He was supposed to wait by the floral arch, beside his best man, until she reached him. But he kept walking and didn't stop until he stood in front of her.

"I'll take it from here," he said to her father.

"All right now," one of her cousins called out. "Go get your woman."

Several people laughed and a murmur filled the room. Brittany was so focused on Daniel that she couldn't make out the words.

Her father kissed her cheek and then relinquished his hold on her. Daniel held out his elbow and she wrapped her arm around his. Smiling, they walked to the front of the room and stood before her pastor. The room and everyone in it faded away as she became acutely aware of the man beside her. The man she was about to join her life to.

"Dearly Beloved," Pastor King intoned, his baritone voice filling the room, "we are gathered here today to join this man and this woman in holy matrimony."

Brittany had heard the familiar words many times in her life, yet now they took on new meaning. This time she wasn't witnessing two other people become husband and wife. This was her wedding. Daniel was about to become her husband and she was about to become his wife. This was real.

Before long they reached the place in the ceremony where they were to exchange vows. Though Daniel had been indifferent to most of the choices, he'd wanted to write his own vows. Initially, Brittany hadn't understood his reasoning. Then it occurred to her that he hadn't wanted to vow to love, honor and cherish her. The thought had pinched her heart a little, but she'd forced the pain away. Why should he say words he didn't mean?

Maybe he was onto something. She didn't want to swear before God and everyone that she would love Daniel forever, so she'd come up with her own vows, too. They hadn't shared what they'd written, so they'd each be hearing the words for the first time now.

Daniel took her hand and looked into her eyes. His voice was firm and steady. "Brittany. You came into my life when I least expected it. Your heart is so pure. So beautiful. You're a treasure I know I don't deserve. I'll do everything in my power to be worthy of you. I can't promise to never make a mistake, because I know I will. But I can promise to learn from them and to do better. Of all the good things in my life, you are far and away the best. Thank you for giving me a chance to experience real love."

Brittany's vision blurred as she listened to Daniel's words. He sounded so sincere she could almost believe that he was in love with her. Though she didn't need a man in her life to complete her, she suddenly wished this was real and that they really were joining their lives and becoming one.

But this was playacting. He'd said his part. Now it was time to deliver her lines.

When she'd written her vows, she'd tried to imagine how a bride who was marrying the love of her life would feel. The words she would use to convey those emotions… After listening to Daniel, her vows suddenly seemed inadequate, but they were all she had.

"Daniel." Her voice was a trembling whisper, so she cleared her throat and started over. "Daniel. I had my entire life mapped out before I met you. I knew where I was going and when I would get there. And then we met. Suddenly my life took a turn along a different path. I'm not certain where the road will lead, but as long as you're by my side, I'm eager to discover what awaits us."

When she finished reciting her vow, she was as breathless as if she'd just run a mile. Reminding herself that none of this was real only worked for so long. She heard people murmuring about true love, and how romantic their vows had been, and she felt a twinge of guilt. That feeling grew as they lit the unity candle, signifying their eternal love for each other, but there was no turning back now.

It was finally time to jump the broom, signaling the end of the ceremony. Tiffany and Stephanie hadn't decorated any old broom, but rather had created one from a branch they'd found in a park near their home. They'd tied ribbons and flowers on it, making it a one-of-a-kind work of art. One of the ushers carried it into the room and handed it to Pastor King.

The pastor turned and spoke to the guests. "In the tradition of our ancestors, the bride and groom will now jump the broom. This symbolizes crossing the threshold into the land of matrimony. It marks the beginning of a new life, sweeping aside the old, and welcoming a new beginning."

When the broom was set before Brittany and Daniel, they joined hands. Then, looking at each other, they hopped over the broom.

"You may salute your bride," Pastor King said.

Brittany had thought about this moment from the time she'd agreed to marry Daniel. Somehow, in all of her imagining, she hadn't gotten the emotion right. As she stared into his dark brown eyes, all thought fled, leaving only one sincere feeling behind. *Desire.*

More than anything, she wanted to feel Daniel's lips pressing against hers.

Her longing must have showed on her face because his eyes flashed for a moment before he lowered his head, bringing his lips into contact with hers. Electricity shot through her body and her knees buckled. Instantly his arms were around her waist, supporting her. Of their own volition, her arms encircled his neck and she moved more closely to him, deepening the kiss. Feelings she'd never experienced—didn't know she could experience—flooded her body and she didn't want the moment to end.

Daniel began to ease away and she moaned in protest. She felt him smile against her mouth and her senses returned. They were in front of their nearest and dearest and she was behaving as if she was a sixteen-year-old in the back seat of her boyfriend's car. She and Daniel eased away from each other and the roaring in her ears was replaced by the cheers of the crowd.

"Ladies and gentlemen, I present for the first time anywhere, Mr. and Mrs. Daniel Dubois," Pastor King said.

While everyone clapped, Brittany did her level best to regain control of herself. Daniel grabbed her hand and winked at her. He was cool as a cucumber. Apparently, the kiss was one-sided, only scorching her lips and all but roasting her insides. Fortunately, there was no time to brood about her embarrassment.

That would have to wait until after the reception was over and the well-wishers had gone home. Now there were pictures to pose for and hugs and congratulations to accept.

Reese whisked the bridal party outside to pose for pictures in the glorious, sunny day. Meanwhile waiters served the guests from trays of appetizers and beverages.

"Smile," the photographer said, pulling Brittany's attention to the here-and-now and away from what was going on inside the restaurant. As they posed for one picture after another, she couldn't help but wonder what the photographs would reveal. Would her inner turmoil show on her face? Would her unexpected desire be revealed in her eyes? Whatever the case, she silently vowed to hide the wedding album forever.

Thirty minutes and hundreds of pictures later, the wedding party went back inside the restaurant. The altar had been replaced by a gorgeously decorated table where Daniel, Brittany and their attendants would sit.

Daniel led her through the maze of tables, greeting their friends and family with an ease that Brittany envied. She was still trying to get a handle on her renegade feelings and could barely manage to smile.

As they reached their table, DJ Traub, the owner

of the restaurant, approached them to offer his congratulations.

"Thanks for letting us have the restaurant on such short notice," Daniel said.

DJ smiled. "Your wife is very persuasive and very hard to say no to."

"I know." Daniel gave Brittany a sexy smile that had her toes curling. "I don't think I'll be able to say no to her for at least a hundred years."

"It really is my pleasure to host your wedding and reception. We'll start serving in about fifteen minutes. Is that okay with you?"

Daniel and Brittany exchanged a look. Daniel nodded. "That's fine."

Brittany was able to see all of their guests from her chair. Her parents were seated nearby. Although this was an adults-only affair, Hailey had been included. They'd requested and received a high chair for her, but she was currently seated on Mallory's lap, contentedly playing with a stuffed horse. Brittany had no doubt that if Hailey became fussy, one of her brothers would entertain her. Lucas and Ethan were currently locked in a battle to become her favorite uncle.

Reese stood in the back, conferring with the new restaurant manager. Brittany wondered if there was a problem. The marriage might not be real, but she still wanted the reception to go off without a hitch.

"Relax," Daniel said, leaning close and whispering into her ear. The warmth from his body caressed her bare shoulders, making her shiver. How could he expect her to relax when his nearness awakened everything feminine inside her? Did he think she could be calm when being close to him made her nerves jangle like wind chimes in a tornado? Of course, she couldn't say that. He was clearly unaffected by her and she needed to find a way to become just as indifferent to him. Until that time arrived, she'd have to fake it.

She couldn't let him know that this whole wedding and the kiss was wreaking havoc with her common sense. Not when, to him, this was simply a part of doing whatever it took to keep Hailey. Brittany did have her pride. She told herself that the feelings she was currently experiencing weren't real. It just turned out that she was a method actor. Pretending to be a besotted bride had turned her into one. Once this was over, she'd go back to being Brittany Brandt—er, Brittany Dubois, calm, cool and collected.

"I'm trying to relax," she told him. "I guess it's the event planner in me."

"But you hired your friend to do that. And she's doing a magnificent job. This room looks like one of the ballrooms in the fairy tales that I read to Hailey."

Brittany looked around. "It really does look magnificent, doesn't it?

"Yes. So smile and enjoy your dinner."

Brittany bared her teeth and Daniel laughed at the face she'd made. "You are so silly, Brittany."

She smiled for real this time, amazed that he'd managed to ease her worry.

Brittany enjoyed every course of the delicious food. She'd worked with DJ to create a special menu for this occasion. Though the restaurant didn't ordinarily serve red wine braised short rib and pan seared salmon, they'd managed to prepare it to her satisfaction.

Suddenly, Brittany became aware of a tinkling sound that clashed with the soft music. When she recognized it as silverware clicking against the crystal glasses, the universal signal guests gave when they wanted the happy couple to kiss, anticipation mingled with dread.

This time she was determined not to make a fool of herself. And she definitely wasn't going to go overboard as if she and Daniel were engaged in a make-out session. Smiling, she leaned over and pecked him on the lips. The guests groaned in protest.

"Surely we can do better than that," Daniel said.

Before she could respond, his lips were on hers in a searing kiss. It only lasted a few seconds, but during that brief time, the earth moved, shifting on its axis. Her heart fluttered and jumped around her chest before settling in its original place.

"I told you we could do better," Daniel said before picking up his fork and turning his attention to his baked potato. Brittany, on the other hand, tried to douse the flame of desire raging inside her by downing her glass of ice water.

Once the meal was finished, the wedding cake, wheeled out on a small table, was set in front of Daniel and Brittany. Grabbing the decorative knife in their hands, they sliced into the cake then set the piece onto a crystal plate. They each picked up a portion and, interlocking their arms, fed each other.

Brittany had never done anything so intimate, much less with an audience, and her hand trembled as it brushed against Daniel's bottom lip. His tongue darted out and touched her finger and she sucked in a breath. He had to know what he was doing to her. But then again, he was playing a role. After all, he had the most to lose if they failed, so he had to give an Academy Award-winning performance of a happy groom. Brittany had no idea how the court case would play out, so it was possible that any of the people in this room could be questioned about their marriage. After watching Daniel's act, the guests would be able to say that she and Daniel may have had a whirlwind courtship, but their relationship was authentic.

After the ever-present photographer snapped even more pictures, the cake was returned to the kitchen where it would be cut and served to the guests.

Amanda approached them. She smiled at Daniel

and then hugged Brittany. "Everything is so beautiful. I hope Holt's and my wedding is as perfect as this."

Daniel caressed Brittany's cheek. "I'm going to check on Hailey. I'll meet you back at the table in a few?"

Brittany nodded.

After he left, she turned to Amanda, who suddenly looked sad. Her smile had faded and the light in her eyes had dimmed. "What?" Brittany asked.

"Nothing. At least, nothing I can talk about in a room filled with your wedding guests."

"Come on. If you can't talk to your best friend, who can you talk to?" Brittany led Amanda to a secluded area of the restaurant. "Talk to me."

"It's just that this wedding is so beautiful. And everyone is so happy."

"So why would that make you unhappy?"

"I was thinking about Winona Cobbs and Josiah Abernathy and their long-lost baby, Beatrix. They never had the chance to be a happy family. Josiah has dementia now and rarely speaks so it was a big deal when he said he wanted someone to find his baby. And from what I understand, Winona isn't doing too well physically. Beatrix would be in her seventies now, so she might not even be alive."

Amanda had been using her social media skills to help their friend Melanie and her fiancé Gabe Abernathy try to locate Beatrix. "I thought that you'd

gotten a response to your query. You were so excited that you might have found Josiah and Winona's child."

Amanda's shoulders slumped.

"Well, it turns out that Bernadette Jefferson
wasn't Beatrix, after all."

"Oh. How disappointing." Amanda was really invested in finding Beatrix.

"Infuriating is more like it. Bernadette was a
fraud. She knew she wasn't Beatrix. She was just
an imposter hoping to shake down the Abernathy
family for money."

"That's awful."

"Yes. Frauds and liars are the lowest of the low."
Brittany winced.

"I didn't mean you. You aren't a fraud or a liar."

"I'm pretending to be a bride," she whispered.

"You are a bride. And you're married to Daniel
Dubois. That's the truth."

"You know what I mean. We aren't in love." She
was tempted to shield her mouth when she spoke
but refrained.

"Maybe not. Yet."

"What do you mean *yet*?"

"There were some serious sparks flying between
the two of you. And that kiss?" Amanda waved her
hand in front of her face. "There was so much steam,
I'm surprised your hair is still curled."

Brittany's face grew hot and she looked around to

be sure they weren't overheard. Nobody was near and they were not attracting unusual attention. "You're imagining things."

"Remember. I'm the one who told you there was something between you and Daniel before any of this occurred. You denied it rather quickly, so I let it go. Maybe I was right all along."

Brittany didn't reply, but inside she hoped Amanda was wrong. The last thing she wanted to do was to fall in love with her temporary husband. Especially since said husband gave no indication that he was falling for her.

"Anyway," Amanda continued, "given your insistence that marriage was the last thing on your mind, I think it's pretty ironic that you've gotten married before me."

"That's one word for it. Have you set a date yet?"

Amanda shook her head. "Still planning for the fall. When we have an exact date, you'll be the first to know."

Brittany was about to reply when she heard a ruckus. Off to the side and away from other guests, she saw Daphne Taylor and her father, Cornelius, arguing—most likely about the animal shelter. Again. Brittany didn't understand how a family could be at odds with each other like the Taylors. Though she and her parents occasionally disagreed, they didn't fight. She'd always believed other families were the same. Looking at the way Daphne and

Cornelius were going at it, Brittany realized how wrong she'd been.

She couldn't let them continue to argue without intervening. Daphne was a friend of hers. Not only that, this was Brittany's wedding reception. She didn't want a scene. "I'll talk to you later."

"Want me to go with you?" Amanda asked.

"No. I'm sure they won't appreciate an audience." Amanda nodded then walked away.

Brittany approached father and daughter, who were so engrossed in their heated discussion that they didn't notice her.

"Is everything okay?" Brittany asked in her sweetest voice.

"Fine," Daphne said, her jaw clenched. "I'm glad I ran into you. I want to extend my heartfelt congratulations, but I won't be staying."

"Oh, don't go. The dancing is going to begin soon. We've hired a great DJ and it's going to be a lot of fun."

"I'm sure it will, but I need to go." Daphne gave Brittany a quick hug then, without giving her father a second look, turned and stalked away.

Sighing, Brittany turned to Cornelius. She didn't want to get in the middle of a family fight, but she wondered why he'd let Daphne walk out when she was so obviously upset. Brittany knew her own father would never do that.

"Will you be staying?" Brittany asked Cornelius.

"Are you asking me to leave?"

"Not at all," Brittany replied smoothly. Asking him to leave would be ungracious. Besides, she was still hoping to land the Taylor account. "As I told Daphne, the party is about to get started. Shall we return to the reception?"

He looked at her with keen eyes then held out his arm to her. "Absolutely."

As they returned to the reception, Brittany's heart ached for her friend and she wondered why Cornelius couldn't have treated Daphne as graciously as he was treating her.

Chapter Eleven

Daniel glanced at Brittany and his heartrate sped up. As the day had progressed, his attraction to her had grown and he'd felt the buzz of excitement each time they'd touched. The first dance had just been announced and now he was about to hold her in his arms again. The very thought made his blood pulse through his veins.

Every head was turned to the dance floor. Brittany stood a few feet away, a shy smile on her face. He knew from spending time with her that she was uncomfortable being the center of attention. He could also tell from the way she nibbled on her bottom lip that the deception was weighing on her. If he could take away her discomfort, he would.

Though she didn't know it, the way her tongue swept across her lip turned him on. Truth be told, everything about Brittany was starting to turn him on. She looked both sweet and sexy in her wedding dress that revealed the shapeliest legs he'd ever seen. They looked even more enticing in her three-inch strappy white shoes.

She'd removed her veil and had freed her hair from the fancy twist it had been styled in. Now her hair floated around her bare shoulders, her curls bouncing whenever she turned her head.

Taking her hand, he led her to the dance floor then pulled her close. She held her body a little stiffly as if unsure of herself. Her sweet scent encircled him, and he closed his eyes in utter bliss.

They'd spent many hours trying to choose the song for their first dance, debating and laughing at each other's choices. It hadn't taken long for them to realize that none of the songs fit their situation. In fact, the song that could adequately sum up their relationship hadn't yet been written. They'd narrowed the choices down to two—with him and Brittany stubbornly sticking to their favorite—and had rock, paper, scissored it. "Always and Forever," a song that had been sung at weddings for a generation or two, was the winner.

As the song played, the lyrics hit Daniel in the solar plexus. The sighs of the female guests were audible, but it was Brittany's sigh that had his heart speeding up. He'd give anything to know what she felt at this very moment.

Did she have any idea just how sexy she was or how desirable he found her? This may be a show wedding, but that didn't make him immune to her. Kissing her had aroused feelings in him that he hadn't expected. And not simply desire. He'd kissed many women in his lifetime, many of them women he'd cared a great deal for, but the reaction he'd had kissing Brittany's lips made the others pale in comparison. Truthfully, there was no comparison. These kisses—like Brittany herself—were in a category of their own.

They'd almost felt like love. But that was crazy. He wasn't in love with Brittany. He couldn't be.

As they danced across the floor, he began to wish he hadn't promised her that their relationship wouldn't be physical. Logically a marriage in name only was the best way to handle this situation. This was a business arrangement. He'd been around long enough to know that business and pleasure didn't mix. Not successfully anyway.

It was imperative that this marriage be successful. So, as he'd done earlier when he'd found himself longing to kiss her deeply, he resisted the urge and thought about something mundane, like his horses' feeding schedule.

The last note of the music faded out and he reluctantly stepped back, keeping contact with Brittany as long as he could. The DJ announced the father and daughter dance, so he relinquished Brittany to her father then went to stand against the wall where he would be able to watch them.

Stephanos came and stood beside Daniel. "I think I might have made a mistake."

"About what?"

"You. Brittany. This marriage. I think there's more between the two of you than you let on."

Daniel looked around before replying. Every eye was focused on the dance floor where Phillip swung Brittany in a waltz. Brittany had told Daniel that when she'd been a teenager, she'd loved watching couples waltz in old movies and she'd convinced her father to teach her the dance. Hopefully, he and Hailey would have a special dance of their own one day.

"You're imagining things."

"Am I?"

"Yes." Daniel shoved his hands in his pants' pockets. "Sure, I like her. What's not to like? But that's as far as my feelings are allowed to go."

"Allowed?"

"The last thing either of us needs is complications." Like kisses that made him feel more than he should.

"True," Stephanos agreed. "But sometimes you don't get what you need. Sometimes you get what you get."

"You're a philosopher now?"

Stephanos laughed and, after a moment, Daniel joined him. It didn't take a philosopher to recognize the truth in those words. That's why it was important to take the hand you were dealt and play the cards the best you could.

Daniel heard footsteps and turned around as Rodney and William joined them. "Why are you guys lurking in the corner? Don't tell me you're in the doghouse already," Rodney joked.

"Even Daniel can't get in trouble at his own wedding reception," William replied, saving Daniel the trouble.

"Speaking of getting into trouble, Brittany has some gorgeous sisters," Rodney said.

"Who are now my sisters-in-law, which makes them off-limits." Rodney was a good guy, but he was a notorious womanizer who didn't remain with one woman for long. Given that Daniel's track record had been similar, he wasn't in a position to judge. But he wouldn't leave Stephanie or Tiffany vulnerable to a guy like Rodney, either.

"All I said was how pretty they are. I'm not planning on seducing either of them—unless I'm asked."

"Don't make me hurt you."

Rodney and William laughed. Daniel noticed that Stephanos didn't join in. There wasn't time for Daniel to ponder his friend's reaction because it was time for the bridal party to dance.

The first time he and Brittany had danced together, she'd seemed almost nervous and unsure. This time, she seemed to be enjoying it. That was good since dancing with his new wife was his new favorite thing. When the song ended, the emcee announced that the floor was open to anyone who wanted to dance.

After a few line dances and the throwing of the bouquet, Daniel noticed a marked difference in Brittany. Now that everything on the reception list had been checked off, she relaxed and truly enjoy herself. She laughed as she danced, enchanting everyone, especially him.

"I need a break," she said after a while.

"Sure." He led her back to their chairs. A passing waiter gave them drinks and, after a few sips, she smiled.

"I needed that."

"I saw you and Cornelius Taylor talking earlier. Does that mean he's going to go along with your Denim and Diamonds fundraiser idea?"

"I hope so. I guess only time will tell."

"He'd be a fool to tell you no."

She leaned over and kissed his cheek. "Thank you. That means the world to me."

His heart skipped a beat as her lips brushed his skin. He wanted another kiss. A real kiss. But that kind of thinking would only get him in trouble.

He'd nearly blown it earlier at the ceremony. Holding her soft body against his had been torture, but kissing her had nearly been his undoing. As much as he craved another taste of her, he had to keep his distance.

After she'd agreed to marry him, they'd covered every topic of their marriage and discussed it to death. They'd thought it prudent to limit their closeness. Heck, just about all of their conversations had involved ways of keeping their distance. Starting with living together. They'd been proud of their extensive planning, which left nothing to chance.

Brittany would move into the bedroom adjoining his master bath, although she'd keep her clothes in his closet to maintain the illusion that they were sharing a bed. None of his household staff lived in the main house, so that was a bonus. Not that either of them expected anyone to go snooping. But Marta wasn't blind, either. Brittany had assured him that she'd make her own bed and clean her room so Marta would never know anyone was occupying it. They'd discussed their upcoming cohabitation ad nauseam, leaving no detail uncovered.

But all that planning hadn't been as comprehensive as either of them had believed. If it had, one of them would have brought up the need to practice touching. And kissing. Had they done so, Daniel would have been prepared for the surge of electricity that shot through his body every time he brushed against her. Or breathed in her sweet scent.

And when he'd kissed her? It was as if a sign

with the word *Wow* had blinked in flashing lights over his head. It was all he could do to keep a goofy grin off his face. He wasn't sure if Brittany felt the same sensation, so he'd played it cool. The last thing he wanted was for her to worry that he'd pounce on her the first chance he got. She was his wife in name only. That's all she'd agreed to. Though he might want to renegotiate a clause in their contract to include kissing, he wouldn't mention it. He couldn't risk that she'd get upset and call it quits. He'd have to stick to the original plan and figure out how to keep his body under control.

"Ready for another dance?" she asked and smiled at him.

"Absolutely."

The DJ played another slow song and he held her in his arms. He'd concentrate on controlling his body later. Right now he was going to enjoy the moment.

Brittany dropped back into her chair. She'd been dancing for half an hour, having a great time. She'd danced with just about every man in attendance. When she'd danced with Brandon and Jordan Taylor, she'd casually mentioned the relationship between their sister, Daphne, and their father. She hoped they'd speak with Cornelius and try to smooth things over with him on their sister's behalf.

Daniel presented her with a glass of champagne then sat beside her. Clinking her glass against his in a silent toast, she lifted it to her mouth and took a sip. She wasn't much of a champagne drinker, but she had to admit this stuff was good.

Daniel looked past her and she turned around. Her mother was carrying a sleeping Hailey in her arms. Her father was right behind, the strap of the diaper bag slung over his shoulder.

"We're about to leave. We just wanted to say good-night," Mallory said.

Daniel stood. "Are you sure about letting Hailey spend the night? We don't mind taking her home with us."

"Nonsense. It's your wedding night," her mother protested. "And she's become comfortable with us."

"But—"

"No buts. She'll be fine. I understand that you two don't want to take a honeymoon trip right now with Hailey being so young, but you need at least one night together as husband and wife. Consider this a wedding present."

Brittany put a hand on Daniel's arm. She knew how protective he was of Hailey. But even so, it would look really strange if he didn't want to spend his wedding night alone with his new bride. Leaning her head against his shoulder, she smiled up at him. "Mom is right. Hailey will be fine. After all the excitement, she'll probably sleep straight through the night."

Daniel smiled at her and then at her parents.

"You're right. I'm being overprotective. Thanks for caring for her tonight."

Brittany was still leaning against Daniel after her parents left, and she didn't feel the need to move. He wrapped an arm around her waist, clearly comfortable with her nearness.

"You know, I guess we should be leaving soon, too," Daniel said. "It might look a little bit strange if we hang around all night."

"True. I'll let Reese know, so she can pass out the birdseed for people to toss at us."

Five minutes later, a laughing Brittany and Daniel ran from the restaurant and hopped into his Mercedes SUV. Brittany waved at the crowd, who watched them leave. She and Daniel had reserved the restaurant for the entire night, so their guests could party until the wee hours of the morning if they so desired. But for them, the party was over.

As they drove out of Bronco and toward Daniel's horse ranch, the reality of what they'd just done slammed into her. They'd really done it. They'd gotten married. For better or for worse, she was now Mrs. Daniel Dubois.

Chapter Twelve

As Daniel drove down the highway to the ranch, Brittany's breath caught in her throat and she forced herself to exhale. This was ridiculous. There was no reason for her to feel jittery. But still, her stomach was filled with butterflies crashing into each other. Her heart pounded and the blood raced through her veins.

Her wedding night was about to start.

Daniel had made it clear that he was willing to change the terms of their agreement. All she had to do was say the word. And right now, sitting beside him in his SUV, inhaling his intoxicating scent with every breath, renegotiation held a certain appeal. She'd love to be wrapped in his strong arms, pressed against his hard chest. But she couldn't give in to the desire to have a real wedding night. Not when she knew the marriage would end as abruptly as it had begun. No, she would stick to the agreed upon terms. This was a marriage in name only.

Daniel pulled into the driveway and parked. Brittany reached to open her door, but he put a hand on her wrist, stopping her. She looked at him.

"I can do that."

"So can I."

"Humor me."

She nodded. Resisting when he was being kind would only raise questions she did not want to answer. How could she explain that she didn't want him to be charming and chivalrous? That his being so gallant gave her ideas about their relationship? She didn't want him to turn into the man that she would have dreamed of—if she'd ever dreamed of a man.

He circled the SUV, opened her door and then offered his hand. She didn't want to appear churlish, so she placed her hand in his and let him help her. Instead of releasing her hand, he tightened his grip and rubbed his thumb over her knuckles as they walked across the cobblestones. He unlocked the door and pushed it open. Before she could step inside, he swung her into his strong arms.

She gasped and her lungs were filled with his heady masculine scent. "What are you doing?"

"I have to carry you over the threshold. It's good luck."

She knew she should protest, but being in his arms felt too good. Just this once, she'd allow herself the pleasure. "I didn't know you were the superstitious type."

"I prefer to think of myself as traditional."

He stepped over the threshold and then kicked the door closed behind them. Instead of setting her on her feet, he carried her into the front room and set her on the sofa. A bottle of wine and a tray of cheese, fruit, fine chocolate and crackers was centered on the coffee table. Vases of pink roses covered every table. It was all very romantic.

"Wow," Brittany exclaimed, looking around. "This is beautiful."

"Yes."

She looked at him. "Did you do this?"

He smiled. "With a little help."

Why would he do something like this? Surely he hadn't forgotten his promise of no wedding night. Given he'd behaved honorably since they'd met, she decided not to jump to conclusions.

He shrugged out of his tuxedo jacket, loosened his tie, unfastened his diamond-stud cuff links and then rolled his shirtsleeves over twice. "Would you care for anything? A strawberry? Truffle? Or, if you're really hungry, there's food in the kitchen. We'll have to cook it since everyone is gone, but I bet neither of us had much chance to eat at the party."

They were alone? Had he sent all the staff home deliberately? Brittany's nerves went into overdrive. She and Daniel had never been alone here before. Even when his employees had gone home for the night, Hailey had still provided a buffer. Her pulse picked up.

Start as You Intend to Continue had always been Brittany's motto. If she acted nervous now, she would no doubt be nervous for the remainder of her marriage. Undoubtedly, that would make Daniel uncomfortable. They didn't need to walk on eggshells for the next few months. Besides, they'd gotten along well for the past couple of weeks. She took a deep breath and forced herself to answer calmly. "This is good for now, but I might want something else later."

"Fair enough."

They each served themselves then leaned back against the sofa. For a moment, neither of them spoke, choosing instead to feast on the fruit and cheese.

"That went well, don't you think?" Daniel asked.

"Are you kidding? We were outstanding. No one suspected a thing. You definitely have a career in theater if this ranch thing doesn't pan out."

He laughed. "You weren't so shabby yourself. Everyone totally believes you're madly in love with me. But then, what's not to love?"

She threw a grape at him. He caught it and popped it into his mouth.

Brittany picked up a square of chocolate. She needed to distract herself from her attraction to him so she changed the subject. "Have you heard from your attorney lately?"

Daniel's smile faded and she wished she could take back the question and just enjoy the moment. "Yes. He said we can expect to hear from a court-appointed social worker who'll be interviewing us as well as the Larimars. Then the social worker will make a recommendation to the court about who should get custody of Hailey. The judge isn't bound by that recommendation, although my attorney says judges generally do what the social worker thinks is best."

"One more person to deceive."

"We aren't deceiving anyone. We're legally married. The details of our marriage aren't anyone else's business. Do you actually believe that every couple acts the same at home as they do in public? Do you think they don't have secrets? Theirs might be different from ours, but believe me, they exist."

"But they're in love."

"How do you know that?" He laughed. "Haven't you heard of staying together for the kids? Or the money? Heck there's that old seventies' song—'It's Cheaper to Keep Her.'"

Brittany laughed as she knew he'd intended.

"You're right. Thank you for reminding me of that. And regardless of how wonderful Hailey's paternal grandparents may be, they can't possibly be better for Hailey than you are."

She'd obviously said the right thing because he smiled. "Thanks for that."

They sat for a while, letting the peace of the quiet night wash over them. Finally, Brittany stood, plate in hand. "I don't know about you, but I'm beat. I think I'll head on up to bed. These past couple of days have been exhausting."

"Okay." Daniel stood and took her plate. "I'll take care of cleaning this up. I'll probably stay down here for a while and watch a little TV."

"I guess I'll say good-night, then."

He kissed her cheek. "Good night."

Brittany managed to act as if his kiss hadn't turned her knees to mush. She felt Daniel's eyes on her as she walked up the stairs, but she didn't turn around to look at him. Feeling as confused as she was, there was no guarantee that she wouldn't go running back for a second kiss. Or a third. When she reached the second floor, she turned and walked down the hallway to her bedroom.

Daniel had showed her the room and explained that the architect who'd designed the house had been enamored of the idea of the master and mistress of the house having their own private bedrooms with a shared master bath in between. Since Daniel had liked the plans, he'd gone along with it. She wondered what he thought of the design now.

Daniel had given her the option of sleeping in any of the other guest rooms, but she'd thought this one would work best. It might have raised red flags if she'd used another bathroom. The social worker might interview the staff. Brittany didn't want the maid to mention damp towels in a guest bathroom that might bring the status of her and Daniel's marriage into question.

Brittany stepped into the room and dropped onto the bed. The mattress was so soft, like sinking into a cloud. She just sat there awhile, letting the enormity of the day slide from her shoulders. Then she took off her dress and headed for the bathroom. What she needed was a good soak in Daniel's gigantic jetted tub.

She spotted a container of bubbling bath salts and gave thanks for whoever had bought them. Deciding she'd rather have the scent and bubbles over jets, she tossed a handful into the tub then turned on the water. While the tub filled, she washed off her makeup. She didn't see a shower cap, so she pinned her hair on top of her head. When the tub was full, she finished undressing and sank into the fragrant water.

Closing her eyes, she saw the images of the day flash in front of her. The sights and sounds of her wedding. The feel of Daniel's arms wrapped around her. Her skin began to tingle as she recalled just how good Daniel's kiss felt. It was almost like being in love, which didn't make a lick of sense.

Brittany didn't believe in love at first sight or anything remotely close to it. Love was something that grew over time. A lot of time. It came from shared experiences and shared values. She and Daniel hadn't done many things together—they hadn't known each other long enough. And it was way too soon to know if they had the same values.

Of course, none of that mattered when it came to animal attraction. Without question, she was attracted to Daniel. How could she not be? He was six feet of male excellence. His muscular body was well proportioned and the result of hard work, not steroids. He was clean-shaved, so none of his gorgeous face was covered by hair—not that a beard or mustache could mask his good looks. Nothing could do that.

His eyes revealed the sharp mind and quick wit he possessed. Though he was occasionally impatient, he had a kind heart. Especially where Hailey was concerned. If he was occasionally abrupt, it was because he was worried about something, not because he was inconsiderate. Once she'd figured that out, she'd been more inclined to give him a little bit of grace.

While she'd been soaking, the water had cooled, and she was getting cold. She hadn't been making excuses when she'd told Daniel she was sleepy. She was beat. Climbing out of the tub, she grabbed a plush bath towel, dried off and then wrapped the towel around her body.

Since her clothes were in Daniel's bedroom, she twisted the doorknob leading to his room. She'd get a nightgown and the clothes she intended to wear tomorrow and scoot into her room while he was downstairs watching TV. She opened the door, took one step and bumped into his bare chest.

Gasping, she jumped back into the bathroom. "What are you doing in there?"

"It's my bedroom. Remember? What are you doing coming in here?" He raised an eyebrow. "I thought we'd ironed out the details of our marriage and sleeping arrangements."

"I thought you were downstairs."

"I was. But the program I was watching ended and there was nothing else on that I wanted to see. You came up here over an hour ago, so I figured you were asleep by now."

"I was taking a bath," she said unnecessarily. She was standing there in nothing but a towel for goodness' sake. She tucked the end more firmly between her breasts. The last thing she wanted was for it to fall off. As it was, very little was left to Daniel's imagination.

And speaking of leaving nothing to the imagination. Daniel was dressed only in his tuxedo pants. The brown skin of his muscular chest looked so good she had to ball her hands into fists to keep from touching it. But that didn't keep her mind from thinking of how good it would feel to caress the muscles of his six-pack abs.

"I can come back later," he offered, turning to go.

"Wait." She grabbed his arm and the heat of his skin nearly burned her hand. She yanked her hand away and took two steps farther into the bathroom. The sensation was so strong, it took a minute for her mind to clear.

"Wait for what?" Daniel asked when she just stood there, her mouth hanging open.

"I'm finished in here. I was going to your room to get a nightgown. I'll get one and you can take your shower."

He leaned against the door frame, effectively blocking her way. "I didn't think this through. This whole clothes thing is going to be inconvenient for you."

"It's not that bad."

He smiled. "You know, you have to be the most positive person I've ever met."

Were they just going to stand there half-naked and talk? Apparently so. "Why wouldn't I be positive? It's not as if this is something that just happened to me. I made a decision that comes with consequences. When I agreed to marry you, my eyes were wide open. Besides, this has to be more inconvenient for you than it is for me."

"How do you figure that?"

"This is your house. You're used to doing everything your way. This is your bathroom, but you suddenly have to share it with me. Same as your closet. You'll have to get used to having me around all the time now that I won't be going home at the end of the night."

"That won't be a hardship. In a house this size, we won't have to see each other unless we want to." He gave her a devilish smile. "And if you're going to wander about wearing nothing but a tiny towel, I can guarantee I won't complain."

She poked him in his chest. "Sure, if you promise to never wear a shirt."

His eyes widened and he laughed. Clearly, she'd surprised him. "You might be on to something."

She grabbed a hold of herself. What was she doing? She couldn't flirt with him. "No, I'm not. Step aside, so I can get my nightgown."

He stepped back and she walked around him and into the master bedroom. Brittany's eyes were automatically drawn to the king bed in front of a wall of windows. The curtains were still open, revealing an Olympic-size swimming pool and patio. But it wasn't the view that held her attention. It was the flower petals scattered across the floor from the door to the bed that had her riveted in place.

She heard the rumble of his deep voice behind her. "I didn't tell Marta to do that. She must have thought it would make the room more romantic for our wedding night."

Brittany couldn't decide if she felt more disappointed or relieved to know the petals hadn't been his idea. "It was nice of her."

"Yes."

"I'll be certain to mention how much I liked it."

"Good thinking."

"What time does your staff usually arrive?" she asked.

"About seven. Why?"

"So I know what time I have to be up and have the bed made each morning. We can't afford slipups."

"If you want, you can always get into my bed," he suggested, making her heart skip a beat.

"I thought we had a deal. No funny business."

"That's not what I meant. It just didn't come out right. I get up early, so if you want to sleep in, feel free to hop into my bed when I get out."

Just like that, Brittany's mind went there. She could imagine lying in Daniel's bed, still warm from his body, her head on the pillow where his head had been only moments earlier and breathing in his intoxicating scent. Those kinds of thoughts needed to be banished before they landed her in trouble.

"And, for the record," he continued with a devilish grin, "there's nothing funny about the way I handle business."

She grinned. She knew he was joking just to keep

things light between them. "I'll keep that in mind. But as far as climbing into your bed, with or without you being there? That won't be necessary. I'm an early riser, too. Besides, I'll need to get to work."

"I thought you took a week off for our honeymoon."

"I did." A honeymoon that would at least in part be spent moving her belongings into Daniel's home. It wasn't exactly romantic, but then, this wasn't a romance. "But I was talking about later. When the honeymoon is over."

He nodded. "That makes sense. I'm usually not this dense. I don't know what's wrong with me right now."

From her perspective, there was nothing wrong with him. But then, she was staring at his bare torso. Or, more specifically, his sculpted shoulders and biceps. When her mouth started to water at the very thought of feeling those strong arms around her in a tight embrace, she knew it was time to grab her nightgown and go.

Once the gown was firmly in her hand, she bade Daniel good-night and dashed through the bathroom to her bedroom. She didn't realize she'd been holding her breath the entire time until it whooshed out of her. She slipped into the scrap of silk and lace her mother had insisted was perfect for her wedding night and then hopped into bed, where she knew she wouldn't sleep a wink. This was going to be one long night.

Chapter Thirteen

Daniel listened to the silence coming from the other bedroom. He'd been awake for an hour, yet he hadn't gotten out of bed, which was unusual for him. Once he awoke, he always climbed out of bed and got to work. There weren't enough hours in the day to get everything done—especially since Hailey had come to live with him—so lying in bed, doing nothing, was a luxury he couldn't afford. Still, today, he didn't move.

Closing his eyes, he pictured how Brittany had looked yesterday at their wedding. She'd been so beautiful. So sexy. Her eyes had sparkled with excitement as they'd danced. And last night, wearing only a navy-blue towel, she'd been a vision. It had taken every ounce of strength he'd possessed to keep from unwrapping the towel from her body and letting it drop to the floor. Of course, doing so would have violated their agreement. He couldn't afford to step across the line. Not just because of Hailey, although her welfare was primary, but because of the kind of man he was.

His word was his bond. He didn't give it easily, but when he made a promise, he kept it. He wouldn't change that now. Dragging a hand down his face, he got out of bed. There was plenty to do and time was a-wasting.

Today he and Brittany were moving her belongings into his house. Although her condo could fit into his house several times over, he had a feeling that adding whatever furniture and other items she wanted to bring to his place wasn't going to be as simple as it sounded. Sure, he had the space, but items with sentimental value deserved places of honor. He wanted Brittany to feel at home in his house. If that meant being surrounded by her knick-knacks, so be it.

A knock on his door pulled him away from his musings.

"You decent?" Brittany called from the other side of the door.

That depended on what she meant by decent. If she meant his thoughts—hell no. Just hearing her voice sent them veering into the X-rated. But if she was talking about his appearance? Maybe.

When Hailey had come to live with him, he'd begun sleeping in pajama bottoms. No matter how hard he tried, he couldn't make himself wear the tops. The bottoms were confining enough as it was.

"Sure." She'd seen his chest before and hadn't fainted. In fact, she'd seemed to like what she'd seen. But then again, he could be projecting how he'd felt seeing her nearly nude.

The door opened and Brittany stepped inside. He took one look at her and his heart practically jumped out of his chest. She was dressed in a pink silk-and-lace nightgown that revealed as much as it covered. For a brief moment, he was willing to throw his dignity and self-respect into a burning Dumpster and enjoy a few hours in his bed with her.

Oblivious to the thoughts he was currently battling, Brittany smiled then crossed the room and sat on his bed. Her sweet scent teased his nostrils. "I was in such a rush last night that I forgot to grab clothes for today."

Apparently she was in no rush to get them because she didn't move toward his closet.

Looking at her beautiful face made thinking hard, but looking at her body made thinking impossible. So he focused on her feet. That should be safe. After all, there was absolutely nothing attractive about toes. One glance had him rethinking that belief. Because her feet were sexy as hell. She'd painted her toenails the same pink color as her fingernails. The skin of her feet was smooth brown and looked soft and touchable. He imagined his feet tangled up with hers and realized there was no distracting himself from his desire for her. The only way to keep from acting on his lust was to stay busy.

"Go ahead and get them," he urged. "I'll get dressed, too. We need to pick up Hailey from your parents. I don't want her worrying that I forgot about her." His voice came out harsher than he'd intended. But it was hard to sound friendly when he was fighting to keep his hands to himself.

"Okay." The hurt and shock in her eyes made his stomach twist with guilt. Just because he was struggling with desire didn't give him the right to be rude to her. His lust was his problem.

"I'm sorry. I didn't mean to be sharp."

"Sure. I doubt that Hailey's awake now, but if she is, she's in great hands. I have no doubt that my parents are spoiling her rotten. They've been on my case about settling down and giving them grandchildren for a while. Marrying you has gotten them off my back."

"Glad I could help."

"Me, too." She went into the closet, grabbed the outfit that she'd brought with her and was gone, leaving him alone with his thoughts. Not entirely alone. Remnants of her sweet scent hung in the air and teased his senses. He inhaled deeply, basking in the floral scent for a moment before he forced himself to stop fantasizing about Brittany. She was off-limits.

This overwhelming longing was new to him. In the past, if a woman was prohibited for whatever reason, he didn't give her a second thought. His mind and his body had always been in one accord. He'd never fought with himself as he was doing now, never had difficulty staying on the right side of the line. But he'd never been married before, either.

Married. Brittany was his wife to have and to hold as long as they both shall live. If only that were true. Theirs was a marriage in name only, so he didn't picture himself being able to wrap her in his arms any time soon. No, there wouldn't be any holding between them and certainly not any having.

He dressed quickly then went downstairs. Brittany was in the kitchen, leaning against the marble counter and sipping coffee as if she'd done it every day for years. Smiling, she filled a mug and handed it to him. He took a sip. Strong and black, just the way he liked it. While he enjoyed his coffee, he looked at Brittany over the rim of his mug. Dressed in blue denim shorts and a pink T-shirt, she looked sexier than she should have. Her curly hair bounced around her shoulders and his fingers ached to run through it. He could get used to seeing her every morning.

"Are you sure you're dressed for moving furniture?"

Brittany laughed softly and his longing returned with a vengeance. "I'm not moving furniture now. My roommate isn't getting married until later in the fall, so I'll just leave everything there until she moves."

"What about your bedroom furniture?"

"I thought about that. But then I looked around here. All of your rooms are fully furnished. There's really no space for my stuff. I could put my bed and dresser in storage, but that really doesn't make sense. Amanda can turn my room into a guest room."

He nodded. That was quite generous of her, but not surprising. Brittany was a very generous and giving person. If there was a selfish bone in her body, he hadn't discovered it.

Not that he believed she was perfect. He didn't. Everyone had flaws, himself included. But Brittany had to be as close to perfect as anyone he'd ever met. That, given his growing attraction to her, wasn't a good thing. He needed her to have more faults. Not the kind that would make living with her difficult, but those that would stem his attraction to her before it got the better of him.

"I just need to pick up my clothes and small items. Everything should fit in the back of your SUV. I think it would be better to leave Hailey with my parents instead of trying to do this with her, but it's obviously up to you."

He nodded. "Let's check with your parents then

decide. If Hailey is fine, there's no reason to disturb her. But if she's missing me, we can pick her up."

"That makes sense." Brittany finished her coffee, rinsed her mug and then set it in the sink. She looked at the wall clock. "I thought you said your employees arrive at seven."

"I gave them the week off. I figured it would be easier to convince people that we were enjoying our honeymoon if we spent the week alone. Getting used to living together will be hard enough without an audience."

She nodded. "You think of everything. And thank you. I'll feel better knowing I'm not being watched."

He downed his coffee then called her parents and spoke with his mother-in-law. He could hear Hailey chattering and laughing in the background, so he knew that she was happy for the time being. Mallory promised to call him if Hailey started to fuss.

"She okay?" Brittany asked when he ended the call.

"Yes. So I'm ready whenever you are."

"I'm ready now. Just let me grab my purse."

Five minutes later, they were in his SUV on the way to her apartment. He'd been there a couple of times, but since theirs wasn't a real relationship, he'd never entered her bedroom. Now he would be walking into the inner sanctum. Despite telling himself they wouldn't be doing anything other than grabbing the belongings she'd chosen to take with her, his heart sped up at the thought.

It was warm, so they'd rolled down the windows to let in the sweet breeze. Birds chirped in the trees, their music filling the air. Despite the beautiful day, he was acutely aware of Brittany sitting beside him and his heart thumped. He reached out to caress her face. Luckily he realized what he was doing in the nick of time and turned on the radio instead, disguising his original action.

He didn't necessarily feel like listening to music—he generally preferred to drive in silence—but he needed the distraction. Brittany hummed along to the song, then began to sing. Though he had a decent if unremarkable voice, he'd never felt comfortable singing in front of others. Brittany had no such reluctance and she sang quite loudly and with gusto. He had to give her credit for boldness. If he had as hard a time staying on key as she did, he wouldn't even sing in the shower.

Maybe that was the flaw he'd been searching for? No. Instead of being annoyed, he found her lack of talent endearing.

Once they reached her apartment, he parked in the underground lot and they took the elevator to her floor. She looked around as they walked through the hallway to her front door. She slowed, as if saying goodbye to a home she'd loved. He wouldn't pretend to know what she was feeling, but he could let her know he was there for her. Reaching out, he grabbed her hand and gave it a gentle squeeze.

"I'm okay," she murmured as they stepped inside. "I packed up the kitchen. I don't cook much but, believe it or not, I have a full set of pots and pans and a bunch of gadgets that I never use. I also have my great-aunt's good china. She gave it to me when she moved into a retirement home. I was born on her birthday, so she always favored me. Crazy, huh?"

"You never know what makes people tick." There was no way he would judge her aunt. He didn't know much about marriage, but he knew criticizing the in-laws never led to anyplace good.

"I guess. She was angry with my mother for a long time because she thought Mom should have named me after her. My mother swore she didn't know it was my great-aunt's birthday."

"What's her name?"

"Grace." Brittany took a step around him and tripped over a box.

He laughed at the irony. "I can see that," he teased. "Was your middle name supposed to have been ballerina?"

She punched him in the arm, which only made him laugh harder. She frowned before she laughed with him.

He added a sense of humor and the ability to laugh at herself to the ever-growing list of qualities he admired about her. At this rate, he'd be able to fill a notebook before the day was over.

They carried down the boxes she'd filled and then headed back up to her bedroom. "I know I should have packed up my clothes and shoes, but I ran out of time."

"No worries."

He stripped her bed and turned to drop the linens into a box as Brittany grabbed a fistful of lacy underwear from her top drawer. Their eyes met and her cheeks grew pink as she tossed her frilly panties into a box. She opened another drawer and began grabbing socks, avoiding his gaze as she emptied the drawers.

When her dresser was empty, she went to work on the walk-in closet, pulling out armfuls of dresses. Had she really told him that all of her belongings could fit in his SUV? Not with the amount of clothes she had. And she didn't appear to be anywhere near finished with the closet.

Not that he was judging the size of her wardrobe. He'd once been a part of the corporate world and knew the importance of projecting the right image. And if she owned all of these outfits simply because she liked to look good? More power to her.

It took several hours to pack up her belongings and three trips to his ranch, but finally part one of moving her in had been accomplished. Putting things away would be more her job than his. It was up to Brittany to decide what went where.

He didn't have any emotional ties to any of his household furnishings. He'd hired a designer to decorate, so nothing had sentimental value. He'd already told Brittany she had free rein to rearrange the furniture or replace items with her own. More than anything, he wanted her to be happy and comfortable, making his home hers.

Once the boxes were piled inside the house, he put the car seat back into the SUV and they headed to Brittany's parents' house to pick up his daughter. As they neared his in-laws' neighborhood his excitement grew. Although it had only been a day, less than that, really, he'd missed Hailey. It hadn't taken long for her to become the most important part of his life. He loved her more than anything in the world and would do anything for her. His marriage was proof of that.

He parked and turned off the ignition. Brittany was reaching for her door handle when he stopped her.

"What?" she asked, looking genuinely perplexed. Then she shot him a mischievous look. "Don't tell me you want to carry me over my parents' threshold, too?"

He laughed. "No. There's no tradition for that."

"Good. That would have been a bit excessive."

"Your parents believe we're newlyweds."

"Technically, we are. At least, that's what you keep telling me." The smirk on her face was cute and he grinned.

"My point is that we need to look and behave like newlyweds."

"You lost me. I know how to act like a new bride, but I have no idea how a new bride looks."

He paused. They had a deal, but still…this was important.

"They hold hands and are affectionate. I need you to feel comfortable with me touching you in front of your parents. I might hug you or kiss you and I don't want you to pull away."

Her cheeks pinked up, but she nodded. "I can do that."

"I know."

He held out his hand and she took it for a moment. Her skin was warm and soft, and he hated to let it go. But he had to…to get out of the car. Once they were out, he wrapped his arm around her waist and pulled her closer to him. He liked the feel of her by his side.

The front door opened before they were up the steps. Mallory stood there, holding Hailey. When his daughter saw him, she let out a happy squeal and lunged for him. He trotted up the last step and scooped Hailey into his arms. He hugged her and she giggled then gave him a sloppy kiss on his cheek. Daniel reached out and took Brittany's hand, pulling her into a family hug. For something that was a sham, he couldn't help but think that it felt so right.

Brittany watched the reunion between father and daughter with a happy heart. The love between Hailey and Daniel was so real. So strong. It would be cruel for the courts to separate them.

"Come on in," her mother said. "Do you have time to visit?"

Brittany met Daniel's gaze. Though he didn't say anything, she could read in his eyes that he would do what she wanted, but she knew that he really wanted to just go home. "Not today. I want to get settled. And I'm sure Hailey would like to be in her own home and play with her toys."

"Okay. But Hailey had a good time with her nana and grandpops."

At the sound of her name, Hailey turned and looked at Mallory. She babbled a few words then lay her head against Daniel's chest. Clearly, Hailey was ready for the fun time she'd had with her new grandparents to come to an end.

Once they were back in the SUV, Hailey began babbling and she chattered all the way to the ranch.

"I thought babies were supposed to fall asleep in the car," Brittany said.

Daniel laughed. "Not after a nap, which I suspect Hailey has just had."

Great. Apparently, Brittany's full-time mommy

duty was going to start immediately with a wide-awake baby.

When they got to the ranch—home, she reminded herself—Daniel took Hailey out of her car seat and grabbed the diaper bag in one smooth motion. Daniel might not have had a baby for long, but he'd mastered some essential skills.

When Hailey spotted the maze of boxes, she was instantly intrigued and struggled to get out of Daniel's arms. Sighing, he put her down and they watched as she crawled to the nearest one and used it to help her stand.

Daniel smiled over at Brittany and her heart lurched. What was that about? She knew she was attracted to him, but if a simple smile could make her heart soar to the sky, she was in danger. Danger of falling in love with him. And under no circumstance could she fall in love with him. What she and Daniel had was a business arrangement and it would behoove her to remember that. When the time came for their marriage to end, she would pack up and leave, returning to her regularly scheduled life while he went back to his. She couldn't afford to let herself have romantic feelings for him. To do so would be disastrous.

A part of her still couldn't believe she'd actually married him. Sure, the idea of having the funds to start her own business had been tempting. As the child of business owners, she'd always wanted to work for herself and be the one in control, the one making the rules and the important decisions. But marrying to achieve that goal was completely out of character for her.

Could it be that there had been something at work in her subconscious? Did she secretly want to be married and have a baby? Not married to Daniel, of course, but married to an imaginary perfect husband.

This marriage was a convenient way to try her hand at being someone's wife and mother; a way to discover if she was cut out for the job. One might say she was trying on the role to see how it fit. If she liked how it felt, she might adjust her five-year plan for her life, penciling in marriage. And if she didn't like it, she could cross that off her to-do list and carry on as planned. She didn't kid herself that it would be as easy as returning an unworn dress, but it was the best she could do. She didn't actually believe she would decide she wanted a husband and kids, but this way she'd be sure she wasn't missing out.

As she watched Hailey tumble onto her diapered bottom, Brittany felt a flood of emotions. She really cared about Hailey and wanted her to have a great future. A happy life. The best way to accomplish that was to live with Daniel.

Hailey enjoyed playing for a few more minutes then, without warning, her pleasure vanished, and she dropped to the floor and began to fuss.

He picked up Hailey and held her against his

chest. "I was about to carry the boxes upstairs, but I guess that can wait."

Brittany looked at her new daughter. She was going to have to step into the role as mother sooner or later. Start as You Intend to Continue applied here, too. "Let me take her. She might need a diaper change. Or want a snack."

"Are you sure?"

"Yes. You just get those boxes where they belong, Muscle Man."

"Muscle Man?" He smiled and preened, flexing his biceps.

Why had she said that out loud? The man didn't need to be reminded of what he looked like. There were mirrors in this house. Not to mention women in this town who weren't nearly as discreet as Brittany wished they were. She'd seen women turn and stare when Daniel came into view. There was no way he'd missed it, either.

"Don't let it go to your head. Your muscles are bigger than mine and therefore better suited to physical labor like carrying."

"I see." He winked at her and then bent to pick up a box, putting it on his shoulder. Though she tried not to look, her eyes drifted down to his backside, which, she noticed, was also toned. She forced her eyes upward across his back and shoulders. She didn't know what kind of regimen this man had, but it was working. She'd need to up her game if she wanted to look as good as he did.

But why? This wasn't a competition. And he wasn't going to be seeing her naked anyway.

Hailey began to make louder noises, stirring Brittany out of her silly musings. "Let's get you a new diaper."

Brittany and Daniel walked to the stairs. He paused and swept out his free arm. "After you."

Suddenly self-conscious, Brittany climbed the stairs with a bit of a sidestep. Then she decided to heck with that and put a little extra swing into her hips. He wolf-whistled and she wondered if she was playing with fire. Maybe, but she was going to be living here for a while. She and Daniel needed to be able to have fun together. After all, there was that social worker to fool. As well as the judge. And the more comfortable they were together, the better their charade would be.

At least, that was what she told herself. Because anything else was unthinkable.

Chapter Fourteen

Brittany dropped onto the sofa beside Daniel and tucked her feet beneath her. She couldn't remember the last time she'd been this exhausted. Hailey had positively worn her out. There'd been moments when she'd wanted to wave the white flag and cry uncle, letting the little girl know she'd won. But she'd been determined to prove to Daniel that he could trust her with Hailey.

Taking care of a baby was a lot harder than her cousins had made it look. But then, none of them had started out with a nine-month-old. They'd learned how to care for babies with infants who didn't crawl away the second you turned your back. None of their first days had been with teething kids who fussed and drooled and gummed everything in sight. Most of Brittany's exhaustion was a result of being on alert for hours on end. If she wasn't checking to make sure that Hailey wasn't about to pull something onto her head or crawl down the stairs, she was watching to be sure that the baby didn't shove something into her mouth. Or nose. Or ears.

But Hailey was now fed, bathed, freshly diapered and sound asleep in her crib where, hopefully, she would sleep through the night. Though it was only eight o'clock, Brittany longed to fall into bed herself. But that would look like she hadn't been up to the task. Daniel, on the other hand, looked fresh as a daisy and not like he'd been carrying boxes around all evening. No, she needed to stay awake for at least two more hours. Ten o'clock or bust.

"Thanks for putting my stuff away," she said then yawned.

"No worries. I needed some special china for the cabinet. The designer had offered to purchase some for me, but I hadn't been interested then. Now I like the way the dishes look in there. I'll have to get some when you move out."

She nodded. Aunt Grace's dishes did look like they'd been made especially for the cabinet. But Brittany couldn't concentrate on china, not after what Daniel had said. *When you move out.* She didn't want to think about her marriage ending. Not tonight.

"So what do you want to do now?"

He looked surprised by her question. "You aren't tired? I love Hailey to pieces, but taking care of her full-time wears me out. But then, you helped your mother with your brothers and sisters, so you have more experience than I do."

She allowed herself to sink deeper into the sofa cushions and released the sigh she'd been stifling. If they were going to have a successful marriage, she needed to answer his questions honestly. That is, as long as the questions didn't involve her growing attraction to him. "Truthfully, she wore me out, too. And I don't ever remember being this exhausted."

"How about we warm up the takeout and eat here while we watch TV?" They'd stopped at DJ's Deluxe on the way home from picking up Hailey and had grabbed a ton of food.

"That sounds good to me."

"You stay here. I'll get it."

He wouldn't get any argument from her. Just the idea of being waited on hand and foot was enough to make her heart smile.

Daniel was back in a few minutes, carrying two overflowing plates. The aroma alone made her mouth water. Daniel set the plates on the coffee table and went back to the kitchen. He returned momentarily, carrying a bottle of wine and two glasses in his hands, two water bottles tucked under his arms.

A minute later they were holding plates on their laps and trying to find something they would both enjoy watching on television. When they couldn't agree on anything, he switched off the TV and turned on the stereo. Fortunately they were both fans of seventies music.

They talked easily while they ate. Brittany was surprised to discover how well they got along. She couldn't remember the last time she'd had so much fun with a man. They'd told funny stories from their childhood and teen years, and Brittany had been endlessly amused by tales of his antics. He reminded her so much of her brothers that she felt as if she'd known him all her life. There was definitely more to Daniel than he let on. Under other circumstances, she'd want to get to closer to him to see where things led. But being temporarily married made that permanently impossible. Still, there was no reason they couldn't enjoy their time together for however long it lasted.

She sipped her wine then looked over at him. "Why Montana? I can understand leaving a successful business you'd started in order to try something new, but why move to an entirely different state?"

He leaned back against the sofa and paused as if weighing his next words before uttering them. "Moving to Montana was about more than business. I was at a place in my life where I needed a total change. There's so much untapped potential here. The possibilities for growth are endless. But that's just business.

"On a personal note, I needed the space to breathe.

And the natural beauty here is unrivaled. I also liked the idea of setting down roots in Bronco. Now that I have Hailey, I know I've made the right decision."

"I grew up in this town and I love it, so you'll get no argument from me about the natural beauty. We're surrounded by it."

His eyes swept over her and she felt her cheeks warm. "I certainly am."

Just like that, the mood turned sensual. A part of Brittany wanted to flirt back. And more. What harm would there be in a few kisses? After all, they were married. And they knew where to draw the line. She knew Daniel's character. He was a gentleman and would take no for an answer. That wasn't the issue. The problem was that, right now, in the dimly lit room with the soft music playing in the background, and feeling relaxed from the wine, Brittany wasn't confident she would say no.

She decided that a wise woman wouldn't put her self-control to the test, so she polished off her wine, set her glass on the table and met Daniel's gaze. The warmth she saw there had her coming close to reconsidering her stand. "Thanks for a lovely evening. I have a feeling that Hailey will be up bright and early tomorrow, meaning we should be, too. So I guess I'll say good-night now."

Standing, she reached for the dishes. He rose, too, and put his hand on hers. Silly tingles skittered down her spine. She tried to convince herself they were the result of the wine and not from the feel of his skin on hers, but she knew that wasn't true. Their gazes met and her breath caught in her throat. For a moment, she thought he might kiss her and her heart sped up with delicious anticipation. Instead, he gave his head a little shake and then dropped his hand. She forced a smile, masking her disappointment.

"I'll take care of the dishes."

Right. The dishes. Odd how she'd forgotten what she'd intended to do just that easily. It was definitely time to end the night. "Thanks. I'll see you in the morning."

She walked from the room on wobbly knees, feeling his eyes on her. She climbed the stairs sedately even though she wanted to race up them like there was a prize waiting for the winner.

Once she reached her room, she sat on her bed and the air whooshed from her lungs. She needed to get a handle on her attraction. How many times did she need to tell herself that Daniel was off-limits before her body got the message?

Daniel looked out the window and frowned. Rain was coming down in buckets. His plan for the three of them to go into town and spend the day together had been washed away by the weather. It looked like he and Brittany would be alone again today. Of course, Hailey would be with them, but she wasn't much of a chaperone. And given his growing attraction to Brittany, it would be nice to have someone else around whose presence would force him to behave.

He knew that flirting with Brittany wasn't wise or in either of their best interests. He hadn't thought that refraining would be a problem. He'd never been much of a flirt in the first place, preferring the direct approach. That way, there were no misunderstandings. If a woman was interested, great. If not, she could say so and he would move on. No harm, no foul. But for some reason he had yet to discover, he caught himself flirting and dropping hints with Brittany. His behavior was out of character and it confused the heck out of him.

Beautiful as she was, he wasn't interested in dating her. They didn't want the same things. She was focused on building a business, not a family. She didn't want kids. He had a nine-month-old. And though Brittany was willing to help him in the short term, she'd made it plain that she didn't want anything permanent. Given that he'd done his share of rejecting women in the past, he wasn't upset with her.

Yet knowing that she didn't see him playing a role in her future hadn't diminished his attraction to her. It was just as strong as ever. And growing. That's why he'd planned to go into town. She was just so appealing that being alone with her would only lead to trouble.

He swiped a hand over his forehead as he recalled

being alone with her last night. The urge to kiss her had nearly overwhelmed him...until he remembered their deal. This was a business-arrangement marriage and not a love match. Kissing and any other shows of affection would only muddy the waters. It was in their best interests that they stick to the rules they'd established.

This entire marriage was more complicated than he'd expected it to be. But since they'd already said their vows in front of scores of witnesses, there was no turning around now. And, truthfully, he didn't want to do things differently. Because, right or wrong, wise or foolish, he was attracted to his bride. Though it had only been a couple of days, he enjoyed being married to her.

"Do you think the rain will stop soon?" Brittany asked, coming into the room, Hailey in her arms. Dressed in what she referred to as cowgirl chic—pink denim shorts, a pink, green and white plaid shirt, and pink-and-white sandals—she made his heart flutter.

She came to stand beside him and look out the window. Her familiar scent wafted under his nose and his imagination switched into overdrive. Her perfume had a vaguely floral scent that appealed to him. But it was her personal scent that turned him on and had him fantasizing about ways for them to entertain themselves here.

"Ba baboo," Hailey said, reaching for him.

"Did you two have fun?"

"That's one word for it," Brittany said dryly.

"I told you I would take care of her today."

"I know, and I had fully intended to take you up on that offer. But one thing turned into another and time got away from us. Besides, we were having fun playing with her stuffed animals. And I know you had work to do."

Truer words were never spoken. When he'd worked at his company, he'd been able to delegate a lot of tasks to his staff. He'd also had complete departments dedicated to advertising and promotion as well as business development. That was no longer the case. He was now an army of one. True, he'd hired Brittany to handle the affair on behalf of his resort, but he was still responsible for every other aspect of its launch. He had the money to hire a full complement of employees, but he didn't want to do that. He relished doing most things on his own and stretching different creative muscles.

"Thanks. I got more done today than I had in a long time, which is why I was planning an outing for this afternoon. The rain has put a damper on that."

"So let's do something else. We might not be able to go outside, but we can have a good time inside."

"Doing what?"

She looked so cute with her furrowed brow as she thought. "I don't know. Hailey just woke up from her nap, so she needs to eat. And I'm a bit hungry myself."

His stomach growled then, saving him from uttering his agreement. But since he'd given his staff the week off, he and Brittany were in charge of cooking, something neither of them did particularly well. "What would you like?"

"What do you have?"

He knew he had a good supply of baby food, but other than that? He didn't have the foggiest idea. Hopefully, his cook had left something in the freezer that they could just warm up. Otherwise they were on their own, something he didn't relish.

While he strapped Hailey into her high chair, Brittany rummaged in the pantry, coming out with a jar of baby food and a biscuit that his daughter loved. While Brittany heated the baby food, he scrounged through the freezer, but nothing he found appealed to him.

"There's nothing to eat," he said.

"Oh. So what's the plan?"

"I guess I could go out for something."

"How about ordering a pizza? Or wings?"

"You'd be okay with that?"

"Of course."

He didn't know why he was surprised by her response. Brittany had showed him on more than one occasion that although she dressed nicely and seemed to enjoy the finer things in life, she wasn't pretentious or demanding.

"I'll call in an order and then swing by to pick it up."

"Okay. Sounds good."

"Or, if you want, you and Hailey can come with me."

"Sort of a family outing, after all?"

It wasn't what he'd had in mind, but it still had appeal. "Yes."

"I'm in. Let me finish feeding Hailey and then we'll be ready to go."

He nodded and watched as Brittany tried to convince Hailey to eat her food.

When Hailey'd first started eating, she'd opened her mouth in anticipation. That was no longer the case. Now she turned her head away whenever Brittany offered her the spoon. She wanted to feed herself. Only, the spoon held little interest for her. She preferred to use her fingers.

Though he knew first-hand how exasperating it could be when Hailey chose not to cooperate, he found the entire scene amusing. But as determined as Hailey was to do things her way, Brittany was just as determined.

"I don't know why she's acting like this. She didn't do this before."

"She's practicing being a woman," he said with a chuckle.

Brittany's hand froze, spoon in the air. "Say what?"

Uh-oh. "She's just not feeling it, so she's exercising her feminine prerogative of expressing her feelings honestly." When Brittany only stared at him, he swallowed. He knew he should stop talking, lest he dig himself a deeper hole, but he continued, hoping for a way out. "She's being her authentic self, which is something we should honor."

"I see." Brittany turned back to the baby, but he could see there was a smile on her face. He didn't know whether it was because she was pleased by what he'd said or because Hailey had decided that she wanted to use the spoon. Whatever the reason, Brittany's joy touched his heart in a way that could be described with one word. Dangerous. Her happiness shouldn't matter that much to him. And it certainly shouldn't make him feel all warm and gooey inside.

"It looks like we're done here," Brittany said, interrupting his musings. "Give me ten minutes and we'll be ready to go."

He nodded. The idea of being in the close confines of the SUV with Brittany was simultaneously thrilling and nerve-racking. He tried to find a neutral emotion but couldn't think of one, so he would just have to be thrilled, which was, in and of itself, nerve-racking.

He really was losing it. But what a way to go.

Chapter Fifteen

Daniel was focused on driving, so Brittany took the opportunity to study him without getting caught. He looked so calm and cool, steering the SUV through the streets. He was dressed in a gray shirt that hugged his torso and jeans that fit his muscular thighs. His appearance set her imagination free and she hoped her reaction didn't show on her face. Though she'd been around him many times over the past weeks, she hadn't found a way to inoculate herself to his appeal. Despite all her rational arguments why becoming emotionally or physically involved with him was a bad idea, her stubborn body zinged whenever he was near. And in the intimate confines of the vehicle, her body was lighting up like the classic pin-ball machine languishing in her parents' basement.

She had hoped that having Hailey around would temper her body's response, but the little girl's presence didn't make an impact. Brittany's insides were humming a happy tune. Worse, her hands ached to run up and down his muscular arms. Not sure how long she could resist the urge, she folded her hands together as if in prayer.

The rain had slowed and it was barely drizzling when they reached the pizza parlor. Daniel held an umbrella over Hailey and Brittany as they entered the restaurant. The place was filled with people who'd had the same idea, but there were a couple of free tables. They had no problem switching from carry-out to dining in. A waitress brought them their hot pizza at the same time she brought their cold drinks.

Brittany settled Hailey into a high chair and gave her a couple of toys that she'd no doubt pick up several times before the night was over.

Daniel was as charming as ever and even a bit flirtatious. Brittany found herself flirting in return, something she'd told herself not to do but couldn't seem to stop. Their hands touched often, as was the case when two people shared a pizza, and she was aware of every touch. Every glance. She noticed every little thing about him. The way his eyes squinted when he laughed. The dimple in his right cheek.

"Well, if it's not the newlyweds," a female voice called.

Brittany turned and smiled at her friend. Rising, she gave Melanie Driscoll a hug. "What a surprise seeing you here."

"I was in the mood for pizza, so Gabe and I decided to brave the rain." She grinned and winked. "Don't tell DJ."

Brittany laughed. Her friend was the new CFO of DJ's Incorporated. "Your secret is safe with me."

"Do you want to join us?" Daniel asked, offering his seat to Melanie.

"No, we're getting ours to go." She looked over her shoulder at her fiancé, Gabe Abernathy, who was holding a pizza box over by the door. "I just wanted to say hello. I miss seeing you now that we're no longer neighbors."

"We'll have to have lunch soon."

"I'm going to hold you to that."

"Give our best to Gabe."

"I will." Melanie took a step then turned back around. "You three really are a beautiful family."

"That couldn't have worked out better if I had planned it," Daniel said after Melanie had walked away.

"Planned what?"

"Running into your friends. Being seen together as a family. We can't stay secluded on the ranch, no matter how much I would like to. We need to be out and about together. It's important that people believe we're a real family and that we belong together."

"Of course," Brittany agreed then took a bite of her pizza. What had been a perfect combination of spicy tomato sauce, gooey cheese and savory sausage now tasted like ashes. She'd been enjoying the evening with Daniel, even the flirting. Especially the flirting. And all the while he'd thinking about how being seen as a besotted husband would work to his advantage.

Brittany forced herself to snap out of it. They had an agreement with terms specifically spelled out. Just because she wasn't as certain as she'd been a couple of weeks ago didn't give her to right to re-negotiate the contract to something that suited her current desires. As a businesswoman she knew a deal was a deal.

So she swallowed her bitterness along with the pizza and adjusted her attitude. If Daniel wanted to convince the town they were in love, that's what she would do.

When they'd finished eating, they boxed up the leftovers and stood. Hailey reached for Brittany and she automatically picked her up. Daniel grabbed the doggie bag with one hand and put the other one on Brittany's waist. His hand was warm and the heat permeated her skin and all but melted her bones. She leaned against her husband just as any new bride would, then concentrated on not going up in smoke.

The ride home was uneventful and Brittany used the time to remind herself that she and Daniel had a plan that included the dinner he'd hired her to arrange. She'd spent so much time organizing the wedding that Daniel's event had fallen by the wayside. It was time to remove it from the back burner and give it the attention it deserved.

When they got home, they played with Hailey for a while. Daniel tossed the baby into the air several times and she laughed loudly. Clearly, she was having the time of her life.

Though Brittany had never dated men with children for obvious reasons, she loved watching Daniel interact with the baby. He was so gentle, giving her one hundred percent of his attention. Her happiness and well-being were the most important things in the world to him. Suddenly the sexiest thing about Daniel wasn't his washboard abs or massive chest. It was the way he adored Hailey.

That thought puzzled her. If she didn't want children, and in fact wasn't sure she even wanted a husband, why did the fact that Daniel would make a great father appeal to her so much? Why did her stomach do loop-de-loops when she heard him sing silly songs or watched him play peek-a-boo with Hailey?

Her changing priorities worried her. She was more at ease when her attraction was limited to his physical attributes. She was even okay with admiring his ambition and business acumen. That was safe. But being pulled to him because of the way he enjoyed being a father? Her heart was skating on thin ice with that one. Too bad it wasn't something she could control.

She'd been lost in thought awhile and it took her a minute to realize the laughter had stopped. Turning, she looked at the floor where Daniel and Hailey had been playing. Now they were sprawled across the blanket. Daniel was lying on his back, his eyes closed. Hailey was lying across his chest, her thumb in her mouth. Brittany's heart squeezed at the sight.

Daniel's eyes opened and he caught her staring at him. She just hoped he couldn't see her emotions in her eyes.

"Let me help you," she said, lifting Hailey from his chest then holding the baby against her own.

"Thanks."

He stood in one graceful moment. "I guess she wore herself out."

"It looked to me like both of you were asleep."

"Nah. I have energy to spare. It takes more than playing with a little girl to wear me out."

Brittany pressed her lips together to keep any inappropriate words from escaping. Instead she rocked back and forth, hoping the motion would keep Hailey asleep until she was in her crib. When Brittany was certain she wasn't going to suggest they burn off their excess energy together in the way most newlyweds did, she spoke. "I'll be right back. I'm going to put her to bed."

Daniel's smile was both mischievous and mysterious and her self-control wavered. Only a moment. Then she forced herself to remember the dinner that was supposed to launch his business as well as catapult her career.

"When I come back, I want to discuss your event. We need to kick the planning into high gear."

Was that disappointment on his face? It couldn't be. Their relationship had started because of the dinner and his dude ranch. She might be his temporary wife, but she was still his event planner.

After she'd settled Hailey, Brittany went back downstairs. Daniel hadn't picked up the blanket, but instead was sitting on it. He looked extremely relaxed reclining against the sofa, his legs stretched out in front of him. He looked even more tantalizing than the tray of fruit and cheese beside the bottle of wine on the table.

He gave her a lazy grin. "I know it's a meeting, but nothing says we have to do it at a desk."

"I don't recall any of our other meetings being this casual."

"Really? Don't tell me you've forgotten about our horse ride already. I'm devastated."

She laughed and sat beside him. Before coming downstairs, she'd stopped in her room to grab the file. Regardless of the setting and the sexual attraction arcing between them, she intended to conduct herself professionally.

Reaching into her notebook, she flipped to a page of suggestions she'd jotted down. She began to explain them to Daniel along with the reasons she'd chosen the path she had. After ten minutes where she was the only one doing the talking, she looked at him. He'd never been so reticent in the past. "Don't you have anything to say?"

"Everything sounds good."

"That's it? You don't want to change anything? You weren't this easygoing before."

He shrugged. "My situation is different now than it was when I first hired you."

She hoped that didn't mean he'd lost interest in the project. She was planning to use it to showcase her skills and convince Cornelius Taylor to hire her. This dinner was a steppingstone to greater things. "How?"

"I'm married now."

"I know. I was there."

"I'm new to being a husband, so I don't know everything." He paused as he rubbed his chin.

She wished he would just get to it. "We have the same amount of time in the marriage game."

"Well, there is a well-known saying. Happy wife, happy life. So if you like it, I love it."

"That's it?" She was flabbergasted. He'd given her such a hard time before. Now that they were married, he no longer had an opinion? She couldn't name the emotions that coursed through her body, but she was fairly certain that none of them were positive. She didn't want favoritism. She wanted her work taken seriously. She wanted to be respected as the professional that she was.

"As flattering as that may be," she said, not bothering to mask the displeasure in her voice, "I'd rather you look at what I've done in the same way you would if we weren't married. I put a lot of effort into this project and I want you to give it proper consideration."

"But we are married and I can't pretend that we aren't."

"But it's not a real marriage."

"It's real enough."

"Regardless, I want your input. You made it clear that this dinner is very important to you and your business. I want it to be everything you envision it to be."

"Okay. But you told me that you could deliver what no one else could. That you are the best at what you do. I already had faith in you and your talent. I wouldn't have hired you otherwise. You wanted me to trust you and now that I do, you aren't happy."

"I still want you to trust my abilities. But I want you to be honest about my plans. I want you to be satisfied with the dinner. If there's something that you don't like, say so. My feelings won't be hurt. I don't want you agreeing just to make your little woman happy. I need you to separate the business from the personal. Can you do that?"

"Certainly, Mrs. Dubois."

She rolled her eyes. "Who said I was going to change my name?"

"No one. It's your right to use whichever name you want."

She nodded. She really hadn't given her name serious thought. And she wasn't going to think about it now. Right now she was going to focus on work.

Once they'd cleared the air, it was easy to get down to business. They discussed her plan in detail and Daniel suggested a few changes. If she thought his idea was better, she altered the plan. If she didn't, she pushed back, which led to quite a few spirited discussions. But when she'd scribbled the last note and closed her file, she was satisfied that they'd come up with the perfect plan. "This is going to be one spectacular dinner."

Daniel smiled. "Yes. Thanks to you. How long will it take to pull it all together?"

"Not long. I've been in contact with several vendors. I just needed your final approval. Now that I have it, I can give everyone the go-ahead."

She started to stand, but he put his hand on hers. "Thank you, Brittany. You've gone above and beyond everything I could have expected. If you weren't my wife and I wasn't afraid of being accused of favoritism, I'd give you a bonus."

"Ah, this marriage is costing me," she joked and then laughed.

He laughed with her, stood and then helped her to her feet. His fingers gripped hers a little longer than necessary before he slowly released her and stepped back. Though disappointed with his withdrawal, she knew it was necessary. They'd established boundaries for a reason. Just because she was attracted to him didn't mean she should start behaving recklessly. In fact, given everything that was at stake, she should reinforce the barriers around her heart before she did something stupid. Like throw herself into his arms and beg him to kiss her the way she'd dreamed of. Dreams were good while you slept but could lead to disaster if acted upon in real life.

"Ah, you've caught on to my devious plan."

"I never took you for a villain."

"Of course, you wouldn't. You're not the suspicious type. If you'd been expecting it, you would have foiled my dastardly plot." He wiggled his eyebrows and twirled a pretend mustache. Then he reached for her and she squealed, barely escaping his grasp.

She grabbed two accent pillows from the sofa, throwing one at him and using the other as a shield.

He dodged the pillow and flashing a devilish grin, he held her gaze as he crossed the room. Her heart pounded as he walked with exaggerated slowness.

Out of nowhere, he jumped and grabbed her, pulling her to the couch beside him.

"Now I've got you," he said. He ran his hands down her back, leaving goose bumps in their wake. When they reached her waist, he pulled her close.

She laughed, struggling to keep from wrapping her arms around his neck. Though she was practically overheating, she forced herself to play it cool. "Well, since you caught me, I'll have to wait for my hero to come rescue me."

"He'll never get past my minions."

She longed to stay in his arms—but knew giving in to that desire would only lead to trouble. So she gently pushed him back, letting her hand linger on his shoulder. "Well, while you're holding down the fort, I'm going to soak in a bubble bath. See you in the morning, my villain."

"Not so fast there, my captive bride. You need to convince me to let you walk away." He cupped her jaw and lowered his head to kiss her, and she knew that nothing would stop her from giving in. As she lifted her face to his, the phone rang.

Except that.

"Hold that thought." He looked at the phone's display and his smile vanished. "It's my lawyer."

Daniel spoke for a few tense moments. When the call ended, he looked at her. "The social worker will be coming to see us tomorrow."

Chapter Sixteen

"How do I look?" Brittany asked Daniel as she burst into his office.

He looked up from his desk where he'd been trying, unsuccessfully, to work. This was the third outfit she'd tried on. Each was as beautiful as the one before. The lilac silk blouse and deep purple cropped pants were elegant yet understated. She looked sexy as hell but, given her curves, that wasn't unexpected. Some things couldn't be disguised. "You look great."

She frowned down at herself. "I want to look motherly, but I'm not sure this works. Maybe I should put the dress back on. Nothing says 'mother' like a peach floral dress."

He grabbed her hand before she could race back upstairs. "You look fine. Not that the social worker will be paying attention to your clothes. What will convince her that we're the right people to raise Hailey is the way we interact with each other. That and how we treat Hailey. We have to make sure this woman knows that we're giving Hailey a happy home so there's no reason to place her with her grandparents."

"This meeting is so important to you. I don't want to blow it."

"You won't. Just be your wonderful self. Act naturally and she won't help but be charmed."

She smiled softly at him and his heart thudded. Though they were putting on this dog and pony show for the social worker, Daniel discovered that he meant every word. Brittany was wonderful and, the social worker would see that, too.

"Thanks."

"Now, how do I look?" he joked.

She laughed, as he'd hoped she would. She was much too tense. Not that he was relaxed by any stretch of the imagination.

Though he ordinarily wore jeans while working on the ranch and a suit in business meetings, he'd put on pressed khakis and a navy button-down shirt. When her eyes traveled over his body, all humor fled him, leaving lust in its wake.

"You'll do," she said, her voice husky. Her cheeks

had grown pink and he knew his attraction wasn't one-sided. He put a finger under her chin and tipped her face towards his as he bent down to kiss her. Before their lips could meet, the doorbell rang, and she shot him a panicked look.

The words that might have encouraged her escaped him, so he slipped an arm around her waist, simultaneously giving and receiving comfort.

Brittany grabbed his hand as they walked down the hall. "We can do this."

He smiled. "You bet we can."

They walked to the front door together and ushered the social worker, who'd introduced herself as Mrs. Kasey, into the front room. He'd imagined the social worker would be a humorless older woman who dressed in bland clothes, sensible shoes and wore her hair pulled in a tight bun in the back of her hair so the woman in her thirties was a surprise.

Despite how friendly the woman seemed, Daniel was suddenly afraid that she'd already decided against them and was merely going through the motions. His little girl was going to be taken away from him by this woman and there was nothing he could do about it.

As if she'd sensed his mind had traveled down a dark road, Brittany squeezed his hand. He glanced at her sweet face and his pounding heart slowed until it beat normally. He squared his shoulders and a sense of purpose and confidence filled him. He wasn't going to give up Hailey without a fight. When the social worker left, she was going to be convinced that he was a loving father who was giving Hailey a good home.

"Welcome to our home," he said.

"Thank you." She looked around the room. Her eyes landed on a framed family photo they'd taken in lieu of engagement photos. "Thank you, Daniel. It's nice to meet you."

"You, too." He introduced Brittany then offered her some refreshment, which she declined. "Would you like to have a seat?"

Mrs. Kasey nodded and sat in the chair he'd indicated. He and Brittany sat side by side on the sofa, still holding hands.

Once they were all settled, Daniel took the lead. "I imagine you want to get right to it. Brittany and I will be happy to answer any questions you have. Hailey is napping now, but she should be awake in half an hour or so."

Mrs. Kasey nodded. "You have a lovely home."

"Thank you," Brittany said. "We're very happy here. I'd be glad to show you around, if you'd like to see more of it."

"That would be nice." Mrs. Kasey pulled a file from her satchel. "I know that the two of you have only recently gotten married. How did that come about?"

Daniel glanced at Brittany, who gave him a warm

smile. The look in her eyes was so loving that, for a moment, he could actually believe she was in love with him and not simply pretending. "I'm planning on opening a dude ranch and resort on part of property. I needed to hire an event planner to help with the announcement, so I hired Brittany."

"Actually, he hired a couple of other companies before me," Brittany said, bumping his shoulder with her own and giving him a teasing look before turning back to Mrs. Kasey. "They weren't from here and didn't know the people. Most importantly, they couldn't come up with a plan that Daniel liked."

"True," Daniel said, playing along.

"When he finally decided to hire a local company, I jumped at the chance. I was determined to show him just what I could do. Daniel started out as a challenging client, but it didn't take long for me to discover that he's really a pussycat on the inside."

"Don't let that get out or my reputation as a hard-nosed businessman will be ruined."

Brittany laughed and Mrs. Kasey chuckled.

"Anyway," Brittany continued, "we began to spend time together working on his project. As we got to know one another, I fell in love with him."

"And I fell in love with her," Daniel added.

"I see," Mrs. Kasey said, and Daniel wondered just what it was she saw. "You got married rather quickly. Why is that?"

He and Brittany exchanged looks. They'd expected this question and had decided to face it head-on, keeping their answers as close to the truth as possible. That way there was less chance of screwing up and being caught. Now the words he'd rehearsed escaped him. He was still trying to recall his speech when Brittany spoke.

"A couple of reasons. First, neither of us is a kid. I'm thirty-three and Daniel is thirty-six. We've had enough experiences with relationships to know what we want and what we don't. And we know the real thing from imitation. Since we both knew our love was real, there was no reason to wait."

Daniel nodded.

"You said two reasons," Mrs. Kasey said.

"Yes. Hailey was the second and, honestly, the most important. Tragically, she's already lost her parents. She's been through so many changes in her young life, we don't want her to have to endure many more. It's important to us that she have a stable home. Since we knew we loved each other, it seemed better to get married sooner rather than later. That way, I could move in right away and become a regular part of Hailey's life. We want her to know she can count on both of us being here every day."

"And how has she adjusted?"

"She's happy," Daniel said. "She loves Brittany just as much as I do."

Before the social worker could ask another question, Hailey's voice came over the baby monitor.

Brittany and Daniel stood.

"I'll get her," Brittany said and then turned to Mrs. Kasey. "That way you can meet her."

"I'd like that."

Brittany left and Daniel sat back down.

"She's lovely," Mrs. Kasey said.

Daniel's response was honest and heartfelt. "Yes, she is. Before I met Brittany, I didn't believe that a woman as good as she is even existed. You may think it suspicious that we married so soon, but after I got to know her, I was determined not to let her get away. She and Hailey are the best things that have ever happened to me."

"You love her," Mrs. Kasey said as if surprised.

"With all my heart."

Mrs. Kasey nodded and didn't reply. They sat in silence and Daniel got the impression that the social worker was sizing him up. He began to second-guess his answers. Had he blown it by overselling his emotions, claiming to love Brittany with his whole heart? He hoped not. The odd thing was…he hadn't thought before he'd spoken. The words had just come tumbling out of his mouth. Just what did that mean?

Before he could ponder that question and come up with a suitable answer, Brittany was back, Hailey in her arms. She'd dressed Hailey in a cute pink dress with white flowers and matching ruffled bottoms. Brittany had insisted on going shopping for Hailey and they'd come home with bags full of adorable outfits with matching hats and barrettes.

She'd also arranged a photo shoot for the three of them with a photographer she knew. Daniel had been resistant at first, but now he was glad he'd given in. The family pictures scattered around the house added a personal feel to the professionally decorated spaces, something Brittany had known the social worker would look for. The enormous portrait hanging over the living room fireplace was a showstopper. With the other changes Brittany had made, the house truly felt like a home.

Hailey was happily carrying on a one-sided conversation. When she saw him, her eyes lit up and, exclaiming, she reached out to him. His heart melted and he stood, wrapping his arm around Brittany's waist for a second before taking Hailey and holding her against his chest.

He and Brittany sat back down. Hailey chattered and laughed for a moment, content to sit on his lap but able to reach out and touch Brittany, which she did frequently.

"Well, obviously she's too little for me to talk to," Mrs. Kasey said.

"Oh, I don't know about that," Brittany said. "She talks quite a bit."

"We just don't speak her language," Daniel added.

"Is she standing yet?"

"She pulls herself up on anything she can," Brittany said proudly. "But when she's in a hurry to get somewhere, she crawls like crazy."

"Is she sleeping through the night?"

"Yes. Although I check on her several times during the night," he confessed. "I just need to be sure that she's fine."

Mrs. Kasey nodded and made a notation in her file. "What will you tell her about her parents?"

He blew out a breath. "I didn't know her father, so, hopefully, her grandparents will share that information with her. They instigated this suit without even trying to speak with me. But rest assured, we want them to be a part of her life. They're her family.

"But I can tell her all about her mother. I'll tell her just how sweet and smart Jane was. And how much her mother was loved by everyone who knew her. I'll make sure Hailey knows how much my sister loved her."

Brittany squeezed his hand. "*We'll* make sure she knows that."

A lump materialized in his throat, leaving him unable to speak, so he nodded.

"Would you like to see the rest of the house?" Brittany asked.

"Yes, but first I'd like to see Hailey's room."

"Sure. I'll show you while Daniel gets her snack. She's happy to sit and play for a few minutes after she wakes up, but if she doesn't get her fruit and bottle soon, she's going to raise the roof."

Daniel watched as his wife led the social worker from the room, his heart in his throat and his mind a jumbled mess. There was too much going on for him to process. He hated being out of control of the situation. Being with him was best for Hailey, but he was powerless to make it so.

Not only that, he didn't have power over his emotions or words. What did it mean that he'd had no problem saying he was in love with Brittany? Why had the words felt so right?

Hailey pulled on his ear, reminding him that it was time for her snack, so he went to the kitchen, glad for a moment to get back to his routine and the little he could control.

Relax. Brittany reminded herself that she had been in plenty of tense situations and had never once cracked under the pressure. She wasn't going to start now. But there was no denying this situation was different. Those other times had been business. This was personal. Mrs. Kasey's opinion of her mattered more than winning a contract or pulling off the perfect event. Only her mind and her ego had been involved then. This time, people's hearts were at stake.

"Oh, this is so sweet," the social worker said when she entered Hailey's room.

"Thank you." Brittany had enjoyed decorating the room. Each item had been selected to pique the little girl's curiosity as well as to make her feel special.

Mrs. Kasey picked up the two-sided picture frame on the dresser. On one side, there was a picture of Hailey with her biological parents. On the other, there was a picture of Hailey with Brittany and Daniel. "This is a nice touch. Not everyone would have been so thoughtful."

"We don't want to erase Hailey's past. We just want to assure her future."

"And you think you can do that better than her biological grandparents?"

Brittany met the other woman's eyes. "I don't know them. I'm sure they think they're doing the right thing by fighting for custody. But they're wrong. Daniel is Hailey's father in all the ways that matter."

"And you? Do you consider yourself Hailey's mother?"

"I'm trying to be. She had her biological mother's love for such a short period of time. I know I'll never be able to replace Jane in Hailey's life, but I hope my love will fill her need for a mother's love."

Mrs. Kasey nodded. "You work?"

"Yes."

"Do you intend to continue working outside the home?"

"Yes. Fortunately, Daniel works from home, so he's here for Hailey when I'm not."

Mrs. Kasey's smile broadened. "That's a little unorthodox, but I like the way you think."

"It works for us."

"Not all men would be willing to do that."

"Daniel isn't just any man. He knows who he is and what he wants out of life, but at the same time he wants to make sure that I get what I need to be fulfilled, too. I have no doubt he'll do everything in his power to make sure that Hailey has every opportunity to set and reach her goals, too."

"You sound like you love him."

"I do."

Brittany heard the words but she couldn't believe her ears. The "I do" had just fallen out of her mouth, without her thinking. What did that mean, exactly? Her body started to tremble, from her toes to her hair. Could it be? Could she truly be in love with Daniel?

Her eyes flew back to the social worker. She couldn't let Mrs. Kasey see her nervousness. But the woman merely nodded. Fortunately for Brittany that was the end of the questioning. She was so stunned by her answer and the truth she'd heard there, she didn't know if she could answer any more questions.

She had to take control of herself. She couldn't be in love with Daniel. Theirs was a pretend romance. A marriage on paper. It wasn't the real thing that came complete with emotions and vows that lasted a lifetime. Daniel had made that clear. It would be foolish of her to pretend otherwise.

Brittany led the way downstairs to the kitchen. As they drew nearer, they could hear Daniel's and Hai-

ley's voices. Daniel was asking Hailey about her favorite toy. She replied in her own language, her voice
sincere. Daniel laughed and Hailey echoed him.

Brittany and Mrs. Kasey stepped into the kitchen
just as Hailey was finishing her snack. She had banana smeared on her face and bits of Graham cracker
on her bib. Daniel was at the sink, wetting a towel.
When Hailey saw Brittany, she leaned in her direction and held out her hands.

"Oh, no. Let's get you cleaned up first," Daniel
said. He wiped the remnants of Hailey's snack from
her face and hands, then removed her bib. Once she
was clean, Brittany took her from the high chair and
held her. Hailey wrapped her legs around Brittany's
waist and leaned against her side.

Mrs. Kasey took in the scene for a moment then
spoke. "I think I have all that I need."

"What happens next?" Brittany asked, hiding the
anxiety she felt.

"I'll make my report and submit it to the court.
It'll be part of the record." Mrs. Kasey looked at
them. "I know this is a frustrating procedure and
even a little nerve-racking. Just be patient and trust
the process. We all want what's best for Hailey."

They thanked Donna Kasey and then walked her
to the door and watched as she drove away. Once
her car was out of sight, Brittany and Daniel sighed
with relief.

"That went well, don't you think?" Daniel asked.

"Yes. And I'm glad it's over."

He put his arm around her shoulder and she leaned against him, grateful for his strength. "You were incredible and very convincing. I don't know how I will ever repay you, but I owe you big-time."

Brittany didn't respond. She couldn't. She'd held it in for the remainder of Mrs. Kasey's visit but now that the pretending was over, she had to admit the truth. To herself anyway. There was no longer any doubt. She was in love with Daniel.

Obviously, she couldn't tell him. It went against every rule in the deal they'd struck.

No, this was her problem and hers alone. And she'd handle it.

Chapter Seventeen

A few days after the interview with the social worker, Daniel suggested that they get out of the house and have some family fun.

"I don't know. I'm not really in the mood to deal with other people," Brittany said. Though Mrs. Kasey had seemed open-minded, the more Brittany thought about the meeting, the more she wished she had done things differently. What exactly, she wasn't sure. But with nothing but time, she wondered if she should have worn a dress. Or perhaps she should have answered the questions in another way.

Though she'd done her best to be convincing, she couldn't stop worrying that the social worker had seen through her. There was no denying that their marriage had come on the heels of Daniel discovering that Hailey's grandparents wanted custody of her. No denying that they hadn't known each other long before the wedding. Even the most trusting person would be suspicious of the timing. Brittany had barely slept a wink stressing over the entire situation.

But worry over the meeting wasn't the only thing that had kept Brittany awake. Realizing that she was in love with Daniel had had her tossing and turning all night. She was past the point of whining about unrequited love. If nothing else, she was a realist who'd entered into this agreement with her eyes open. Still, knowing that Daniel didn't feel the same hurt. She knew he liked her, that he admired her—he'd told her that often enough. And there was no denying that he was physically attracted to her. But all that didn't equal love.

"Well, I know," Daniel said firmly. "We need to get out of this house. Sitting around and brooding won't change a thing. Besides, I think you were fine. Better than fine. You were awesome."

"Thanks." Maybe he was right. Maybe they needed to get out. "Okay, let's have some fun. And I know the perfect place."

"Where's that?"

"Happy Hearts Animal Rescue."

He nodded. "Sounds good. I'll get Hailey ready."

In minutes, they were in the car and Brittany

couldn't stay down in the dumps. Not with a cheerful baby singing in the back seat.

They were a few miles from the rescue when Daniel flashed her a grin. "I was just thinking. Maybe we should get Hailey a puppy."

"Are you kidding?"

"No." He stopped at a red light and then looked over at her again. "From the tone of your voice, I take it you don't think this is a good idea."

"You've got that right. You already have one baby. The last thing you need is a second." He didn't look convinced. The light turned green and he turned his attention back to the road, but she knew he was listening. "Puppies need a lot of love and attention. Like children. At this point, I don't think either of us has the spare energy to give it."

"I have the energy," he said instantly, but his voice lacked conviction.

"Really? Are you hiding it under your bed? Because I haven't seen it."

He laughed and her insides quivered. "Just give me the go-ahead and I'll show you how much energy I have."

Suddenly the air crackled with heat. Suddenly they weren't talking about the puppy any longer. Her body felt damp, but she turned away, not wanting to let him know how hot and bothered she was. Or how tempted she was to give him the go-ahead.

Then he sighed. "I guess you're right. No puppy for now."

His abrupt change back to talking about the puppy was a relief. And a disappointment.

She cleared her throat and pulled herself together. "I know I am. But that doesn't mean Hailey won't have a good time at the rescue. Happy Hearts has a lot of animals that she'll enjoy seeing."

They'd reached the rescue and Daniel turned into the parking lot. Once she was in the stroller and could see all the animals, Hailey began chattering a mile a minute in her secret language.

"You were right," Daniel said. "She's going to enjoy this."

Happy Hearts, which had been started and was run by Daphne Taylor, sat on several lovely acres. The animal rescue was a bone of contention between Daphne and many of her family members. They were cattle ranchers and to them the rescue was an affront and criticism of the family business. Sadly, many other ranchers in the area harbored similar feelings for Daphne, who was only trying to do good. Thanks to her efforts, abandoned or otherwise homeless animals ranging from house pets to horses and goats had a safe home. And since the animals could be adopted, they often found families and forever homes.

Brittany hadn't talked to her friend since the wedding and made a mental note to seek her out. As she recalled the scene between Daphne and her father,

her heart ached. Brittany truly hoped that the two of them would reconcile.

"Where should we go first?" Daniel asked.

Brittany looked at Hailey. She was twisting in her seat, straining to get a clear view of the pigs and goats. "I think we have our answer."

They headed down the path to the area where the farm animals were housed. A bunch of little kids swarmed a volunteer who was holding a baby goat. The children jostled and shoved each other in an effort to get closer.

"No need to push," the young woman said firmly. "Everyone is going to get a turn."

Brittany watched as each child took their time petting the goat. When it was Hailey's turn, she kicked her feet and squealed in delight as she rubbed the goat's back. When Hailey had gotten her fill, Brittany whipped out a baby wipe and cleaned the baby's hands, ignoring her loud protests. No way Hailey was getting sick on her watch.

Next they strolled over to the pigs, where they repeated the process. They encountered some friends and neighbors and stopped to converse. Daniel and Brittany accepted congratulations on their marriage and received invitations to get together in the near future. Then Brittany spotted Daphne in the distance. Although Daphne was smiling, Brittany had a feeling the smile masked an aching heart.

"I'll be back," she said to Daniel. "I want to talk to Daphne."

"Take your time. Hailey and I are going to find the puppies. We'll be there when you finish catching up with your friend."

Brittany quickly walked up to Daphne. "Hey."

Daphne looked up and smiled as Brittany approached. "Hey, newlywed. I'm surprised to see you here. I thought you'd be on your honeymoon."

"With a baby?"

"I imagine that would put a damper on things."

Brittany laughed and looked over at Daniel and Hailey. Daniel caught her eye and smiled at her, pausing momentarily before continuing to the dog barn. Brittany's heart skipped a beat. Realizing she hadn't replied to Daphne's comment, she pulled her eyes away. "Slightly. But Hailey is a real sweetie. I can't imagine life without her."

Daphne poked Brittany's shoulder playfully. "You know, you keep a secret better than anyone I know."

"What do you mean?"

"You and Daniel. I had no idea you were dating. In fact, I didn't know the two of you even knew each other. And the next thing I know, you're married."

Brittany didn't like deceiving her friends and family, but it was necessary. Especially now that the social worker had interviewed her and Daniel. Mrs. Kasey might make her way to friends and family soon. It was better to stick with the story they'd agreed on. "It was a whirlwind affair."

"Yes. But it's obvious that the two of you belong together. The love between you is visible from a mile away."

Brittany's stomach flip-flopped at her friend's words. Though she had begun to face up to her feelings for Daniel, it shocked her to hear someone else remark on them. It was especially jarring when her feelings were growing and becoming stronger each day while Daniel's appeared unchanged. "We're happy together."

"And I'm happy for you both. I don't know Daniel very well, but he seems like a great guy."

"He is," Brittany replied automatically. And honestly.

A volunteer approached, needing to speak with Daphne, so Brittany knew it was time to say goodbye. She hugged her friend. "You're busy. And I'd better get back to Daniel and Hailey."

"Thanks for stopping by. It was good to talk to you. I hope you and your family have a great time."

Your family. The words echoed through Brittany's head as she walked away to join Daniel and Hailey. Her family.

Daniel and Hailey were watching the puppies tumble over each other as they played. Hailey's happy laughter made it easy for Brittany to find them. When she reached them, Daniel wrapped an arm around her waist, pulling her close. Smiling, she leaned against his side. When Hailey tired of the puppies, they went outside to the dog runs and watched the dogs chase each other. They appeared to be racing, so Brittany cheered on a black Lab that she thought would win.

After a while, Hailey became cranky, so they decided to skip the cat house and call it a day. A quick diaper change and they were on their way back home. Throughout the ride, Daphne's words repeated through Brittany's head. Daniel and Hailey were her family. Those words took on a new meaning now and she knew that whenever this marriage ended, her life would never be the same.

The next days passed in a flurry of activity as Brittany spent hours at the office working on every detail of Daniel's party. She checked and double-checked everything right down to the afternoon of the event. Satisfied, she went home to get ready for the party that evening, looking forward to wearing the new dress and shoes she'd bought for the occasion.

She couldn't stop her mind from racing as she showered and dressed. So much was riding on this dinner. Though Daniel had gotten to know several of her friends over the past few weeks, it was his formal introduction to the community. More importantly, he was going to announce his new venture.

Brittany had no doubt that, once people watched the presentation she and Daniel had put together, they would be on board.

Taking a deep breath to calm her nerves, she checked herself one last time in the mirror.

She heard a wolf whistle and turned around. Daniel leaned against her open doorway and crossed his ankles. Her skin began to tingle as his eyes, alight with desire, traveled over her body. "There are no words to describe just how good you look."

"Thank you." Brittany ran her hand over her formfitting red dress, smoothing out an imaginary wrinkle, and gave him the once-over. Dressed in a navy suit and crisp white shirt with a blue-patterned tie, he was the personification of sexy. "You look pretty snazzy yourself."

He gave her a mischievous look. "I'm ready. Are you?"

Brittany felt her cheeks warm at the double entendre. He'd been a lot more flirtatious the past few days. "I am."

He held out his arm and as she took it, his scent wrapped around her like a lover's embrace. Hailey was spending the night with Brittany's parents so they wouldn't have their tiny chaperone tonight. With Daniel's flirting becoming intense each day and the wall she'd built around her heart weakening with each passing moment, she wondered just what the night would hold for them.

They'd rented DJ's Deluxe again and Brittany's nerves jangled as they neared the restaurant. Daniel parked and they went inside. The guests would be arriving soon and they wanted to be there to greet them.

She'd always had a flair for design and she'd pulled out all the stops to make DJ's even more elegant than it had been for their reception. DJ's wait-staff was top of the line and she knew the service would meet her very high expectations.

She made a quick circuit of the room, checking each centerpiece and place setting to be sure everything was perfect. This event was important to Daniel, but it mattered to her just as much. Her reputation as an event planner would either get a big boost or take a hit, depending on the outcome.

She joined Daniel at the front of the room. He smiled at her and her heart skipped a beat. "Everything up to your standards?"

"Yes."

He took her hand and gave it a gentle squeeze. "Then relax and enjoy yourself."

She smiled at him then turned her focus to the door as the first guests stepped inside—Amanda and her fiancé, Holt. Brittany gave her former roommate a quick hug. "Thanks so much for coming."

"You knew I would be here to support you. Plus, I'm seriously curious about this new secret venture. I believe everyone is." She glanced over her shoulder at Cornelius Taylor, who was standing inside the doorway. "I'd better let you get to it. We'll catch up later."

Cornelius walked up to Brittany and Daniel and looked around. "Very nice."

"My wife planned the entire event," Daniel said. Brittany's heart filled at the pride evident in Daniel's voice. But that was nothing compared to the tingles that raced up and down her spine at his use of the word *wife*. Though she knew they were legally married and nothing else, the sound of the word made her giddy.

"Well, I'm interested to see how it goes. So far, so good." Cornelius then nodded and walked away.

Daniel wrapped his arm around her shoulders and gave her a squeeze. "By the end of the night, he won't be able to resist your Denim and Diamonds idea."

"I hope so."

Brittany had scheduled everything to the second and, right on time, the waitstaff began circulating with beverages and finger food. Daniel was at his most charming, and the guests responded to his warmth in kind.

At precisely thirty minutes past the hour, dinner was announced. She joined Daniel at their table and looked around. The staff stood in their assigned stations. Brittany signaled and they brought out the first course.

"Everything is great. Relax."

"I want to be sure that everything goes off without a hitch. There's a lot riding on this night." For him and for her.

"Well, you'd better eat or people will start to think there's something wrong with the food."

Brittany laughed. She knew the food was perfect, but she picked up her fork anyway. As she enjoyed her meal, she looked around the room, noting her guests' behavior. If anyone displayed even the slightest bit of unhappiness, she wanted to be able to address it immediately. To her satisfaction, everyone looked happy.

Once dessert and coffee had been enjoyed, Daniel straightened his tie. "Wish me luck."

She caressed his cheek and their eyes met. Held. "You don't need luck. You've got skills."

"Thanks." He kissed her briefly, then rose and went to the front of the room.

"Thank you all for coming tonight. I enjoyed meeting those of you I hadn't met before. I hope to get to know all of you even better in the future. I'd like to spend the next few minutes telling you about the Dubois Guest Ranch and Resort."

He gave a short speech then stepped aside and a short video detailing his upcoming venture played on a wide screen Brittany had set up. When the video ended, the waitstaff passed out glossy brochures containing detailed information. Daniel once more stood in front of the gathering. "It's my belief that the resort will benefit all of Bronco and I welcome discussion on how the resort can further benefit our community. On that note, I'll step aside and let the band play. Please feel free to dance. And of course, I'm available to answer any questions you have."

The applause was thunderous and Brittany was filled with pride. Watching him mingle with their guests, Brittany understood why Daniel had been so successful in business. He was absolutely fantastic, giving each person his undivided attention, listening more than he talked. As much as she wanted to stand around and admire her husband, she still had work to do.

She took two steps and noticed that Cornelius Taylor was walking in her direction. He was smiling broadly and holding a glass of champagne. "This has been an excellent night. I was impressed by your wedding and reception, but this was even more impressive. I'm rarely wowed, but I was tonight. I want to hire you to organize the Denim and Diamonds fundraiser."

Brittany smiled. "Thank you. You won't be sorry. I have great ideas."

"I'm sure you do. Call my office on Tuesday morning to schedule a meeting."

"Will do."

After that conversation, Brittany practically floated on air. She couldn't wait to share her good news with Daniel. Needing a moment in private to bask in her happiness, she stepped into a secluded alcove. She was there less than a second when Melanie and Gabe happened to step inside.

"Hi," Brittany said. She glanced at Melanie, who looked troubled. "Is something wrong?"

Melanie and Gabe exchanged a look before Melanie answered. "I don't want to be a downer on such a happy occasion."

"Okay, now I'm worried. You two aren't having troubles, are you?"

"No, it's nothing like that," Melanie said. "It's about Beatrix. I don't think we're ever going to find her."

"Oh. I'm sorry," Brittany said. She knew how important finding Beatrix was to Melanie.

"Don't give up," Gabe said, looking down at his fiancée. "There's still a possibility that something might turn up."

"From where? The only people who responded on the internet were a bunch of frauds or weirdos."

"True. But that doesn't mean the real Beatrix won't reply," Gabe said. "Give it time."

"Gabe's right," Brittany added. "Give it time."

"Time is the one thing we don't have. Winona Cobbs was recently hospitalized—they had to take her to Kalispell. I'm afraid we might lose her before we can tell her that her baby didn't die all those years ago like she'd been led to believe."

"Think positively," Gabe said.

Having nothing to add, Brittany gave her friend a comforting hug before walking away.

She returned to the party and her eyes sought out Daniel. He was standing alone, looking confident and devastatingly handsome and intense longing surged through her. When she joined him, he swept her into his arms and led her to the dance floor. She closed her eyes and placed her head against his muscular chest. If only she could stay in his embrace all night.

After a couple of dances, they reluctantly released each other and made the rounds again. Daniel received many congratulations and requests to discuss his new venture further. Once the last guest had left, Brittany felt safe to say the evening had been a great success.

When they finally arrived home, they looked at each other and grinned. Brittany turned in a circle, her arms over her head. "Yes!"

Daniel took off his jacket and loosened his tie. "That went superbly. Thank you so much for all of your hard work."

Feeling the effects of the champagne she'd consumed, and buoyed by the success of the night, Brittany smirked. "I told you that I was the best."

"That you are, dear wife. That you are." Daniel pulled her into his arms. "Thank you."

He kissed her lips gently. It was butterfly-soft, but its impact was strong. What was no doubt intended as a simple gesture of gratitude quickly morphed into something else. It was as if a stick of dynamite had been lit inside her and she instantly went up in flames.

Within seconds, the kiss grew more intense. Brittany leaned against his chest, needing to get closer. He started to pull away, so she wrapped her arms around his neck, pulling him back to her. The weeks of simmering desire had boiled over and she didn't want to control it. Being kissed by Daniel felt terrific and she didn't want it to end.

He kissed her a moment longer, as if his emotions were as out of control as hers, then gradually pulled back and leaned his forehead against hers. She was breathing heavily and it took a moment for her heart to slow down.

"I'm sorry," he said. The guilt written on his face also dripped from his voice. "That was entirely inappropriate."

"Don't apologize. I liked it."

"But we have a deal. We agreed our marriage would be in name only."

"I know. But this is what I want now."

"And later?"

"Later can take care of itself."

"Are you sure?"

"Yes."

He kissed her again. Then he pulled back and offered her his hand. There would be no "getting carried" up the stairs tonight. She had to walk into his bedroom, removing any lingering doubt that she wanted to make love with him.

Her heart thudded loudly in her chest and her blood pulsed through her veins as desire and excitement filled her. With each step, the longing and need expanded inside her. By the time they reached his bedroom, Brittany thought she would explode. She reached up, removed his loosened tie and draped it over a chair, then began to unbutton his shirt. He returned the favor, unzipping her dress.

When they were both undressed, they fell onto the king-size bed. Brittany might not have been ready to put her feelings into words, but she wasn't shy about showing Daniel just how she felt.

This was what had been missing from their relationship. Now their marriage was complete.

After making love with Daniel, she didn't think she would be able to go back to a marriage of convenience. Nor would she want to. The question was—did he feel the same?

Chapter Eighteen

Daniel stretched and looked down at his wife, who was snuggled close to his side. Last night had been the best of his life. It was as if every dream he'd ever had, and some he hadn't, had come true. Brittany was a generous lover. Given the nature of their relationship—their marriage was a business arrangement, after all—he'd expected her to be a little bit shy. He'd been wrong. She hadn't been the least bit bashful. They'd made love all night, until the wee hours of the morning, and Brittany had been a confident lover. They'd fit together so perfectly, it was as if she'd been created especially for him.

After a moment, guilt began to poke holes in

his joy, and the sense of well-being began to seep away. How would Brittany react today? Would she be happy or filled with regret? Last night they'd been swept away by the success of the event. Everyone had been enthusiastic about his plan and Brittany had landed the account she'd worked so hard to get. They'd been flying high. Mix in the champagne they'd consumed and it was easy to see how they'd ended up making love all night.

The night was over and the sun was rising. Brittany would be waking soon. She'd already begun to stir, so it would soon be time to face the music. He didn't know how she would feel in the cold light of day, so he'd watch her closely and pick up on her mood. Hopefully, by following her lead, he'd say the right thing.

He didn't delude himself into believing that one night spent making love would change the course of her life. She'd been clear that she didn't want to be a mother. And he had Hailey, so that ruled him out as playing a permanent role in her life. If he'd even dared to hope the past weeks together had changed her mind about the kind of future she wanted, her joy at landing the Taylor account killed that hope. Brittany had the right to create the kind of life she wanted. If she wanted to live her life without children, then she should. Sadly, that meant they had no future together. But Daniel refused to make her feel guilty about her choices. She'd upheld her end of the bargain. She didn't owe him anything else. He wouldn't try and hold onto her no matter how desperately he wanted to.

But she was here now, and he intended to make the most of the time he had. Her eyes opened and she looked at him. Though he tried, he couldn't decipher the expression on her face. Her lovely brown eyes were unreadable. That meant he couldn't tell whether she regretted last night or if her body was still humming with contentment as his was.

Before he could decide what to say, his phone rang. He picked it up immediately.

"Hello?"

"Daniel, it's John Kirkland." His lawyer's normally calm voice sounded excited.

"What's up? Do you have news about the case? Have you seen the social worker's report?"

Brittany's eyes widened and she sat up, pulling the sheet over her perfectly round breasts and momentarily distracting him.

"No. It won't matter now anyway."

"Why won't it matter?"

"What's happening?" Brittany asked.

Realizing she had nearly as much at stake as he did, Daniel put the phone on speaker so she could hear, too.

"I just received word that the Larimars have withdrawn their custody suit."

"Say that again," Daniel said. His head was spinning. Despite the fact that Brittany had just let out a joyous cheer, he couldn't believe his ears.

John laughed. "You heard me. They're no longer trying to take Hailey from you. I'm going to make a motion asking the judge to grant you permanent wardship and custody of Hailey. And I advise you to proceed with your plans to adopt her as soon as possible to prevent anything else like this from happening again. But it's over."

"So that's it. They disrupt my life, threaten Hailey's security, and then drop everything. No apology. No nothing." Daniel was at once angry and grateful. He expected he'd run the whole gamut of emotions before the end of the day.

"Why? Why are they dropping the suit now after putting me through all this? It doesn't make sense."

"Apparently, Mrs. Larimar was recently diagnosed with cancer and her husband doesn't feel capable of raising a baby right now."

"I see."

"I'll forward the documents. Congratulations again."

"Wait," Daniel said abruptly before his attorney could hang up. He exhaled the bitterness he felt. Hailey's happiness was still his number one priority. "If they want to maintain contact with Hailey, they can. We can arrange visitation in the future. In the meantime, I'll bring Hailey to visit them if Mrs. Larimar is up to it."

"I'll pass on your offer and get back to you."

Daniel ended the call and turned to Brittany. Her bright smile was a balm to his soul. "I'm so happy for you, Daniel. And for Hailey, too. You're a family and you're going to stay together. You should be happy."

"I am happy." He noticed that she'd excluded herself from the family. She was already distancing herself from them. Perhaps she was mentally returning to her regularly scheduled life.

"You don't look happy."

"I am. I was angry for a second, but I'm not anymore," he insisted.

"That's good. But something else is wrong. I can tell."

"It's just…" He blew out a breath.

"Just what?"

"This is another loss for Hailey. I don't know the kind of cancer her grandmother has or her prognosis, but that's one more person she can potentially lose."

"That's not necessarily so. People are surviving cancer these days. She could live for a very long time and be a positive part of Hailey's life."

He nodded. Naturally, Brittany would think of something that hadn't occurred to him. "True."

An awkward silence settled over them and he searched for something to say. Before he could find a subject, Brittany spoke.

"So, I guess that's the end of things for us. Now

that you aren't at risk of losing custody of Hailey, you don't need me anymore."

He didn't need her anymore? He only wished that were true. In the short time they'd been married, he'd grown close to her. He enjoyed every moment they spent together and had anticipated sharing many more in the future. After last night, he'd begun to hope theirs would become a marriage in every sense of the word. That hope was now completely dashed. Brittany wanted out.

He could tell her that he wanted her to stay, but he wouldn't. He knew her too well. He knew she might stay for his and Hailey's sakes, sacrificing what she wanted to keep him happy. That wouldn't be fair.

Not only that, he could ask her to stay and she could say no and leave. She had every right. There was no need to open himself up for the agony such a rejection would bring. His heart had been battered enough in this lifetime. It had hurt to be rejected by a sister he'd loved so much, devastating to be shut out of her life only to lose her forever. And he was still recovering from the loss of his parents. He couldn't open his heart again when he knew it could be pummeled.

Oh, he was sure Brittany would do her best to let him down easy—she was too sweet to do anything else. But she was also too honest to pretend to want a life with him when she didn't. And he wasn't going to put her in a position that would leave both of them uncomfortable. So he decided to tell her the part of the truth that didn't leave him open to hurt and that would set her free at the same time.

"I will never be able to thank you enough for what you've done. Though our marriage is ending a lot more quickly than either of us anticipated, I hope that you'll stay in our lives. Hailey really does love you."

He was wrong when he thought that would save him from being hurt. The pain of those words nearly undid him.

Hailey really does love you. Brittany had to give him credit for being subtle. His statement of Hailey's feelings with no mention of his own might as well have been yelled from the rooftop. She heard him loud and clear. Daniel didn't love her and was too considerate to utter the words. Not that the situation required he make such a declaration. She'd gone into this marriage knowing that it would be in name only. The fact that they'd somehow ended up making love last night didn't change the agreement or his feelings, obviously.

Though she was disappointed and maybe even a little bit hurt, she understood. He might have made love to her with such tenderness that she'd begun dreaming of a future where their vows become real, but wanting something to be true didn't make it so. And he'd been very clear from the beginning why he'd wanted to marry her. A future with her wasn't one of them. Since she'd insisted that their marriage be in name only and end once he'd gotten custody, she had no right to be upset that he wanted to stick to the terms.

She might want to see if their marriage could last, but that was her problem. She wasn't going to try to change his mind or to make him feel guilty. She was a big girl and would act like one.

She pulled the sheet higher on her chest and wiggled up on her pillow. "I enjoyed myself. And, of course, I'll keep in touch. Hailey is important to me, too."

She hadn't been the least bit self-conscious last night, but now she was uncomfortably aware that she and Daniel were completely naked beneath the sheet. The dress she'd worn to the party was on the floor in a puddle of red silk. She couldn't reach it without getting out of bed and baring her nude body was out of the question now. But she couldn't lie there so close to him that she inhaled his masculine scent with every breath. The heat of his body had her longing to get closer, but she wouldn't. Last night's sweet magic was gone, leaving only the bitter taste of disappointment behind.

Daniel stared off into the distance, as if lost in thought. Perhaps he'd moved on mentally and had already forgotten she was there. But he was the one with a robe on the foot of the bed, not her. Well, since he didn't seem inclined to move, she scooted to the edge of the bed and managed to grab his robe without revealing too much of herself. Not that he was looking.

Once she'd put on his robe, she stood and tied the belt around her waist before glancing at him. His eyes were a mixture of humor and confusion. Apparently, she hadn't been as graceful or inconspicuous in real life as she'd been in her mind.

"I think I'll shower and get dressed. Then I guess we can go to my parents' house and get Hailey."

He nodded.

"Then I'll come back here and pack. Good thing we didn't bring everything I own."

"There's no hurry, Brittany. It's not as if I'm evicting you."

"Maybe not, but there's no reason to draw things out unnecessarily, either. Besides, my place is a lot closer to my office. Now that I've landed the Taylor account, I'll be super busy. I'll need the extra time I'll save on the commute."

His eyes narrowed and, for a minute, she thought she'd seen pain flash in them. But then he smiled and she knew she'd imagined it. Why would he feel anything remotely resembling pain? He'd gotten everything he'd wanted and, as far as he was concerned, the contract had been fulfilled. No need to prolong the inevitable goodbye.

"Okay, then," he said. "I guess I need to shower and get dressed myself."

"I'll bring back your robe in a little while."

"Sure."

With that awkward conversation now over, Brittany gathered her discarded clothes and shoes and then went to her room. When the door was firmly closed behind her, she sat on the bed and ordered herself not to cry. There was no reason for her heart to be breaking. No reason at all. But then, love wasn't ruled by reason.

Chapter Nineteen

Daniel walked past the now empty bedroom for the umpteenth time. Brittany had been gone for five days, but he still missed her like crazy. The hint of her perfume lingered in the air, making him long for her even more. She'd forgotten one of her scarves and he'd placed it in his sock drawer where he saw it every morning. He knew he was being ridiculous and that he should return it to her, but that scrap of silk made him feel closer to her.

He shouldn't have let her go. But what choice had he had? She didn't want a family. She'd been clear about that. Brittany had married him for the money that he'd promised to give her so she could start her own event planning company. She'd lit out of here so fast he hadn't had the chance to hand her the check he'd written for the agreed-upon amount. When he'd noticed it on his desk two days later, he'd torn it up, filled out a check for twice the amount and dropped it in the mail. He could have delivered it to her in person, but he was afraid if he saw her, he might beg her to come back to him.

Hailey began rousing from her nap and he went to her nursery so he'd be there when she was fully awake. He stood by her crib, wishing that Brittany was there beside him as she'd been over the past weeks. Though he had Hailey, his heart still ached from loneliness. And unrequited love.

He sucked in a breath and was momentarily dizzy. What? Had he just thought that he was in love with Brittany? He couldn't be. But as he pondered the words, the truth sank in and he couldn't avoid it. *He was in love with Brittany.* He probably had been for quite some time. He'd just been too blind to see it.

But in his defense, it had happened so gradually, he hadn't noticed when his feelings changed. One minute he'd thought her a competent employee. Then he'd thought of her as a friend. And, finally, a lover. She was beautiful, so his attraction hadn't been unexpected. But love? That had caught him off guard and he hadn't known what name to give it. And now it was too late.

He'd been so sure his growing feelings would disappear if she wasn't around. Instead he found himself prowling the house as if she would magically materialize in the family room. Or better yet, in his bed. The night they'd made love had been more than he could ever imagine, and he wanted to duplicate it every night for the rest of his life.

It had almost killed him to let her go. Standing by silently with a fake smile on his face while she'd packed her belongings, and then helping her load his SUV so she could leave him, had been a colossal mistake. But what was he supposed to do? She was the one who'd said it was time to leave the morning after they'd made love. The night that had changed everything for him hadn't affected her at all.

The phone had still been in his hand when she'd announced that she was leaving him. She'd made up some lame excuse about her condo being closer to her job and then turned her back on him. She'd said he'd gotten everything he'd wanted. The truth was, she'd gotten everything she'd wanted. Or she would have, the minute she cashed the check.

He fought against the bitterness welling inside him. Brittany hadn't done anything wrong. In fact, she'd given more than she'd agreed to. Falling in love hadn't been a part of it. Nor had staying with him. So he shouldn't be upset that she'd gone.

Once he'd changed Hailey's diaper, he carried her downstairs and gave her a snack. He hadn't tried to find a new nanny since Brittany had left. Instead, he'd made room for Hailey in his office. He'd brought in a playpen and some of her favorite toys so she could play while he worked. He wasn't as productive as he'd been when he'd had help, but he enjoyed her company. Now, after settling her in the playpen, he picked up the mail.

He tossed aside the junk mail and then looked at the envelope addressed in his own hand. The check he'd sent to Brittany. She'd written "Return to Sender" and sent it back unopened. That didn't make sense. The money was his part of the bargain. She'd earned it. She needed it to start her business. Yet she'd sent it back to him. What did that mean? Why would she toss away the opportunity to make her dream a reality?

Daniel set the check aside and continued to go through the mail. After reading and rereading a three-paragraph letter without being able to comprehend a word, he knew it was futile to continue. His mind was too filled with thoughts of Brittany for him to focus.

He'd always been able to think clearly when riding a horse. Unfortunately, given that he had yet to put Hailey on a horse with him, and there was no one she was comfortable with enough to watch her, that was out of the question. So he did the next best thing. He called Stephanos. His best friend possessed the ability to help him see things he couldn't see.

Once he'd reached Stephanos and explained the

situation, Daniel listened for what seemed like forever while his friend laughed. He was starting to regret calling him and was in the middle of saying so when his friend spoke.

"I don't know what you want me to say," Stephanos said once his laughter had died down.

"I don't know, either, but I certainly didn't expect you to laugh at me."

"I always laugh at the ridiculous. You know that."

"What's so ridiculous?"

"This whole thing. You marry a woman you don't love—a woman you barely know—because you're worried about losing Hailey. Then it turns out that you don't need to be married, after all, so she leaves. And now you're upset with her. Am I missing anything?"

"No."

Stephanos laughed again. "Oh, I think I am."

"What?"

"The fact that you've fallen in love with your wife and are too scared to let her know."

"I'm not scared." He just didn't want to put Brittany in a bad spot.

"Tell that to someone who doesn't know you as well as I do."

Daniel dropped his head into his hands. He should have known better than to call Stephanos. They'd been friends too long to be able to deceive each other. "What should I do?"

"I can't believe you're asking me that."

"Neither can I."

Stephanos laughed again and Daniel seriously considered finding a new best friend. "It's easy. Go get your woman."

Go get your woman. That thought stuck with Daniel throughout the rest of the day. It echoed through his mind as he tried to sleep that night. *Go get your woman* was the first thing he thought of the next morning. And though he'd been hesitant at first, by the time he'd finished giving Hailey her breakfast, he knew what he had to do.

Brittany sat on the sofa and adjusted the pillow behind her back yet again. Though the condo had felt like home from the day she'd moved in, she felt out of place. The bed she'd slept in until she'd moved in with Daniel no longer felt familiar. While in the past she'd rested easily, she now tossed and turned all night and woke with a feeling of unrest that followed her throughout the day.

She'd managed to get started on the Denim and Diamonds fundraiser for Cornelius Taylor. While she was excited about the possibilities the future held for her professionally, she was no longer certain about the direction of her personal life. Even though marriage and children hadn't been part of her life plan, being with Daniel and Hailey had changed her. She suddenly felt herself longing for her husband and child. Their relationship might have been short, but it had been wonderful. What had started out as a pretend marriage had turned into a marriage so real she couldn't even think about its loss without crying.

Whenever she felt weak and considered returning to the ranch, one thing held her in place. Daniel didn't want her. He'd been almost cheerful as he'd helped her move back into the condo. She'd half expected him to dance a jig on the way to his SUV after he'd carried in the last box. And all the while her heart had been breaking. But she'd kept it together and had given him her best smile.

She didn't know how long she would be able to keep up the act. No one at work knew her marriage had ended. Every day she pretended to be a happy newlywed. Amanda knew something was up, but she hadn't asked questions. She'd simply let Brittany know she was there if she wanted to talk. Worse, she hadn't told her family the truth, either. They still had the impression that she and Daniel were together. She knew she needed to come clean and stop living a lie, but she couldn't. But not just because of her pride. To do so would mean accepting that her marriage was over and the man she loved didn't love her in return. She wasn't ready to face that yet.

One thing was certain. She couldn't continue to live in the condo. It no longer felt like home. Now it felt like failure. Sadly the ranch that felt like home would never be home again.

There was a knock on her door and she forced herself to her feet. Though she wasn't in the mood to deal with anyone, she was sick of her own company, too.

"Coming," she called when the knock came again. Apparently, her uninvited guest was anxious to see her.

She ran a hand over her hair, then glanced through the peephole. Her mouth fell open. *Daniel.* She hurriedly unlocked and opened the door. "Hi."

"I need to talk to you."

He seemed panicked and her heart skipped a beat. "Where's Hailey? Is she okay?"

"She's fine. I dropped her at your parents' house before I came here. She could do with a little spoiling today." He shifted his feet and shoved his hands into his pockets. "Can I come in?"

"What? Oh, sure."

"Thanks."

She led him to the living room and they sat on the sofa. He didn't speak, and with every passing second she grew more uneasy.

Was he here to talk about getting a divorce? Perhaps he'd already hired an attorney—something she hadn't been able to bring herself to do—and wanted to tell her in person. She searched for something to say to break the silence. "Would you like something to drink?"

"No, thanks." He looked around and she got the feeling he wasn't seeing her condo but was rather using the time to gather his thoughts. He didn't seem his usual confident self. "I guess I should just get to the point."

She nodded.

"I made a mistake and I need your help. You're the only one who can help me fix it."

"Okay." Her heart sank as she realized she'd hoped that he'd come here for personal reasons. Instead, it was business. Thank goodness she hadn't said or done anything to let him know how she felt. That would be too embarrassing for her to ever live down. "How can I help?"

He rubbed his hands over his denim-clad thighs. "I—" He cleared his throat. Obviously he was nervous which only made her more uncomfortable. She needed him to spit it out already before she lost what little composure she had.

Daniel inhaled and blew out his breath then spoke quickly, the words running together. "I made a mistake and let someone that I love walk away."

"What?" He'd spoken so quickly Brittany wasn't sure what he'd said.

He sighed and looked her in the eyes. The emotion she saw there made her heart skip a beat. "I said, I made a mistake when I let you go without telling you that I love you. I should have told you the morning after we made love, but you wanted to leave, and I knew it would be unfair to hold you. But I do love you, Brittany."

Her heart began to soar.

"I know that marriage and motherhood weren't in your plans," he continued. "And I've tried to respect that and let you live the life you chose. The thing is, I can't live without you."

"What?" Brittany knew she was repeating herself, but she couldn't believe what she was hearing. Did he really mean it?

"I love you."

The simply spoken vow healed the hurt that had been piercing her heart ever since they'd parted.

"You're right, Daniel. I never planned on getting married and having children. My career was all I'd needed. All I'd imagined wanting." The hope in his eyes faded and he stiffened, seeming to withdraw into himself. She realized how easily a carelessly spoken word could hurt him which was the last thing she'd ever want to do. "But that all changed when I married you and became Hailey's mother. Then I realized there was room in my life and my heart for more than a career."

His eyes warmed and his smile grew as she spoke. "Does that mean you'll consider giving us a second chance? I'll do the best that I can to be a good husband and show my love to you every minute of every day. Do you think you might want to try being married again? For real this time."

"Yes! Oh, yes."

They reached for each other and kissed. The love

she'd been feeling for him filled her heart to over-flowing. The life that she'd planned was nice, but it was no longer the one she wanted. Now she wanted a life that included Daniel and Hailey and the love they'd found.

They joined hands and walked to her bedroom together. She had a feeling that her bed was going to be a lot more comfortable with him in it.

Epilogue

November...

Daniel stepped into the front room, then stopped and looked at Brittany and Hailey. The two special women in his life were playing with one of Hailey's favorite toys, the plastic doughnuts. Brittany held up the rings one at a time and told Hailey the color. Hailey babbled or laughed in return.

The past few weeks had been the best of his life. Once he and Brittany had confessed their love for each other and pulled down the walls that they'd each been holding up, their marriage had become even better than he'd ever dreamed. Every day was happier than the one before.

As planned, Brittany had started working on a business plan for her own event planning business. For now, she was busy at Bronco Elite, but eventually she wanted to be ready to go her own way.

She'd been working diligently on the upcoming Denim and Diamonds fundraiser, which would take place in two weeks. Cornelius Taylor had been thrilled by her proposals and had been singing her praises far and wide. Brittany was well on her way.

Brittany looked up as he entered the room. The radiance of her smile rivaled that of the sun. He couldn't believe his luck in finding her.

"How did the fence repairing go?" she asked, standing and giving him a hug.

"Fine. It feels good to be back working the ranch."

"Even with the resort guests?"

He laughed. "We'll see. The first guests won't be arriving for a few more weeks."

They returned to where the baby played and sat back down. He set Hailey on his lap.

"How do you feel about tomorrow?" Brittany asked.

"I'm excited. And a little bit nervous." The Larimars were coming for a weeklong visit tomorrow. He and Brittany had been in touch with them ever since the older couple had dropped the custody suit. They spoke on the phone regularly. Daniel had offered to bring Hailey to see them, but they'd preferred coming to Montana. Daniel had a feeling they wanted to see where Hailey was living. Best of all, the social worker had filed her report approving Hailey's adoption by Daniel and Brittany.

"They're going to love you," she said, cupping his cheek.

He turned his face, kissing her palm. "*Us*. They're going to love us."

The doorbell rang and he gave her Hailey and then jumped to his feet. A minute later he returned to the room. "What's behind your back?" Brittany asked as she stood up, Hailey in her arms.

He revealed a bouquet of red roses. "It occurred to me that I've never brought you flowers or given you gifts."

She kissed Hailey's forehead. "I beg to differ."

His heart warmed knowing that she considered Hailey a gift. Of course, she'd proved that several times over these past weeks. Together they'd managed to balance work and caring for Hailey.

"I guess it's more accurate to say that I didn't woo you. Our marriage began as a business arrangement. We fell in love, but that doesn't change the way things started. I know our marriage is real, but I want to do some of the things I would have done if we'd had a more traditional beginning. I would have courted you. I would have given you flowers and candy. I would have taken you out to dinner. Bought you jewelry. You deserve those things."

Brittany stood on her tiptoes and brushed a kiss against his lips. Her lips lingered against his, giving him a taste of what he would enjoy that night. Anticipation was a wonderful thing.

"Thank you."

He handed her the bouquet and she handed Hailey to him. She sniffed the roses and closed her eyes for a moment, as if in bliss.

"You're welcome."

Brittany smiled at Hailey and pointed at Daniel. "Who's that wonderful man?"

Hailey looked from Brittany to Daniel. Then she grinned and said clearly, "Dada."

* * * * *

COMING SOON!

We really hope you enjoyed reading this book.
If you're looking for more romance, be sure to
head to the shops when new books are
available on

Thursday 3rd
September

To see which titles are coming soon, please visit
millsandboon.co.uk/nextmonth

MILLS & BOON

Coming next month

CHRISTMAS REUNION IN PARIS
Liz Fielding

She straightened from her task, took one last glance around. The man was staring out at Paris, already ablaze with lights for the Christmas season, but she didn't see the view, only the face mirrored in the glass.

Chloe gasped his name.

'James...'

It was no more than a whispered breath, but his gaze flickered from the lights of the city to her own image mirrored alongside him.

For a moment, as they looked into the reflection of each other's eyes, her heart stood still. Would he recognise her? Remember her?

The thought had barely formed before he spun around so fast that, as if he had disturbed the earth's rotation, the room rocked.

She flung out a hand as her world tilted, throwing her off balance but there was only air to grasp until strong fingers clasped hers, his body steadying her world as he stepped into her, supporting her, holding her, saying her name.

Not a ghost, but the living man with whom, a lifetime ago, she had shared an intense, passionate teenage love.

A doomed romance that had brought disaster down on both their heads but, in his arms, she had forgotten reality, naively blanked from her mind the future planned for her by ambitious parents.

For a few short months, lying spooned against his body, feeling the slow, steady thud of his heart beating against her ribs, the softness of his sleeping breath against her neck, anything had seemed possible.

Now, unbelievably, he was here, grown into the promise of the youth whose every kiss, every touch had stolen her senses, his fingers entwined in her own, a hand at her back, holding her safe against the breadth of wide shoulders, their bodies touching close. Looking at her as if he could not believe what he was seeing.

His eyes were still that thrilling swirl of grey and green that, for years, had haunted her dreams. To look at his wide, sensuous mouth was to feel his lips angled against hers, feel the heat of his need echoed in the desire pounding through her veins and for a moment, weakly, she leaned into him.

'Chloe…'

Continue reading
CHRISTMAS REUNION IN PARIS
Liz Fielding

Available next month
www.millsandboon.co.uk

LET'S TALK
Romance

For exclusive extracts, competitions
and special offers, find us online:

f facebook.com/millsandboon

🐦 @MillsandBoon

📷 @MillsandBoonUK

Get in touch on 01413 063232

For all the latest titles coming soon, visit
millsandboon.co.uk/nextmonth

JOIN US ON SOCIAL MEDIA!

Stay up to date with our latest releases, author news and gossip, special offers and discounts, and all the behind-the-scenes action from Mills & Boon...

 millsandboon

 millsandboonuk

 millsandboon

It might just be true love...

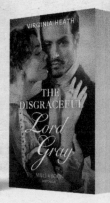